SHANE MALONEY is deputy director of the Brunswick Institute, a weather board think-tank financed by his wife. *The Brush-Off* was awarded the 1996 Ned Kelly Prize for best Crime Novel, and short-listed for the 1996 Vance Palmer Prize for Fiction. He is also the author of *Stiff, Nice Try* and *The Big Ask*.

THE
BRUSH-OFF
A MURRAY WHELAN NOVEL

SHANE MALONEY

CANONGATE

First published in 1996 by The Text Publishing Company,
Melbourne, Australia

First Published in Great Britain in 2002 by Canongate Crime, an
imprint of Canongate Books Ltd,
14 High Street,
Edinburgh EH1 1TE

This edition published in 2003

10 9 8 7 6 5 4 3 2 1

Bristish Library Cataloguing-in-Publication Data
A catalogue record for this book is available on
request from the British Library

ISBN 1 84195 356 3

Typeset in Sabon by Palimpsest Book Production Limited,
Polmont, Stirlingshire

Printed and Bound by
Cox & Wyman Ltd, Reading, Berkshire

www.canongate.net

For Wally and May,
for their forbearance
and their grandparents

'I can't think of a single Russian novel in which one of the characters goes into a picture gallery.'

W. SOMERSET MAUGHAM

THE TWO cops were virtually invisible. Only the bobbing white domes of their helmets, floating like ghostly globes through the thick summer night, and the muted clip-clop of their horses gave warning of their approach. She hadn't mentioned the mounted patrol when we came over the fence.

'Look out,' I whispered. 'Here comes the cavalry.'

'Ssshhh.' Salina clapped her hand over my mouth, trembling with the effort of stifling her own laughter. 'Get down.'

I got down. On my knees in the leaf litter, nuzzling the pom-pom fringe of her mu-mu. It was the mu-mu that first drew my eye to Salina Fleet. The mu-mu with its palm-tree motif. Then the apricot lipstick. And the terry-towel beach bag with hula-hoop handles. So playful among all those business shirts and bow ties. 'Rode one when I was ten,' I mumbled.

The pub was closed, the crowd from the art exhibition dispersed. And there we were, in possession of two stolen wine glasses and a filched bottle of chardonnay, hidden in a thicket of shrubbery inside the locked gates of the Botanic Gardens. This, I already suspected, was a decision I might come to regret. For now, however, I was game for anything. Ten or twelve drinks and I'm anyone's.

'Rode a what?' Sal whispered.

'Rhododendron,' I repeated. '*Rhododendron oreotrophes*.' It was written on a little plaque hammered into the ground beside my foot. I said it out loud, just to see if I could.

'Ssshhhh!' Again her hand closed over my face. 'You'll get us arrested, Murray.' Beneath the press of her palm, I opened my mouth. My tongue tasted her skin. The horses passed, so close we could have reached out and stroked their flanks. I stroked Salina's instead.

'Quick.' She grabbed my hand and dashed across the path, a wood sprite disappearing into a tunnel of undergrowth where the overhanging branches were too low for any horse to follow. Her legs flashed white, darting ahead.

Playing hide and seek in the Botanic Gardens was not where I'd imagined our acquaintance might lead when Salina and I were introduced at the Ministry for the Arts earlier that evening. I was the new minister's political adviser. She was the visual arts editor of *Veneer* magazine. The two of us should probably have been discussing post-modernist aesthetic theory and its impact on social policy. I fixed my eyes on her bare legs, took a deep breath and plunged into the darkness.

'You like it?' Sal whirled, showing her secret place. A fern gully. Dark, moist, prehistoric. Round and round she spun, noiseless, abandoned, crazy, even drunker than me. She grabbed my hand again and took off, leading me on at breakneck speed. The path forked and twisted, becoming a maze. She let go, disappeared. The night was tropical, full of sounds, water running, the hypnotic thrum of a million cicadas, bird calls, a high-pitched squeaking like a gate swinging on its hinges in a breeze. I plunged on, running headlong downhill, the momentum irresistible.

A grove of bamboo reared up, the canes as thick as my arm, a kung fu forest. She lay there on a bed of leaves, waiting. I threw myself on my back beside her, and she rolled onto me, straddling my thighs. She could scarcely have been unaware of the effect this produced. '*Pinus radiata*,' I said. '*Grevillea robusta*.'

We did not kiss. It would have seemed soppy. My hands glided up her ribs, thumbs extended to trace her anatomy through the fabric of her dress. Belly, sternum, ribs. Nipples as hard as Chinese algebra. Her neck arched, her mouth hung open. Dirty dancing in deep dark dingly dell. Above, high above, the sky was a pale blur, immeasurably distant, framed by branches festooned with hundreds of brown paper bags that rustled gently in the still night air.

My shirt was open. Her dress was runched up around her waist. Fingers tugged at my belt – hers or mine I couldn't tell, didn't care. 'Where is it?' she gasped. 'Where is it?'

'In your hand. It's in your hand.'

'Not that, stupid. A condom.'

If she didn't stop doing what she was doing with her hand, I wouldn't need a condom. I didn't have one. What sort of boy did she think I was?

Warm liquid trickled out of the sky and splashed the ground beside us. Rainforest soma, warm and dank.

Salina arched her neck again, staring up to where the paper bags shifted and shuffled, fluttering from branch to branch, chattering among themselves, a hundred squeaky gates.

'Bats!' she shrieked.

Hundreds of them. Fruit bats, flying foxes, roosting high in the tops of spindly Moreton Bay figs. She leaped to her feet and we ran, she convulsed with the giggles, me stuffing myself back in my pants.

We exploded out of the fern forest into a circle of lawn. The night sky, drenched with humidity, shone like a sudden spotlight after the jungle depths. We rolled together on the grass, kissing now, all the imminence of the previous moment gone, the compact implicit, a slow build-up ahead of us. Sweet, sweet, sweet. I came up for air. 'You think any of these are rubber trees?'

Salina pulled the wine from her bag and we drank from the bottle, getting sensible, keeping un-sober. 'My place,' she said. A loft. In the city. Safety tackle, more booze. I pulled her to her feet. 'Let's went.'

Easier said than done. Melbourne's Botanic Gardens are approximately the size of Uganda. At the best of times, finding your way out takes a compass, a ball of twine, and access to satellite navigation. We sat down and drank some more. She watched me graze her lowlands, then we started up the hill, hugging the dark fringes, cutting through the densest thickets.

Here and there we stopped, pressed against each other in beds of flowering succulents, stamen brushing pistil, inhaling nectar. Pissed to the eyeballs. My fingers were sticky with liquidambar. My aching prick was as hard and smooth as the trunk of the ghost gum,

Eucalyptus papuana, planted here by Viscount de Lisle, Governor-General of Australia, 1961–65.

Eventually, unpollinated, we found the fence at the top of the hill and followed it. An open-sided rotunda capped the crest, its cupola resting on columns topped with stag ferns cast in concrete. My sentiments precisely.

Below was the river, its banks hidden by trees. The occasional swish of a car wafted up from Alexandra Avenue. In the distance, tipping the foliage, the neon sign above the Richmond silos told the hour. NYLEX 3.08. The pub had closed at one. Time was meaningless. Across the river, the lights of the city glowed. A loft, she'd said.

'Princes Bridge.' She cocked her head towards where the fence was concealed in a border of hardy perennials. Princes Bridge was the nearest point we could cross the Yarra. Bliss was a twenty-minute walk away. Never again, I swore by the sacred name of Baden-Powell, never again would I be caught unprepared.

We climbed the fence and began our way across the treed lawns of the Queen Victoria Gardens. The heehaw of an ambulance siren washed through the night towards us, echoing the pulse of my horny urgency. As we headed for the bridge, the sound grew louder, insistent in the stillness, urging us forward.

At the floral clock, where the trees ended and the lawn met the broad boulevard of St Kilda Road, the sound abruptly stopped. We stopped, too, and stared.

Across the road sat the National Gallery, its floodlit facade looming like the screen of a drive-in movie, a faceless wall of austere grey basalt. Extending along the foot of the wall was a shallow ornamental moat, walled by a low stone parapet. In the moat stood a gigantic multi-hued beast with three legs and a head at each end.

This sight was not, in itself, remarkable. The gallery with its moat and its sculptures was a prominent civic landmark. A tourist attraction, a cultural resource. We'd both seen it a thousand times before. But neither of us had ever seen it like this.

An ambulance was drawn up at the gallery's main entrance, a dark mouse-hole in the blank wall. Both of the vehicle's rear doors were flung open. Its light was flashing. Giant shadows, thrown up by the spinning flare, played across the facade of the building like characters from a half-glimpsed puppet show. Like the figures in Plato's cave. Two men were kneeling on the parapet of the moat. Their heads bobbed. Their arms jerked rhythmically. A little cluster of figures moved about the ambulance, engaged in some obscure task. The sudden silence, the lack of passing traffic, was absolute. The tableau was compelling in its mystery.

Drawn irresistibly, we crossed the road. It was a pointless detour, a distraction. Stupid.

The paramedics parted as we arrived, as if to display their handiwork, as if our mere presence entitled us to a view of the proceedings. Except they weren't parting for us, but were clearing a way to wheel a stretcher towards the yawning doors of the ambulance.

On the stretcher was a body. Alive or dead, man or woman, it was impossible to tell. All I could see were legs, clad in wet black jeans. Then my view was blocked by a gallery security guard. His trousers, too, were soaked. Water trailed across the footpath. Someone had been pulled out of the moat.

There was a kind of bleak formality to the scene. Sombre work was being undertaken by those trained to its demands. The climax, whatever it was, had already been played out. We had no business here, gawping at its aftermath. I turned away, embarrassed, a little ashamed of my curiosity. Besides, I had more vital concerns. That loft in the city was only ten minutes away.

But Salina had slipped between two of the uniforms. 'Hey, Marcus,' she called, like it was all an elaborate joke being staged for our benefit. 'What's going on?'

Then I saw what she had seen. A pair of cowboy boots, tooled leather toes pointing at the sky, jutting from the end of the stretcher.

Things happened very quickly after that. A police car disgorged two uniforms, one male, one female. A security guard, some toy copper with pissant insignia, grabbed at Sal, caught one of her hula hoops. I pushed forward, but one of the cops got there first. She had Salina by the arm, holding her back. 'You know this person?'

In the staccato explosions of light, I saw Salina's face as it bent above the stretcher. Saw it change, frame by frame. Recognition. Shock. Panic. Her eyes were wide with dread. 'He's my . . .' The words hooked in her throat.

'His name?' The policeman was in no mood to be stuffed about by a half-drunk dolly bird. One of the security guards had handed him a wallet, and he was reading a plastic card.

'Marcus Taylor.' Salina's tone was defiant now, as she fought for control. The officer nodded, acknowledging her right to be there, conceding nothing else. The stretcher was almost all the way into the ambulance. Even without looking, I knew who he was, this Marcus Taylor.

'He's my boyfriend,' said Salina. Then she corrected herself. 'Fiancé. He's my fiancé.'

The policewoman drew her back, making room for them to close the ambulance door.

Salina turned then and looked at me like it was all my fault. 'Bastard,' she swore.

I'D BEEN given the brush-off before, but this was a bit rich. I could see that the woman was upset, but she could hardly blame me for what was happening.

Twelve hours earlier I'd never even heard of Salina Fleet, or this Marcus Taylor who was being fed feet-first into the ambulance. Twelve hours earlier, the idea of romping in the rhododendrons with a blonde cultural critic in a pom-pommed mu-mu was as remote as my chances of being appointed ambassador to the Holy See. Seeing a floater being pulled out of the moat of the National Gallery had not been pencilled into my diary.

Half a day earlier, I wasn't even on this side of town. I was stuck in a stifling room behind a shopfront in Northcote, being given the hairy eyeball by Leonidas Mavramoustakides. It was the last Friday in January 1989, the stinking hot end of an overheated decade, and I was waiting for a phone call. I wished it would hurry up and come.

Mavramoustakides was once a major in Greek army intelligence. That was twenty years earlier, during the military regime. He still cultivated the style. Crisp white

9

shirt, hairline moustache, dark tie, gimlet eyes. The dye he used to keep his hair jet black was beginning to run in the heat and little dribbles of it were trickling down beneath his collar. But I wasn't going to tell him that. Not with the attitude he was taking.

He was sitting behind a tiny imitation baroque desk made of plywood. Most of it was taken up by a voluminous white marble ashtray, and by two pompously over-flowing correspondence trays, one weighted down by a small plaster bust of Aristotle. Mavramoustakides crushed the tip of his cigarette cruelly into the ashtray, put his elbows on his desk and smiled a mirthless smile. 'If we don't get your co-operation,' he said. 'We can make things very uncomfortable for you.'

It was difficult to conceive just how he proposed to do this. I was already about as uncomfortable as humanly possible. The air of the minuscule room was thick with stale cigarette smoke. My shirt was drenched with sweat and stuck to the back of a vinyl chair. My teeth were caked with grounds from the cup of muddy coffee in front of me. And Jimmy Papas, Mavramoustakides' overweight sidekick, looked like he was about to lumber to his feet and smack me across the chops with his fat hand.

'Remember,' warned Mavramoustakides. 'We are more than half a million Greeks in this city.' The way he said it, you'd think he was claiming personal responsibility for the fact. 'You can't afford to upset that many people.'

Actually there were only 326,382 Greek-speaking residents of Melbourne and scant few of them paid any attention at all to Leonidas Mavramoustakides. The only reason we were having this conversation was because he and Jimmy Papas were getting to be a pain in the neck. They'd been ringing around and writing letters and two weeks earlier Papas had confronted my boss, Angelo Agnelli, at Kostas Manolas' daughter's wedding and threatened to make a scene. Angelo, naturally, had immediately agreed to an appointment. Then, naturally, he found he had an unavoidable engagement elsewhere and deputised me to solve the problem.

'Piss off, Leo,' I said, staring at the phone, willing it to ring. 'You're talking crap and you know it.'

We were in the editor's office at *Nea Hellas*, a Greek-language tabloid with an ultra-conservative political line and a weekly readership of about ten thousand. Leonidas Mavramoustakides owned and edited the paper and Jimmy Papas was its business manager, a job that consisted largely of convincing delicatessen owners and fish-roe importers to buy advertising space they didn't really need. This task was proving increasingly difficult, which explained why the two of them were getting so pushy.

'We only ask what we entitled to,' growled Papas, doing to his worry beads what he'd like to do to my testicles. '*Neos Kosmos, Il Globo, El Telegraph*, all these papers get government advertising. How come we don't get our share? If we don't, our readers will not vote Labor at the next election. You tell your boss Agnelli that.'

A little respect would not have been out of order. For me, and for my boss. The Honourable Angelo Agnelli was a Minister of the Crown, the Minister for Ethnic Affairs. Ours was a Labor government, democratic in temper, so obsequiousness was unnecessary. Just a little less contempt, that was all I asked. The kind of scorn that Mavramoustakides displayed was the prerogative of colleagues and associates, not superannuated torturers.

'Get real, Jimmy,' I said. 'None of your readers vote for us anyway. Most of them can't even read.'

The function of the Minister for Ethnic Affairs was to spread a microscopically thin layer of largesse over every ethnic community in the state. My task, as his adviser, was to help wield the butter knife. On a day like this, dealing with pricks like this, it was a job whose appeal was limited.

Fortunately, before I could say something undiplomatic, Sophie Mavramoustakides stuck her head around the door. 'Phone call for Murray Whelan,' she chirped, in the manner of a hotel bellboy paging a guest. 'You want me to put it through?'

Sophie had a hair-do like a haystack and a lot more va-va-voom than she could burn off working as a typist at her fascist father's rag. She splashed some of it over me. She was wasting her time. I was single but I wasn't suicidal.

Only Trish at the office knew where I was, so this was the call I'd been waiting for. But the last thing I needed was Leo and Jimmy breathing down my neck while I got the news. I unpeeled myself from the plastic chair and indicated I'd prefer to take the call in private. Mavramoustakides grunted. My preferences were beneath his dignity. He'd wanted to talk to the organ grinder, not be fobbed off with the monkey. As far as Leo was concerned, I could go climb a tree.

Sophie, utilising as much of her bottom as possible, led me upstairs to the chaos that passed for the *Nea Hellas* production room, indicated which phone I should use and returned Eurydice-like into the Stygian realm below.

Nea Hellas was on the Northcote hill, one of the few elevated points in the otherwise flat expanse of Melbourne's inner-northern suburbs. The view out its first-floor window swept in a broad arc across the baking rooftops of houses and factories, all the way to the glass-walled towers of the central city, a shimmering mirage on the far horizon. Above, an un-broken blue sky beat down with the full power of a forty-degree summer afternoon. Below, a metropolis of three million lay prostrate beneath its might.

For much of the decade, the state of Victoria, of which this city was the crowning jewel, had been ruled by a Labor government. For a while things had gone well. More recently, the auguries were less auspicious. The previous year's election victory had been snatched from the jaws of defeat only by the narrowest of margins. In politics, as in our city's notoriously fickle weather, nothing is certain. When things change, they change quickly. From the direction of Treasury Place, at the foot of the towering office-blocks, wraiths of heat haze ascended to the remorseless heavens like smoke from a sacrificial altar.

It must have been the weather. All this Greek shit was going to my head. I picked up the phone. 'Break it to me gently,' I said.

For the past sixteen months, since the '87 stock-market crash, the Economic Development Ministry had been haemorrhaging money. What had started as a trickle had become an unstoppable torrent. The government was losing money faster than it could raise or borrow it. A gesture was required. A head must roll. Bill Hahn, the Deputy Premier, had drawn the short straw. The fag end of January met the timing requirements perfectly. Half the population was too shagged out from the heat to be interested in politics. The other half was busy folding its tents and returning from holidays. When the Premier called an unscheduled Cabinet meeting earlier that after-noon, the agenda was only too obvious.

'It's over,' said Trish. 'Angelo's just come back.'

Behind her voice I could hear the mechanical whirr of a document shredder. Which could mean only one thing. There had been a major reshuffle. Angelo Agnelli was no longer Minister for Ethnic Affairs. 'Don't keep me in suspense.' I tried to make it casual. 'What happened? Did he get the sack or did he get a new portfolio?'

Trish was Agnelli's private secretary. I thought I could detect a suggestion of distance in her tone, a hint that old alliances could no longer be taken for granted. The flux was running, changes were afoot up there in the ministerial suite. 'You're going to love this,' she said. She could afford to be flippant. She'd be okay. Whatever happens, they always take their secretaries with them. 'He's been given Water.'

'Christ!' I said. 'Minister for Water Supply.' The very thought of it made my mouth go dry. I looked about the *Nea Hellas* production room for something to slake my sudden thirst. The only cup in sight contained the congealing dregs of ancient Greek coffee. My future was suddenly as black as that bitter beverage. I touched it to my lips. At least it was wet.

I'd been at Ethnic Affairs for four years. Employing me as his principal adviser had been one of Agnelli's smarter moves. In a state whose two major ethnic power blocks are the Greeks and the Italians, giving the job to a man with an Irish name was a masterstroke of impartiality. And since I'd once been party organiser in Melbourne Upper, Agnelli's electorate, home to the highest concentration of migrants in the country, it wasn't as though I didn't have some pretty solid credentials in the field of dago-wrangling. But Water Supply? All I knew about Water Supply was it happened when you turned on a tap.

'And the Arts,' said Trish.

Water Supply and the Arts. My heart plummeted. Not only had Agnelli failed to win substantial promotion, he'd managed to put me in very ticklish situation. Local Government I could do. Community Services, no problem. But Water Supply and the Arts? I knew as much about rocket science.

'The Arts?' I repeated dismally. 'That means I'm fucked.'

Now that I had embraced my fate, Trish could afford to allow a little more of the old warmth back into her voice. 'Yeah,' she said cheerfully. 'I reckon.'

The odds that Agnelli would retain me as his adviser on hydraulic affairs were low. But the very idea that a man named Agnelli might employ someone called Whelan to advise him on cultural matters was inconceivable. The fact that Ange had been born in the Queen Victoria Hospital, not five kilometres from where I stood, was immaterial. What possible assistance could an Australian bog-wog provide to a man through whose veins surged the blood of Tintoretto and Tiepolo? A man sprung from the race of Boccherini and Vivaldi. Dante and Boccaccio. Bramante, Caravaggio, Raphael, Michelangelo, Donatello, Leonardo and all those other fucking turtles. 'What do you know about Water Supply?' I begged, no longer bothering to conceal the desperation in my voice.

Trish and I went back a long way. She was a tough cookie who had run the electorate office in Melbourne Upper in the days before Agnelli got the pre-selection. If it walked in off the street, whatever it was, Trish could handle it. 'Can't be too complicated,' she said. 'Dams don't go on strike. Pipelines don't stack committees at party conferences.'

She had a point. Water seeks to find its own level. Even as Minister for Water Supply, Agnelli would still need a man with my skills. Someone to write his speeches. Fend off lobbyists. Crack the whip over the bureaucrats. Sniff the air. Test the water. Help him go with the flow. Maybe he'd keep me on, after all.

'He wants to see you,' said Trish. 'Now.'

It wasn't as if I didn't appreciate the political realities of the situation. The government was skating on thin electoral ice. A Cabinet re-jig was essential if we were to keep the show on the road. But what was good for the party could hardly have come at a worse time for me personally. Not to put too fine a point on it, with the interest rate on my mortgage nudging 16 per cent, I was no candidate for early retirement. It wasn't just the money, either. Family matters needed to be considered.

'Oh, another thing,' added Trish. 'Wendy called. She says to ring her urgently.' Wendy was the mother of my ten-year-old child Redmond. They lived in Sydney where Wendy ran equal opportunity for Telecom. 'Not in trouble with the ex again, are you, Murray?'

'*Malacca fungula*,' I said. A Mediterranean expression meaning 'Don't be silly'.

Trish, who'd picked up a smattering of Southern European at the Electoral Office, pretended to laugh and hung up. Pressing down the phone cradle, I quickly dialled Wendy's mobile. Trust Wendy to have one, the latest toy of the corporate high-flier. At five dollars a minute, *Nea Hellas* could cop the tab.

'Yes.' Wendy's phone manner was brisk, but she wasn't fooling me. Somewhere in the background was the gentle lap of Sydney Harbour, the flapping of yacht sails in the breeze, the lifting of shirts. Wendy was probably at Doyle's, finishing a long lunch. I could see the sucked-dry shells of pink crustaceans piled before her. 'Oh, it's *you*,' she said. 'About time, too.'

Four years before, I'd assumed the prime parenting role while Wendy took a temporary secondment to the Office of the Status of Women in Canberra. Before I knew it, she was the big cheese in gender equity at the Department of Education, Employment and Training, our marriage was finished, and I'd become the non-custodial parent. By the time she got her fancy new job in Sydney, Red's access visits had dropped to four a year. One was scheduled to begin that evening. But not before I was subjected to the customary lecture on my deficiencies as a parent.

'I've got all the details already, Wendy,' I told her.

'How many times have I not been there to meet Red's plane?' A couple, actually, but they weren't my fault and the kid had agreed, for a price, that they'd be our little secret.

'He won't be arriving,' she said. 'His orthodontist appointment was changed and there isn't another flight until two tomorrow afternoon.'

'Orthodontist?' I said. 'What does he need with an orthodontist?' Red's teeth were fine last time I'd looked. This was clearly a pretext to cut short my son's first visit in more than three months.

'Just a check-up,' said Wendy. 'But this guy's the best overbite specialist in the country. You don't want second-rate treatment for your child's teeth do you?' I let that one go by. 'Besides which, school doesn't start until Tuesday, so he can stay until Monday evening.'

'I'll be at work on Monday.' I was trying to make a point, but as soon as I spoke I knew I'd walked into a trap.

'Well, I suppose there's always another time. He'll be very disappointed, of course.'

If I missed this chance, it might be months before I saw Red again. 'I'll take Monday off,' I said quickly. The way things were shaping up, I probably wouldn't have a job to go to anyway. Not that I had any intention of sharing that hot little item with Wendy.

'I daresay the place won't fall down if you're not there for a day,' said Wendy. Telecom, of course, ceased to function every time Wendy stepped out of the room. 'And don't forget to see that he wears a hat in the sun. He nearly got burned at Noosa. Richard had to keep reminding him to put one on.'

Just like Wendy had to keep reminding me that she had successfully recoupled and I had not. And that her salary allowed her to take Red to fashionable resorts for his holidays, when the best I seemed to be able to do was take him to the cricket or the movies. And the cricket wasn't even on this weekend. 'Two o'clock,' I said. 'I'll be there to meet him. Tell him I'm looking forward to it.'

'Two o'clock is the departure time, Murray,' she said. 'The plane doesn't arrive down there until 3.20.' Her maths were top-notch. 'It's an eighty-minute flight.'

I knew that. 'Three, then,' I said cheerfully and hung up. I know when I'm licked. I went back down the stairs, past travel posters of old women with faces like hacksaws standing beside piles of picturesque rubble.

The air in Mavramoustakides' office, what there was of it, was thicker than ever. And not just with cigarette smoke. Sophie came out the door blowing her nose into a tissue, looking like she'd just been betrothed to a donkey. She flounced back upstairs.

'Okay,' I announced. I hadn't driven all that way in the heat to trade pleasantries. 'This is the deal. You report the government in a more balanced way and *Nea Hellas* gets a regular advertising contract with a major government campaign.'

Mavramoustakides looked like he'd never for one moment doubted his newspaper's capacity to strike fear into my heart. Papas wanted details. 'What campaign?'

I'd brought a bone with me, hidden up my sweaty sleeve. I pulled it out and tossed it. 'Keep Australia Beautiful,' I said.

Leo and Jimmy lit up with a mixture of avarice and

incomprehension. As far as I was concerned, Australia the Beautiful could look after itself. I was more interested in keeping my job. That, and a three o'clock appointment at Tullamarine airport the next afternoon.

We sealed the deal with a handshake beneath a poster of Mount Olympus. The gods, if I had bothered to look, were laughing.

MELBOURNE'S WEATHER teeters forever on the brink of imminence. If it is warm, a cool change is expected. A day of rain bisects a month of shine. Spring vanishes for weeks on end. Summer arrives unseasonably early, inexplicably late, not at all. Winter is wet but not cold, cold but not wet.

So far, that summer, all we'd had was heat. Through a city limp and surly beneath its oppressive demands, I steered my butter-yellow 1979 Diahatsu Charade towards my waiting fate. Past the airless bungalows of Northcote and the tight-packed terraces of Collingwood, through the reek of molten asphalt and the baked biscuit aroma of the brewery malting works, I drove to Victoria Parade, a boulevard of canopied elms marking the northern boundary of the central business district.

Laid out by city fathers with Parisian fantasies and strategic interests, Victoria Parade was where the young gentlemen of the Royal Victorian Mounted Volunteers would have drawn their sabres if ever the working-class mob had come storming up the hill from its blighted shacks on the flat below. As it turned out, the tide of history had run the other way. It was the slums that had fallen, captured by the gentry. And me, for my sins, rapidly becoming one of them.

The Ministry for Ethnic Affairs occupied the top three floors of a brick-clad early-seventies office building overlooking the elms. I drove around the block and parked on an all-day meter beside the Fitzroy Gardens. The Charade was a step in the direction of anonymity I'd taken after a demented constituent ran my previous vehicle into a lake one dark and stormy night several years before. It was less conspicuous than my old Renault, but it didn't do a thing for my image.

Short of walking around the block in the blazing sun, the quickest way into the Ethnic Affairs building was via its basement carpark. Suit jacket hooked over my shoulder, I advanced down the ramp into the half-darkness. The carpark was small, its twenty-odd spaces reserved for the building's more important tenants. Agnelli parked there on the odd occasion he drove himself to work. The Director of the Ministry. The Commissioners of the Liquor Licensing Board. Senior managers from the private companies which occupied the building's middle levels.

Taking up two spaces at the bottom of the ramp was a huge silver Mercedes, top of the range, an interloper among the familiar collection of managerial Magnas and executive Audis. At the far end of the garage, next to the lift, was a luminous white blob, Agnelli's official Fairlane. Beside it, wiping the windscreen, was Agnelli's driver, Alan.

Not Alan, I realised, as my eyes adjusted to the gloom. Alan was in his mid-fifties, a fastidious ex-corporal who spent his off-road moments burnishing the Fairlane's duco and picking dead insects out of its chrome work. But, apart from sharing his general height and build, this guy bore no resemblance whatsoever to Alan. Nor was he cleaning the Fairlane's window. Palm cupped, he was scrutinising the car's interior with what I instinctively took to be no good intent.

He was somewhere around my age, mid-thirties, and he affected the style of a spiv. His dark hair was sleekly combed, his trousers and tie black and too narrow. The sleeves of his white shirt were rolled to mid-forearm. He carried himself with the loose-limbed posture of a man who wants it understood that he is handy at close quarters. The only thing missing was the jemmy in his hand. As I drew near, he leaned insolently against the Fairlane's door and tracked my approach through the twin mirrors of aviator sunglasses with an air of casual menace.

I had neither reason nor inclination to respond to the implicit challenge of his stance. Carpark monitor wasn't my job – if I still had a job. The security of Agnelli's vehicle was Alan's responsibility, not mine. Unfortunately, the stranger was between me and the lift, making no effort to move aside. To get past, I'd virtually have to brush against him.

As I closed the last few paces between us, the man's features became more distinct. I realised, with dismay, that I knew him. Nearly twenty years had passed, but it was impossible not to recognise Spider Webb. Mr and Mrs Webb may have called their little boy Noel, but at school he was always the Spider.

Despite his nickname, there was nothing arachnoid

about Spider. No spindly limbs or jutting canines. On the contrary. He had an athletic build, high cheekbones and fleshy, petulant lips. He would almost have been handsome if not for his ears. You only had to look at Noel Webb to know why they called them jug ears. Chrome-plated, his head wouldn't have looked out of place in a trophy cabinet. Wing-nut would have been a better nickname. But Spider, despite Noel's dislike for it, was the one that stuck. It suited him. There was something predatory about Spider, cold-blooded, self-serving. He'd been like that at sixteen, and he was still like that. You could read it in his pose. We'd been friends once, or so I thought. Then things had happened, violent things that gave me no reason whatsoever to want to renew our boyhood acquaintance. Especially since Spider had clearly fulfilled the criminal promise of his youth. I hoped to Jesus he didn't recognise me.

As I approached, he massaged a piece of chewing gum loose from its pack, tossed it into his mouth and rolled his head like a prize-fighter readying himself for a bout. I resigned myself to our reunion, waiting for him to speak.

But Spider said nothing, gave no explicit sign of recognition. It had been a long time. With luck, he might not remember me. If he didn't speak, I decided, neither would I.

Back to the wall, I sidled past, head up, eyes straight ahead. We were almost exactly the same height and so close that my own face stared back at me from the mercury pools of Spider's sunglasses. Stereoscopic reflections, I thought, of a man not quite succeeding in mastering his loathing.

Spider straightened a little to allow me passage but still he said nothing. His face had slackened into a sphinx-like inscrutability. Only the muscles of his jaw moved, flexing almost imperceptibly around his gum, a gesture of contemptuous amusement at the discomfort of a stranger. Still an arsehole after all these years.

I pressed on. As I crossed the final few paces to the lift, I heard a dismissive, barely audible grunt and felt hidden eyes boring into my back. Then the lift doors yawned before me and out stepped Alan, a polystyrene cup in his hand, his gaze darting towards the Fairlane. Nodding, I stepped into the lift. As the doors whoomphed closed behind me, I felt a shudder of what could have been either relief or foreboding.

If ever there was a bird of ill omen, it was Spider Webb. Loosen up, I told myself, pushing the button for the top floor. It's only a job. It's not the measure of your worth as a human being. There's always the slow descent into alcoholism and penury to look forward to.

The door slid open to a re-enactment of the evacuation of Saigon. Boxes of documents littered the corridors. Base-grade clerks from the Translation and Information sections bustled about, pushing trolleys in and out of rooms. Trish stood feeding files into the shredder. I recognised one of mine, *Current Issues in the Macedonian Community*. It was a slim document and held no state secrets, but that wasn't the point.

Agnelli had been at Ethnic Affairs long enough to generate more than enough stuff-ups to provide ammunition to his political enemies. Especially those from his own party. So before his replacement arrived everything short of the potted plants would be fed into the shredder. By the end of the day, some of my most skil-fully wrought briefing papers would be reduced to a pile of fly-specked tagliatelle in the ministerial dump-ster. I prayed that I wouldn't be in there with them.

Back when she ran the electorate office, Trish had been a rough diamond, well-upholstered and ready for anything. She was efficient, smart and knew her stuff. Eventually, Agnelli was persuaded to overlook her rougher edges and reward her loyalty with a promo-tion. A monster was born. Within a month of being made his private secretary, she'd joined Gloria Marshall and taken a course in fire breathing. Success, in accor-dance with the fashion of the day, had gone straight to her shoulders. She glanced up from the papery gnashing of her task and tossed a nod in the general direction of Agnelli's shut door. 'Take a number and wait,' she commanded.

I took it into my office and had a cigarette with it. Ours was a smoke-free environment, but what the fuck – as of now I didn't work here any more. Out the window, across the wilting greenery of the gardens, glass-walled towers quivered in the heat haze, molten swords plunged into the heart of the city. In the gaps between, ant-sized men plied construction cranes. Hardier men than the likes of me.

The building boom sustained by Labor's rule was at its peak, a relentless reordering of the skyline that was the most tangible evidence of the government's success. Everywhere the old was being jackhammered away and replaced with the spanking new. So headlong was the charge of money into real estate that slow-footed city shoppers risked being knocked down in the rush to build yet another office tower or luxury hotel. Anything more than twenty years old was obsolete. Yesterday's skyscrapers were today's holes in the ground. Tomorrow's landmarks had lakes in their foyers and computer-monitored pollen filters and the city council was putting little lights in the trees so we'd think it was Christmas all year round.

Not that I, as I pondered my options, had anything to celebrate. My attachment to Agnelli, like his loyalty to me, was contingent on the political realities. Bypassed for pro-motion this time, Ange would need plenty of runs on the board if he hoped to impress the Premier next time around. My employability depended on how useful he thought I could be in achieving that outcome. This we both understood.

Anybody working in politics who claims to be without personal ambition is a liar. That I hadn't yet quite formulated the nature of my own particular aspirations was beside the point. The fact that I'd placed my political loyalties at Agnelli's disposal for the previous four years didn't mean I had no interests of my own. If Agnelli thought I'd go quietly, he could think again. At the very least he should find me a new position appropriate to my skills. Try to throw me out with the dirty bath water, and he'd soon find that I had plenty of influential friends in the party who'd take a dim view of that sort of behaviour. Plenty. I tried to think of several.

While I was waiting for a name to come to mind, I finished my cigarette. Our smoke-free environment, naturally enough, provided no ashtrays so I took the butt into the executive washroom and stuffed it down the basin plughole. The executive washroom was what we jokingly called the small private bathroom off the minister's inner office. Supposedly for Angelo's exclusive use, it was also accessible from my office. Since it had an exhaust fan, I'd sometimes slip in for a quick concentration-enhancing puff when no-one was looking.

The door leading into Angelo's office was open a crack and I could hear his voice. He sounded keyed up. 'A new broom,' he was saying. 'Energetically wielded.'

I was history.

'**M**ONEY IS the key.' Just the sort of thing you'd expect to hear Agnelli barking down the phone. 'All the policies in the world won't save us if we don't go into the election with a decent campaign fund.'

Party matters were the subject, so he wasn't speaking to a bureaucrat from one of his new ministries. Whoever it was, my employer was warming to his topic. 'It's time to start getting serious.'

'The finance committee's doing everything it can, Angelo.'

Ange wasn't on the phone. He had a visitor. I knew the voice. Duncan Keogh, one of a number of assistant state secretaries from party headquarters. Keogh was a smarmy popinjay, a twenty-seven-year-old smarty pants who could barely remember when Labor wasn't in power. He approached politics as though its exclusive purpose was to provide a career structure for otherwise unemployable graduates of Monash University.

Why, I couldn't help but ask myself, was Agnelli closeted with a mid-level machine man like Duncan when he should have been more concerned with the pressing business of the day, the outcome of the Cabinet reshuffle?

'Duncan,' I heard my boss say wearily. 'You're our third finance committee chair in eighteen months. I'm not saying you aren't competent, otherwise I'd never have supported you for the appointment. But you just don't have the sort of clout you need to be effective.'

Keogh needed more than clout. He needed a brain transplant and a personality upgrade. He was a non-performer who had inveigled himself into the finance committee chair by singing some bullshit song about new blood and fresh ideas. Agnelli had bought it, against my recommendation, and seconded Keogh's nomination. Duncan's subsequent performance had been conspicuously ordinary. With any luck, Agnelli had summoned the twerp to tell him he'd better start delivering, that he should either shit or get off the pot.

'Cabinet-level influence is what you need, Duncan. And that's what I'm proposing to give you,' he said. 'With you in the chair and me setting the agenda, we can move our fund-raising efforts to a whole new level.'

I didn't like the direction this conversation was taking.

Raising the cash needed to run election campaigns was a chronic headache. Last time we'd gone to the polls, we had to mortgage party headquarters to cover the cost of the how-to-vote cards. And, lacking the conservatives' traditional allies in big business, we were forced to scratch for cash wherever we could find it. But rattling the tin for money was a task best undertaken at a very long arm's length from the positions occupied by people like Angelo Agnelli. It was a job best done by more anonymous members of the party apparatus. Collectors of membership dues. Organisers of mail-outs. Conductors of wine-bottlings and quiz-nights. Men like Duncan Keogh. Not Cabinet ministers.

'I'll still be the chairperson,' said Keogh. 'Right?'

I could hear his tiny mind ticking over. Letting Agnelli pull the strings, he was thinking, would be a good idea. He would win a big friend and move a little closer to the centre of the action. Agnelli could do all the work and Duncan would still get to put 'Chairperson, Finance Committee' on his CV.

'Absolutely,' said Angelo. 'So, how much have we got in the kitty right now?'

'Just over four hundred thousand,' said Keogh. 'Union affiliations and membership levies, mostly. Half in Commonwealth bonds, half on deposit at the State Bank.' A safe player, our Duncan. If this was his idea of a fresh approach, no wonder our finances were in such a parlous condition.

'We're going to need a shitload more than that,' said Agnelli. 'A million five, minimum. What about corporate donors?'

Keogh cleared his throat nervously. 'Barely a pat on the head, so far. About ten grand all up. But we're setting up a sub-committee to look at a strategy to improve that figure.'

'A committee!' Agnelli snorted derisively. 'The skyline's full of cranes. Fucking sunrise industries left, right and centre. People making money out of our polices hand over fist. And ten grand is the most they can cough up. What's wrong with these pricks?'

Keogh was really on the ropes now. 'It's a sensitive

area. Either they give or they don't. Mostly they don't.'

Another voice weighed into the discussion, soothing, placatory. 'Duncan's right, Angelo,' it said. 'This is a sensitive area. Go blundering around putting the hard word on the business community, you'll end up being accused of peddling influence.'

For the life of me, I couldn't put a face to the voice. But whoever he was, he was talking sense.

'See,' said Keogh, vindicated. 'It's not as easy as you seem to think.'

But the other speaker hadn't finished. 'That's not to say that there aren't ways of approaching these matters. Take your new portfolio, for example, Angelo.' The voice was of a man used to being listened to, someone at ease in a minister's office. 'Your accounts department alone employs, what, four or five hundred people.' He was speaking, he wanted it understood, hypo-thetically. 'That's a lot of office space. Property developers pay sweeteners to private corporations to secure long-term leases on their new buildings. If some of them were to get the idea that the Water Supply Commission was thinking about moving house . . .'

'Jesus,' groaned Keogh. 'We're treading perilously close to the line here.'

'You don't think the Liberals wouldn't be even more cosy with their business cronies if they had the chance?' said Agnelli.

The more I heard of this, the faster my disquiet turned into outright anxiety. Knowing Angelo as well as I did, it didn't take too much mental exertion to figure out what he was up to. He'd decided to do a bit of lateral thinking.

Like the weather, campaign finances were something that everybody complained about, but nobody did anything to fix. Angelo, evidently, had decided he'd be the one to grasp the nettle. Even the most outstanding performance in Water Supply and the Arts could only earn him a limited number of brownie points with the Premier. But if he succeeded in filling the party war chest, some big favours would be due next time the hats went into the ring. Obversely, the consequences of failure did not bear thinking about.

'We're all agreed, it's a sensitive area,' said the voice, conciliatory again. 'And there's no rush. The election is two years away.'

'Quite right,' said Agnelli, getting the hint. 'First things first. What sort of interest is the State Bank paying us, Duncan?'

Keogh rustled some paper and named a percentage. It was about ten points lower than what I was paying them on my home loan.

'Shit,' said Agnelli. 'My cheque account pays more.'

'The money could definitely be working harder,' agreed the other man, business-like now. 'Managed properly, 20 per cent or higher isn't out of the question. That's another $50,000 a year, straight up. And no favours required.'

The intercom buzzed. 'Premier's Department on line one,' squawked Trish's voice. 'About the swearing-in of the new Cabinet. And Murray has just arrived.'

At the sound of my name, I scurried back into my own office and lit another cigarette.

Agnelli was heading straight into the kind of troubled waters he paid me to steer him away from. Why hadn't he discussed his foray into fund-raising with me first? And who was this guy in his office? Knowing exactly who Agnelli was talking to, about what, and why, was what I got paid for. At least it had been, I reminded myself. Angelo's problems were not necessarily mine any more.

Sitting behind my artificial-woodgrain desk, gazing between my shoes into the reception area, I tried to concentrate on my own immediate predicament. What I needed was a bit of instant expertise. Just enough to make Angelo think I might still be of some use, despite the changed circumstances. A couple of tantalising scraps of inside info on the Amalgamated Tap Turners and Dam Builders Union could go a long way. I opened my teledex and started scanning, hunting for a contact who could provide a crash course in the finer points of H_2O.

At that moment, Agnelli's door opened and Duncan Keogh strutted out, a pocket battleship in an open-necked sport shirt that strained at the thrust of his barrel chest. The shirt had a design like a test pattern and looked like Duncan had bought it at one of those menswear shops with a rack outside on the footpath. Any two shirts for $49.95 plus a free pair of pants. He was probably under the impression that he'd got a bargain. Not for the first time, I thought that maybe the Australian Labor Party should consider instituting a dress code.

Close on Keogh's heels came a man who didn't need any fashion advice. His lightweight summer suit was so well tailored it made Keogh's clothes look like he was wearing them for a bet. He could have been anywhere between his late forties and his early sixties, depending on the mileage, and he had the self-assured air of a man who didn't muck around. What he didn't muck around doing wasn't immediately apparent, but he'd made a success of it, whatever it was. His tie was red silk and so was his pocket handkerchief. He was fit, well-lunched and towered over Keogh like a gentleman farmer walking a Jack Russell terrier on a short leash.

He was laughing at something Keogh was saying, but only with his mouth. His eyes, up there where Duncan couldn't see them, were saying dickhead. Whoever he was, I liked him. He looked like he'd be a handy man to have on a lifeboat. While the others were singing 'Abide With Me', he'd slip you his hip flask of Black Label. He and Dunc went into the lift, doing the doings.

'Who was that?'

Trish, standing at the shredder, pretended she couldn't hear me, giving nothing away until she knew whether I was in or I was out. Jerking her head in the direction of Agnelli's door, she gave me leave to enter.

The great panjandrum's inner sanctum was as dark as a hibernating bear's cave. The air conditioning was on high and the heavy drapes were drawn against the glare of the day and the wandering gaze of the clerical staff in the Ministry for Industry and Technology next door. Through the cool gloom I could just make out the shape of Agnelli himself, a ghostly presence in shirt sleeves etched against the cluster of framed awards and diplomas on the wall behind his desk. Seeing him there like that – surrounded by his Order of the Pan Pontian

Brotherhood, his Honorary Master of Arts from the University of Valetta, the little model donkey cart presented with gratitude by the Reggio di Calabria Social Club – made my heart go out to him. Three years at the epicentre of political power and his office looked like a proctologist's consulting rooms.

His back was turned and he was reaching up to unhook one of the framed certificates. His University of Melbourne law degree. He studied it for a moment, then laid it carefully in an empty grocery carton sitting on his desk. Across the room I could read the box's yellow lettering. Golden Circle Pineapple, it said. This Way Up.

Shivering at the sudden drop in temperature, I stepped forward. Agnelli turned to face me. 'You heard?'

I nodded. 'Water Supply and the Arts.' I showed him my palms. Ours not to reason why, ours but to do and die.

Angelo indicated I should sit at the conference table, then crossed to the drapes and tugged them half-open. Harsh daylight swept away the conspiratorial shade. He got a couple of cans of beer out of his bar fridge, kicked his shoes off and sat down opposite me. So, he seemed to be saying. Here we are. Two men who know what's what. He slid me one of the cans – my poison chalice, I took it. And so it was, as it turned out. But not in the way I thought at the time.

He shrugged. 'I won't say I'm not disappointed.'

Power had improved Ange, the way a couple of drinks do to some people. It had smoothed down his more abrasive anxieties, made him more mellow, less in need of having constantly to assert himself. But his forties were well upon him, and he could no longer pass for a child wonder. His smooth black hair still came up well in print, and his cheeks still bulged with chipmunk amiability, but the good fairy of middling high office had scattered ashes at his temples and given him slightly more chins than were absolutely necessary. His heart remained where it had always been, though. Marginally to the left of centre, and closer to his stomach than his brain.

'This will mean some changes, of course,' he said.

I popped the tab off my can and waited for the bullet. Agnelli's gaze loitered in midair, among the dust motes playing in the beams of sunlight, as though they might offer him the right form of words.

'Tell me, Murray,' he said, at long last. 'What are the Arts?'

THIS WAS very disheartening. Why go through the pretence of having me fail the job interview? I sucked on my can. Bitter, beer, but fortifying.

Agnelli's question, it turned out, was entirely rhetorical. He didn't want my opinion. He wanted an audience. The axe was too brutal. There must needs first be a little armchair philosophising. A deep and meaningful on the complexities inherent in public intervention in the cultural sector.

'Let me bounce this off you,' he said. A little bouncing before the big bounce. 'The Arts are the measure of how far we have come and how far we have yet to go. A resource to be developed, an economic as well as a social asset. When I hear the word culture I think excellence and I think access . . .'

I wasn't sure where this was going, but at least he wasn't reaching for his revolver. 'Not bad,' I shrugged. 'Bit vague.'

'Then you'd better sharpen it up for me,' he said.

'You want me at Arts?' I must have sounded a little incredulous.

'If you don't mind.' Ange had a way of making you

feel like it was your decision, even if he was making it. 'For the time being. Until things settle down.'

'And then?'

'And then we'll see.' No doubt we would. If, he was making it clear, I didn't botch it.

So, here I was, my fortunes again leg-roped to Angelo Agnelli. Less than a minute before, I'd been merely apprehensive about my future. Now I had real cause for concern. 'I'll line up a departmental briefing, then,' I said, by way of acceptance.

'Fine.' Ange tossed his can at the waste basket, scored. 'You know Lloyd Eastlake?'

I shook my head. 'Should I?'

'He chairs the Cultural Affairs Policy Committee.' In theory, policy committees shaped the party platform and guarded it from the expediency of ministers. In practice, they were ineffectual talking-shops and magnets for inconsequential schemers. That did not mean, however, that due lip-service did not need to be paid. 'Bit of a mover, from all reports,' Agnelli said. 'Well connected in the unions. Not factionally aligned. Seen quite a few arts ministers come and go.' That wouldn't have been hard. The arts ministry changed hands more frequently than a concert pianist with the crabs.

'There's some sort of art gallery thing he's invited me to this evening. The Centre for Modern Art.' The policy committee chairman wasn't wasting any time cosying up to the new minister. 'Reckons it could be a good opportunity to start developing links with the cultural community.'

'Could be,' I agreed tentatively. No skin off my nose what Agnelli did with his Friday nights.

'I told him I couldn't make it, got a family function it's more than my life's worth to miss.' In other words, he planned to spend the evening on the phone, doing his factional arithmetic, figuring out where his esteem in the eyes of the Premier had turned to water. 'I told him you'd represent me. Standard booze and schmooze, you know the drill. He'll pick you up in front of the National Gallery at 6.30.'

Luckily, Red's deferred arrival meant I had a free evening. Not that disrupting my personal arrangements had ever unduly concerned Agnelli. 'This Eastlake and I don't know each other from a bar of soap. Do I wear a white carnation and carry a furled umbrella, or what?'

'I told him to look for someone who can't believe he's still got a job.'

I backed off, not complaining. Stroking the relevant policy committee chair was one of a ministerial adviser's chief chores, after all. And the Centre for Modern Art, whatever that was, had to be a step up from the Maltese Senior Citizens' Association annual dinner-dance, the sort of delegated duty that normally occupied my Friday and Saturday nights.

'Anything else I should be aware of?' I was steering him towards the conversation I had just overheard.

'Matter of fact, there is.' Agnelli ambled back to his desk and resumed his packing. 'See if you can't get me some tickets for *Don Giovanni*. You have heard of *Don Giovanni*, haven't you?'

'Shit, yeah,' I said. 'Big in the concrete business, isn't he?'

'It's a small portfolio, Murray,' said Agnelli, signalling

that our interview was at an end. 'Let's not make a meal of it.'

I drained my beer and beat a path to the door, grateful for small mercies. I might not yet have Agnelli's confidence on this fund-raising caper, but at least I was still in work. My fist was closing on the door handle when something crossed Agnelli's mind. 'Lots of rich you-know-whats involved in the arts, aren't there?'

What was that supposed to mean? 'I've heard rumours,' I said. 'Would you like it covered in the briefing?'

Agnelli turned back to his packing. 'Piss off,' he said, not entirely without wit.

I did, too. I immediately rang the Arts Ministry to confirm that the director was in, stuffed a couple of taxi vouchers in my pocket and went downstairs to Victoria Parade. The Charade could stay where it was until I'd scouted the parking situation at Arts. Besides which, I'd probably be offered a drink or two at this modern art joint. No point in risking the prospect of being invited to blow into a little bag on the way home. A Silver Top cab arrived. 'Hut,' said the driver, a wizened Ethiopian. 'Very hut.'

The city centre swarmed with schoolkids making the most of the dying days of their summer vacation. We skirted the soaring steel skeleton of the half-completed Karlcraft Centre and crossed the Yarra, glassy beer-bottle brown under the baked enamel sky, and found another Parisian boulevard, St Kilda Road. On one side it was bounded by the expansive park-land of the Domain, on the other by the brutalist boxes of the Arts Centre, squatting on the bank opposite

Flinders Street railway station like a gun emplacement guarding the strategic approaches of the town.

Once upon a time, the riverside had been a jumble of run-down warehouses and obsolete factories, an eyesore enlivened only at night when a huge neon sweet unwrapped itself over and over again in a blaze of coloured lights. But the electric lolly was long gone, replaced by Arts City. Here – in the National Gallery, the Concert Hall, the State Theatre, the Ballet Centre – the blue-collar Labor constituencies to the north and west of the city paid for the Liberal voters of the leafy eastern suburbs to have their self-esteem massaged.

Not, I thought, the proper attitude to be taking. Think centre of excellence, I told myself. Think vibrant treasure house of national identity. Think better than unemployment.

Behind the National Gallery, even newer cultural edifices were rising from bulldozed construction sites. A new HQ for the symphony orchestra, studios for the ABC, a resplendent cultural precinct rising from the flattened ruins of ancient industry. Soon, according to the architects' models, little stick figures would sip cappuccinos here under little stick umbrellas before ambling into the Concert Hall to soak up a bit of moral improvement. Of the uncouth past, only the mouldering 1920s edifice of the old YMCA survived, crouching behind the Concert Hall as if it hoped to dodge the wrecker's ball.

Haile Selassie deposited me in front of the National Gallery and I headed straight for the moat. Its shallow ornamental pools flanked the entrance forecourt, separated from the footpath by a low wall of square-cut stone. Originally intended to mirror the building's blank facade, its austere lines were now a little cluttered with an embarrassment of artistic riches. First had come a trio of dancing water fountains. Then an iron and polypropylene sculpture modelled either on the inner workings of a spring-scale or a trash-can fish skeleton from a Hanna Barbera cartoon. Then a gravity-fed spiral based on the anatomy of a mollusc. Finally, an enormous ceramic creature, a kind of bifurcated llama that straddled the water like an aquatic mutation of Dr Doolittle's pushmi-pullyu.

But the moat was still cool. Resisting the temptation to strip off and plunge my head into it, I pulled my tie down a couple of notches and splashed a handful of the wet stuff over my face. It smelled faintly of soda ash. I trickled a second handful down the back of my neck. Then I lit a pause that refreshes and took in the scene, servant of the master of all I surveyed.

The facade of the gallery rose behind me, a smooth basalt cliff, unbroken by windows. 'We need the space for hanging,' explained the Premier who commissioned the building, or so legend has it. His idea of a joke, in those days of capital punishment. Henry the Hangman, they called him. But that was twenty years ago, a benighted age, a time of human sacrifice. We're more civilised now. We know that the dark forces are better propitiated with social justice impact statements and ongoing consultative processes.

It was just past three o'clock and, despite the heat, the place buzzed with activity. Air-conditioned coaches lined the kerb, disgorging tourists. Elderly matinee-goers swarmed blinking into the daylight. A queue snaked towards the ticket window at the gallery's arched entrance, clinging to the shade. Gelati vans did a roaring trade, dispensing ice-cream that tasted like it came from cows with silicone tits. Frazzled mothers pushed grizzling toddlers past a banner advertising the current blockbuster exhibition. In the midst of all this activity, a glistening supermarket trolley lay abandoned on its side, a found object, far from home.

Beside me, ranged along the parapet of the moat, was a gang of pubescent boys, their sprayed-on jeans and rat-tail haircuts indicating that they, too, were out of place. Marauders from distant suburbs, they were scavenging for submerged coins, their arms plunged shoulder-deep into the water. Egged on by his friends, one swung his legs over the edge and lowered himself waist-deep into the water. Wading out to the middle, he bobbed swiftly to the bottom and surfaced with a twenty-cent piece in each hand. His mates roared uncouth approval. I, too, applauded this community-based initiative in the redistribution of cultural wealth. But I did so silently. These facilities, after all, were now within my purview.

The kid was about twelve, by the look of him, a couple of years older than my son Red. Little kids are easy. An ice-cream cone, a roll down a grassy hill, that's enough to satisfy them. But then they get older, their threshold shifts. They start wading about in public foun-tains, cheered by their hoon mates. They get drunk and steal cars. But not just yet. Not at ten, I told myself. That was something to look forward to.

Last time Red came to stay, I'd taken a week of leave and we'd headed down the coast. We bought every useless gewgaw in a dozen bait-and-tackle shops, slept in cabins in caravan parks, lived on chips and Chinese takeaway, and fished off beaches and jetties from here to the Cape Nelson lighthouse. But the initial enthusiasm had soon waned. I was trying too hard and we both knew it. After four days we came back to town where Red could do what he'd wanted to do all along. Hang around outside the nearest skateboard shop with his dopey friend Tarquin Curnow.

This time around, I'd made no special arrangements, except to check that Tarquin would be in town. Tark was an utter dill, gawky and buck-toothed with year-round bronchitis and a tendency to play up when his mother wasn't looking. But his company took the awkwardness off Red's visits and for that I was grateful. Splashing a last handful of water over my face, I doused my fag, slung my jacket over my shoulder and hied myself hence to the cultural coalface.

The Arts Ministry was across an elevated walkover that connected the rear of the National Gallery to the Ballet Centre, home of the national silly dance company. A gaggle of ballet-school students were clustered around the doorway, anorexic girls with their hair in chignons, lithe boys with flawless skin, none of them older than twenty, all of them smoking. Fifteen years of mandatory package warnings, a total ban on television advertising, a Quit campaign, and the fittest, brightest, most privileged young people in the country were tugging away like racetrack touts. If I hadn't just put one out, I'd have been tempted to join them.

'I was just sooo embarrassed,' I heard one of the boys say as I passed. The others all giggled. Scratch the bit about brightest. On the top level, the lift opened directly into the Arts Ministry foyer, an expanse of parquetry with beige walls and rows of little track-lit pictures. The receptionist was fielding a phone inquiry. 'What's it in conjunction to?' she was saying. Off to the side was a glass door marked 'Minister'. I pushed it open and went in.

ON THE other side of a glass partition, two men faced each other across a small conference table.

The one I recognised was Ken Sproule, senior adviser to the man Angelo Agnelli was replacing, Gil Methven. Ken's boss punched in a heavier weight division than Angelo and had come out of Cabinet that day holding Police and Emergency Services, one of the big ticket ministries. That made Ken Sproule one of the big boys, too. He was a tough cookie with more suspicion than imagination, an indispensable quality in any major player's personal fixer. And for all the factional differences between our respective masters, he had yet to do me serious personal injury. Which, in our party, is tantamount to bosom friendship.

Spotting my arrival, he beckoned me inside. 'Ah! The changing of the guard,' he rasped. He wore a short-sleeved business shirt and a no-nonsense polyester tie. He gestured grandly towards the other man. 'Phillip Veale, meet Murray Whelan, aide de camp of the infamous Angelo Agnelli.'

Phillip Veale stood up and surveyed me with benevolent curiosity. Where Ken Sproule was fidgety and thrusting, Veale was suave and reticent. He was some-where in his fifties, smooth-skinned, silver-haired, pink with the exertion of carrying just a tad too much good living. A man without angles or apparent malice who wore his two-toned business shirt, French cuffs and matching tie with all the assurance of a mandarin's robe. Which well he ought, since Phillip Veale had been Director of the Arts for as long as anyone could remember. Ministers came and went, but Phillip Veale abideth forever. We shook hands, his skin soft but his grip firm.

'I'm looking forward to working with the new minister,' he said, managing in some intangible way to impart the impression that the change could only be an improvement.

'And Angelo is keen to get started,' I reciprocated. 'Would Monday morning be convenient for a briefing?'

'Perfectly,' Veale said, not entirely able to conceal the humour in his eyes. 'Shall we say nine?'

This exchange of niceties brought Ken Sproule's dial out in a big smirk. I was the sheepdog type of minis-terial assistant, there to keep the departmental flunkeys all trotting along in more or less the same direction. Ken was primarily a backroom mathematician, one of those blokes who can't see a head without wanting to sink his boot into it.

'And perhaps while I'm here,' I suggested. 'We can go over the minister's diary.'

'Of course,' said Veale, backing out the door. 'It's been a pleasure working with you, Ken.' For sure.

'I think you've won a heart,' said Sproule as the door closed.

I sat down, leaned back in my chair and took in the surroundings. The office was an airy, glass-walled space, a definite step up from the vinyl and laminate world of Ethnic Affairs. A row of floor-to-ceiling windows opened onto the Arts Centre tower and overlooked a rooftop garden at the rear of the gallery, a rectangle of lawn upon which sat an enormous white ball, as though God were about to tee off. The furniture was pale and waxy, crafted from some rare and expensive timber, soon to be extinct. Sproule followed my gaze out into the fiery afternoon light. 'Not bad, eh?' he said. 'For the booby prize.'

'I'll think of you, Ken,' I said. 'Arm-wrestling the Police Association while I sit here contemplating the finer things of life.'

Sproule went over to the minister's desk and cleared a drawer into his briefcase. 'A word to the wise, Murray. Those wogs you've been duchessing at Ethnic Affairs have got nothing on the culture vultures. Tear the flesh right off your bones, they will.' Ken had climbed into the ring with some hard-nosed bastards over the years, and he spoke with genuine awe.

'Going soft?' I said.

Sproule gave me a pitying look. 'The first thing you should know about this job, pal, is that in this town the arts are a minefield. Everything from the pitch of the philharmonic to the influence of landscape painting on the national psyche is a matter of public debate. We've got more experimental film-makers, dramaturges and string quartets than you can poke a conductor's baton at. And every last one of them has a direct line to the media. You've never seen so much colour and movement in all your life. Tell you, pal, it's more than a can of worms, it's a nest of vipers.'

The purpose of this sob story, I took it, was to deflect any blame that might arise from unfinished business left by the departing team. 'In other words,' I deduced. 'A time bomb is about to blow up in Agnelli's face.'

Sproule was innocence itself. 'Keep your wits about you, that's all I'm saying. Within a week you'll be Mr Popularity, up to your arse in invitations to opening nights and gala exhibitions. The glitterati will be lining up to wine and dine you so they can piss in your pocket about how much public money their pet project deserves.'

So what was new? Fending off lobbyists was a ministerial adviser's bread and butter. Sproule had finished his packing. I shook his hand, formally accepting the helm. 'Good luck with the coppers,' I said. 'See you round.'

'Not if I see you first.'

The instant that Sproule was gone, Veale reappeared with a folio-sized leather-bound diary and a well-stuffed manilla folder. We ran through the ministerial appointments for the next week, a predictable round of flag-showings and gladhandings. Nothing so pressing that Trish couldn't take care of it when she arrived with Agnelli on Monday morning. Only one engagement was listed for the weekend. *Karlin. 11.30 Saturday.*

'A small brunch,' explained Veale. 'To mark the acquisition of a rather significant painting by the Centre for Modern Art. The former minister agreed to say a few words of blessing. Given the changed circumstances, Max Karlin will doubtless understand that the new minister is unable to attend.'

'Max Karlin?'

'He's hosting the occasion.' Veale didn't have to tell
me who Max Karlin was. His name was in the paper
every five minutes. A millionaire shoe salesman who
had lately expanded out of footwear into property
development. The half-completed Karlcraft Centre I'd
passed on the way was his baby, a multi-storey retail
and office complex rising on the site of his original
downtown shop. 'Karlin's been collecting Australian
modernist painting for more than twenty-five years.
It's one of his pictures the CMA is buying.'

It suddenly occurred to me that this little luncheon-
ette might serve a useful function. The conversation I'd
overheard in Agnelli's office had been replaying itself
in the back of my mind, still ringing alarm bells. If
Agnelli had indeed decided to re-invent himself as a
bag man, Max Karlin would strike him as an obvious
mark. Hard experience had taught me that Agnelli did
not respond well to direct disagreement. But if I got
the two of them together and kept a close eye on what
ensued, I might be able to confirm how serious Agnelli
was about his new sideline. And once I was clear on
that point, I might stand some chance of putting an
end to any such foolishness. If Agnelli had a high
enough opinion of my abilities to keep me on the
payroll, the least I could do was curb his more suicidal
impulses.

'Angelo is very interested in the visual arts,' I said.
'I'll let him know about Mr Karlin's invitation. Just in
case.'

Veale was inscrutably professional. 'Very good,' he
said, closing the diary and handing me the manilla folder.

It contained an avalanche of snow so deep it would take me weeks to dig myself free. Organisational charts, committee membership lists, advisory board structures, policies, draft policies, potential draft policies, terms of reference, annual reports, strategy plans, treaties with foreign potentates, fixtures for the staff association cricket club, a list of recent grant recipients. Heaving a heavy sigh, I took unenthusiastic possession.

'Anything here on the Centre for Modern Art? I'm going to some sort of exhibition there tonight and I really don't know much about the place.' Precisely zip, in fact.

Veale dealt me the relevant document. 'Lloyd Eastlake's not wasting any time taking you under his wing, I see.'

I thought Veale must have been reading my mail until I opened the CMA annual report and scanned its list of office-bearers. Eastlake was the chairman. 'I haven't met him yet,' I said. 'But I've been told he's very well regarded.'

'Very,' said Veale. His arid neutrality betrayed a hint of sniffiness. 'Lloyd Eastlake chairs so many committees it's a wonder he finds time to make a living. The CMA. The Music Festival. The Film Development Corporation. The Visual Arts Advisory Panel. The ALP policy committee, of course . . .'

All political appointments, in other words. This Eastlake, whoever he was, was clearly making the most of his opportunities. On the league ladder of policy committees, Cultural Affairs was about as low as you could go. A clout-free zone. A sheltered workshop for no-hoper Upper House backbenchers. Old farts from the Musicians' Union who once played the saxophone in three-piece wedding combos and now spent their declining years haunting thrash rock clubs trying to sign up roadies. Eastlake, alert to the perquisites of his chairmanship, had clearly set about making himself Labor's man in the garden of culture.

'A retired union official?' I asked. 'With a taste for trad jazz and the French New Wave?'

'Financial services, actually,' said Veale. 'Started as a carpenter. Joined his father-in-law's building firm back in the fifties, turned it into a major player in the housing industry, then sold up to concentrate on investment consulting.' An ex-chippie made good. No wonder he got up Veale's aristocratic nose.

A large colour-field painting hung on the wall behind the minister's desk. It was hard-edged, all surface, a bled-out pink with a broad stripe of yellow running right through the middle. Not unlike many in the party. Veale saw me looking over his shoulder and turned to follow my gaze. 'Taste in pictures is such a personal matter,' he said, as though he'd never seen the thing before in his life. 'Does our master have a liking for something in particular?'

Human blood, I nearly said. 'Perhaps something to match his mental processes,' I suggested.

'Nothing too abstract then, I take it,' said Veale, cocking a jovial eyebrow. I had a feeling that he and I were going to get along like a house on fire.

Veale left me alone with my homework. I took it over to the big desk and started in. As well as the National Gallery, the State Theatre and the Concert Hall, all of which I could see out the window, Arts was the overseer-in-chief of everything from the State Library to a regional museum so small the brontosaurus skeleton had to stick its neck out the window. All up, the annual budget topped forty million. Not in the major league by any means, but enough to have some fun with. And enough to generate some pretty vocal squabbling, if Ken Sproule was to be believed.

The list of recent grant recipients revealed some familiar names. The Turkish Welfare League had scored a thousand dollars to run traditional music classes for Turkish Youth. In my experience, your average Turkish youth preferred heavy metal to Anatolian folk songs. Doubtless the dough would go to pay a part-time social worker. At the other extreme, the Centre for Modern Art had copped three hundred grand for a 'one-off extraordinary acquisition'. I wondered what you could acquire for that sort of cash.

I closed the folder. Plenty of time for that sort of thing later. Reminding myself of more pressing realities, I rang Agnelli and caught him on the way to Government House for the swearing-in of the new Cabinet. I told him about the Karlin brunch invitation, making it sound like a minor formality, and asked for his okay to decline. Right on cue, at the magic words 'Max Karlin', he was dead keen.

'It's important that we maintain continuity of appointments during this transition,' he said.

'You're the boss,' I told him.

By then, it was just on five o'clock. I was feeling a little parched in the back of the throat, but it was ninety minutes before I was due to meet this Lloyd Eastlake bloke. I was flicking absently through the Centre for

Modern Art annual report when Phillip Veale's well-barbered mane appeared around the door. 'Drinkie winkies?' he mouthed.

I COULD TELL immediately that I'd have to pull my socks up in the duds department if I ever hoped to cut the mustard in this culture caper. Aside from Phillip Veale's two-tone shirt, I counted three bow ties, a pair of red braces and a Pierre Cardin blazer. And that was just what the women were wearing.

All up, about fifteen people were milling about the conference room, enjoying what Veale described as the ministry's customary end-of-week after-work convivial for staff and visiting clients. In no time at all, a glass of government-issue fizzy white had been thrust into my hand and the director had waltzed me about the room and presented me to sundry deputy directors and executive officers. The natives seemed affable enough and bid me welcome with the wary amiability of practised bureaucrats.

Three drinks later, I was cornered by a large woman wearing a caftan and what appeared to be Nigeria's annual output of trade beads. 'Does the new minister have strong interest in anything in particular?' she asked. Her name was Peggy Wainright and she'd been introduced as the executive responsible for the visual arts.

'The visual arts,' I said. 'Naturally. And puppetry, of course.'

My lame wit fell on deaf ears. The woman grabbed my elbow and began to drag me through the throng. 'In that case,' she said. 'You simply must meet Salina Fleet. She's the visual arts editor of *Veneer*.'

'*Veneer*?'

'The leading journal of contemporary cultural criticism.' In other words, an art magazine. Peggy was shocked I hadn't heard of it. 'Very influential.' In other words, an art magazine with very few readers.

One of the occupational hazards of working at Ethnic Affairs was the tendency it encouraged to categorise people on the basis of their names. In the case of, say, Agnelli or Mavramoustakides this was not difficult. Fleet was pure Anglo. Fleet as in First, as in Street. The Salina bit was definitely an exotic ring-in. I allowed myself to be propelled forward, already a little curious. 'Here's Salina now.'

Salina Fleet was a gamine blonde with apricot lipstick and dangly white plastic earrings, her slightly tousled hair growing out of a razor cut. Her limbs were bare and lightly tanned and she was wearing a mu-mu with a fringe of pom-poms and a palm-tree motif. Slung over her shoulder was a terry-towel beach-bag with hula-hoop handles. A surfie chick from a Frankie Avalon movie. She was about thirty, old enough to know better, so her intention was clearly ironic.

'Salina's on the Visual Arts Advisory Panel which makes recommendations on grants to artists and galleries,' said Peggy, by way of introduction. 'This is Murray Whelan. He's on the new minister's personal staff.'

Salina Fleet turned from pouring herself a drink, cocked her budgerigar head and gave me a long, intelligent and frankly appraising look. 'Really?' she said. She reached into her beach-bag and drew out a pack of Kool. 'How interesting.' You had to admire her attention to period detail. I didn't know they still made Kool.

'The new minister has a strong interest in the visual arts,' added Peggy. 'And puppetry.'

'Really?' said Salina. A flicker of mischief played between her eyes and the corners of her apricot lips. 'How interesting.' She took a cigarette out of the pack.

'You're not going to smoke in here?' said Peggy Wainright with alarm.

'Mind if I have one of those?' I said. I hated menthol cigarettes.

Salina did some jokey huffy wiggly stuff with her shoulders. 'I suppose we'd better be good boys and girls, then.' She nodded towards a sliding glass door that opened onto a narrow balcony overlooking the trellised white tower of the Arts Centre. 'Coming?' She was certainly a live wire.

We took our drinks outside, just us smokers. It was like stepping into an oven. 'Hope you don't mind.' Salina broke out the camphorated stogies and we both lit up. 'Peggy's a dear but she's never off duty.'

'Frankly I'm relieved,' I said. 'For a minute there I thought I'd have to pretend to know something about art.'

'Pretence is essential in the art world.' Salina exhaled a peppermint-scented cloud. Her fingernail polish was apricot, too. Perfect.

'Any other tips for a novice?' I was trying to pretend that my cigarette didn't taste like fly spray.

'The most important thing is always to keep a straight face. As long as you do that, anything is possible.'

I accepted this advice with a grateful dip of my head. 'Salina?' I said. 'Unusual name.'

Too late, I realised that this must have sounded like a very lame come-on line. Do you come here often? What star sign are you?

She didn't seem to mind. 'Literary,' she said. 'Lyrical, at least. The result of having an academic for a father.'

The literary/lyrical reference was over my head. Troilus and Cressida. Tristan and Isolde. Starsky and Hutch. Salina and . . . ?

She came to my rescue. '*Out in the west Texas town of El Paso*,' she began to recite:

'*I fell in love with a Mexican girl*
Night time would find me in Rosa's cantina
Music would play, Salina would whirl.'

Either Salina's father lacked all academic rigour or he was hard of hearing. I knew the song. Marty Robbins was on every juke box in every bar I'd ever worked in. As a publican's son who had paid his way through university pulling beers, I had an acute ear for bar-room gunfight references in popular music. The Mexican maiden who did the whirling at Rosa's cantina was called Felina, not Salina.

'Your father's academic discipline,' I asked. 'What did he teach?'

'Three-point turns, mainly,' she said. 'And reverse parking. He was chief instructor at the Ajax Driving

Academy. I followed in his footsteps. I teach cultural studies, part-time, at the Preston Institute of Technology.'

PIT used to be a trade school for the motor industry. Not much call for that sort of thing any more. Not unless you were a Japanese robot. 'Really?' I said, like she might be having me on. 'How interesting.'

'Salina's a bit prissy,' she said. 'You can call me Sal. But never Sally.' No, she definitely wasn't a Sally. And I didn't care if she was having me on. At Ethnic Affairs, the only women who flirted with me either had moustaches or fathers with shotguns.

'*Her name was McGill*,' I said. '*And she called herself Lil*.'

'*But everyone knew her as Nancy*,' she replied. 'The Beatles' *White Album* is on my students' required reading list.'

Having a cigarette was one thing. Standing in a blast furnace was another. We ground our butts underfoot, toe to toe. '*Let's twist again*,' she said.

'*Like we did last summer*,' I closed the couplet.

As we slipped back into the air-conditioned relief of the conference room, Phillip Veale materialised at my side. He pinged a fingernail on the rim of his glass. The crowd fell silent and turned our way. It was a jolly little speech, delivered in administrative shorthand.

'Welcome to those just back from summer hols. A new year awaits. Exciting developments. Fresh challenges. Not least of which, a new minister, Angelo Agnelli, whose commitment is well known.' Veale's ambiguity raised an appreciative chuckle from the assembly. 'A minister so keen he's already sent his right-hand man to join us.' Eyes darted my way, measuring my response. I tried to look sly. 'So,' Veale raised his glass, staring directly at me. 'The king is reshuffled. Long live the king.' It was blatant flattery. Always the best kind.

I glanced about for Salina Fleet but she must have slipped out under cover of the formalities. Pity, I thought. Still, I had no cause for complaint. Semi-secure employment, congenial surroundings, a drink or three, a little light buttering-up. A man could do worse.

Outside, the late afternoon sun was turning the harsh concrete of the Arts Centre a glowing fauvist orange. Warning-light amber.

It had gone 6.15 and the drinks crowd was thinning to a hard core. I took one last snort for sociability's sake, slung my hook and headed downstairs. By rights, if my day had gone as planned, I should have been at the airport, meeting Red's flight from Sydney. Instead, I was headed for the front of the National Gallery, under instructions to find a total stranger named Lloyd Eastlake so we could go look at some modern art together. Half an hour, I'd give it. Tops.

A slab of shadow had fallen across the forecourt of the gallery. The mouse-hole curve of the gallery entrance dozed, a half-shut eye in a blank face. The crowds were gone, the tourist buses departed, the gelati vans pursuing more lucrative business at the bayside beaches. Later, theatre goers would begin to arrive. For now, apart from a trudging trickle of home-bound pedestrians and a pair of teenage lovers having a snog on the moat parapet, the place was deserted.

Out on St Kilda Road, the tail end of the rush-hour traffic crawled impatiently towards the weekend, raising a desultory chorus of irritable toots. I propped on the edge of the moat, trailing my hands in the cool water, and waited for Lloyd Eastlake, Our Man in the Arts, to arrive. At least he wouldn't have any trouble finding me.

A slow five minutes went by. Romeo and Juliet broke off their tonsil hockey and wafted away, hand in hand. The passing trams became less crowded, less frequent. A silver Mercedes pulled into the Disabled Only parking bay in front of the gallery entrance, its interior concealed behind tinted windows. It sat there for a long moment, too late for the gallery, too early for the theatre. Then the back door opened and man in a suit got out. Well-heeled, self-assured, brisk. I recognised him instantly. The man I had seen coming out of Agnelli's office earlier that afternoon.

He crossed directly to me. 'Murray Whelan?' he said, not much in doubt about it. 'I'm Lloyd Eastlake.'

He was quite handsome in a conventionally masculine way. Close-up, I pegged him for a well-preserved fifty-five, fit as a trout even if the good life had tipped the bathroom scales a smidgin over his ideal weight-to-height ratio.

Shaking off the moat water, I accepted his offered handshake. His grip was competitively hard, as though advertising the fact that he had once worked with his hands. But not for some time. The nails were manicured.

'Don't let the National Gallery trustees catch you paddling in their pool,' he warned. 'They think it's a bloody holy water font.' He indicated the open door of his car. 'C'mon. This'll be fun.' Flash wheels but still one of the boys.

The interior of the Mercedes was so cool it could have been used to transport fresh poultry. I followed Eastlake into the back seat, sinking into the soft leather upholstery. Agnelli's Fairlane was impressive in a high-gloss velour-seat sort of way, but it had a utilitarian aspect that never let you forget that it was public property out on loan. This car said private wealth, personal luxury, a separate reality.

As I pulled the door closed behind me, the big car purred into life. 'Centre for Modern Art,' said Eastlake. 'Thanks, Noel.'

My eyes darted forward to the driver. He was wearing a white shirt and a chauffeur's cap. The cap fooled me for a moment, made me think that the Mercedes was hired. Then I registered the pair of fleshy flanges protruding from the sides of the man's skull, and the wire arms of the aviator sunglasses hooked over them.

'Certainly, Mr Eastlake,' said Spider Webb. 'Coming up.'

'YOU'RE NOT one of the sanctimonious ones, are you?' Eastlake sprawled back, observing me with good-natured amusement, misreading the nature of my reaction to his driver. His red silk tie was patterned with little pictures of Mickey Mouse. The sort of tie that says the man wearing it is either a complete dickhead or he doesn't give a flying fuck what anyone thinks of him. 'You don't take a dim view of a man because he's earned himself a few bob?'

His few bob's worth of German precision-engineering purred gently and Spider eased it into St Kilda Road, joining the traffic stream headed away from the city centre.

'Not at all,' I said. 'It's just that you're the first Labor Party member I've ever met with his own chauffeur-driven Mercedes.'

'How do you know?' said Eastlake agreeably. 'You'd be surprised how well off some of the comrades are.'

Doubtless he was right. If Labor really governed for everyone, not just for its traditional blue-collar base, then a millionaire should feel just as much at home in the party as any boilermaker ever did. If the Prime

Minister had no problem with that concept, why should I? A decade in government at state and federal level had smoothed over a lot of the old class antagonisms, ideological and personal. Getting real, we liked to call it.

We veered left and headed up Birdwood Avenue into the manicured woodland of the Domain. A late-afternoon haze had turned the sky to burnished steel, bleeding the shadows out from beneath the canopies of the massed oaks and plane trees. Geysers of water sprang from sunken sprinkler heads in the lawn and hissed across the roadway. Not that I could hear them. The cocoon of the Mercedes was a world apart.

'Old loyalties run deep,' said Eastlake, catching my mood. 'I'm a Labor man, born and bred. You don't change your football team just because you change your address.'

This Lloyd Eastlake was not at all what I had expected. A wheeler-dealer ex-carpenter with a penchant for modern art. A party player with a back-stairs fast-track to ministerial ears. I toyed with the idea of asking him how his meeting with Agnelli had gone. Shake the tree, see what fell out. I decided to sit, not give anything away until I had a clearer sense of the lie of the land.

'You'll have to tell me all about the Cultural Affairs Policy Committee,' I said, making myself comfortable, putting both of us at our ease. 'I'm on something of a steep learning curve here, as Angelo no doubt told you. And what's the story on this Centre for Modern Art?'

Eastlake took a blank card out of his wallet and scrawled a couple of telephone numbers on it with a small gold pen. Private numbers. High-level access. 'Call me next week and I'll bring you up to speed on the policy committee.' He tucked the card in my breast pocket. My backstage pass.

'As for the Centre for Modern Art, it's a bit of a pet project of mine, to be frank.' He reassumed his relaxed posture and proceeded to expound. 'The National Gallery is all Old Masters and touring blockbusters. And the commercial galleries are little more than the unscrupulous peddling the unintelligible to the uncomprehending. The CMA's mission is to fill the gap, to provide public access to the full range of modern Australian art, from its originators through to the creative work of contemporary young artists. Being relatively new, we don't yet have our own collection, but we're working on it.'

Art really turned the guy on. I could sense the genuine enthusiasm. For art, and for the games that went with it. The pleasures of collecting. And of getting someone else to pay.

'Quite successfully too, judging by the government's $300,000 contribution to your acquisition fund.'

Eastlake looked at me sideways, crediting my homework, sensing criticism. 'Good art costs money,' he said. 'Do you have any idea how much government money the trustees of the National Gallery have got over the years? The nobs are never slow to stick their hands out, believe me. The old masters are more than happy for the public to pay for their Old Masters. Isn't it time that someone else got a fair suck of the sausage? Newer artists. Or the forgotten ones the art establishment has written out of history?'

He wasn't going to get any argument from me on

that point. He saw that and got down off his high horse.

'I started off as a carpenter, you know.' He slipped into an avuncular tone. 'It's a cliché, I know, but when I first began to succeed in business, I felt that people were contemptuous of me. Not that I particularly cared what they thought, but I didn't want anyone thinking they had the edge on me just because of my background. I'd always had a bit of an interest in art, so I cultivated it. I started going to exhibitions, asking questions, buying pictures. Eventually, I got invited onto exhibition committees and boards of directors. Not the National Gallery, of course. I'm still a bit beneath its dignity. I don't entirely flatter myself that it's because my taste and judgment are held in high esteem. I know it's partly because of my business and political connections. But nobody looks down his nose at me any more. Art is an even greater status symbol than having a chauffeur. Isn't that right, Noel?'

'That's right, Mr Eastlake.' Spider was smarmily obliging, sharing a little private joke with the boss.

I raised my eyes to the rearview mirror and found him observing me, stony faced. He tilted his head upwards and literally looked down his nose at me. Making a point. He'd recognised me all right, back in the garage, and knew that I'd recognised him. There was no mirth in the gesture. None whatsoever. I stared back into his mirrored eyes until he returned them to the road.

'The thing to keep in mind' – Eastlake had resumed his briefing mode, oblivious – 'is that most arts practitioners, the creative people, are Labor supporters.'

We passed the squat pyramid of the war memorial and turned down an elm-lined side road. The Mercedes cruised to a gentle stop outside a small white house standing by itself in the middle of the park, complete with a front veranda and an old-fashioned rose garden.

'We've arrived,' Spider announced. Eastlake opened the door and stepped out. As I made to follow, Spider slung his elbow casually onto the seat back. 'Haven't we?' he said, pointedly. 'Mate.'

'Hello, Spider,' I said.

He didn't like to be reminded. 'Bit of a snob these days, Murray? You didn't say hello this afternoon. And a bit of an art buff, too. Moving in all the best circles. Haven't turned into a poofter, have you?'

'Even if I had,' I said, feet on the footpath, 'you'd be safe.'

The Centre for Modern Art looked more like the lawn cutter's residence than the cutting edge of the avant-garde. Its function as an art gallery was betrayed only by a rather inconspicuous sign on the gate and people spilling out the front door with drinks in their hands. Clearly Labor voters to a person.

Eastlake led me up the garden path, nodding hellos. He surged into a narrow hallway with a polished-wood floor, track-lighting, and white walls hung with pictures of dwarfs with enormous penises. Through archways opening on either side I could see people milling about, drinking, chatting and pretending to look at crucified teddy bears and scrap-iron dingoes. 'I'm just the front man here,' Eastlake was saying. 'The real work is done by the our director, Fiona Lambert. You'll like Fiona. Everyone does. Bright as a button. Darling.'

Darling? Eastlake and I were getting on pretty well, but it seemed a little early in our relationship for this degree of affection.

'Dahling!' The word echoed back from the far end of the hall. A woman of export-quality glamour elbowed her way through the crowd towards us. She was somewhere in her late twenties. Her skin was extraordinarily pale, translucent almost, and lustrously moisturised. She was wearing a little black dress with spaghetti straps, its colour exactly matching her finely arched eyebrows and the precisely engineered bob of hair that framed her face. It was a face with too much character to be called pretty, but it was still well worth looking at. Her legs were bare and went all the way to the floor where they ended in a pair of low-heeled brilliantly shiny shoes, one black, one white. If it hadn't been for the slash of postbox red at her mouth, she could have got a job as a pedestrian crossing. But not one I'd ever cross. She was so far out of my price range she might as well have been the Hope diamond. She offered Eastlake one of her cheeks.

'Fiona, darling.' He pecked the air beside her ear. 'I've brought you a present.' He meant me.

Fiona Lambert inspected me with shrewd green eyes, and politely showed me some teeth that must have cost daddy a pretty penny. Her LBD was cut low to display a divine declivity, dusted with barely visible pale-yellow freckles. Not that I noticed.

Eastlake was right, she was as bright as a button – as neat, as highly polished, and just as hard. He introduced us, explaining the change of ministers and embellishing my credentials somewhat. Ms Lambert smiled non-committally and extended her fingertips. The hand-shake was slight, barely making contact, but there was a firmness of muscle there that made me think of ballet points and horses. I felt like a politician's yes-man in a cheap suit.

Eastlake promptly bailed out. 'Why don't you induct Murray into the mysteries, Fiona darling, while I get us a drink.' He merged into the throng, waving ineffectually at a disappearing waitress. More people were arriving. I felt conspicuously overdressed in my workaday collar and tie. The only other men in suits were very old and slightly bewildered. The rest of the crowd was haphazardly casual, the women with styl-ishly eccentric spectacles, the men meticulously louche.

Fiona Lambert put her hand lightly on my elbow and steered me out of the hall. We went into a room hung with minimalist paintings so well executed I had to look twice to make sure they were really there. The room was filling and there was a slight crush of bodies. Fiona Lambert stood disconcertingly close. Sooner or later I would be asked my opinion of the stuff on the walls. There was bound to be some sort of formula, but I didn't know what it was. A heavy bead of perspiration broke from under my arm and trickled down inside my shirt. 'Lloyd was somewhat vague about the occasion,' I said, groping for small talk.

'Primarily, it's an opportunity for some of the more promising newcomers to show what they can do.' Fiona Lambert was nothing if not well-bred, and she knew her job. 'More of a social thing, really. So our friends and supporters don't forget us over the summer.'

'You make it sound like the night football,' I said. Might as well play the part.

She forged a mechanical little smile. Her attention was elsewhere. A couple were walking through the door, making an entrance. He was well into his sixties, gnomically stocky and almost completely bald. His heavily lidded eyes and well-tanned skin made him appear simultaneously indolent and cunning. He was wearing a sixty-dollar white t-shirt under a nautical blazer. He looked like a cross between Aristotle Onassis and a walnut. She was fortyish, twice as tall and whipcord thin, with leathery skin and a helmet of red hair that had been worked on by experts. The man's eyes scanned the room until they found Fiona Lambert.

'Speaking of friends and supporters,' she said, her fingers fastening around my elbow. 'Come and meet the Karlins.'

As we crossed the room, Lloyd Eastlake sailed into our orbit with a glass of champagne in each hand. He spotted our destination and arrived first, thrusting the drinks ahead of him. 'Max and Becky Karlin.' He smooched the air beside the woman's earhole. 'Meet Murray Whelan, trusty lieutenant to our new Arts Minister, Angelo Agnelli.'

Karlin bent slightly forward at the waist and offered me his hand. My fingers disappeared into an encompassing embrace of flesh and Karlin pumped them softly, as though gently but firmly extracting some essential oil. He fixed me with oyster eyes, my hand still encased in his paw. For a moment I thought he was going to ask me what size shoe I wore. 'You tell your minister that this con man is robbing me blind.'

'Con man? Robbing you?' Eastlake reeled back in mock outrage. 'Six hundred thousand is not what I'd call robbery.'

Karlin let go of my hand and waggled a chubby finger in my face. 'Don't trust this fellow,' he clucked dryly. 'Do you know what he has done to me?'

I made no attempt to reply. My job, I could see, was to play the straight man while these two went into a well-rehearsed double act.

'What I have done,' said Eastlake, 'is agree to pay you one of the largest sums ever paid by a public collection for a work by a twentieth-century Australian painter.'

Karlin flapped his jowls in dismay. 'This talk of money, it insults the picture's true value. Isn't that right, Fiona?'

Fiona Lambert gave every indication of having seen this little song and dance before, but she played along. 'Its a wonderful painting,' she said.

'Fiona,' said Karlin in an aside for my benefit. 'Fiona is our greatest living expert on the work of Victor Szabo. She was very close to him before his death.'

Fiona was suddenly very interested in the track-lighting. I'd get no help from her. The name Szabo meant nothing to me. I was out of my depth and sinking fast. Meanwhile, Eastlake and Karlin continued their Mo and Stiffy act.

'Max here is cranky because his bluff has been called,' Eastlake told me. 'For years he's had what is arguably Victor Szabo's best work hanging in his office, a picture called *Our Home*. But Fiona realised its significance, identified it as the perfect cornerstone for our permanent collection here at the CMA. Max likes to be thought of as a philanthropist, so he couldn't refuse outright to sell us the picture. He just asked a price so high he thought he'd scare us off.'

So, this Victor Szabo was a painter, evidently one big enough to warrant a six-figure price tag. Karlin was finding this all very entertaining, this story in which his taste and acumen were the starring characters. 'I'm practically giving it away,' he told me.

Eastlake was getting to the bit he liked. 'But I called Max's bluff. I told Gil Methven that a picture of this significance really ought to be in a public collection. He agreed that the Arts Ministry would provide half the funds if I could raise the other half. Which is exactly what I did. So Max had no option but to agree to the sale. Now all he does is bitch about how he's being swindled.'

'Bah,' Karlin waved a thick finger in the air. 'Money was never the issue. I love that picture. It's like one of my children. Twenty years ago I bought it, long before most people had ever heard of Victor Szabo.'

Most people? 'I'm afraid I'm not very familiar with Szabo's work,' I confessed. 'Is the painting here?'

'We take possession on Monday.' Fiona Lambert made this a question, arching her eyebrows at Karlin.

He nodded confirmation. 'Until then,' he said, 'it remains my private pleasure. At least until the formalities are completed.'

Eastlake explained. 'Max is holding a little going-away event for the picture, brunch tomorrow. Gil Methven was going to do the honours but what with the Cabinet reshuffle, the short notice and so on . . .'

It was my turn to flash a little rank. 'Oh, I think I can persuade Angelo to attend,' I said. 'He's particularly keen to meet' – here I gave my attention entirely to Karlin – 'such a prominent supporter of the arts.'

Karlin merely smiled indulgently. 'Yes, fine.' Across the room Becky Karlin and another lizard-skinned bat were scrutinising what was either a visual discourse on the nature of post-industrial society or the wiring diagram for a juice extractor. Nodding a brisk farewell, Karlin took off towards them, a politely hunched Fiona Lambert on his arm.

'You did well to wangle three hundred grand out of Gil Methven,' I told Eastlake admiringly. I didn't want the policy committee chairman taking my little exercise in one-upmanship amiss. 'Spending the taxpayers' money on modern art is not exactly a sure-fire vote-winner, you know.'

'Couldn't agree with you more,' he said with unruffled equanimity. 'But wait until you see this particular picture. The public will love it. It'll become a national icon, just you wait. You think a hardhead like Gil Methven wouldn't have considered the political implications?'

'Just as long as it's not twenty metres wide and made of bullock's blood and emu feathers,' I grudgingly allowed. 'Angelo's in the hot seat now.'

'Believe me.' Eastlake snaffled a couple of fresh glasses off a passing tray and thrust one into my hand. 'Agnelli will love it. He'll think he's Lorenzo bloody Medici. And the public will lap it up.'

Eastlake could afford to be optimistic about the judgment of the people. He'd never have to face it. I didn't tell him that, though. Instead I let him wheel me around the room and introduce me to more names than I could hope to remember and more glasses of Veuve Clicquot than I could reasonably be expected to digest on an empty stomach.

In due course, I found myself standing alone, contemplating one of the pictures. It was a portrait of the Queen constructed entirely out of different varieties of breakfast cereal. Corn Flake lips, Nutri-Grain ears, Coco Pops hair. I had, I decided, done my duty for the day. It was getting on for 8.30. Time to scout for an out.

I sidled through the nearest door and found myself in an enclosed garden, a green rectangle of lawn bordered by high shrubs, a cool refuge from the clamour inside. A lavender-hued dusk was beginning its descent. The slightly overgrown grass was littered with dead marines and ravaged canape trays. Little clusters of people sprawled about languidly with their shoes kicked off. At the far end of the lawn, near a pile of rusty ironwork from the Turd of a Dog with a Square Arsehole school of sculpture, stood Salina Fleet, *Veneer* magazine's spunky visual arts editor.

The palm trees on her mu-mu swayed. Pom-poms brushed her bare thighs. A lipstick-smeared wineglass sat athwart her bosom. All up, she looked a damned sight more edible than the wilting sushi circulating inside. Unfortunately, she was not alone.

Her companion was a male. He was somewhere in his mid-thirties, with lank unkempt hair, heavy-rimmed Roy Orbison glasses and an attempt at sideburns. The sleeves were sheared off his western shirt and he was wearing grimy, paint-speckled jeans. A creative type, no doubt about it. And judging by the intense way he leaned into Selina when he talked – he was doing all the talking – more than a casual acquaintance. He was reading expressively from a tatty piece of paper, as though reciting a poem.

Salina, I noted with some pleasure, didn't appear to be buying it, whatever it was. My hopes soared. The guy was probably some mendicant artist, putting the hard word on her for a grant or a favourable review. But then she stepped closer and put her hand on his forearm. The gesture was so intimate, her demeanour so affectionate, that I mentally reached for the chalk to scratch myself from the race.

The guy jerked his arm away as if stung. No soft soap for him. He spun on his heels and strode towards the doorway where I was standing. Salina watched his progress across the lawn, less than impressed. She shook her head ruefully and drained her drink.

Here was my chance. The bar table was just through the door. I dived back inside and hit the waiter for a quick two glasses of shampoo. As he wrestled the wire off a fresh bottle, the artist-type came bustling up beside me, his eyes glinting through his spectacles with madcap determination. He slapped his hand down on my shoulder. 'Excuse me,' he said, his voice piping with emotion.

Before I could respond, he pushed downwards. Using me for support, he hoicked himself up onto the bar. His tooled leather boots skidded on the wet surface. A loaded tray of empty glasses careened over the edge and hit the floor. They shattered with an almighty crash.

Every head in the room turned our way.

'Shut up, everybody,' declaimed the weedy cowboy. He brandished his piece of paper at the upturned faces like he was Lenin addressing the Congress of People's Deputies. 'And listen. You're all being conned. This whole edifice is built on a lie.'

He made a gesture so expansive he had trouble arresting its momentum. And when he took a steadying sideways step, it was immediately obvious that he was drunk. Not legless perhaps, but a good three sheets to the wind at the very minimum. His voice was pitched high with nervous exultation at his own boldness. 'The people behind this place don't care about art.'

Backs turned dismissively, and the hubbub of conversation resumed. There's one in every crowd, the murmur said. Just ignore him.

Seeing his audience's attention begin to slip away, the would-be Demosthenes raised his voice against the resumption of normality. He succeeded only in sounding hysterical. 'Listen, everybody,' he pleaded. 'This is important.'

I almost felt sorry for him, standing there in all his horrible vulnerability, flapping his skinny arms about, his pearls cast before swine, a teenage barman in a clip-on bow tie tugging at his trouser leg. Not sorry enough to forget my mission, though.

Salina Fleet, drawn by the ruckus, was standing in the doorway observing the spectacle with wide-eyed alarm.

Taking advantage of the waiter's distraction, I filched the still-unopened champagne bottle, grabbed a couple of glasses and began in her direction. 'You'll see,' the cowboy warned. 'You can't dismiss me so easily.'

And, as if to prove his point, and to me in partic-ular, he promptly staggered forward and toppled off the table. He landed on top of me.

It isn't every day I get strafed. I folded like a cheap banana lounge, flat on my backside, glassware skit-tering, dignity out the window. The demented speech-maker's face pushed into mine, flushed with humiliation and too much to drink. 'Sorry, mate,' he mumbled, scrambling to his feet and rushing for the door. Salina Fleet, seeing him coming, pursed her mouth into a furious slit and folded her arms in an emphatic gesture of disavowal.

The hands of solicitous strangers dragged me to my feet. 'Watch out!' squealed someone. 'Blood!'

MY NEW-FOUND friends all jumped backwards as if jet-propelled. The offending bodily fluid was mine. The stem of a broken wineglass had nicked my forefinger. The cut was small and there wasn't a lot of blood, but that wasn't the point. Who knows what fatal contagion I may have been harbouring?

Whipping a cocktail napkin from my pocket, I hermetically sealed the offending digit. The traumatised bystanders cast me nervously apologetic looks. Fiona Lambert arrived, the scandalised hostess. 'How ghastly,' she clucked. 'Are you all right?'

'Fine,' I said, bravely displaying my ruby-tinged bandage. 'Who was that guy, anyway?'

'Nobody important,' sniffed Fiona, dismissively. 'These would-be artists, they're always complaining about something. Are you sure you're all right?'

Lloyd Eastlake closed from the other side, trapping me in a social pincer. 'You okay?'

Nothing was damaged but my prospects. Salina Fleet was nowhere in sight.

'Let's get out of here,' said Eastlake keenly, clamping my biceps. He was quite shaken, a lot more disturbed by the amateur dramatics than I was. He scanned the room as though my inadvertent assailant might be about to launch another attack from the cover of the crowd. 'People are going across to the Botanical,' he said.

I'd read about the Botanical Hotel. It was a chichi watering hole and noshery on Domain Road, not far away. Before Fiona Lambert could object, he clamped her arm, too, and marched us out the front door.

Night had fallen over the parkland, filling it with the drone of cicadas and the heady fragrance of damp lawn. A straggling gaggle of exhibition-goers meandered through the trees ahead of us, blending into the twilight in the general direction of Domain Road. To my relief, I could make out the bird-like silhouette of Salina Fleet among them. The tormented artist was nowhere in sight. Perhaps my prospects were salvageable.

Eastlake noticed the way I was gripping my fore-finger in the roll of my fist. 'Wounded in action,' he said. 'You need a Band-aid on that. Doesn't he, Fiona?'

A Band-aid would be useful, I admitted. The cut was small but it was bleeding profusely. I couldn't walk around all night clutching a bloody cocktail napkin. 'Fiona's place is practically on the way,' insisted Eastlake. 'You've got a first-aid kit, haven't you, Fiona?'

Fiona looked like she'd prefer to save her medica-ments for a worthier cause. 'Only if it's no trouble,' I said.

Domain Road delineated Melbourne's social divide. It was the point where the public parkland ran out and the private money began. Marking the border were the playing fields of Melbourne Grammar, a school for chil-dren with problem parents. Beyond, were the high-rent suburbs of Toorak and South Yarra. Toffsville.

We crossed the road and walked half a block, turning into the entrance of a pink stucco block of flats. A dog-faced dowager with a miniature schnauzer under her arm was coming out. Eastlake held the door open for her, and the old duck nodded regally but didn't say thanks. It was that sort of a neighbourhood, I guessed.

We climbed a flight of steps to the second floor, where two doors with little brass knockers faced each other across a small landing. One of them had a Chinese ceramic planter beside it, sprouting miniature bamboo. Fiona began to rummage in her handbag, searching for her keys. The bag was an elaborate leather thing with more pockets than a three-piece suit. After she'd been rummaging for what seemed like an eternity, Eastlake said something about dying of thirst, tilted the Chinese pot, slid a key from beneath it and unlocked the door.

Irritation flickered briefly across Fiona Lambert's face, whether at Eastlake's presumption, his casual breach of her security, or merely at the time she'd wasted searching her bag, I couldn't tell.

Fiona's domestic style was tastefully relaxed – what *Vogue Living* would describe as 'a professional woman's inner-city pied-à-terre'. The building dated from sometime in the forties and the best of the original features had been retained – the ornately stepped cornices, the matching plasterwork chevron in the centre of the ceiling, the onyx-tinted smoked-glass light-fitting, the severely square fireplace, the rugs – well-worn but far from threadbare, geometric patterns in black, turquoise and dusty ivory. Aztec jazz.

To these had been added a huge box-shaped sofa,

heavily cushioned and covered in cream cotton duck, plain and inviting, a dining-table of honey-coloured wood with matching bentwood chairs, and a marble-topped coffee-table piled with art books. The only lapse into period was a pair of low-slung tubular-steel armchairs, the kind that look like they're too busy being design classics to offer much comfort.

'Make yourself at home,' she said, her hospitality perfunctory at best. 'I'll get your Band-aid.' Eastlake had charged ahead into the kitchen where he was making ice-cube and bottle-top noises. I crossed to the window. The view was of the darkening expanse of the park, and the lit-up towers of the city centre beyond. A tram clattered by, its wheels chanting a mantra. Location, location, location. Eastlake's car stood at the far kerb, Spider beside it, his jaw working mechanically.

Eastlake reappeared, bearing iced drinks. 'Gin and tonic,' he said. 'Nature's disinfectant.' Fiona handed me a Band-aid. 'Bathroom's down there.' It was perfectly preserved, all green and cream tiles and curved edges, the bathtub big enough to float the Queen Mary. I unwrapped my finger and found the bleeding already stopped.

When I wandered back, Fiona was sprawled on the sofa, almost horizontal. A monochromatic odalisque, bare legs stretched out before her, feet on the coffee table. 'What a week,' she groaned. 'Cheers.' Ah, the gruelling lot of a gallery director.

The heat of the day had permeated the flat, and an air of lassitude filled the room. We sipped without conversation. Lowering myself into the design-benchmark chair, I faced Fiona across the coffee table. The

seat was very low and her toes nearly touched my knees.
I couldn't help but see her knickers. White cotton. She
yawned and ran the bottom of her glass over her forehead. Maybe that's how it works around here, I
thought. Averting my eyes, I scanned the title on the
spine of one of the art books. *A Fierce Vision: The
Genius of Victor Szabo 1911–77* by Fiona Lambert.

On the wall behind her, lit to good effect, hung a
large painting in an understated frame. A highly real-
istic bush scene, pared down to the most basic elements
of sky, earth, trees. The work of someone who knew
his subject and hated it with a vengeance. Above the
mantelpiece hung a smaller painting, clearly by the same
hand. A reclining nude.

Lloyd and Fiona exchanged knowing glances,
expecting me to say something. Let someone else make
an idiot of themselves, I thought. Besides which, I'd
already seen enough pictures that day to last me quite
a while. Art would keep. My appetites at that point
were more basic. 'If I don't eat soon,' I said, sociably,
'I won't be answerable.'

The phone rang. Fiona went into a little study opening
off the living room. 'Hello.' She listened for a moment,
then reached back with her foot and hooked the door
shut. I stood up and sucked my piece of lemon, beginning to get impatient, not sure why we were still here.
Pacing to the window, I saw Spider leaning against a
tree, a mobile phone pressed to his ear. Wanker.

Lined up on the mantelpiece was a row of framed
photographs. Family snaps. Incidental mileposts in life's
little journey. Me, Mummy and Toby the pony. Provence
on a hundred dollars a day. I took my drink over and

picked one up, a five by eight colour print. This Fiona was a good ten years younger. A real little chubby-bubby. Her hair was longer, still brown, her dress a shapeless shift. She was smiling at the camera, close-lipped as though hiding braces. An old man had his arm around her shoulder. He was maybe sixty-five, barrel-chested, with a round face and a bare scalp, tufts of grey hair sticking out above his ears, grinning like a wicked old koala. The background was blurred, providing no clues to the setting.

I held the frame up. 'Her father?'

Eastlake nearly choked on his G & T. 'Christ no!' he spluttered, glancing furtively back at the closed door of the study. 'That's Victor Szabo.' He took the photo-graph out of my hand, regarded it with ill-concealed amazement and returned it to its place on the mantel. His eyes swivelled upwards, to the nude, and his mouth opened to say something. The study door opened and Fiona reappeared, frowning.

'Bad news?' said Eastlake, turning quickly to face her.

She made a dismissive gesture and shook her head. 'Nothing.' She yawned – it looked forced – and tugged off her earrings, plain pearl studs, one black, one white. 'I'm sorry,' she said. 'I really am, but I'm exhausted.' She was trying hard to sound tired, but there was a tight brittleness in her voice. 'Would you think I was terribly rude if I begged off dinner?'

Frankly, it suited me fine. Eastlake made some dissuading noises, thankfully to no avail, I expressed more gratitude for the first aid than was warranted and two minutes later we were back in the street. 'Think I'll give it a miss, too,' said Eastlake, looking at his watch.

The night was young and I was half-cut and fancy-free. A hundred metres up the road women with back-sides by Henry Moore were entering the most fashionable wet-throat emporium in town. As soon as Eastlake began across the street towards the Mercedes, I hastened to join them.

Shuffling down the footpath towards me was my nemesis, the flying cowboy. All the stuffing had gone out of him. He was lost in thought, mumbling to himself. 'Jus you wait,' he was saying, repeating it under his breath. As poignant a solitary drunk as ever I had seen. I gave him a wide berth and went into the pub.

So much fashionable architecture had been inflicted on the Botanical Hotel that it could have passed for the engine room of an aircraft carrier, all distressed boiler-plate and industrial rubber. Business was booming. Salina Fleet was in the far corner of the bistro section, at a raucous table crowded with faces from the CMA back lawn. Down boy, I told myself. Read the mood. Take it slowly.

I ordered a beer, examining myself in the bar mirror. Uglier men were stalking the earth. The barman was one of them. 'Grolsch?' he said. I thought he was clearing his throat. He handed me a tomato sauce bottle of pale brown liquid. *Grolsch Premium Lager*, read the label. *Brewed in Holland*. 'That'll be four eighty,' he said.

That explained the balance of payments deficit. Time was when you could get paralytic for four dollars eighty. On Australian beer, at that. I put my hand on my hip pocket and discovered my wallet was gone.

There was a limited number of places I might have

mislaid it. Mentally retracing my steps, I got as far back as that low-slung designer chair in Fiona Lambert's apartment. I went back down the street, took the stairs two at a time, and rapped on Fiona's little brass knocker. Five minutes, ten at the most, had elapsed since Eastlake and I had left, so it wasn't like I'd be waking her up. There was no answer. I rapped again, the sound reverberating down the stairwell. Either Fiona Lambert was a very sound sleeper or there was no-one home. Somewhere inside, the phone began to bleat. When it finally rang out, I raised the edge of the Ming Dynasty shrub tub. The key was back in its hiding place. I let myself in.

Streetlight lit the living room. The remains of our drinks sat on the coffee-table condensing dribbles of water. My wallet was on the floor, just where I hoped it would be. As I bent to pick it up, my eye was caught by the picture hanging above the mantel, the nude. I stood and studied it.

Its subject was the younger, plumper Fiona Lambert, the one in the photograph. The artist's approach was clinical, lurid and without a shred of sentimentality. Superbly confident, the picture captured not just Fiona's likeness but her narcissism as well. The pose was blush-makingly provocative, anatomically explicit. The artist just had to be bonking her teenage ears off.

I did some quick mental arithmetic. At the time he painted the picture, Victor Szabo must have been at least sixty-five. The old goat.

Five minutes later I was back at the Botanical with four dollars eighty worth of Dutch courage in my hand, making eye contact with Salina Fleet.

She waved me over, making space at the table. 'What did you say your name was, again?' she demanded, her way of being smart. I didn't doubt I was already tucked away in Sal's mental Filofax, cross-referenced against future contingency. Everyone was talking at once, bellowing into the general din. Art scene party time. 'Saw you at the CMA,' she half-shouted. 'Thought you were gone.'

'So did I,' I said. 'When that guy landed on me.'

She laughed and bit her lip at the same time, a cornered look in her eyes. I rapidly changed the subject to the only other thing I could think of. 'Got side-tracked by Fiona Lambert.'

She relaxed. 'The Black Widow, we call her.' I bent closer, the better to hear her, and the bare skin of our forearms touched. A little spark of static electricity shot between us. 'Better watch yourself there.'

'Why?'

She was even tighter than me. Not that we were drunk. And so what if we were? The waiter came and stuck a menu in front of my face. It was the sort you read right to left. Everything on offer was either char-grilled, stir-fried, snow-pead, or came with sheep's cheese. What I really wanted to taste was the waxy fruit of Salina's apricot lips.

'Go on,' I urged. 'Tell me.' Keep her talking until we found some common ground, that was the strategy. 'Why do you call Fiona Lambert the Black Widow?'

A thin-lipped, imperious-beaked bloke was squeezed in on the other side of Salina. I'd met him at the CMA but his name escaped me. When he heard Fiona Lambert's name, he pricked up his ears and leaned over.

'They call her that,' he whispered in an accent that sounded like it came from the same place as my beer, 'because of the rumour that Victor Szabo died, shall we say, on the job with her.'

He had a bracket like a Borgia pontiff in a Titian portrait. To hear him properly, I had to lean even closer to Salina, so I kept up the questions. 'They were lovers, were they?'

'She modelled for him, slept with him, buried him, wrote the book on him, is curating his retrospective,' said Salina with what sounded suspiciously like envy. 'She practically invented him.'

'And now he's about to be the next big thing, eh?' I said.

'Bigger than Sir Ned Kelly himself, if the Black Widow has anything to do with it,' confirmed the Pope's nose.

By that stage, I could've eaten a nun's bum through a cane chair. We moved on to the Koonunga Hill cabernet shiraz. Food arrived, cross-hatched from the grill, and I sawed into my fillet of salmon.

'A brutal deconstruction of mordant reality,' declaimed Salina.

'Beg pardon?' I chewed.

'A sundering of the constituent components of antipodean materiality.' She sucked in her cheeks and tried to look severe and authoritative.

'Eh?' I popped a french fry into my mouth.

'The insertion into a distinctively Australian sensibility of the universalising impulse of an internationalist form.'

At last I got it. She was doing a Fiona Lambert

impression. Quoting, I took it, catchphrases from her book on Victor Szabo.

'An unflinching critic of the mundane,' piped up the schnoz, getting in on the act.

'*A Fierce Vision*,' we all chortled in chorus.

Holding it up with the best of them, I was. Who'd've known that three hours ago I'd never heard of this Szabo bloke. This art business was turning out to be a piece of piss. While we ate, Sal and the other guy kept up a running patter about Szabo. He was quite a mystery man from what I could glean – a refugee from Europe, a misanthropic recluse who had done most of his work in the fifties and sixties while holed up in rustic squalor. 'A total output of what, fifty or sixty paintings,' Sal said at one point. 'Not exactly prolific.'

'Forty *known* paintings,' the accent corrected her. 'Now that he's getting better appreciated, who knows how many more will emerge?'

The conversation soon meandered elsewhere, and I was happy to go with it. I would have been happy to go anywhere, given the encouragement I was receiving under the table. At the salad, Salina's hand brushed on my knee. By the tiramisu, it was lodged between my thighs.

When the liqueurs and coffee arrived, I knew I was going places. 'Have you ever been exploring?' she asked, dipping her forefinger in Sambuca and offering me a taste. 'In the Botanic Gardens at night?'

IT WOULD have been churlish to refuse. What I didn't realise – could not possibly have realised – was that the expedition that followed would lead me much further than over an iron railing and into a thicket of *Rhododendron oreotrophes*. Further than an exploratory probe in the depths of the fern forest. Further even than the searing flare of an emergency light beside the moat of the National Gallery.

And, before it was over, more than one body would be wheeled into the back of an ambulance.

But right then, in the dead of the night, the itch of crushed leaves still on my skin, all I could see was Salina Fleet's contorted face.

'Bastard!' She said it again.

Not an accusation this time. Not thrown in my face, but muttered under her breath. Her eyes followed the movement of the gurney into the back of the ambulance, the trail of water across the pavement left by the lifeless black legs. Her head shook with the movement of it, emphatic in denial. Despite the heat, she was trembling.

Abruptly, slow motion became fast forward. The

flashing light went off. Doors slammed. The ambulance began to draw away. I moved towards Salina, wanting nothing except to comfort and to calm. The policeman blocked my path with a hand to my chest. He gestured towards the rear of the departing vehicle. 'Friend of his, are you?'

Salina was moving out of reach, being led towards the police car. She wasn't looking back. The air was humid, cloying. I shook my head. 'Not really.'

The cop was about ten years younger than me. His shirt had two stripes on the sleeve, and he had a howitzer on his hip. 'Don't you think you've had enough, mate?'

I looked down and saw that I still had the bottle of wine we'd pinched from the hotel. We'd been swigging out of it as we crossed the lawn and I was holding it by the neck. Barely a tepid mouthful remained in the bottom. The Botanic Gardens suddenly felt a very long way away. The taste on my tongue was bile, not apricots.

Beyond a pair of security guards, Salina was being helped into the back seat of the police car. The cop followed my line of sight. 'You with her, are you, mate?'

Salina stared back towards me. She was calmer, regaining control, her face as bloodless as marble. Guilty and contrite. She gave a little rueful shake of the head. Goodbye, Murray, it said.

I shook my head slightly, mirroring her movement. 'Not any more,' I said. It seemed like the right thing. Only later did it feel like cowardice.

More police were arriving. Another two squad cars and an unmarked Falcon. A security guard, fishing in the moat, pulled a pair of thick-rimmed glasses out of the water. Another had the discarded shopping trolley from earlier in the afternoon and was dragging it out of the gutter. The car with Salina went.

There were maybe six cops, as many security guards. I was the only civilian. I dropped the wine bottle into a rubbish bin. It was empty and the bottle hit the bottom with a blunt thud that went straight to my temples. 'Go home, pal,' ordered a honcho in an Armaguard uniform. 'The show's over.'

I could, I supposed, have identified myself, claimed some small entitlement to information. A pretty picture that would have made. A crumpled suit, grass stains on my fingers, a gutful of souring wine, trying to throw my rather limited weight about. And for what? To find out how come my hot date had been cut short?

Snatches of radio chatter and snippets of half-over-heard conversations gave me more than enough clues to satisfy my immediate curiosity on that point. The body in the cowboy boots had been found by a security guard. He'd come outside for a cigarette and noticed a dark shape lying on the bottom of the moat, in the shadow of the retaining wall. He thought it was a roll of carpet. Idiots were always dumping things in the moat. He shone his torch into the water and saw what it was. He called another guard and they attempted resuscitation. It was no use. The guy could have been lying there for hours. An empty scotch bottle was found beside the body.

I trudged across Princes Bridge to the dormant railway station, laid my cheek upon the rear-seat uphol-stery of the only cab at the rank and murmured my address to the driver, a Polish scarecrow in tinted plate-glass hornrims. 'Hot,' he said. 'Wery hot.'

'Gdansk, it ain't,' I agreed.

Chauffeured for the third time that day, the pulse of the passing streetlights throbbing at my temples, the grog finally catching up with me, I succumbed to a headachy doze. And in my waking sleep, I found myself thinking unbidden thoughts of a time long gone.

My father had just taken the licence of the Olympic Hotel, his fourth pub in ten years. Apart from the name, there wasn't anything sporting about the Olympic, not unless you counted the horse races droning away on the radio in the public bar. Mum hadn't been dead long when we made the move, and Dad had taken me out of St Joseph's and put me in the nearest government secondary school. It was a haphazard choice. He said he wanted me near him. More like he didn't want to keep paying the fees.

That was okay with me. Compared to where I'd been, Preston Technical was a breeze. Nobody gave a flying continental about academic results. Soon as they got to fifteen, most of them were straight out the door and into apprenticeships or factory jobs. Plenty of work for juniors in those days, the sixties. But not much teenage entertainment. Not unless you could get your hands on some piss. Not unless you knew how to handle the kid whose father owned the pub.

At St Joey's the only real source of fear was the Brothers, pricks with leather straps, a weight advantage and the high moral ground. At the tech we had the Fletchers, fifteen-year-old twins and their older brother, ferret-faced thugs who hunted in a pack and made the Christian Brothers look like the Little Sisters of Mercy. There was an older Fletcher still, but he was in Pentridge prison. The initial charge was manslaughter but the magistrate believed him when he said that if he'd been seriously trying to hurt the bloke he'd have worn his kicking shoes. So he got off with reckless endangerment and grievous bodily harm. Five years.

The Fletchers lived on the Housing Commission estate, prefab concrete boxes built in 1956 to accommodate the Olympic athletes and already falling to bits when the welfare cases moved in after the Games were over. When you rode your bike to school through Fletcher territory you needed steely nerves, strong thighs and tough friends. That's what they told me at school, anyway. But I was the new kid. I didn't have any tough friends. Not until I was adopted by the one they called Spider. Then I had a friend. Just my luck.

General Jaruzelski woke me long enough to dump me on my doorstep and extract his fare. Then I was face down in my own empty bed, dreaming again. But not of Spider Webb, or the Fletchers, or the bad business with the stolen bottles of bourbon. This dream was more promising.

A wood nymph was tugging at my toga. One more fold and I would spring free and plunge into her grotto. But my toga was tangled and there was a thyme-drunk bee in my ear. Buzz buzz, it went, buzz buzz. I swatted it and it stung my eyes. Daylight poured into the wound and pierced my brain with a red-hot poker. The campfire ashes of a thousand marauding armies filled my mouth. Buzz buzz, said the persistent bee. Then a voice started shouting about the weather. Hot. Again. As if I didn't know that already.

Untangling myself from sweat-drenched sheets, I swung my feet onto the floor, slammed one hand down on the clock-radio and picked up the phone with the other. What prick would ring me at 7.04 on a Saturday morning?

Agnelli.

'Urgghh,' I said. The glass of water beside my bed had been there so long it had formed a skin. When it hit my tongue, sea monkeys hatched, spawned, died, and shed their exoskeletons down my throat. I fumbled for a match and fumigated my oesophagus with cleansing smoke.

'You heard about the National Gallery last night?' My boss was wide awake, keyed up.

'What?' I grunted, my head throbbing from the effort. Had I missed something? 'Somebody swipe a Picasso?'

'Some idiot drowned himself in the moat. I've had three different reporters on the phone since 6.30, wanting a comment.'

Even in my fuddled state, I got the point immediately. To the press – reduced to reporting the weather – a body in the moat of the National Gallery would be a story straight from heaven. In a city without distinguishing landmarks – no opera house, no harbour – the Arts Centre was the closest thing to a civic icon. Its picture was on the cover of the phone book, in every tourist brochure and glossy piece of corporate boosterism. Melbourne, City of the Arts. Look. See. Naturally a death in the moat would be a sensation. And if a political angle could be found, so much the better.

But what political angle? By covering my head with a pillow and closing my eyes, I could just about see to think. 'Why call you? What's it got to do with you?'

'According to the journos who rang me,' Agnelli said, 'this whacker committed suicide in protest at the lack of government support for the arts.' At least it wasn't because his girlfriend was rolling around in the hydrangeas with the responsible minister's major-domo.

'What makes them think that?' There'd been no mention of a protest motive at the death scene, not that I'd heard. And I couldn't see any immediate point in informing Agnelli that I was there when they dredged up the body.

'He left a note.' There was more than a hint of anxiety in Agnelli's voice. 'A manifesto, the press are calling it.'

I realised why Agnelli was aerated enough to have called me at this ungodly hour. Two years before, a Picasso really had been swiped from the National Gallery. It was held hostage by hijackers demanding more government funding for the arts – a motive so cryptic as to bamboozle the police utterly. The ransom negotiations were conducted on the front pages of the daily press. In a series of manifestos, the Arts Minister was described successively as a tiresome old bag of swamp gas, a pompous fathead, and a self-glorifying anal retentive. Subsequent insults were so erudite they had millions rushing for their dictionaries. Eventually, the painting was recovered, abandoned in a railway station locker. But the thieves were never caught.

So it wasn't hard to infer whence Agnelli was coming.

Public ridicule and ministerial amour-propre make a poor mix, and mere mention of the word 'manifesto' was bound to set a cat among Agnelli's pigeons. I took a deep breath and started again. 'Just exactly what does this manifesto say?'

'Jesus Christ, Murray, that's what I want you to find out.'

'Has this alleged suicide note been released?' By ratcheting the terminology down a notch I hoped to quiet the quivering antennae of Agnelli's ego.

It didn't work. 'Not according to the journalists who rang, but the general gist is being bandied about. And I'd rather not find out the details by seeing them on television. No surprises, Murray. I thought we were clear on that. No surprises.' Meaning that I should pull my finger out and have something reassuring to contribute to the overview. Pronto. 'I'll pick you up behind Parliament House at eleven. You can bring me up to speed on the way to this Max Karlin brunch thing.'

I told him I was on the case, buried my head in the pillow and tried to get back to sleep. It was a waste of time. Twenty litres of used booze were backed up in my southern suburbs, leaning on the horn. On top of which, a pounding noise was now coming from outside in the street.

Reaching across the mattress, I eased a chink in the curtains. Sunlight stabbed my frontal lobes. Across the narrow street, a guy in shorts and a carpenter's belt was fixing a For Sale sign to the facade of the house immediately opposite. The letters on the hoarding were as big as my hand. *Inner City Living*, they read. *A Gem from the Past. An Investment for the Future.* No room to swing a cat, in other words, but the market is buoyant.

From the front, the house was identical to mine, a single-storey, single-fronted terrace. The whole street was the same, all twenty houses. A cheese-paring speculator had built them as a job lot back in the 1870s. Workingmen's cottages they were called at the time – as distinct from the grander two-storey terraces in the surrounding streets with their cast-iron balconies and moulded pediments.

This neighbourhood was once considered a slum – such an affront to the national ideal of the suburban bungalow that whole blocks of it had been bulldozed in the name of progress. But those days were gone. Thanks to the miracle of gentrification, dingy digs in dodgy neighbourhoods had become delightful inner-city residences with charming period features in cosmopolitan locales. It was truly amazing what a lick of paint, a skylight and an adjective or two could do for real estate values.

This was the fifth time in the two years I'd lived there that a house in this street had been put on the market. I couldn't help but wonder what this one would fetch at auction. Mine had set the bank back nearly a hundred and fifty thousand dollars. A pretty penny – and a bargain at that – for two bedrooms, a kitchen–living room and a back yard the size of a boxing ring. And, with my variable interest rate bobbing around at 16 per cent, a very good reason to get out of bed and go to work.

I padded to the bathroom, fine grit beneath my bare

soles, wind-borne detritus of our island continent's blasted interior. A reminder to give Red's room a quick dusting before he arrived. As I crossed the lounge room, I reached into the bookcase, pulled out the dead weight of *101 Funniest Australian Cricket Stories* and tossed it onto the couch where Red would see it when he arrived. He'd sent it to me for Christmas, a boy's idea of the right sort of gift for his dad, and I treasured every page, even though I'd never read a word of it. Just as well Wendy hadn't done the buying for him, or I'd have got *Cooking for One*.

Not that it wouldn't have been handy, I reflected as I rinsed the forlorn breakfast bowl that had been soaking in the sink.

Next Christmas he'd give me *Home Maintenance Made Easy*. And it, too, would go into the bookcase unopened. Right beside *The Rise and Fall of the Great Powers*. That one I bought myself. Got bogged down in the War of Spanish Succession. One night soon I'd try again, get right on top of Metternich.

Red gave me what he thought a boy should give his father. But he needn't have worried about my home maintenance needs. I had none. After seven years with Wendy, fruitlessly wrestling with cross-cut saws and counter-sunk wood screws, all I wanted was to change the odd light globe. That's why I'd bought a renovated house.

So what if all the bench tops were apple-green and the cupboards burnt-orange? So what if all my furniture came from the Ikea catalogue and looked like it was designed for Swedish dwarfs? So what if the walls were still bare after two years? I could walk to work whenever I wanted. Red had a room of his own when he came to stay. And perhaps my new-found friends in the arts could recommend something suitable to adorn my vacant hanging space. Home is where the heart is, after all. Even if it did get a little lonesome from time to time and the shelves in the fridge could've done with a good wipe.

My heart and I went into the bathroom, stood under a hundred icy needles of cold water and started making plans. The first item on my agenda was to forget about last night as soon as possible. Salina Fleet had been a bad idea, even without the business at the moat. In fact, the business at the moat may have been a blessing in disguise. A Salina Fleet was not what I needed at this juncture in my life.

What I needed was groceries. A ten-year-old kid can go through a hell of a lot of groceries in three days.

Hit the oracle, make a few calls, raid the super-market, meet and brief Agnelli, take in Max Karlin's brunch, then out to the airport to pick up Red. After that, maybe the local swimming pool. Cool down, then take in a movie. Play it by ear.

My first call was to Ken Sproule. Half past seven on a Saturday morning was not the ideal time to go shop-ping for favours, but I remembered that Sproule had a two-year-old daughter. If he wasn't out of bed already then two-year-olds weren't what they used to be.

As a rule of thumb, personal networks are always preferable to official channels. Sproule would under-stand implicitly why I was calling. His boss Gil Methven may have been Police Minister for less than a day, but Ken was fast on the uptake and I preferred to be steered informally around police procedures than to go dropping Agnelli's name into the loop at this early stage.

Sproule was up all right, monitoring *Cartoon Connection* and cutting toast into fingers. He was thankful for the distraction and when I drew the map he laughed out loud. 'Agnelli's only had the job twelve hours and already artists have started killing themselves.'

'Maybe the guy hadn't heard about the reshuffle,' I said. 'Maybe he couldn't stand the thought of Gil Methven staying in the job.'

We went on like this for a while until Sproule was in a thoroughly good mood, then I asked him to suggest the least conspicuous way for me to find out what was in the suicide note. Surprisingly, he volunteered to make the calls himself. Under normal circumstances getting someone like Sproule hitting the phone on my behalf would have taken a fair amount of horse-trading. But the idea of a corpse in the moat of the National Gallery stimulated his morbid curiosity. 'Fifteen months in that job, the only bodies I ever saw were in the last act of *Hamlet*,' said Sproule. 'I'll call you back in a couple of hours.'

It was closer to a couple of minutes. 'Something just occurred to me. The name Marcus Taylor rings a bell. Don't quote me, but I think he might have applied for a grant.'

'Did he get one?'

'That's the part I can't remember.'

'If I'm not here when you call back,' I told him, 'try the Arts Ministry.'

I hiked over to Ethnic Affairs via a cup of coffee,

picked up my car and drove to Arts, twiddling the radio dial across the eight o'clock news bulletins. The top-rating commercial station had already picked up the story. *Melbourne's arts community*, it said, *was deeply shocked by the apparent suicide of the promising young painter Marcus Taylor* – the young part was encouraging, given that Taylor had looked to be about my age – *in protest at lack of government support for the arts*. Salina, identified as a prominent art critic, was quoted as describing Taylor's death as a shocking waste.

As I passed the National Gallery, a television news crew was shooting background footage of the moat. The vultures were circling.

The ministry was locked, but Phillip Veale's name worked magic at the stage door of the Concert Hall. Keys were immediately conjured up and I was escorted to the top floor of the Ballet Centre and admitted to the deserted offices. The list of grant recipients was where I had left it. And Marcus Taylor's name was on it. Professional support, $2000.

Not exactly a king's ransom, but as a free gift it was a damned sight more generous than a poke in the eye with a burnt stick. By the standards of Joanna Public and her overtaxed consort, it might even teeter dangerously close to the edge of government extravagance. A layabout artist could be drinking red wine out of the public trough for six months with a cheque like that.

Swinging my feet up onto the desk, I let a contented smile settle over my lips. From a PR point of view, Agnelli now had an ace up his sleeve that could be played if the media decided there was mileage to be

had from the starving-artist-versus-government-indif-
ference issue. Not that it was likely it would ever come
to that. My advice to Ange would be to keep his head
down for a couple of days and wait for the whole thing
to blow over.

I picked up the list again. While I was on the job,
I might as well do it properly. So far, all I knew about
this Marcus Taylor was that he tended to histrionics,
had a poor sense of balance and had ruined my plans
for the previous evening. Quietly aching parts of my
own anatomy told me that much. Information of an
official nature might be more useful. You can't have
too much information. Beside the names on the grants
list were reference numbers. Everything I had seen so
far of Phillip Veale suggested he ran a tight ship.
Somewhere in these offices would be a file containing
Taylor's application form.

A cluster of glass-walled boxes, the last word in office
design, occupied the whole top floor. At intervals, the
layout was punctuated by small sky-lit enclosures,
carpeted in white gravel, containing sculptural objects.
Ministry management, slaving over a hot memo, needed
only raise its jaded eye to find inspiration in an artful
agglomeration of whitewashed driftwood or fluorescent
space junk. The central registry, down the back beside
the lunchroom, held a less encouraging sight – the latest
in filing systems, securely locked.

But the offices of the executive staff were wide open.
Within half an hour I was sitting at the desk of the
Deputy Director Programs, thumbing through an over-
stuffed file containing the recommendations of the
Visual Arts Advisory Panel. Attached to Marcus

Taylor's application form was an envelope containing a set of colour slides and an assessment note from Peggy Wainright. She was the one, if memory served me right, in the kinte cloth headdress and Ubangi jewellery.

I took the file back to the minister's office and started reading. I'd got as far as lighting a cigarette when the phone rang. 'What do you want first?' It was Ken Sproule. 'The forensics or the hysterics?'

T HE CORONER'S office, alert to the attention a death like this would draw, had been working overtime.

'One of two things can happen when you drown,' explained Sproule. 'Either you take a great big gulp and fill your lungs with fluid. Or you thrash about sucking in air and fill your plumbing with froth and foam until you choke. This bloke did the first. He also had a blood alcohol content of .35 per cent, which means he was pretty whacked when he hit the water. On the medical evidence, opinion is currently divided as to whether the death was accidental or intentional. It's up to the coroner to decide. The balance of probabilities, however, tends to favour suicide, given the note found near the body.

And so to the nub of the matter. 'What's it say?'

'Nothing you might call brilliantly lucid. Lots of crossing out, spelling mistakes, abbreviations. But then the guy was a painter, after all. It's a wonder he could read and write. But he had a chip on his shoulder about something, that's for sure. Listen to this.

'*You so-called experts of the art world,*' Sproule quoted. '*You curators and bureaucrats who hold your-*

selves up as the arbiters and judges. You big-spending speculators and collectors who do not even know what you are buying. You are all allowing yourselves to be deceived and defrauded.

'I take this action to arouse public attention to this pretence, perpetrated in the name of art. Those with their hands on the levers of power are the most corrupt of all.

'You who have seen fit to dismiss my work yet do not recognise what is before your very eyes. Who is embarrassed now?'

As I rapidly jotted this down, it was as though I could hear again the hysterical voice of the figure on the table at the Centre for Modern Art. And I could see, too, the hang-dog look on his face as he passed me in Domain Road, trudging towards his death.

'In short,' concluded Sproule. 'The immemorial whine of the failed artist. I dunno where those journos got their bullshit line about a protest against lack of funding. The stiff didn't say anything about the government. Not so much as a whiff of swamp gas.'

Back at the electorate office, I'd heard plenty worse from disaffected punters every day of the week. And none of them had killed themselves, even if they sometimes made me wish they would. 'Anything else of interest turn up? Personal background, psychiatric history?' Perhaps the artistic temperament was more fragile.

'No criminal priors. Always the possibility he was a registered nutcase, I suppose,' said Sproule, optimistically. 'We won't know for a few days yet. What about the grant application?'

'You were right,' I told him. 'No reason for him to be feeling sorry for himself on our account. We gave him $2000 last November. Nothing more life-affirming than free money.'

That about covered the political aspect, such as it was. Any journalist trying to claim that Marcus Taylor had a legitimate grievance against the government would be drawing a very long bow indeed. 'The story will blow over in a couple of days,' said Sproule. 'If the press try to shift any shit our way in the meantime, we'll be ready.' On that up-beat note, he rang off.

Sproule had come up with a pretty fair haul. Any other useful background would be in the grant assessment file in front of me.

This is Taylor's fifth application for a Creative Development Grant in the last five years, wrote the Visual Arts Executive Officer. *He is a proficient draughtsman whose work is executed in a highly technically competent manner. There is, however, general critical agreement that it lacks originality and vision. Very derivative. Applicant has been unable to secure representation by any commercial gallery. Recommend reject application.*

Poor prick. It was enough to make anyone want to slash his wrists. According to the application form, he'd shown his work only a couple of times in the previous year, at group exhibitions in regional civic centres – only a short step away from hobby painter shows in shopping malls. DOB 1953, Katoomba, NSW. An unfinished fine arts diploma at Sydney Tech. Address: care of YMCA building. Although he claimed to be painting full-time, his principal source of income was cited as unemployment benefits. The grant was sought to pay for materials.

Despite the executive officer's negative recommendation, the panel had approved a small grant, less than a quarter of what Taylor had asked for. Reading between the lines, I detected a kiss-off, a few crumbs of conscience money to get rid of a nuisance. Either that, or Taylor knew someone on the panel prepared to go into bat for him. I flicked to the front of the file and read the membership list. There were only two names I recognised: Salina Fleet and Lloyd Eastlake. Salina, presumably, had persuaded her fellow panel members that her boyfriend's talent was worth throwing a small bone at.

A sad story but a closed book. When I met Agnelli in two hours, I'd be able to advise him that Taylor's potential nuisance value was negligible.

Tossing the file back where it belonged, I shut the office door behind me and headed down three floors to the carpark. Now that I knew a little more about Marcus Taylor, I found myself increasingly sympathetic to the poor bugger. The man was obviously a social misfit. Spurned by the critics, ignored by buyers, barely qualifying for an official handout, snubbed by a gallery full of art-lovers, dumped by his girlfriend. Talk about suffering for your art. The only thing missing was the garret.

Or was it? The address he gave on his grant application was the YMCA, the ruin next door, so close it would've been cheaper to hand-deliver the letter than pay the postage. And certainly faster. But the YMCA had been derelict for years, slated for demolition as part of the Arts City development. Surely he wasn't living there? Shit, I could just see it: Drowned Artist Squatted in Shadow of Lavish Arts Bureaucracy.

I rode the lift to street level, walked through the parked cars, turned left and looked up. In its heyday, the Y must have been an impressive pile. Seven storeys tall, V-shaped, city views. But the tide had long since gone out, and now it had nothing to look forward to this side of demolition. Peeling grey paint and a hundred grimy windows. But apparently still in use. Although the street-level doors were bricked up, a set of stairs led to a first-floor entrance, a heavy door painted with the Ministry for the Arts logo: a pair of tragi-comic masks surmounted by dancing semi-quavers above a crossed pen and paintbrush.

The door was locked. As I turned away, it abruptly swung open and a hunched spine backed out. It belonged to a spotty youth with an armload of music stands. He propped the door open with the stands, went back in, re-emerged with a violin case in each hand. 'Do you mind?' He held the cases out from his sides and nodded at the music stands. I tucked them up under his armpits, holding the door open with my shoulder. 'If you're looking for Environmental,' he said, pleased to be the bearer of bad news. 'They've already left.'

'I'm looking for someone who lives here,' I said.

He gave me a queer look. 'Bit late for that. Nobody's lived here for years. It's cheap storage now. Rehearsal rooms. Office space for low-budget arts organisations. Artist studios.' He stood there, waiting for me to close the door.

'I might just look about, then,' I said.

'I'm afraid I can't allow that,' he said pompously. 'Tenant access only at the weekend.'

What was he going to do? Deck me with a Stradivarius?

'Won't be long.' I stepped sideways into the building and the door swung shut behind me.

An ill-lit vestibule faced an ancient cage-type elevator, its oily cables caked with grime. Exhausted linoleum covered the floor. Stairs ran up and down on either side of the lift and a poky corridor extended back into the building, punctuated by doors at regular intervals. The whole place had been painted with mushroom soup at the time of the Wall Street Crash and not swept since the Fall of Singapore. About twenty tenants were listed on a directory board, the names spelled out in movable letters, subject to availability. Th* Orph*us Ch*ir, J*llyw*gs The*tre *n Educ*tion Tr*up*, Comm*nity Ar*s *nform*tion *esource *ntre, Let's D*nce Victor, Environ Men*l Puppets, Ac*ss Stud*os.

This last item, third floor, struck me as the best prospect. The elevator seemed a bit iffy, so I took the stairs. The third-floor corridor was a dingy passage indistinguishable from those on the floors below, a receding horizon of peeling lino and numbered doors with smoked-glass panels. I started knocking, raising an echo but nothing else. The whole building had a forsaken air. 'Hello,' I called, tentative at first, then hiking up the volume. My voice came back at me, unanswered. I'd worked my way nearly the full length of the corridor, knocking and trying door handles, before one of them gave.

What I found could not have looked more like an

artist's studio if the Art Directors' Guild had whipped it up for a production of *La Boheme*. Every inch of the place was crammed with canvases, crinkled tubes of paint, jars of used brushes, step-ladders, casually discarded sketches, stubs of charcoal. Paint spills Jackson Pollock would have been proud of lay thick on the floor. Mounted on an easel in the centre of the room was an example of the resident artist's work.

The subject was the quintessential suburban dream home of the nineteen fifties. Cream brick-veneer, red tile roof, green front lawn, cloudless sky. The style was photo-realist, hyper-realist, super-realist, whatever they call it. An exact rendering, anyway. Sharply vivid. Perfect in every detail, a real-estate agent's vision splendid. Crowning this ideal, a lovely finishing touch, was a lawn-mower, a spanking new Victa two-stroke, sitting in the middle of the lawn. Although its topic was utterly banal, the picture was oddly disturbing, as though this commonplace scene contained within it a secret of some deep malevolence.

But I wasn't there to immerse myself in art. I tore myself away and continued my search. Half-concealed behind a heavy curtain was a hole in the wall, a short cut into the adjacent room. This was furnished as living quarters, rough but not entirely squalid. There was a small enamel sink, a trestle table with a gas camping-stove, a microwave oven and a rack of op-shop crockery. A futon on a slatted wooden base. A vinyl-covered club armchair. A brick-and-board bookcase filled with large-format colour-plate art books, filed by artist, Australians mainly. Brack, Boyd, Nolan, Pugh, Williams. Empty bottles, six wine, two vodka. An overfilled garbage bag, a little on the nose in the heat. At the window, a metal two-drawer desk and typist's chair. Home sweet home. But whose?

Moving quickly now, feeling like a burglar, I crossed to the desk. It was covered with loose sheets of doodled-on tracing paper, drafting pens, erasers, crayons, chinagraph pencils, note pads. Nothing to indicate the occupant's name.

I slid open the top drawer. A bulldog clip of receipts from Dean's Artist Supplies. An art materials price-list. Envelopes containing colour transparencies of artworks, pictures of pictures, each labelled with a name. Familiar names from the bookcase. Beneath this clutter, held together by a paperclip, were three photographs. The first was old, the print dog-eared, square, black-and-white, a Box Brownie snap. A pretty teenager, full-faced, her hair permed for home defence. The next was also black-and-white, but glossier, a fifties feel. A man and a woman standing at a scenic lookout, a row of mountain peaks arrayed along the horizon behind them. The Twelve Apostles, the Seven Sisters, the Three Musketeers, somewhere famous. It was the same woman, now a twenty-year-old sophisticate in twin-set and pleated skirt, the man in baggy trousers and a beret. The pair of them relaxed, joky, hamming it up for the camera. Lovers. I had no idea who they were.

The last print was colour, curved corners. A young man with shoulder-length hair and wire-rimmed glasses standing in a row of corn, hoe in hand, bare to the waist, the original ninety-pound weakling. Beside him, leaning on a fork, an older man, barrel-chested, high-scalped.

The face unshaven, bags under the eyes, but the same comic tufts above the ears, the same brazen stare as I had seen on Fiona Lambert's mantelpiece. Victor Szabo.

The hippy could have been Marcus Taylor. He had the same elongated face, the same feral intensity. It could have been anyone. I held the photo motionless, observing from a great height, staring down like a bird floating on a thermal, waiting for something to reveal itself.

Nothing did. I was asleep on my feet, miserably hungover. I opened the second drawer, working quickly, feeling furtive. A stamp album, most pages still empty. The few stamps it held were all Australian, low denominations. All bore the Bicentenary logo of 1988. Last year's issues. Hand-written annotations in tiny print. Whoever lived here was no great philatelist. A new hobby, perhaps, the interest unsustained. Wedged into the back of the album was a bank passbook. I slipped it out of its plastic cover, flipped it open and read the name.

Marcus Taylor. Bingo.

The dead have no privacy. I thumbed blank pages, looking for a balance. Thunk. Whirr. Somebody had started the elevator. It shuddered and lurched upwards, the sound magnified in the deserted building.

Startled by the sudden noise, I dropped the bankbook. It fell down the gap between the desk and the wall. I began to go down on my knees to retrieve it until it occurred to me that this was probably the police, come to examine the deceased's effects. I felt like a tomb robber. Not that I was doing anything wrong. It's just that I would have been hard put to explain exactly what I was doing. It was, I rapidly concluded, one of those situations where discretion was the better part of anything else you might care to mention.

Dumping the rest of the stuff back into the drawer, I stepped out the door. Down the hallway, the lift groaned and shuddered to a halt, a vague shape behind the grille. Immediately in front of me, a rubbish bin propped open a door marked Fire Escape. The layout of the building suggested these stairs opened onto the adjoining lane. I took them two at a time, scattering litter.

Three flights down, where the street exit should have been, the wall had been bricked up. Half a flight further, they ended at a large door. *Environ Mental Puppet Company*, it said. Beyond, a broad corridor lined with age-speckled white tiles extended towards the vague glow of daylight.

I pressed on, and had taken perhaps a dozen steps when a sudden draft of air stirred the grime at my feet. A pneumatic woomph sounded in my ears. I swung around just in time to see the door slam shut behind me. It was some sort of fire door, steel, fitting snugly into a metal frame. There was no handle on my side.

'Hey,' I shouted, and banged the palms of my hands against the flat metal plate. 'Hey.' There was no answer.

I BALLED MY fist and banged again. The heavy steel reverberated with a dull echo, but there was still no answer. Either a draught in the stairwell had slammed the door shut or somebody was playing funny buggers. If I wanted out of this dump, I'd have to find another way.

Giving the door one last futile kick, I turned and headed along the corridor. Its white-tiled walls, even in their grimy state, reminded me of a hospital or a science laboratory, a place of bodily messes and antiseptic solutions. Even the air seemed to have a faintly pervasive chemical odour, as fusty as the cracked porcelain of the tiles. I soon discovered why.

The wide passageway opened abruptly into a cavernous basement, also lined with decrepit white tiles. Sunlight, struggling through a row of frosted windows high up in one wall, illuminated the room with its pallid wash. Occupying almost the entire space was a gigantic cement pit.

Great scabs of peeling green paint clung to its walls like clumps of dried lichen. Overlapping the edge of the huge trough, at the far end of the room, was a tangle of corroded pipes. Attached to the decaying metalwork was a sign. DANGER, it said. NO DIVING. POOL CLOSED. Lying on the bottom of the empty swimming pool, right in the middle, was a body.

Numerous bodies, actually. But the one that grabbed my attention was the whale. It was life-sized, aqua blue and made of fibreglass. Scattered around it was a pod of papier-mâché dolphins, several dozen polystyrene starfish mounted on bamboo poles, innumerable cardboard scallop shells, piles of flags and pendants embroidered with sea-horses, and a pair of hammerhead sharks made of lycra and chicken wire.

But none of these were as compelling as the whale. Painted across its deep-sea dial was an idiotic anthropomorphic grin. I was buggered if I could figure out why it was smiling, though. It was high and dry, and so was I.

The only other exit was a roller door, big enough for a truck and battened down with more locksmithery than Alcatraz. Through the narrow gap at the bottom, I could just make out the surface of a laneway. Blasts of hot air were already rising from the asphalt. I rattled the roller a few times and gave a yell, but there was nobody outside to hear.

Next door was a long-disused changing room with vandalised lockers and ancient urinals full of desiccated deodorant balls. I tore a length of iron pipe from the wall of a shower recess. When I bashed it against the fire door, it produced considerably more noise than anything I'd been able to raise with my bare hands. Loud enough to make the blood in my temples throb and showers of sparks shoot into my eyes. But not loud enough, apparently, to be heard by anyone else in the building. I bashed away for a fair while, but all I got was a tired arm and an even more aggravated headache. The door was thicker than a Colleen McCullough novel. I could have banged away all day and not got a result.

I carefully explored the whole place again. The only potential exit was the windows. They appeared to be unlocked. They were also six metres up a sheer wall.

It had just gone 9.15 a.m. The situation was beginning to give me the shits. This whole spur-of-the-moment garret-rifling expedition had been of questionable value in the first place. And taking off like a sprung burglar had only made things worse. At this rate, I'd be locked in all weekend. I slumped down beside the wall and lit an aid to clear thinking, my second last.

Bone weariness and enraged irritation fought for control of my body, equally matched. I jumped up, sat down, jumped up again. That little smartarse with the armful of violins had done this. Finally, I collapsed back against the wall and drew what comfort I could from my cigarette. If I'd been the Prime Minister, I'd have cried from sheer self-pity.

Agnelli had got me into this mess, waking me up with his paranoia, sending me to hose down imaginary threats to his public image. Nor was the Premier blameless. If he hadn't decided to reshuffle the Cabinet, I wouldn't have been compelled to change jobs. And if that hadn't happened, I wouldn't have a hangover and be locked in the storage facility of a marine-fixated puppet company.

Who was I trying to fool? Sleuthing around in a

brain-dead state for no good reason, it was my own damned fault that I'd managed to get myself in this situation.

In a little over ninety minutes I was due to meet Agnelli, brief him on Taylor's suicide note and escort him to Max Karlin's brunch. A side trip to the supermarket in the interim was beginning to look unlikely. Not that Red would need any groceries, not where he'd be. Standing in an airport lounge waiting in vain for his father to arrive. 'I was only two days late,' I could hear myself grovelling down the phone to Wendy. 'You didn't have to tell the airline people to put him on the next plane back to Sydney.'

When my cigarette was smoked down to its stub, I ground it out on the dirty cement floor and began gnawing at my fingernails. For the first time since the previous evening in Fiona Lambert's flat, I thought about the cut on my finger. Peeling away the flesh-toned plastic strip, I examined my wound. The skin was wrinkled and bleached, the cut shrivelled to a tiny slit. My finger looked like a sea slug, horrible little mouth and all. Very appropriate, I thought. The way things were going, I might as well be part of the flotsam and jetsam in the bottom of the pool.

Hard against the wall immediately beneath the windows was a work bench littered with piles of fabric, tangled chicken wire, bits and pieces of half-made piscine puppets. Maybe I could find enough timber among all this parade-float junk to rig up some sort of ladder. If I got as far as window level, I could perhaps find a handy drainpipe to climb down. On a building this old, the plumbing was bound to be external.

But the only timber at the bottom of the pool was bamboo, flimsy shafts with polystyrene starfish jammed on the end. I went around the back of Willy the Whale and stuck my head into his rear-end aperture. More parade paraphernalia had been dumped inside – jellyfish costumes of green and blue lycra, papier-mache fish masks, plastic sheeting cut up into seaweed shapes, bicycle helmets with fin attachments. Beneath all of this, I found two lengths of aluminium tubing.

Thick as my wrist and about three metres long, they were painted a mottled greyish-blue and tipped with rubber. This was promising. Grabbing a pole in each hand, I backed out the whale's bum, dragging them after me. First came the poles. Then a set of rubberised fishing waders. Then a bulbous blob covered in blue and grey fabric. Then some kind of bodysuit covered with strips of coloured plastic. Then a tangle of foam-covered wire.

I hauled the whole rigmarole up beside the pool and examined it. Metal plates in the insoles of the waders were riveted onto matching plates welded onto the aluminium struts. The bodysuit, complete with foam-rubber midriff, was sewn securely onto the waders. The result was a octopus costume on stilts. The artistry was truly execrable, but the engineering was superb. So much so that it was impossible to detach the poles. Great. Just what I needed. An Oscar the frigging Octopus suit.

Propped against the wall, the aluminium shafts reached only halfway to the windows. My ladder project was shaping up as a dead end. At this rate, I'd be here for the rest of my life. I returned to the fire door, picked up the iron pipe and pounded away in futile rage. Then I spent fifteen minutes trying to lever the bolts off the roller door. I smoked my last cigarette and realised I was hungry. If this Prisoner of Zenda crap went on much longer, I'd be reduced to drinking my own urine. Eventually, like a dog to its dinner, I went back to Oscar.

All my previous stilt experience had been on jam-tin-and-string models when I was about six years old. Octopus costume aside, these babies were the real thing, fully three metres tall. Even if I managed to get myself upright, I'd still need to be standing on the bench to reach the window sill. A fall from that height would do nothing to improve my general well-being.

On the other hand, I had to do something. The Environ Mental Puppeteers might not be back for days. The jerk with the violins said they'd left already. He didn't say where to. Maybe they were on an international tour. Taking the best of the worst of Australian artistry to the world.

Oscar was mostly foam rubber. A big foam rubber cocoon. So if I fell, as long as I didn't topple over the edge into the pool, the damage would probably be limited. A fractured skull, a broken neck. Nothing I couldn't live with. In a wheelchair. If only I had a few more cigarettes. Just one, even.

I sat on the floor, took my shoes and pants off, stuck my legs into the trouser part of the waders and hoisted the engorged champignon bit up around my waist. The toes pinched, but the fit wasn't too bad. Tugging the straps of the overall part over my shoulders, I wiggled my arms down the sleeves and into the washing-up gloves sewn on the ends. A cowl sort of thing fitted over my head, held in place by velcro tabs. The rubbery waders made my legs tacky with sweat and a necklace of tentacles dangled to my knees. I felt vaguely fetishistic. Christ alone knew what I looked like.

So there I was, disguised as a giant cephalopod, flat on my back beside a dehydrated aquatic facility in a derelict cultural resource centre, with absolutely no idea of what to do next. When I'd taken on the job of adviser to the Minister for the Arts, I somehow hadn't imagined myself in such a position. If this didn't work, I swore, I would make it my personal mission as a senior government functionary to see that the Environ Mental Puppet Company never again received a penny of public funding.

Now that I was togged up, there was nothing for it but to proceed. Grabbing a leg of the bench, I dragged myself upright. Then, flailing my many appendages, I swept the tabletop clear and climbed aboard. By extending the blue poles behind me and pressing my palms flat against the wall, I could form a reasonably stable triangle.

Thus I advanced, palms splayed out before me. Little hop, inch. Little hop, inch. Palming myself along like Marcel Marceau trying to get out of that fucking invisible box of his. The trick with stilts, in case you ever need to know, is to stay in motion. Much like a bicycle. Or politics. Stand still and you're stuffed. Keep moving or you take a dive.

By the time I was five metres up, my priorities review committee had urgently convened. Second thoughts were in the majority. I was bathed in sweat, my arms were aching from the effort, and my sea slug was throbbing. But it wasn't just the prospect of crashing to the floor in a welter of shattered vertebrae and ruptured organs that was urging me to reconsider my strategy. A structural flaw in the plan had became obvious. The transom was rigged to open only part of the way. Even if I managed to get as far as the sill and push the window open, the gap was too narrow to admit a man with a blue rubber mattress strapped to his midriff.

Just your head and shoulders will be enough, I told myself. Even in a precinct teeming with cultural offerings, the spectacle of a man in an octopus suit sandwiched into a window frame could not pass unnoticed for long. Eventually a passer-by would see me, realise I was not an art object and mount a rescue effort.

Grunting, I pressed on. Finally my fingers closed around the metal of the window frame. Pushing the transom open with my beak, I wriggled forward. Somewhere far below, my stilt feet lifted off the floor. My head and shoulders poked through. My position was as tenuous as the Liberal Party leadership, but at least now I had an outside chance of hailing somebody.

Immediately across from my vantage point was the saw-toothed roof of a warehouse, closed for the weekend. Below me was the narrow street I had glimpsed from beneath the roller door. It was an access lane to the warehouse. Not much hope of passing traffic at this hour on a Saturday morning. Not that I knew the hour, not with any precision. My watch, along with my wrist, was encased in latex. But I knew that if I didn't get noticed soon, I might as well throw myself from the window and be done with it. If I didn't meet Agnelli I wouldn't have a job. And if I wasn't at the airport on time my life wouldn't be worth living. Except that I couldn't even get far enough into the window frame to defenestrate myself.

My only hope was the building next door, the Ballet Centre. Its parking levels were faced with vertical steel slats. By pushing myself out the window as far as possible and swivelling sideways, I could just make out a row of parked cars. Event-ually somebody would come to collect one of them. Then all I had to do was shout loudly. And hope that whoever heard me would have the sense to stick his head over the edge of the parking deck and look sideways.

As luck would have it, I didn't have to wait long. My vigil had scarcely begun when a figure appeared, an indistinct shape bobbing between the cars. 'Hey,' I yelled, and waved my tentacles.

The shape passed out of sight, then appeared again, partly obscured by a concrete column. He was bending, his head in the boot of a car. Then he stood up. He was hard against the periphery of my vision but there was no mistaking that rear profile, that head like a wing-nut.

'Hey,' I bawled. 'Over here. Noel. Mate.'

AT FIFTEEN, Spider was a seasoned drinker, or so he claimed. A man with established tastes. Southern Comfort, he reckoned, was cough syrup. Cat's piss. A man of his experience knew what he wanted. Bourbon. Jack Daniels. In return, I need never worry about the Fletchers again. The Fletchers kept a respectful distance from Spider. He'd done boxing. 'You look after me,' he said. 'I'll look after you.'

Southern Comfort would be easier, I argued. Or Bundaberg rum. The pub sold a fair bit of those. But protection never comes cheap. So, in the end, bourbon it was. Jim Beam. A 'breakage' off the top shelf, syphoned into a Marchants lemonade bottle while I was polishing the mirrors in the saloon bar and Dad was downstairs tapping a keg. Not Jack Daniels but I hoped Spider wouldn't notice the difference.

The handover was to be in the Oulton Reserve, the local football oval, after training on Thursday night. Not that either of us was in the team, but going to watch the Under-19s train was a good thing to tell a father. What could be more innocent? It was all pretty innocent, I suppose. Until the Fletchers turned up.

'Hey, you,' I bellowed desperately, wrenching the sound up from the bottom of my lungs and waving a blue rubber glove. 'Over here. Noel.' At least I thought it was Noel. He'd moved out of sight again.

'Spider!' I tried, hoping to trigger a primal reaction. 'Help! Heeelp!' The cry was as loud as I could make it. My head spun from the effort. It sounded pretty loud to me, but so did the trucks shifting gears on City Road. Oblivious to my impassioned cries, the figure was moving away. 'Help,' I bawled.

It was a waste of breath. The head bobbed down, a door slammed, a moving vehicle flickered momentarily in the shadows behind the screen of steel slats and the carpark was still again.

It remained that way for what seemed a very long time. Nobody else came. Nobody else went. Not in the carpark, at least. Down below in the laneway, a minibus drove briskly by, a cricket team of teenage boys hanging out the windows. I waved my tentacles at the flash of upturned faces, but all I got in return was the collective finger.

Unless somebody saw me soon, I'd be spending the rest of my life on my knees before Wendy with gravel rash on my forehead. No, to do that I'd have to get down first. I didn't even have a cigarette to console me. And even if I did, I wouldn't be able to get my tentacle up to my beak to inhale. I decided I had better prospects at floor level, banging on one of the doors.

To descend from my perch, I had to turn around, press my back to the wall, and execute a controlled slide. Controlled being the key word. Halfway down, the foot of one of the stilts caught in a snarl of chicken wire lying beside the work bench. Off balance, I pitched forward. Suddenly, I was standing upright, clear of the wall, with no way of maintaining my balance but by taking the next step. Then the next. Then the next.

I was stilt-walking. Look Mum, no hands. No place to go, either. Arms helicoptering madly through the air, I tottered forward – towards the rim of the empty pool.

Then Willy rose and swallowed me whole. One moment I was looking down at him from a great height. The next I was in his belly, staring up at a gaping hole in his back. There was a sharp but momentary pain in my left ear. Plunging over the edge, I had crashed straight through the whale's thin fibreglass shell. Luckily, Oscar's copious contents helped break my fall. I had landed on a pile of stuffed squid. I was winded, upside-down and my legs were twisted together, but otherwise I was intact. Willy, for his part, was now the only whale in captivity with a sunroof.

All but hysterical with relief, I jettisoned my ludicrous padding and crawled out the whale's backside. I could have been killed. I was lucky to be alive.

I clambered out of the pool and put on my trousers and shoes. My hands were palpitating so wildly I could barely tie the laces. I breathed deeply to calm down and gave myself a quick once-over. No broken bones, but my explosion through Willy's carapace had done something to my ear. It was bleeding profusely.

I found a crumpled rag and clutched it to my earhole. Then I picked up the iron pipe and began bashing the fire door. I guess I must have lost it there for a while. I was stir crazy. Cabin fever had me in its grip. I may have even been howling. I wanted out and if need be I'd bludgeon my way through three inches of steel plate. I bashed until my arm went numb and bells rang in my brain.

Eventually, worn out, I collapsed against the door. Through the metal, I heard the grind of a bolt being drawn. 'Yeah, yeah,' a woman's voice was saying, irritably. 'Take it easy.'

The door swung backwards to reveal Salina Fleet.

But not the Sal I'd been fumbling in the forget-me-nots. Nor the freaked-out Salina lit by the ambulance light at the moat. This Salina was very sober and very proper. A woman who had made up her mind about something. Gidget was gone. This Salina wore calf-length culottes, a fawn blouse and black button earrings, not a hair out of place. This Salina was so composed she could have read the Channel 10 news.

She took a step backwards. In my panting, dishevelled state, I must have been quite a sight. And not a welcome one. 'What are *you* doing here?'

Snooping through your deceased boyfriend's personal effects did not, somehow, seem like the appropriate answer. Already it was clear that what had occurred between us last night was ancient history, a dead letter. The fire was well and truly out. Our little nocturnal nature ramble was a temporary lapse to which neither of us would again refer. Nothing had happened. Nothing ever would.

'The minister wants a report,' I said, self-importantly. 'On under-utilised Arts Ministry facilities.' Hand pressed to ear, I must have looked like a harmonising Bee Gee. 'I was sent on a tour of inspection. A tenant got hostile and locked me in. You didn't see him, did you? A guy with an armful of violins.'

Salina shook her head, and cocked it sideways in disbelief. To think, her eyes seemed to say, I nearly took this lunatic to bed.

'What about you?' I asked. The pretence begun, I had no option but to continue. 'What are you doing here?'

She cast her gaze downwards and adopted a sombre tone. 'Marcus's studio is upstairs.'

I nodded understandingly and stepped forward, moving us onward from the doorway. 'He was the one at the exhibition last night, on the table, wasn't he?' I said. 'I'm sorry. I didn't realise, I mean . . .'

She maintained her aloof solemnity. 'No need to apologise. You weren't to know.'

'I mean I'm sorry about Marcus,' I said, gently correcting her. As far as I knew, I didn't have anything to apologise for.

'Thank you.' She spoke formally, bowing her head slightly. Rehearsing, I realised, the role of the grieving widow graciously accepting condolences.

'It was on the radio. You were mentioned, too.'

'Ah.' This information did not entirely displease her. 'So soon?'

She turned and began back up the stairs, as if trying to put an interruption behind her. She was carrying a folio case, the sort art students and advertising types use. Evidently she had just arrived at the YMCA and my banging had distracted her from her objective. When we reached the ground floor corridor, she stopped at the open door, anticipating my departure. Up in the harsher light, there was a fragility to her. She'd probably got even less sleep than me. The strain was showing. I reached over and touched her arm. 'You okay?'

She jerked away, then softened. 'I'm fine. Really I am.' She squeezed out a pained little smile.

I didn't want her thinking I was coming on to her. We stood uncomfortably in the doorway, each waiting for the other to move. I could feel her impatience growing. 'Here to collect some personal things, are you?' I asked.

She nodded, relieved at the explanation. At the same time, she shrugged the fact into wounded insignificance, as though I was trampling on a small private grief.

It was 10.30. That gave me just enough time to get to Parliament House to meet Agnelli. But not with a bloodied rag gripped to my auditory apparatus. I needed water and a mirror and the only place I knew for sure I'd find them was Marcus Taylor's room. 'I'll give you a hand,' I said. 'The artists' studios are on the third floor, aren't they?' I started up the stairs. 'According to the board at the front door.'

Helping myself to the dead boyfriend's personal facilities was not, I knew, the most sensitive move possible. On the other hand, all this holier-than-thou stuff was beginning to rankle. I'd be buggered if I was going to be made to feel like the guilty party here.

'No. Don't.' Salina dashed after me. 'I'll be okay, really,' she protested.

The door of Marcus Taylor's bedroom sat open to the corridor. 'This it?' I said. I headed directly for the small enamel basin. Drying blood caked my ear but a little water confirmed that the damage was only skin deep. My eyes were sinkholes and I had the complexion of a piece of candied pineapple.

Over my shoulder in the mirror, I saw Salina come in and glance around anxiously. As far as I could see, there was no evidence of feminine habitation in the place. For rough-and-ready accommodation, the joint had a certain masculine sufficiency. But I couldn't imagine a woman here. A forest floor was one thing, but this was the pits.

'Don't mind me,' I said. The tin cabinet behind the mirror held shaving gear, out-of-date antibiotics, Dettol, cotton-wool, a roll of adhesive bandage. Salina laid the folio case flat on the futon bed. 'Just a few private effects, is it?'

For some reason, she resented this remark. 'Now that Marcus is dead,' she said, defensively, 'people will be curious about his work. The least I can do is see that it is presented to the world in a favourable light.'

Without turning, I held my hands up in a placatory gesture. 'Hey,' I agreed. 'You don't have to explain yourself to me.' The sharp bite of antiseptic brought tears to my eyes.

Suddenly, all of Salina's freshly cultivated reserve was gone. She slumped down on the edge of the bed and began tearing the wrapper off a pack of cigarettes. 'I should have seen it coming,' she said, her voice thick with self-recrimination. 'Marcus was so depressed and moody lately, drinking a lot, complaining that everyone was against him. I did what I could, even used my influence to get him a grant, but it didn't make any difference. You saw what he was like last night. I told him

I was sick of his self-indulgence. Now I keep thinking that's what pushed him over the edge. It's all my fault.'

Black smudges ringed her eyes. Exhaustion and rattiness engulfed both of us. She lit a cigarette, sucked at it hungrily, openly trawling for sympathy. Considering what had almost happened between us, I owed her that much.

Tearing the adhesive tape with my teeth, I patched my ear as best I could. Then, compelled by a weariness as irresistible as gravity, I sank down on the other side of the bed. 'Don't blame yourself,' I said. 'Perhaps it was an accident. He was pretty drunk. He could have fallen in. Perhaps he didn't mean to kill himself.'

She tried without success to make her bottom lip quiver. 'Oh, no,' she said firmly. 'It was definitely suicide. The police showed me a note he left, asked me to identify the handwriting. It was definitely his. His style, too. That litany of complaints. I told them I thought he was probably a manic depressive. He certainly had a tendency to self-dramatisation. That's why I didn't take any particular notice last night. More of the usual crap, I thought. Told him I'd had enough, it was over between us.'

I helped myself to one of her cigarettes, drawing sustenance from it, oblivious to the vile taste. A scarifying sunlight poured in the window, the window at which Taylor must have conceived his own death, his artistic auto-da-fé. It was a strange feeling, sitting there amid the scant domesticity of a dead man I had never really met.

'He was illegitimate, you know,' Salina blurted, offering the fact as if in mitigation. 'A lot of unresolved emotional trauma bubbling away. And his work. He felt the rejection of his work deeply.'

She was veering dangerously close to the maudlin. I sensed that, now the facade was down, she'd keep talking until she got it all out. Not that I was insensitive or anything, but my time was not entirely my own. If I didn't start disengaging, I'd be there all day.

'Forget the souvenirs.' A few scraps of paper weren't worth the aggravation. What she needed was to go home and sleep. 'Come back another time.' Grinding my fag underfoot, I hauled myself into the vertical and held out my hand.

Salina remained where she was. She shook her head. 'You've been sweet,' she said. 'But if you don't mind, I'd like to be left alone.'

I'm not an entirely insensitive person. I nodded and turned to leave, stepping towards the curtain covering the hole into the studio. 'I'll go this way.'

Sal was on her feet in a flash, interposing herself between me and the curtain. 'I feel so bad,' she said. 'About last night.'

She stood very close and put her hand on my arm. Sliding it downwards, she found my hand and squeezed it. Then her head was against my chest, looking upwards into my eyes. Her body moulded itself to mine. She sighed deeply.

Her change of mood was abrupt and disconcerting. But, like I said, I'm not an entirely insensitive guy. I put my arms around her.

Her hand snaked up my back. She stood on tiptoes and pressed the back of my head down towards her closing eyes and opening lips. I kissed her. Compassionately at first. Then, at her insistence, the other way.

Then she peeped and I could see it in her eyes. It wasn't me that Salina desired. Nor was it my pity. She wanted my complicity. Complicity in what, I couldn't tell. But whatever it was, I didn't want any part of it. I prefer to save my cynicism for politics.

Putting my hands gently on her shoulders, I prised my face free. Salina stared up, not comprehending. 'It's okay,' she reassured me. 'My relationship with Marcus was all but over anyway. We weren't even sleeping together. Hadn't been for months.'

The last thing I wanted was the sordid details. I took a step backwards. 'I'll leave you to it,' I said, sweeping the curtain aside. 'Make sure you get everything before you go.'

I don't know why I said it. Taylor's lonely death, his relationship with Salina, had nothing to do with me. But my remark wasn't just sanctimonious. It was superfluous. There was nothing for her to get. The paintings that were strewn about Taylor's studio in such ill-ordered profusion just an hour before were gone, stripped off their stretchers or roughly cut from their frames. The easel in the middle of the room was empty, the suburban dream house vanished. While I'd been downstairs impersonating a seafood dinner, someone had cleaned the place out.

Salina stared at the looted room. On her face was the same appalled expression with which she had responded to Taylor's drunken speech at the Centre for Modern Art.

I didn't have the time, the energy or the inclination to keep up with Salina Fleet's emotional gymnastics.

Stepping around the discarded struts of timber and upended jars of brushes, I continued into the hallway and down the stairs.

Marcus Taylor's work, it seemed, was finally in demand. Suicide was beginning to look like the smartest career move he ever made.

'**I**T'S ABOUT time!'

Agnelli cleared a pile of briefing papers off the back seat of the Fairlane and made room for me. We were due to meet at eleven. It was 11.09. Under the circumstances, I thought I'd done well.

'Jesus,' he said, as I finished giving Alan the address of Karlin's brunch and slid into the back seat. 'What happened to your ear? You look like Vincent bloody Van Gogh.' I wasn't going to begin to answer a remark like that.

And Agnelli didn't really want to discuss my aural health. His own welfare was preying on his mind. Ministerial impatience suffused the car's interior like oxygen in a bell jar. 'Those journos have been on the blower again. Now they're talking about allegations of corruption in the arts bureaucracy.'

We glided out the back gate of Parliament House and Alan turned the Fairlane towards West Melbourne. 'Those with their hands on the levers of power are the most corrupt of all,' I quoted.

'Who?' said Agnelli. 'What?'

'I think I've got it right.' I fished my scrawled copy

of Taylor's note from my pocket.

Agnelli seized it, avid for the worst. A policy crisis, accusations of pork barrelling, being caught misleading parliament, these he could take in his stride. They were but grist to the mill of everyday politics. But a suicide note, a city landmark, a potential media feeding-frenzy – this was a volatile combination. Agnelli's most defensive political instincts were aroused. His lips moved as he read.

'This is the sort of story the press are going to milk for every possible angle,' I said. 'They're just rattling your cage, trying for a reaction, hoping to drum up a political angle where there isn't one.'

Agnelli corrugated his brow and peered down at the note as though he'd been dealt a very bad hand in Scrabble. 'This is garbage. Who is this guy anyway?'

'An unemployed artist,' I said. 'Possible psychiatric history.' Salina called him a manic depressive. I should have pressed her for details. 'We'll know for sure in a couple of days. The guy was broke, depressed about his work and shit-faced drunk. There's even a school of thought that the whole thing was an accident and the note just a circumstantial furphy. But given the location and the fact that he was a painter, a certain degree of media interest is inevitable. My bet is they'll swarm in the direction of the most obvious cliché – anguished artist dies of broken heart, his talent unrecognised in life.' Particularly with the nudge in that direction that Salina Fleet was already giving them. 'The whole thing will have blown over by this time next week.'

'Maybe.' Agnelli's brow unfurrowed slightly. 'But

keep a close eye on it anyway. This sort of drivel is tabloid heaven.'

'If absolutely necessary,' I tossed in the clincher, 'we can discreetly let it be known that shortly before his death Taylor was allocated a small but generous Arts Ministry grant.'

A foxy light came into Agnelli's eyes. 'Now why didn't I think of that?'

The idea that I was being devious was doing wonders for Agnelli's morale. 'And to think I had reservations about offering you this job,' he muttered.

While I pondered that point, he moved on to the topic of our imminent destination. 'So what about this Max Karlin? The Jew from Central Casting, eh?' Two years in Ethnic Affairs had done nothing for Angelo's rougher edges.

'I met him briefly last night,' I said. 'Quite the philanthropist apparently.' This was intended as a fairly obvious prompt for Agnelli to come clean about his self-appointed fund-raising role. It didn't work. He kept his cards pressed silently to his chest. 'I told him how delighted you'd be to meet such a prominent contributor to the public good,' I tried.

'And so I will be.' Agnelli remained impenetrably bland. 'Better give me my starting orders.'

Madness, I told myself, sheer insanity. Here I was, stage-managing an encounter between a minister in an increasingly fragile government, a man to whom I owed my employment and my loyalty, and a wealthy businessman about whom I knew next to nothing. All with no better objective than having my fears confirmed that Agnelli was planning a new career as a bag-man.

'Essentially this is just a low-key meet-and-mingle,' I told him. 'Karlin is something of an art collector and the Centre for Modern Art has recently copped a fairly decent Arts Ministry grant to buy one of his pictures. Lloyd Eastlake, who chairs the CMA, is keen to see that the government gets its share of the credit. Understandably so, since he was also on the Arts Ministry committee that recommended the purchase.'

Eastlake's name was another obvious cue, a little reminder to Agnelli that he had not yet told me about the threesome in his office the previous afternoon. If Angelo wanted to limit my role to strictly arts matters, that was his prerogative. He was the minister. He was perfectly entitled to make all the unwise decisions he liked. But the least he could do was take me into his confidence.

Agnelli pricked up his ears, but not in the way that I hoped. 'What's Eastlake's connection with Karlin?'

'Aside from them both being on the board of the Centre for Modern Art, I don't know. Eastlake showed me his art gallery last night, but he didn't take me into his confidence.' I paused pregnantly.

My delicate condition was of no interest to Agnelli. He was too busy figuring the angles. 'We're funding this picture deal on Eastlake's say-so, right? How much is Karlin getting, and what are we getting in return?'

'Our kick-in was $300,000, towards a total purchase price in excess of half a million dollars. What we, in the form of the publicly owned CMA, are getting in return is a painting by Victor Szabo.'

Agnelli whistled lightly under his breath. 'For that sort of dough we could get a Matisse.'

'Possibly,' I said. 'But Matisse wasn't Australian.'

'And Victor Szabo was?' Ange was probably finessing the point. I suspected he knew even less about Victor Szabo than I did.

'Szabo's background was, er, European, of course,' I ventured. 'But the CMA seems to feel that his contribution to the development of Australian art warrants the price.'

'That may well be,' said Agnelli. 'But he's not exactly a household name, is he? And we're the ones footing the bill. Big-ticket art buys are hardly a guaranteed vote-winner, you know.'

My sentiments precisely, I told him. But the fact that Gil Methven, neither a conspicuous risk-taker nor a notorious art lover, had okayed the deal suggested that the decision was unlikely to be controversial. 'Eastlake raised half the total purchase price from corporate donors. Not only does that spread the risk, fallout-wise, it also gives us the "government in partnership with private enterprise to promote culture" line.'

Agnelli's mental gears went into overdrive. 'Corporate donors? Who exactly?'

I shrugged. 'Dunno, yet. They'll probably be at this brunch, though. Maybe you could take the opportunity to put the hard word on them for a contribution to the party.'

He didn't rise to the bait. 'Good idea.' He straightened his tie and concentrated on assuming his most commanding demeanour.

Fine, I thought. Have it your own way, pal. Just don't come crying to me when you get into strife, expecting me to clean up the mess.

Max Karlin's corporate headquarters was a backstreet Cinderella, one of a hundred work-worn industrial facades tucked away in a factory precinct abutting the Queen Victoria market on the north-western edge of the central business district. We might have missed it completely if not for the logo of Max's chain of shoe stores, Karlcraft, above the entrance and the expensive wheels parked bumper to bumper at the kerb outside. From here Karlin had built his retail empire. From here he now oversaw his ultimate creation, a vast hub of shops and offices that would one day be the Karlcraft Centre.

Max, looking like an admiral in his navy blazer, materialised on the pavement as the Fairlane drew up. I made the introductions. Glancing at me only long enough to look askance at my mangled ear, Karlin swept Agnelli inside.

The external shabbiness of Karlcraft House belied the maxim about flaunting it. Max had it, all right, but he kept it discreetly out of sight, waiting until the moment you stepped through the door to clobber you with it. Everything about the building's interior was calculated to obliterate any distinction between substance and style. Here was a lush world of working wealth where good taste was a capital asset.

'Darling,' I heard. 'Smooch, smooch,' as the rest of the already assembled guests mingled in the foyer. Women with tennis tans and pre-stressed hair milled about, drinks in hand, chatting with men in oversized shirts buttoned to the neck and tasselled moccasins with no socks. Pouty waitresses, meanwhile, lurked in door-ways with trays of glasses, like cigarette girls at the Stork Club refusing to be impressed by anyone less than

F. Scott Fitzgerald. Nobody could keep their eyes off the walls.

They couldn't help it. Neither could I. Max Karlin had filled his company offices with paintings whose authorship and authority were unmistakable, even to a yob like me. Definitive works by the who's who of modern Australian art hung everywhere. Each picture seemed so perfectly to exemplify the style of its creator that I almost had to stop myself saying the names out loud. Here a Tucker, there a Boyd, a Dobell, a Perceval. A pair of Nolans faced each other across the lobby. Halfway up the stairs on either side were a Whiteley and a Smart.

I ran out of names long before Max ran out of pictures, but by then I had the message, loud and clear. When it came to aesthetic judgement, there were no flies on Max Karlin. And anyone with the dough to lavish on ornaments of this calibre had to be worth an absolute mint.

As the big boys advanced up the stairs ahead of me, there was a polite cough at my shoulder and I turned to find myself facing Phillip Veale. His eyes flickered over my suppurating ear with a droll twinkle. 'Body art?' he said. 'It's all the rage, I hear.' In the interest of weekend informality, he'd shed the French cuffs for a pastel-yellow polo top with a crocodile on the tit. 'But not as enduring as this kind.' He tilted a glass of kir royale at the nearest wall. 'Impressive, aren't they? It's not every day that Max opens his collection to the public. And only in the worthiest of causes. Today it's the CMA acquisition fund. The donation is a hundred dollars a head.'

I blanched and nearly tripped over the bottom stair.

'You and I needn't worry,' he smiled, dryly. 'The help get in for free. As for the rest' – he indicated the beau monde around us – 'they're only too happy to pay. It makes them feel special.' Offices led off the foyer, their doors open to display well-hung interiors. Veale cocked his head towards the nearest. 'A quiet word in your Vincent-like, *s'il vous plaît*.'

The office held Perry White's desk, cleared for the occasion but for four phones and two computer terminals. Apart from the desk and a big caramel landscape by someone whose name hovered on the tip of my tongue, we had the room to ourselves. 'This dreadful moat business,' Veale clucked. 'The minister's heard, I take it.'

'Had the press on the phone at dawn.'

'They have his home number?' Veale was aghast.

'It's in the book,' I told him. Angelo's idea of democratic accessibility. 'He told them to piss off.'

'Quite properly so,' said Veale. 'All press enquiries are to be handled by the Acting Director of the National Gallery. Not that he'll have anything to tell them, apart from confirming that it was gallery staff who found the body. You, of course, know that already.'

In other words I was not the only one who had spent the morning apprising myself of the facts. 'The dead man was a client of the ministry, I understand,' I said.

Veale's eyebrows went up. Evidently not all the facts were yet in his possession. 'Really?'

'Got a little grant in the last funding round. Two thousand.'

A departmental director could hardly be expected to

be aware of every teensy-weensy item of expenditure. But he knew how to draw an inference. 'Ahh,' he exhaled.

'And he was living at the old YMCA. One of our facilities, isn't it?'

'Temporarily. Pending demolition. The rooms are made available to certain worthy causes and individuals. But nobody *lives* there.' The sheer squalor of the idea seemed to appal him.

'At any rate, this Taylor had a studio there,' I said. 'It'd be interesting to know if he had any other connection with the ministry.' This was unlikely, but I was far enough ahead of Veale to have him on the defensive. A good place for a departmental head, however efficient and congenial, to be. 'Indeed,' Veale hastened to agree.

Come Monday morning, deputy directors would scuttle. In the meantime, Veale's prompt attention to the sensitivities of the issue should not go unrecognised. 'I don't believe you've met Angelo yet,' I said, leading him back into the foyer.

'Plenty of time for that on Monday.' He made a self-deprecatory gesture that suggested he would not be entirely upset to be found minding the shop on his day off. We went up the stairs to the mezzanine.

Agnelli and Karlin were getting on famously, a couple of well-rounded high-achievers basking in the cloudless skies of each other's company. They stood shoulder to shoulder in front of a painting while Karlin laid on a monologue. Agnelli jiggled with pleasure at his every bon mot. Ange's hands, I was relieved to see, were firmly in his own pockets. Beside Agnelli, very close, stood Fiona Lambert. And at Karlin's right hand, with the look of a successful matchmaker at an engagement party, stood Lloyd Eastlake.

Veale and I went into a holding pattern, waiting for a suitable break in Karlin's soliloquy. 'This Szabo purchase,' I said to him, passing the time. 'Inheriting such a large grant allocation, sight unseen, may tend to make Angelo a little uncomfortable. If he could meet one or two of the corporate participants in the project, I'm sure it would reassure him immensely.' Not chatting. Pimping. In the hope of catching Agnelli *in flagrante*. Madness, I told myself, sheer insanity. Stop it.

'It looks as though he's beaten us to it.' Veale nodded towards the official entourage. 'Obelisk Trust, contributor, if memory serves me right, of $150,000. Various other donors gave smaller amounts. Fifty thousand here, twenty there.' He dropped his voice, confidentially. 'Clients of Obelisk, I daresay, keeping in good with their line of credit.'

I'd heard of Obelisk Trust – vaguely – and felt it somewhat remiss of me not to know more. It was some kind of financial institution, that much I knew, part of the free-wheeling money market that had erupted onto the scene since deregulation and the floating of the dollar. Merchant banks, brokerage arbitrageurs, futures dealers, entrepreneurial wheeler-dealers – the media was giddy with them. You couldn't turn on the television without some egg-headed pundit leaning earnestly into the camera and whispering about the FT-100 or the ninety-day bond rate. It was all so hard to keep up with. Fluctuations in share prices and currency exchange rates were reported with greater frequency than the weather outlook.

Reading the paper was like trying to watch a sport without knowing the rules.

Veale responded to my blank look. 'Lloyd Eastlake,' he said. 'Obelisk Trust's executive director.'

Wheels within wheels. Hats upon hats. 'Handy,' I said. And precariously close to conflict of interest.

Veale's voice took on a slightly miffed tone. 'As far as the Centre for Modern Art and the Visual Arts Advisory Panel are concerned, all procedural guidelines have been rigorously observed.' No funny business on any committees in Phillip Veale's jurisdiction. Not on paper, at least. 'As to the Obelisk Trust, I have no reason to assume other than that Lloyd Eastlake conducts himself with the utmost probity.'

One hand washes the other. While we stand by, holding the soap. But there was no point in ruffling Veale's feathers. 'So where's this Szabo picture,' I said, gawking around. 'It must be quite something.'

Veale loosened up again. 'You mean at six hundred thousand dollars it had better be.'

'The last picture I bought was on the lid of a box of shortbread. Five dollars fifty and I got to eat the biscuits.'

Karlin, Agnelli & Co had ambled along the mezzanine into a spacious boardroom hung with more pictures. A horseshoe-shaped table ran down the middle, invisible beneath a sumptuous buffet of fresh fruit and architect-designed pastries. The aroma of excellent coffee perfumed the air, making my mouth water. 'I doubt if anyone ever expected a Szabo to fetch such an amount,' Veale was saying. 'Arguably, his contribution to Australian art might have gone largely unremarked if not for Fiona Lambert's tireless work in developing his reputation and bringing him to public notice.'

'And what better measure of a man's significance,' I said, 'than the price of his work.'

Veale pursed his lips, pitying me my cynicism. I conceded him the point, sort of. 'Ironical, though, isn't it,' I remarked. 'So many artists never get to enjoy the fruits of their own success.'

'True,' conceded Veale. 'I never met Szabo myself, but I used to know his dealer, Giles Aubrey, quite well. I doubt if Karlin paid Giles more than five or six thousand when he bought the picture back in the early seventies.' A steal. Only a year's take-home pay for one of Max's employees at the time.

Much of the crowd had followed the official party into the boardroom and were tucking into the mille-feuilles and moka blend. I helped myself to a hair of the dog out of a bottle marked Bollinger, poured one for Veale, and sniffed at a tray of dainty pink-and-white sandwiches. 'Caviar?' I wondered.

'Strawberries,' said Veale.

Christ. Strawberry sandwiches. Now I'd seen it all. But I hadn't. Not by a long chalk.

'Ladies and gentlemen,' Karlin began, his voice barely above conversational volume. As if by magic, the chatter of voices and scrape of forks across plates faded. It was Karlin, at least as much as his artworks, they had paid to be near. His entrepreneurship, luck and taste were legendary. Famous, at the very least. Stand close enough, listen attentively enough, and perhaps some of it might rub off.

'Welcome to today's open-house in aid of the CMA's acquisition program.' Karlin's public voice was both smooth and gravelly, a combination of wet cement and washed silk, conveying a mixture of amenability and conviction. The expression 'If madam would just care to try this on' sprang to mind.

Karlin pressed on. 'And an especially warm welcome to our new Arts Minister, the Honourable Angelo Agnelli, who has made a special effort to be here, which I think speaks volumes for his commitment to the visual arts . . .'

Just in case anyone didn't quite know which one he was, Ange took a half-step forward, smiled bashfully, and let the gaze of the congregation fall gently upon him. There was a shuffling that might have been applause. Ange nodded, recognising in all humility that it was the office, not the man, to whom acknowledgment was due. But conveying, nonetheless, a distinctly personal pleasure at finding himself among like-minded people. A photographer circled, flash popping.

Karlin allowed Ange his moment of grace before continuing. 'Because, thanks to the vision of the government, a great painting hitherto seen only by a fortunate few will soon hang in the Centre for Modern Art where it will be accessible to all. I refer, of course, to Victor Szabo's *Our Home*.'

As he delivered this phrase, Karlin moved slightly to one side, offering the painting on the wall behind him to the perusal of the assembly. Unfortunately, Phillip Veale was in my line of sight, obstructing my view, and all I could see of it was a bit of blue in the top right-hand corner. As Karlin continued to speak, informing us that the occasion was tinged with regret at the departure of a cherished possession, I popped the last of the strawberry sangers into my mouth, craned my neck over the bureaucrat's gelati-hued shoulder and feasted my eyes.

My jaw froze in mid-chomp. You could have knocked me down with an ermine bristle. The picture I beheld, hanging on the wall of Max Karlin's boardroom, was strikingly familiar. So much so that I thought my eyes were playing tricks with me. It depicted a cloudless Australian sky and a swathe of vivid perfectly manicured lawn. In the middle of the lawn sat a Victa Special two-stroke motor-mower. Behind it was a red-roofed double-fronted brick-veneer house, brooding with malevolent intensity.

I MIGHT NOT know much about art, but I've been a member of the Labor Party long enough to recognise the aroma of rodent when it wafts my way. So, when the speechifying was over, I introduced Veale to Agnelli and left them exchanging pleasantries while I examined the Szabo at closer range.

An expert might have detected subtle differences – the demeanour of the brushstrokes, the gradation of the colour, the intangible aura of genius – but on face value I was buggered if I could tell this picture from the one I had seen scarcely two hours before in Marcus Taylor's studio.

Eastlake noticed my close interest and joined me. 'Following in the footsteps of Van Gogh?' he said. This joke was beginning to wear thin.

'Angling accident,' I said. 'You should see the fish.'

He inclined his head towards *Our Home*. 'Come on,' he beamed. 'Admit it. It does have a certain *je ne sais quoi*, doesn't it?'

'Oh, I dunno,' I shrugged.

But Eastlake was right. And not just about there being nothing in the painting to provoke outrage. He'd been right that people would genuinely warm to it. It did for suburbia what nineteenth-century Australian painters had done for the bush – made it a worthy subject for art. And, by inference, made heroes of those who dwelt there. *Our Home* was the Parthenon of tract housing, with a bit of laconic satire chucked in for good measure. And an edge of the mysterious, so you knew it was proper art.

'I used to build houses just like this,' Eastlake confided with a proprietary sentimentality.

And millions grew up in them. I dipped my head in acknowledgment of his superior judgment. 'How does it get from here to the CMA?'

Administrative detail didn't interest Eastlake. 'In a crate, I imagine.' His contrivance at being both amiable and patronising could easily have grated. But compared with the unremitting dullness of most of the business types I met, Lloyd Eastlake's candour was disarmingly refreshing. 'Fiona handles that sort of thing.'

Fiona Lambert was across the room, thick as thieves with Becky Karlin and a helmeted honeyeater I recognised from the CMA. 'That guy who got up on the table last night and tried to make the speech,' I started. 'The one who fell over.'

Eastlake's attention was elsewhere. Max Karlin had detached Agnelli from Phillip Veale and was leading him out onto the mezzanine, steering him towards one of the offices. The holy of holies, I took it. Eastlake made a must-rush noise and headed after them.

I should have too, I suppose. Monitoring what passed between Agnelli and Karlin had, after all, been the whole point in bringing them together. To have my suspicions confirmed, wasn't that why I was here? But now something else was exercising my mind, something that took me instead down into the melting heat of the street, to the row of up-market cars lining the kerb, to crack open the seal on the refrigerated interior of Eastlake's big silver Merc. 'Morning,' I said, 'Noel.'

Spider didn't turn. He just sat there, fish-faced behind his shades, contemplating the sporting section of the *Herald*, his hat on the ledge above the dashboard. Even when I slid in beside him he didn't look around. A knob low on the instrument panel might have been the cigarette lighter. I put my thumb on it and pushed until it clicked into place. Agnelli didn't let me smoke in the Fairlane.

We sat there, me side-on, Spider gazing into the V of his paper. Profile was definitely Noel Webb's better angle. Made him look less like a plumbing fixture. 'So,' I said. 'Long time no see.' Long time no answer, too. More than long enough for me to get a smoke out and tap it on the side of the pack. Pop went the lighter. Spider's hand shot out. He held the glowing element short, so I had to bend across to fire up, offering the nape of my neck. A gold pinky ring glistened on his little finger, fat and square, set with a crescent of tiny rubies, a real tooth-breaker. Quite the primitive, Spider. 'This job suits you,' I said. 'You've got the silent menace bit down to a tee.'

Spider tossed his chin in the general direction of the Karlcraft building. 'Won't you be missed?' he said, unimpressed. 'Big shot.'

'Never too busy to catch up with old friends,' I said, absently flicking a molecule of ash onto the car's pale grey carpet. 'Funny, isn't it?' I stretched my legs out and leaned back against the headrest. 'Twenty years since we've seen each other, now our paths cross all the time. Down at the Ballet Centre carpark this morning, for instance.'

Spider very slowly closed his newspaper, folded it neatly in half and laid it beside his hat. 'MOAT DEATH PUZZLE,' read a column-wide headline on the front page. He turned his mirrored face towards me, at last. 'I dunno what you're talking about.' His delivery was flat, sneering. 'And neither do you.'

The big car's interior felt suddenly very claustrophobic. Noel Webb had been a tough kid. And if he was acting the hard man maybe it was because that's exactly what he was. Spider wasn't the sentimental type. Never had been. And any tenuous connection between us was long gone. My feet were getting colder by the second.

For nearly an hour I'd waited at the Oulton Reserve, clutching that contraband bottle of bourbon under my duffel coat, its neck sticky and warm in my hand. Footy practice ended, the oval emptied, and still I sat, half of me ashamed, the other half defiant. Ashamed for the theft, for I'd never before stolen from my father. Ashamed for my reason for doing it, to buy friendship. Defying my father to catch me out, defying Spider Webb to doubt that I could deliver. As I waited, I took little sips. The liquid was fiery and harsh, but it kept me warm. Kept me waiting.

When Spider finally arrived, he came out of nowhere, looming out of the leaden dusk. 'Got it?' he said, sinking down beside me. I hesitated then, kept the bottle hidden beneath my coat, wanting some spoken confirmation of our pact.

'You haven't, have you?' His scorn was wounding. 'You didn't have the guts, did you?'

That's when the Fletchers exploded out of a clump of tea-tree edging the football oval. Georgie, the big one, had a steel fencing picket in his hand. The twins trotted at his heels. Like Attila and his horde, they swept down upon us.

Twenty years is a long time. People change. But if Noel Webb had, I couldn't see it. Maybe I'd underestimated him, though, pegging him for a car thief. Maybe he'd graduated to something more sophisticated.

'Nice car,' I said, running an eyeball over the walnut inlay. 'Been Mr Eastlake's chauffeur long? His status symbol, that's what he called you, didn't he?'

'What's it to you?' Annoyance had crept into Spider's voice, evidence that communication might be possible.

'Probably nothing at all,' I agreed. Probably nothing more than ancient adolescent resentment, octopus-induced irritability, and a suspicious mind. But if I stirred the pot a little, something more might come bubbling to the surface. 'It's just that there are points where your employer's activities and my employer's interests overlap. And proper attention to my employer's interests requires that I keep myself broadly informed. I rather hoped you'd understand that, us both being in the service sector.'

He snorted contemptuously. 'Haven't you got anything better to do with your time?'

As a matter of fact, I did. It was nearly 12.30. Red's plane was due in little more than two hours and, apart from picking up a pack of cigarettes, I still hadn't done any shopping. 'I guess I can always ask Lloyd,' I shrugged. 'Just thought I'd ask you first, not wanting to embarrass an old friend and all.'

'I'm shitting myself, Whelan,' Spider said, brimming with schoolyard disdain. But he tilted his head a fraction and I knew his eyes had gone to the rearview mirror.

The Mercedes had power windows. Mine made a little whirring noise and let in a wilting gust of heat. I stuck my head out, looked back at the stragglers drifting out of Karlcraft and whirred it back up. 'Have it your own way,' I said. 'Mr Eastlake will be along soon.'

Spider puffed his cheeks and blew a long steady breath, like I was a deliberately obtuse child, trying his patience. Then, shaking his head as though reluctantly coming to a decision he already regretted, he leaned across in front of me and casually opened the glove compartment. The lid fell down to reveal a shiny, chrome-plated pistol.

This was not something I saw every day. In fact, I'd never seen one before. Not for real. It wasn't so long ago that not even cops carried guns. And now that they did, they certainly weren't guns like this. This was an automatic, chrome-plated with a cross-hatched grip. I'd seen enough movies to know that. Whether it was the current release Baretta .44 with Dolby sound and merchandising tie-in, I neither knew nor cared. Guns did not interest me. They scared the shit out of me, but they didn't interest me. Beside the gun was an unopened packet of Wrigley's Arrowmint gum. Spider let my gaze linger for a moment on the pistol, then he picked up the chewy and snapped the glove box lid shut.

I got the point. Noel Webb was no mere opener of doors, no low-grade flunkey. Nor was he just there for his good looks, his obsequious manner and his masterful grip on the steering wheel. He was there because Lloyd Eastlake's taste in fashion accessories ran to keeping a bodyguard.

If an arsehole like Noel Webb thought he could intimidate me by showing me his penis substitute, he could think again. It took more than a flash of metal to impress Murray Whelan. On the other hand, I'd just as soon not have anything to do with guns. Spider unwrapped his chewy and proffered the pack. Take it or leave it.

I was shagged out, hungover, lied to, pissed off, earmangled and behind schedule. It was none of my business if Brian Eastlake thought he needed an armed minder. Nor was the fact that he'd seen fit to give the job to Spider Webb. As to the matter of the vanished duplicate of *Our Home*, it suddenly seemed unimportant. The main game was being played by the big boys upstairs in Max Karlin's office, not down here in the gutter with a pistol-packing dipstick. Instead of keeping my eye on the ball, I was chasing a chimera. My duties didn't run to this kind of crap.

'See you, Spider,' I said wearily and opened the door.

Webb already had his nose back in the paper. 'Not if I see you first.'

I wished people would stop saying that to me. A man could get paranoid. At least he hadn't said anything about my ear. For obvious reasons. Even with one in tatters, mine weren't half as conspicuous as Spider's.

I turned back towards Karlin's office. Agnelli's Fairlane had pulled away from the kerb and was heading down the street. Wonderful. Agnelli was going without me, the prick. Not only had he probably bitten Max Karlin for a little campaign donation, he was leaving me in the lurch. My Charade was back at Parliament House, a dozen blocks away.

My best shot at a cab was back towards the Queen Victoria market. A shopping list marshalled in my head. Bending beneath the glare of the burnished sky, I made haste through the empty sun-blasted streets. The market closed at 12.30 on Saturday and it was already that.

The century-old fresh-daily aroma of the open-sided sheds advanced to greet me. Hot sugared doughnuts, bananas on the turn, the rustling exhalations of onion skins, the pungency of soy sauce and live poultry. All mixed together, emulsified with forklift fumes and baked under the grill of sheet-iron roofs. Then came the sound – the murmur of shuffling feet, the shouted offers of last-minute bargains, the street-sweepers' hard-bristled brooms, the play of hose-stream on steaming gutters.

The top shed stalls were already closed, their mountains of lush produce reduced to a range of grey tarpaulin foothills. Downhill, across a street shrill with the beeping of reversing trucks, I found a late-closing Chinaman prepared to risk his vendor's licence with the offer of dew-misted nectarines and fat knuckles of ginger. At a premium, I bought mangoes, mandarins and firm tomatoes. Red liked avocados. I bought six. From a Greek woman clearing a till behind the last glass counter in the delicatessen section, I inveigled fetta, ham and walnut bread. Then I schlepped my supplies to the cab rank. Every other bastard in Melbourne had got there first.

There was still two hours until Red's plane touched down. The dusting could wait. An overloaded plastic carry-bag in each hand, I began up the hill towards the State Library.

ALITTLE KNOWLEDGE is a dangerous thing and if you really want to live dangerously the State Library is a good place to start. Even on a quiet Saturday afternoon, its obliging staff can take your vaguest apprehensions and turn them into a swarm of disturbing possibilities.

The domed reading-room was hushed and serene, bathed in the cool submarine light that filtered down from its huge cavernous hemisphere high above. The long tables radiating from its centre were like the spokes of a wheel, an imperceptibly moving cog in wisdom's silent mill. I delivered my victuals into the custody of the cloakroom attendant and moved from the general to the specific, starting with *Art Sales Index*, the annual digest of works passing under the hammer in the world's major sales rooms.

International art prices were going systematically batshit. In the preceding five years, total world turnover on everything from archaic bronzes to zoological watercolours had doubled then doubled then doubled again. And it wasn't just the Yasuda Fire and Marine or the Getty Museum. The whole world was at it. Firms of

English auditors were snapping up Soviet construction-ists, Brazilian livestock agents were trying to corner the Flemish rococo and a former signwriter from Perth had just paid £43 million for Van Gogh's *Sunflowers*. For that sort of money, you'd want the ear as well. Almost overnight, scraps of pigmented fabric of virtually no intrinsic value were being transformed by the logic of the marketplace into commodities whose prices could have fed all of Africa.

Not to be outdone by New York and London, domestic prices were hot on the heels of the global trend. According to the gazette of Australian auction records, modest little pictures by well-known Australian artists that could've been snapped up any time in the previous two decades for a couple of grand were suddenly fetching five or ten times that amount.

Victor Szabo's name appeared infrequently, in some years not at all. But then, according to what I'd heard at the Botanical Hotel, his life's work amounted only to forty or so known paintings. Eleven of these had been offered at auction in the previous few years, six more than once. The prices had risen slowly at first, barely keeping up with the general trend. Then, more recently, the pace had quickened. This improvement was in line with a general tendency of the market to seek out previously underrated artists as the value of the big names went stratospheric.

One hundred thousand dollars was the top price listed for a Szabo. Nothing remotely like the figure Karlin was charging. Either there was more to *Our Home* than met the eye or somebody was being taken for a walk.

A Fierce Vision: The Genius of Victor Szabo 1911–77 by Fiona Lambert was a handsomely produced coffee-table job published two years previously. Plentiful text, lavish illustrations and a one-paragraph biography of the author on the inside flyleaf. Exhibition curator, gallery director, BA(Hons). Fluff.

Flipping through, I found what I was looking for. *Our Home: Oil on canvas, 175 cm x 123 cm, 1972. Private collection.* I pored over the plate's glossy surface, searching for some previously unnoticed detail that would spring out and distinguish this image from the one I had seen in Marcus Taylor's studio. It was useless. The two paintings had converged in my memory.

Two pictures, two dead men. One an artist of growing repute, dead ten years. The other an unknown loser, dead twelve hours. Two things linked them. One was a picture of a house with a lawn-mower in the front yard. The other was a dog-eared photograph among a suicide's pathetic collection of personal effects. Something about all of this didn't feel right. Disturbing possibilities rattled around in my brain, nagged at me. The missing painting. Salina's emotional game-playing. Spider's menacing evasions. Something was cooking and it didn't smell right. It smelled of egg on Angelo Agnelli's face. I decided to keep sniffing.

Taylor, Marcus was listed nowhere in Lambert's index. I waded into the body of the text. *The literalness of Victor Szabo's work deploys a multi-layered, almost compulsive, disjunction of a myriad of identities,* it began. *Its vocabulary welds the specificity of circumstance to the logic of allegory so as to create a bridge between the depersonalised formalism of abstraction and the narrative poetics of an uninhibited quest for the archetypically mundane.*

Well, she wasn't going to hear any argument from me. I read on. It didn't get any easier. In comparison with art criticism, the mealy jargon of bureaucracy sparkled like birdsong. Not even in the mouth of the Leader of the Opposition did words convey so little. Scanning and skipping, attempting to draw a thread of comprehension from the furball of Fiona Lambert's prose, I jotted the few biographical facts I could garner on a library call-slip with a pencil someone had mislaid on top of the catalogue cabinet.

The bare bones, as far as I could make them out, were that Szabo had been born in Hapsburg Budapest, had studied art in Paris in the thirties and arrived in Australia as a displaced person after the Second World War. Isolated from the local art scene by circumstances and temperament, he found work as a railway fettler in the Blue Mountains west of Sydney, sketching and painting intermittently. By the late fifties he had moved south and was living on the outskirts of Melbourne, painting full-time, occasionally exhibiting his work, even sometimes finding a buyer. His trademark realism and suburban subject matter began to emerge. Painting constantly, he destroyed most of his output, retaining only his most highly finished pictures. Anti-social and reclusive, he made contact with the outside world only through his dealer, Giles Aubrey. Eventually he fell out even with him. His talent, Fiona Lambert put it, could no longer endure the constraints of the relationship.

About this time, '77 or '78, Lambert herself appeared. And not a moment too soon. Up until that point in the story, no woman had been mentioned who was not another artist, an artist's wife, or a critic. No wonder, if Fiona's version of Victor Szabo's life story was to be believed, the old coot expired in her arms. Sheer astonishment at his change of luck.

If there was some clue to connect Szabo and Taylor, it certainly didn't lie in Fiona Lambert's text. I flicked through the illustrations again. Sketches, draughtsmanlike renderings of landscapes, architectural details, life-studies in charcoal, the finished paintings.

Two of the sketches, dating from the early fifties, were female nudes. Where had he found his models, I wondered, this New Australian railway labourer? One was a rear view, rough-hewn, a few broad strokes outlining the curve of a back, a fall of hair, the droop of buttocks. The other was a pencil sketch, highly finished, face and shoulders turned in three-quarter profile.

The resemblance was unmistakable. It was the woman in the photograph in Marcus Taylor's desk drawer. In the souvenir snap she was more carefree. But the woman in the sketch knew he would go soon, her artistic European lover. That happy time when the camera had captured them together on the mountaintop lookout was already fading fast. Her belly was distended, her expression resigned. Marcus Taylor's birthplace, according to his grant application form, was Katoomba, Jewel of the Blue Mountains, gateway to the original Australian bush.

Before I left the library, there were a couple more publications I wanted to consult. *Veneer: A Journal of Contemporary Cultural Criticism*, appeared quarterly.

I went straight to the list of editorial credits. *Veneer*, said the tiniest possible type, *acknowledges the financial support of the Visual Arts Panel of the Victorian Ministry for the Arts*. I attributed no significance to this fact. I was just interested, that's all.

The second book I consulted had printing almost as small. It was thick and yellow and lived in a metal bracket under the pay phone in the foyer. Under Art Dealers, between Atelier on the Yarra and Aussie's Aborigine Art was a listing for Aubrey Fine Art. I dialled the number and asked for Mr Giles Aubrey.

There was a moment's silence, then a sound that could have been eyebrows being raised. 'Giles Aubrey has not been associated with us for quite some time,' said a snooty male voice.

'You don't know how I can contact him?'

'Not really. He sold the business and retired several years ago. This is the current proprietor speaking. May I be of assistance?' Meaning, can I sell you a picture, and if not piss off.

'It's a rather delicate matter,' I said, 'concerning the provenance of an item bought some time ago, when Mr Aubrey was in charge. Before beginning legal proceedings, I'd prefer to speak with Mr Aubrey. If, however, that's not possible, what did you say your name was . . .'

'Just a moment, sir.' After a few seconds, he came back with a phone number. The first three digits, denoting the local exchange, were unfamiliar. Somewhere in the eastern suburbs gentility belt, I assumed.

'That's Eaglemont, is it?' A locale of faintly arty pretence.

'Coldstream,' said eyebrows, eager to send me packing.

Coldstream, of course. Eltham, Kangaroo Ground, Christmas Hills, Yarra Glen, Coldstream. Out where the Food Plusses and the Furniture Barns gave way to plant nurseries and pottery shops. A bushland bohemia of mudbrick and claret in whose sylvan glades colonies of free-thinking artists once made their abode, sculpting wombats out of scrap metal, listening to jazz, swapping wives and growing their beards. Where shadow Cabinet ministers in turtle-neck sweaters once went to have their portraits painted by polygamous libertarians. Long before art was an industry, when it was a talisman against the triumphant philistinism of encroaching suburbia, these scrubby hills on the urban fringe were its Camelot.

Not a lot of Camelot left out there any more, not since art had decamped to the inner city, gone post-modern, started pleading its multiplier-effectiveness and cost/benefit ratios before the Industry Assistance Commission. Not since the bird-watching suburban gentry had parked their Range Rovers in its driveways and paved its bush tracks with antique-finish concrete cobblestones available in an extensive range of all-natural designer colours. Only the artists' half-feral chil-dren remained, gone thirty, still barefoot and stinking of patchouli oil. And old Giles Aubrey, retired to some bend in the river.

His phone rang a long time, long enough for me to rehearse my approach, long enough for me to think he wasn't going to answer. 'Giles Aubrey speaking.' A voice with rounded vowels and clipped diction, the sort of voice that would once have been called educated, that suggested I forthwith state my business and heaven help me if I was a fool.

Anyone hoping for Giles Aubrey's assistance would need to play it deferential, keep their wits about them. I apologised for disturbing him at the weekend, inferred that I was calling at the express instructions of the Minister for the Arts, and wondered if he might spare me a few moments of his unquestionably precious time to provide some background on Victor Szabo. 'The minister is currently reliant on a limited number of sources of expertise. Ms Lambert, Szabo's biographer, has been very helpful, naturally.'

For all the archness in his voice, Giles Aubrey deigned not to rise to the temptation of petty rivalry. 'Exactly what is it you wish to know, Mr Whelan?'

'It's more the personal aspect. Family details, children, that sort of thing,' I told him.

'I'm not sure I follow you.' His voice quavered with age, but he was following me all right.

'Victor Szabo is still largely unknown to the general public.' I was groping my way here. 'So naturally there will be a great deal of interest in his background when it is announced that a government-funded gallery is spending six hundred thousand dollars on one of his paintings.'

'That much? For one of Victor's? Really?' Behind the patrician disbelief was something else. Vindication, perhaps. 'Which one, may one ask?'

I told him. There was a long silence and when finally he spoke it was as if recognising the arrival of something long anticipated. 'Oh dear,' he said. 'Oh dearie, dearie me.'

Coldstream was a good ninety minutes away. 'I'll be in your area a bit later this afternoon,' I said. 'Perhaps I could drop around?'

'Very well.' His acquiescence was immediate, total. 'Some things *are* better discussed face to face.' The last house, he told me, bottom of the hill.

But first things first. The fruit of my loins was making his descent. I hiked my purchases up to Parliament House, tossed them into the Charade and made the airport with seconds to spare.

Tullamarine was thick with Italian families, there to meet the Alitalia flight from Rome, cooling their heels while customs frisked their grandmothers for contraband salami. Red's flight was running ten minutes behind schedule – which gave me a chance to read what the Saturday paper pundits had to say about the Cabinet reshuffle.

Rearranging the deck chairs on the Titanic was the recurrent phrase. Since these were the same luminaries who'd confidently predicted our defeat at the previous election, I tried not to take offence. We had, after all, won by two seats. The *Herald*'s Moat Death Puzzle story ran to five paragraphs, covered only the bare bones and took the anticipated line. A side-bar profiled famous artistic suicides.

All up, I'd been waiting at the gate lounge for half an hour by the time the flight landed and the last of the exiting passengers streamed through the door. Red was not among them.

It was definitely his flight. Definitely. The airline woman at the service counter verified it, ratting her glossy nails across a keyboard, consulting her monitor.

Unaccompanied child, Redmond Whelan. Ticketed, confirmed and boarded. Might I have simply missed him in the crowd, she asked? There were quite a lot of families on the flight, returning from holidays. Had he perhaps proceeded directly to claim his baggage?

'He wouldn't do that,' I said, anxiety mounting, and turned with a sweep of my arm to prove my point.

'Tricked ya!'

Red stood behind me, grinning from ear to ear.

WE EMBRACED, his cheek on my sternum, the bill of his baseball cap obscuring his face. It was a solid hug, but brisk. Even a ten-year-old has an image to think about.

'So,' I said, holding him at arm's length the better to examine him. Every time I saw Red, he'd changed in some subtle, inexpressible way. His face still had the same cherubic quality as always, but the body below was whippier, carried less puppy fat. His eventual shape, I allowed myself the conceit, would owe more to me than to his mother. 'How you been?'

'Good.'

'How was the flight?'

'Good.'

'How was your holiday?' Three weeks on the beach at Noosa Heads with Wendy and her barrister boyfriend. I didn't want the details.

'Good.'

So far, so good. 'Good,' I said.

Quite the frequent flier, Red travelled light. A back-pack and a Walkman were his total luggage. Everything else he needed – several hundred comics, a skateboard and a change of clothes – was waiting in his room at my place. *Our* place, I thought, brimming with the fact.

Back when Red was seven and his mother was in Canberra securing her future in the affirmative action major league, the boy and I had lived together for the best part of a year. Wendy had returned home at regular intervals and phoned frequently, but for weeks at a time it was just the two of us, living the life of Riley. Okay, so we ate out often enough to have our own table at Pizza Hut, slept in the same bed to cut down on house-work and missed the odd day of school. But I always ordered pizzas with a high vegetable content, insisted Red brush his teeth at least once a week and kept him relatively free of parasite infestations. And it was only by unavoidable accident that Wendy discovered him home alone one morning when she arrived earlier than anticipated. The olive-skinned beauty in my bed and the Hell's Angel on the roof with a crowbar had a perfectly innocent explanation, if only she'd stuck around to hear it.

'What did the orthodontist say?' I asked as we headed for the carpark.

Red indicated the problem, open-mouthed. 'E ed I eed a ate.'

'Why do you need a plate?' Aside from further enriching some overpriced gum-digger, I was already sending Wendy five hundred dollars a month. Not that I begrudged a penny.

'E ed I ot a oh a ite.'

'You haven't got an overbite,' I said. 'Your face is the same shape as mine. I look okay, don't I?'

Red eyed me sceptically. His gaze lingered on my

bandaged ear. He didn't say anything, but I could already sense them gift-wrapping my birthday copy of *First Aid for the Home Handyman* at the Sydney branch of Mary Martin.

'You think Tark's home today?' This was Red being sensitive, not wanting me to think it wasn't me he was here to visit. Tarquin Curnow was his best mate in Melbourne, possibly the world, and doubtless the two of them had already been on the phone, cooking up plans for the weekend. Whenever Red came to stay, he headed directly to Tarquin's place and the two of them hung out like Siamese twins.

I took no offence. Tarquin Curnow had been Red's friend since kindergarten, and the clincher when I bought my house was that it backed onto the same lane as the Curnows' big terrace. Tarquin's parents, Faye and Leo, were old friends and better ones than I deserved, especially Faye who tended to worry about my unattached status. It affronted her sense of the natural order. I was beginning to share her sentiments.

The temperature had long hit the forty-degree mark and my shopping was beginning to go whiffy by the time we tracked down the Charade and blew the carpark. We headed straight for Tarquin's place. Not much point in going home just to put a piece of cheese in the fridge. Faye's would be just as cold.

The Curnows' front door was opened by a four-year-old girl in a pair of faded pink cottontails. Ignoring me, she took one look at Red, pirouetted on the hall-runner and bolted into the shadowy interior. 'He's here. He's here. Red's here.' This was Faye and Leo's youngest, Chloe. No wonder Red liked it here. If Chloe had a basket of rose petals, she'd have strewn them in his path.

At its far end, the hallway opened into a haphazardly furnished room, part kitchen, part lounge, scattered with the customary detritus of family life and heavily shuttered with matchstick blinds. The blinds made about three degrees worth of difference, so the room felt like it was in Cairo rather than Khartoum. Torpor blanketed the house. Tarquin unfurled himself like a praying mantis from a beanbag in front of the television and the boys scooted upstairs in conspiratorial glee. Chloe dogged them optimistically.

Leo was upstairs, napping. Faye was standing at the sink in a shortie kimono thrashing a handful of greenery under a running tap. I opened the fridge. 'I'll have one, too,' said Faye.

The fridge was a cornucopia of everything from anchovies to zucchini. I deposited the ham and fetta, ripped the tops off a couple of stubbies of Cooper's Pale Ale and sank into the nearest beanbag, beginning to unwind at last.

A ferociously modish cook, Faye was a journalist by profession. She wrote for the *Business Daily* – one of those papers that runs stories with titles like 'GDP Gets OECD OK' and 'Funds Pan Mid-Term Rate Hike' – while Leo did something obscurely administrative at Melbourne University. Neither of them were what you might call high fliers and the contrast between Faye's billion-dollar subject-matter and her modestly anarchic personal circumstances never ceased to amuse me.

'So.' She added a baptised lettuce to the profusion in the fridge, dried her hands on her kimono and lowered her big-boobed frame into a cat-scratched armchair. 'You still got a job, or what?' The question was both personal and professional. Ever solicitous of my personal welfare, Faye also wanted the good oil on the Cabinet reshuffle.

'Pending satisfactory performance indicators,' I told her.

'Arts Ministry, eh?' she whistled appreciatively. 'That explains the ear. Trying to wow the art crowd, eh?'

'And not succeeding.' I gave her a quick rundown of the previous evening, all the way to the scene at the National Gallery moat. The business about the dead body interested her only mildly – she wasn't that kind of journalist – but my unconsummated experience with Salina Fleet elicited a sympathetic cluck. 'Not having much luck lately, are you, Murray?'

'How come I never seem to meet anyone sane?' I asked, relaxed enough now to feel philosophically sorry for myself.

'What about Eloise? You can't say she's not sane.'

Eloise was Faye's most recent exercise in dinner-party matchmaking. A waif-like book editor, she laughed so nervously at my little jokes that the beetroot and orange soup came out her nose. Then she burst into tears on her doorstep when I tried to do the right thing.

'She was pleasant enough, I suppose,' I said, not wanting to sound ungrateful. 'Just not my type.'

'And what is your type, Murray?' Faye was beginning to regard me as major challenge. She was constantly inviting me to meals and seating me beside some loudly ticking biological alarm clock. So far, she'd tried to pair me off with a workaholic paediatrician who left when her beeper went off during the osso buco, a lecturer in linguistics who couldn't stop talking about Pee Wee Herman, and an up-and-coming corporate lawyer with the inside-running on the bottom-line, real-estate wise. And then there'd been Jocasta, about whom the least said the better. The name, I think, speaks for itself.

'I don't know,' I said. 'Someone I don't have to impress or compete with. Someone who isn't assessing my genetic material over the entree. Someone nice. Goes off like a rocket.'

'Someone you can inflate when required?' said Faye. 'You don't want much, do you?'

The boys erupted down the stairs, towels over their shoulders. 'Can we go to the pool, huh? Huh, can we, huh, can we?'

'Even better,' I said. 'Let's go up the bush, find a waterhole.' Coldstream, I supposed, might technically qualify as the bush. Red looked keen.

'Do we have to?' whined Tarquin. He'd be a politician one day, our Tark. As a matter of principle, he never did anything without being pressured into it first.

'I'd take Chloe, too,' I said, winking at Tarquin, 'but the seat belt's broken.' That sealed the deal. A boys-only expedition into the wild.

'You stay and help Mummy,' Faye told the crestfallen girl. 'And we'll all have a picnic dinner tonight in the gardens, okay? You can invite your friend Gracie, okay?'

I went upstairs to the Curnows' bathroom and removed the bandages from my ear. It was scabbing up very nicely. I'd certainly come out of my ear-sundering experience better than Vinnie Van G. In two or three days, with a bit of fresh air, my lobe would be good as new.

Smeared with sunscreen, the boys and I piled into the car. 'Stay in the shade, careful of submerged branches, and don't get lost,' suggested Faye helpfully. 'And watch out for snakes.' I passed her my squishy fruit, terminating her bushcraft advisory service before Tarquin could chicken out.

We tooled out the freeway, singing along with the radio, the windows wound down. Hits and Memories. Ah bin cheated. Bin mistreated. When will ah be loved. 'Were you a mop?' Red wanted to know. 'Or a rotter?'

Within half an hour we'd cleared the built-up area and entered open countryside, paddocks of stubble the colour of milky tea. At the turn for Kangaroo Ground, the road ran between two vineyards and the boys let me think I'd conned them that there really were kangaroos bounding between the rows of vines. The road crested rolling hills and dipped into lightly wooded valleys, winding through tunnels of dappled darkness. At the top of a bare rise stood a peeling weatherboard church surrounded by moulting cypresses, a dilapidated sign out front: 'EEK AND YE SHALL FIND'.

'That reminds me,' I said. 'I've got to drop in on someone for a few minutes.' Acquired with parenthood, the habit of compulsive deception is not easily shed.

'Aaww,' the boys groaned in unison, but the wind buffetted the sound away.

At the Christmas Hills fire station, a zincalum shed, volunteer fire-fighters awaited the worst, stripped to the waist in the shade of a concrete water tank, moving only to fan the dust raised by our passing. At the far end of an unmade road, as instructed, I found Giles Aubrey's house in a tinder-dry forest of stringybark saplings.

THE ARCHITECTURAL style was the local specialty, Mudbrick Gothic. Clay-coloured adobe walls set with clerestory windows, the whole thing slung low into the slope. Somewhere down below, the river wound between the trees. We went around the side, looking for the door. Dry leaves crackled under our feet and bellbirds pinged loud in our ears. 'Careful of snakes,' I reminded the boys. It would be typical of Tarquin to get himself bitten.

'I trust you're not referring to me.' The man who spoke was sitting at a garden table beneath the shade of a pergola on a wide terracotta-tiled terrace. Behind him, glass doors opened into a house filled with pictures, rugs and books. In front of him, spread on old newspapers, was a punnet of tomato seedlings.

He was a desiccated little old rooster, with alert rheumy eyes and a complexion hatched with spidery blood vessels. The draw-string of his wide-brimmed straw hat sat tight under his neck and he wore a pair of canvas gardening gloves. Stripping off the gloves, he stood up and put his hand out, laying on the charm. 'Giles Aubrey,' he announced. 'And you are?'

It was Red he addressed and for a moment it looked like the kid was going to disgrace me. Then he took Aubrey's hand and pumped it gravely. 'Redmond Whelan,' he said. That about exhausted his supply of etiquette.

'Well, Redmond Whelan,' said Aubrey, relinquishing his hand. 'If you two boys go down that path, you'll find a very good place to swim. No matter if you haven't got a costume. It's my secret spot.'

The boys, braced to run, waited on my okay. 'It's quite safe,' Aubrey assured me. 'And I'm well past being a risk to anyone.'

I nodded and the boys bolted down the hill. Aubrey picked up a duck-headed walking-stick and pointed to the tray of seedlings. 'Would you be so kind as to bring those.' Walking gravely with the aid of the cane, he led me to a vegetable patch down a set of steps made from old railway sleepers. The earth was hard packed, the lettuces going to seed. A steep track ran down the slope and sounds of splashing and laughter wafted up through the trees. Aubrey lowered himself to his knees and jabbed the dirt with a small trowel.

'I heard about young Marcus on the radio,' he said. 'Tragic. Didn't quite make the connection at first. He used to be Marcus Grierson. Grierson's the mother's name, of course. Had a bad feeling about it, all the same. Then when you rang and mentioned the painting, it all fell into place. Szabo means 'tailor' in Hungarian. Rather predictable that way, Marcus was. Now I suppose the genie is out of the bottle. It was all in this suicide declaration they mentioned, I take it?'

Well, well, well. 'The note did make some allegations,' I said. 'But we'd like to hear what you have to say before we take the matter any further.'

'To lose one's reputation' – Aubrey tamped the ground around the seedlings, taking his time – 'at my age.' Tomatoes planted this late in the season would probably not ripen.

'If you could start at the beginning.' The impersonal bureaucrat, that was the approach to take.

Aubrey gripped my knee and levered himself upright. His weight was so insubstantial I could barely feel the pressure. The horticulture was for my benefit, a demonstration that age had not wearied him. 'I'll put the kettle on.' Hospitality required certain rituals. He watered in the seedlings and we went back up the slope.

Aubrey's domesticity was an eclectic mixture of quality heirlooms and superseded modernity. Earth-toned paintings, over-framed. A French-polished sideboard bearing blobs of runny-glazed hand-wrought pottery. Persian rugs. Well-used Danish Deluxe armchairs. Giles Aubrey had once danced on the cutting edge.

A place for everything and everything in its place. The tea things were already laid out. 'Shall I pour?' he said. 'Gingernut snap?'

I sat my cup on my knee, cleared my throat and waited. Confession, too, had its protocols.

'The early seventies could have been a very good time for Victor Szabo,' he began. 'There was a growing appreciation of his work, thanks mainly to the popularity of the American photo-realists.' He gave a resigned shrug. The cultural cringe must have been an occupational hazard in Aubrey's line of work. 'But

Victor was a difficult man, a perfectionist, neurotic and unpredictable. And a drunkard. He'd work on a picture for months, then go on a bender and burn it. What he did produce was good work, but I was lucky if I could get three or four paintings a year out of him. I had him on a retainer, not uncommon in those days. A hundred dollars a week to cover his living costs and materials, recouped from his sales. Costing me a fortune, he was. He was renting an old farm house, up at Yarra Glen. It's gone now, a housing development.' He was meandering off.

'Marcus?' I said.

'Turned up in mid '72. Just twenty, he was. Victor was quite awful to him, denied ever knowing his mother, even though Marcus had pictures of them together. Denied he was the boy's father, even though the resemblance was unmistakable. Marcus didn't want anything, mind you, except to be an artist. He'd sought Victor out contrary to his mother's wishes. I think he'd rather imagined himself as Victor's protege. Brought his folios with him, laid them at his father's feet. Quite competent he was too. Skilful, anyway. That appealed to Victor's ego, I think. So he let Marcus stay on as a kind of unpaid slave. I'd go up there and find Victor raging around his studio with a paintbrush in one hand and a bottle in the other, Marcus on his hands and knees on the kitchen floor preparing his canvases for him. Marcus was there for nearly two years and his presence seemed to have a good effect. Victor didn't drive, but Marcus had an old station wagon and every few months he'd turn up at my gallery in South Yarra with three or four pictures in the back. Never quite enough for a exhibition. I suppose I should have suspected something, but Victor had cost me so much money by then I just didn't want to think about it.'

The tea had gone tepid. I glanced out the open door, cocked an ear to the river, heard no sound of the boys. Aubrey levered himself up and picked up his walking stick. 'Perhaps the bunyip got 'em,' he said.

Just beyond the vegetable garden, we stopped at the top of the track. The river was immediately below us, shallow over a gravel bottom. Red and Tarquin lay side by side, face-down on the pebble bottom, letting the water ripple over them. Their naked skin showed white against the dappled brown gravel.

Aubrey took in the sight with a sigh. '*Quam juvenale femur!*' he exclaimed.

My grip on the third declension had only ever been tenuous, but I got his drift. Old Giles was a leg man. 'Your suspicions,' I said. 'When were they confirmed?'

'When I arrived unannounced one day and found Victor passed out drunk and Marcus working in the studio. He admitted then that most of what he'd delivered in the preceding year hadn't been Victor's work at all, but his own. Victor had no idea what was going on. Marcus begged me not to tell him.'

'And one of those pictures was *Our Home?*'

'The best of them, by far.'

'But you sold it to Max Karlin anyway.'

'Karlin had already bought it. I should have told him, I know. But the subject matter, the execution, everything except its actual authorship was classic Victor Szabo. And I did insist that Marcus stop it. Even offered him his own exhibition. Embarrassing it was. Pretentious art-school abstract expressionism. The only thing that sold, I bought myself out of pity. Victor wouldn't even come to the show. Soon afterwards they had a big blow-up and Victor turned him out. They never spoke again. Two years later I sold the gallery and retired.'

'So you and Marcus Taylor were the only ones that knew that *Our Home* was a fake?'

Aubrey winced at the word. 'As far as I know. I was afraid it would all come out at Victor's death. The will was a bitter blow to Marcus, but when he didn't say anything at the time, I put it to the back of my mind and it's been there ever since.'

'The will?'

'Marcus harboured hopes that Victor would eventually acknowledge him in some way. But he didn't even mention him. Not a word. Left everything to that Lambert woman. Marcus was devastated.'

What a depressing little saga. Father-and-son relationships are notoriously vexed, even at the best of times. This Victor Szabo sounded like a worst-case scenario. Marcus Taylor must have been lugging around enough psychological scar tissue to sink anybody, the poor prick. Fortunately, my own son had already won his Oedipal battle. Half of it anyway. I couldn't vouch for his mother.

'He was susceptible to women, Victor, and Fiona Lambert was scarcely a third of his age. Not that he had a lot to bequeath, just a few pictures and a growing reputation. But she made sure she milked that for all it was worth.'

'The Black Widow.'

Aubrey snorted derisively. 'Don't believe a word of it.

She made that up herself. Shameless self-promotion. Victor died of liver disease, the result of poor personal hygiene and a surfeit of cheap wine.'

I struggled to assimilate the significance of what Aubrey was telling me. The news that the CMA's Szabo was not a Szabo at all was dynamite. It had the potential not merely to embarrass Fiona Lambert, the self-declared expert, but to expose to ridicule the competence of the government which had funded the purchase. 'Legal proceedings are inevitable, I suppose,' said the old man, wilting on his cane.

'That's not for me to say. May I suggest we keep this conversation confidential at this stage?'

He nodded penitently, as though receiving conditional absolution. There were other questions I should have asked Aubrey while I had the chance. But his tale of Taylor and Szabo had pricked my parental conscience. Down below, Red and Tarquin were swinging off an overhanging branch into dangerously shallow water. So I thanked Aubrey for his candour, assured him of my discretion and left the shrivelled old bird standing there, Tiberius among his tomatoes.

Shedding my clothes on the sandy bank, I hit the water running, scattering Red and Tarquin before me like startled cranes. Thigh-deep in mid-stream, I plunged to the bottom, luxuriating in the water's cool embrace.

Was it really possible to drown yourself in water this deep? Could any sense of grievance, any urge to self-dramatisation, be strong enough to overcome the body's fundamental instinct for survival? I kicked forward, propelling myself along the dappled gravel, holding my breath by sheer force of will. Could anyone really master that reflexive lunge for air that was propelling me so inexorably upwards? I broke the surface, scattering water, gasping.

No, Salina Fleet was wrong. Marcus Taylor hadn't killed himself. His death was an accident. It just couldn't have come at a better time, that's all.

F ORTY KILOMETRES downstream, the Yarra berthed oil tankers and container carriers in the biggest port south of Singapore. Closer to its source, at the height of summer, it was little more than a series of shallow pools strung out along a narrow bed that meandered through the low hills.

We went exploring. The banks rose steeply on either side, thick with pencil-straight stringybarks and scrubby undergrowth, punctured with granite outcrops. Giles Aubrey had no immediate neighbours and within minutes we might have been in some trackless wilderness. Here, in the eternal bush, man and boy could test their masculinity against the challenges of raw nature.

'Ow,' said Tarquin. 'That tree scratched me.'

Pushing on intrepidly, we clambered over boulders and along bridges of fallen tree-trunks. 'But aren't there snakes?' insisted Tarquin.

'Keep your eyes open,' I said, drawing on my inherent knowledge of bushcraft. Pioneer blood flowed in my veins. My father's grandmother had once run a pub in Ballarat. 'Make plenty of noise as you go.' The advice was superfluous. If Tarquin managed to get himself bitten, it would be nothing short of miraculous.

'What do you do if one bites you?' Red wanted to know.

Snakes weren't exactly my forte, not in the zoological sense anyway. But the habitat did seem custom-made – sun-warmed rocks, cracks and fissures everywhere, plentiful frogs and other creatures coming down to the water to drink. I owed it to the boys to pass on the time-honoured lore of the bush. 'You have to get somebody to suck out the poison,' I explained. 'That's the standard treatment. Except if you get bitten on the backside.'

'What happens then?' said Tarquin, apprehensively scrutinising the riverbank.

'You put your head between your legs,' said Red, racing me to the punch line. 'And kiss your arse goodbye.'

Where a massive red gum overhung the water, I lingered in the shade and smoked a cigarette while the boys scouted ahead. A crystal stream bubbled at my feet. Dragonflies flitted hither and thither. The scent of eucalyptus perfumed the air. Kookaburras carolled distantly. Luxuriating in the tranquillity of the bush, I banished all thoughts of work – of Agnelli, of the press and Marcus Taylor, of Spider and the duplicate Szabo. I let my eyes close.

'Help!' came a scream from around the bend. 'Come quick.' Red. Not mucking around either, by the sound of it.

It was black, thick as my wrist, coiled at Tarquin's feet. Red was circling at a distance, stick in hand, bellowing for help. Tarquin stood frozen with fear. He must nearly have stood on the thing. 'Don't move,' I yelled. 'If you die, your mother will kill me.'

Grabbing the stick from Red's hand, I lunged forward and smashed downwards at the repulsive black spiral. At the same time, I shoved Tarquin out of harm's way. The snake bucked under the blow, bounced upwards and revealed itself to be the inner tube of a bike tyre.

'Tricked ya!' Red and I cackled simultaneously, high-fiving each other in the time-honoured Australian tradition.

'My ankle,' writhed Tarquin, prostrate on the ground. 'You've broken my ankle.'

It took me nearly an hour to carry him back downstream and up the hill to the car, slung over my shoulder fireman-style. His foot wrapped tight in my shirt, he whimpered right up to the moment I lowered him onto the back seat. 'Can we have an ice-cream on the way home?' he said.

'Shuddup, Tark,' said Red. But he didn't mean it. I suspected he was in on it all along.

It was well past eight when we arrived back in town. A note from Faye instructed us to proceed to the Exhibition Gardens, five minutes away, where a picnic awaited us. While the boys rummaged for frisbees and skateboards, I nicked home, changed into shorts and a t-shirt and put a bottle of pinot vino in a plastic carry-bag.

The shadows were lengthening as we walked to the gardens. The doors and windows of the houses had been flung open to admit the buttery dusk. Cooking smells and guitar-riffs emerged, and the old Italian and Greek remnants of the former demographic had come outside to hose down their footpaths and sit fanning themselves on their minuscule front porches. *Arms for Afghanistan*, said the fading grafitti. *Legs for Tito*.

Faye had not been the only one to think of dining alfresco that evening, and the lawns of the gardens were liberally peppered with picnickers and amorous couples. From the direction of the tennis courts came the pock-pocking of furry balls beating an intermittent rhythm to the chorus of innumerable cicadas.

Chloe appeared from between the trees to guide us to the others. She had a girl the same age with her, shy with big eyes. They led us towards a vast Moreton Bay fig, at the foot of which a blanket was spread. It was all very *Dejeuner sur l'Herbe*. Leo, tall and darkly bearded, lay propped on one elbow, plastic wineglass in hand. Faye was removing containers from a cooler and laying them out. Seated between them, knees drawn up, glancing over her shoulder to keep a weather eye on the girls, was a woman I didn't know. She was not unlike the woman in Manet's painting except, of course, that she was not nude. Her loose summery dress only hinted at what she might be like underneath. More your full-figured Gauguin sort of thing was my guess.

Apart from me and Leo, there was no other man in sight. Bloody Faye, I thought. Playing go-between again, setting me up.

'Murray Whelan,' beamed Faye, butter not melting in her mouth. 'This is Claire Sutton.'

Claire Sutton had a mass of chestnut hair, pulled back into a bushy ponytail, and a high round forehead. We nodded perfunctorily. Lowering myself to the ground, I shot a sideways glower at Faye.

'I've just been telling Claire that you work in the arts,' she persisted. 'Claire's in the arts, too.'

'Uh-huh.' With Faye on the job, that could mean anything from riding bareback in a circus to running macrame classes. I passed my bottle of wine to Leo who, as usual, was handling the drinks. Faye's spread of salads and cold-cuts was straight out of the culinary pages of the colour supplements, much of it mysteriously so.

The children rushed the food, Tarquin suddenly began hobbling again. 'Guacamole?' said Red. Sydney was doing wonders for his education.

'Zhough,' said Faye. 'A Yemenite dip of coriander, cumin and garlic. What's wrong this time, Tarquin? You put it on the chicken.'

'He made me go rock climbing.' Tarquin jiggled up and down on one foot, dangling the other in front of his mother. Red piled a paper plate with everything in reach. Leo stood with the bottle squeezed between his thighs, straining at a corkscrew.

'I'm not really in the arts.' I met Claire eye-to-eye for the first time. She was, I saw, just as ambushed as me. 'The politician I work for has just been given that portfolio.'

The shy-eyed girl, obviously Claire's daughter, climbed across her to reach for a bread roll. 'Off you go and play, Gracie,' she said. Claire had a wide mouth, a slightly turned-up nose and watchful brown eyes that hinted they might, if she so decided, laugh. 'I used to be a conservator' – she flicked me a quick glance to see if I knew what that meant – 'at the National Gallery. But now I've got a print and framing business.' This was an exchange of credentials rather than conversation.

'Artemis, it's called,' enthused Faye. Tarquin limped off, ankle in remission, plate in hand. 'In Smith Street. Try the tapenade.'

I'd driven past Artemis, on the way to Ethnic Affairs. Awning over the footpath. Window full of pre-Raphaelite maidens. The tapenade was black stuff that tasted like a cross between seaweed and Vegemite. I rolled it round on my tongue. 'Artemis?' The reference escaped me. Something literary, perhaps.

'Amazonian moon goddess,' said Faye. 'A mixture of olive paste, capers and anchovies.'

'Red or white?' said Leo. 'Capinata? Frittata? Aioli?' Amazonian moon goddess? My heart sank.

'It's a joke!' Claire rushed to her own defence, spilling crumbs into her abundant decolletage, brushing them away self-consciously as she spoke. 'A pun. Arty Miss. My former husband's idea of being smart. He registered the business in that name and it stuck, even if he didn't.'

The deficiencies of ex-husbands were, in my book, a topic best avoided. 'Guess what I had for lunch, Faye? Strawberry sandwiches. Went to this brunch at Max Karlin's corporate HQ. His art collection is unbelievable. Must be worth millions.'

'He might not have it for much longer,' said Faye, unable to resist shop talk. 'From what I hear, this Karlcraft Centre project of his has turned into a bottomless pit. He's hocked to the eyeballs against the prospect of future commercial tenancies, but by the time the building is completed, there'll be a glut of downtown office space. Unless he can get some long-term tenants locked in pronto, he risks going belly-up.' Faye loved to talk like that. 'Word is that his creditors are getting pretty jumpy. Try the mesclun, Claire. Chloe, Grace, come and get a drink.'

The mesclun was a mixture of nasturtiums, dandelions and marigolds. 'Do I eat it?' whispered Claire behind her hand, making common cause against our mutual tormentor. 'Or put it in my hair?'

When I arrived, I'd wanted nothing so much as to succumb to the torpor of the evening. Now I wasn't so sure. Perhaps it was the wine. 'You've excelled yourself, Faye,' I said. 'Who are his creditors?'

'Various financial institutions. Guarantee Corp, Obelisk Trust. Walnut pesto?'

'I've heard of Obelisk,' I said, trying very hard to avoid looking down the front of Claire's dress when she reached for the crudites. 'What is it exactly?'

'Dip your pita in it. It used to be the Building Unions Credit Co-operative. Then a guy called Lloyd Eastlake took it over, restructured it into a unit trust and changed the name to Obelisk. It's what the Americans call a mutual fund. Manages a pool of funds on behalf of its investors. Unions mainly.'

'Claire mounted our Jogjakarta trishaw-drivers, you know, Murray,' said Leo.

Blow-ups of Faye's arty holiday photos lined the Curnows' hall, flatteringly framed. 'The ones inside the front door?' I said, admiringly. 'You did that?'

'Mounting street-vendors is my bread and butter.' Claire permitted her eyes a small smile, beginning to relax.

Before I could ask her if she'd mind taking a look at my etchings, the kids swarmed over us, Indians storming the fort. We ate. Ravenous, nothing in me but a coffee and a berry sandwich, I fell on the food. Faye and Claire talked kindergarten politics.

When we'd eaten, Leo got out a bat and we played cricket with the kids, using the No Ball Games sign for stumps. Claire hit a six off my first ball. In time, the shadows meshed together and the night fell gently from the sky. We crept through the velvet darkness, feeding cautious possums pieces of leftover fruit.

'Well?' Faye hissed into my ear, behind a tree. 'Thirty-three. Owns her own business. Not bad looking.'

What did she expect me to do, jump the woman on the spot? 'Where's the father of the child?'

'Left them a year ago. New cookie.'

'Coffee?' said Leo. 'Sambuca? Port?'

We walked back to Faye and Leo's, slapping mosquitoes. I swung Grace up onto my hip. She took it as her due and twined her arms around my neck. Her sleepy head nestled in the crook of my shoulder. A daughter, I thought, would be nice. Eventually.

'She's not usually so trusting,' said Claire.

'I wouldn't trust Murray as far as I could throw him,' said Faye.

Cleopatra was on television. We sprawled in the dark before the flickering set, draped with drowsy children. The girls, curled like kittens in their mothers' laps, were soon rendered unconscious by Richard Burton's narcotic vowels. Elizabeth Taylor, fabulously blowzy, seethed and ranted. Leo lay bean-bagged on the floor, Tarquin using his shins for a pillow. Red slumbered against my shoulder. 'This film,' observed Claire, 'is longer than the Nile.' She made, nevertheless, no move to leave.

What were the poor people doing tonight, I mused. Max Karlin, for all his outward trappings, was teetering on the brink. Desperate to find those elusive big-ticket tenants, those precious million-dollar customers willing and able to sign on the line, ten floors for ten years. Multinationals. Public utilities. Government departments needing accommodation for hundreds of pen-pushers, sitting there at their desks sending out those millions of water bills.

By the time the credits rolled, Claire and I were the only ones still awake. Perhaps all that on-screen sensuality had given me the wrong idea, but her posture seemed more than accidentally provocative. She lay draped languidly at the other end of the couch, errant corkscrews of hair framing her face. The fabric of her dress moulded to her body. She could not possibly have been unaware how wanton she looked.

She wasn't. From behind lowered lids, she was measuring my reaction. No longer concealing my interest, I ran my gaze lazily over her body. Then watched her reciprocate.

Our eyes devoured each other. The time had come to act, to grasp the transient moment. Gingerly, I prised Red's sleeping head from my lap. My hand edged towards Claire's extended leg.

Red's eyes sprang open. 'Tricked ya!' he yawned. His arm flung out in a stretch and connected with my sore ear.

'Ow,' I said. Faye woke with a start, activating Chloe.

'Huh? snuffled Leo, inadvertently letting Tarquin's head fall to the floor. 'Is it over?'

'My ankle,' groaned Tarquin. 'You kicked my ankle.'

Instantly, there was more barging around going on than Cleopatra ever dreamed of. 'Is it time to go home yet, Mummy,' pleaded Grace, rubbing her eyes.

'Yes, darling,' sighed Claire. 'I guess it is.'

SUNDAY'S DAWNING came sticky with humidity, heavy with the prospect of rain. By dawning I don't mean the sun's rosy-fingered ascension. Nor do I mean the day's first blossoming when I reached for my winsome sleep-mate while thrushes warbled outside my window. I mean eight, when I shucked off the sheets, checked that Red was still asleep in his room and padded to the corner for the papers. I'd slept as deeply as the heat allowed, but my choice of dreams could have been better. Again, I'd been visited by Noel Webb.

Again, we were sitting in the wintry twilight on a park bench in the Oulton Reserve, Spider's contempt ringing in my ears, the three Fletcher boys looming over us.

The Fletchers were weedy runts but they'd been raised on a diet of belt buckles and brake fluid and they had us at unfavourable odds. They were sharpies, an amorphous tribe of terrifying reputation, precursors to the skinheads. In an era when every adolescent male in the world yearned for longer locks and tighter pants, the sharpies wore close-cropped hair and check trousers so perversely wide they flapped like flags. Rumoured to carry knives, they were less a gang than an attitude of casual violence looking for somewhere to happen. And now they had found me.

The moment I most dreaded had arrived. And Noel Webb, my as-yet-unpaid protector, was edging away. Flanked by his twin brothers, Geordie, the seventeen-year-old, thrust his face into mine. 'What are you looking at?' he snarled. His denuded skull occupied my entire field of vision.

A craven bleat issued from my mouth. 'Nothing.'

The twins snickered. 'Nah-thing, nah-thing.'

They acted like idiots, but that didn't make them any less dangerous. The kid their brother kicked to death wasn't much older than me. Trying to fight back would only provoke them. Not that fighting back entered my mind. My guts had shrivelled into a queasy lump and my legs were jelly. The contraband booze beneath my coat was my only hope.

But before I could get it out, offer it up in supplication, Geordie grabbed the crook of my elbow and jerked me upright. The twins closed from either side, pistoning their bony kneecaps into my thighs. 'Ow,' I said. Piss weak. A heel swung behind mine and swept my leg away. Wayne and Danny were pressed so close that I stumbled first against one then the other. Pinning my arms, they buffeted me sideways, setting me spinning like a top, biffing and slapping me as I turned, yelling encouragement to each other.

A circle of faces flashed before me. Fletcher faces. Noel Webb's face. Denied his mercenary price, Spider had gone over to the enemy. Or worse. A set-up all along. The tough men of the district had found some fresh meat. Round and round I spun, all the while attempting to wrestle the bottle from beneath the folds of my coat. Dizzy, strait-jacketed, sweaty with panic. That's when I woke up.

Both the Sunday papers had given the Suicide in the Moat story a run on page three. Both featured Salina Fleet in her widow's weeds, wistfully gazing at one of Marcus Taylor's sketches like it was the shroud of Turin. I took fresh croissants back to the house for Red's breakfast and rang Ken Sproule.

He'd seen the paper. 'As predicted,' he said. 'Angelo can stop peeing his pants.' Despite his crack at Agnelli, Sproule had thought it worth keeping his own ear to the ground. 'This suicide stuff's a load of crap. They found bruising to the back of the skull consistent with a fall. The cops tend to think he was walking along the parapet, tripped over, knocked his head and fell in.'

'What about the manifesto?'

'Could mean anything. Or nothing. The fact that it was found on the body doesn't necessarily make it a suicide note. But an anguished suicide makes far better copy than a clumsy drunk. Particularly with the girl-friend pushing that line. You watch. By this time next week, he'll be a great unrecognised talent and his work will start turning up in the auction houses. Not a bad looker, the girlfriend, eh? She's on some committee at the ministry, you know.'

'While you're on the line,' I changed tack, 'I met Lloyd Eastlake last night. What's a hot shot like him doing on a minor policy committee like Cultural Affairs? He fits that scene like a pacer at a pony club.'

'Parliamentary ambitions,' Sproule said. 'Same reason

anyone gets themselves onto a policy committee. If you're not a union official, it's the best way to get yourself noticed, find out how things work. My guess is that Eastlake has targeted the arts to build a profile as something other than just another penny-ante money man.'

'He didn't look too penny-ante to me.'

'That's because you've led a sheltered life, Murray. That chauffeur-driven stuff might impress his investors, but it doesn't mean much in the big picture. For every Alan Bond or Robert Holmes à Court, there's a hundred Lloyd Eastlakes. They're a sign of a buoyant economy, springing up like mushrooms after rain. We need them to make the system work. But don't confuse Eastlake with serious money. You could probably count his millions on one hand.'

'Not a bad result for a humble chippie, though.' I ashed my cigarette in a saucer, sipped cold instant coffee from a cracked cup and wondered what I'd be doing if I had even a lousy one million dollars. 'So why does he want to get into parliament?'

'Why does anyone? If we psychoanalysed every parliamentary candidate we'd have full nut-houses and empty legislatures.'

An operator like Ken Sproule could never be taken on face value. He could be poisoning the wells. He could be giving me the good oil. But he was right about one thing. In our line of work, it was best not to think too much about people's motives.

'Tell me something else,' I said. Since Ken was in a talkative mood, the least I could do was listen to him. 'What's the story on this Centre for Modern Art acquisition? Three hundred thousand dollars was a pretty generous grant, wasn't it?'

'Piss off,' said Sproule. 'If I start to background you on last year's grants, you'll be pestering me every five minutes.'

'Don't be like that, Ken,' I said. 'Angelo's got to live with this decision, so I might as well know the reasoning behind it.'

'What's to tell? The CMA applied for funding. The Visual Arts Advisory Panel recommended the application be approved. Gil Methven accepted the recommendation. End of story.'

'I might have lived a sheltered life,' I said. 'But I didn't come down in the last shower. Eastlake is chairman of both the CMA and the Visual Arts Advisory Panel.'

'So what? Eastlake absented himself from the chair and left the room while his panel voted on the grant.' This was no more than the standard procedure for fending off any suggestion of conflict of interest.

'Eastlake's committee could only recommend the grant. Ultimate approval lay with the minister.'

'You trying to make a point here, Murray?'

'It's a big grant. Lloyd Eastlake must have done a lot of arm-twisting to convince Gil to approve it.'

'Gil agreed to provide half the funds if the CMA could find the other half. He didn't think they'd be able to raise that sort of dough for an unknown artist. But Eastlake came up with the money and Gil had no option but to keep his part of the bargain. The Centre for Modern Art is Eastlake's main hobby horse, but he wears a lot of other hats. Not much point in putting the chairman of the Cultural Affairs Policy Committee offside, not with the friends Lloyd Eastlake has in the unions.'

'His financial clients?'

'Eastlake has been dealing with the unions since back when he was in the building game,' said Sproule. 'What with all these mergers and amalgamations, some unions have found themselves sitting on sizeable assets, as well as having to manage their members' superannuation funds. They need financial expertise. The word got around that Eastlake had the magic touch and he ended up holding the kitty for quite a few of the comrades. You ever heard of Obelisk Trust? That's Eastlake.'

'And Obelisk donated the CMA's half of the purchase price for this picture they're buying?'

'Correctomundo.'

'Helping an art gallery to buy a painting hardly seems the ideal way for an outfit like Obelisk to target its sponsorship money,' I said. 'Isn't Eastlake just using union money to buy himself a bit of kudos with the art crowd?'

'Possibly. He's also engaging in a bit of mutual pocket pissing with Max Karlin. Obelisk has a lot of money riding on the Karlcraft project and paying top dollar for one of Max's pictures could be construed as a gesture of confidence in the project, a way of shoring up the commitment of other investors.'

At last we were getting to the nub of it. 'In other words, the Ministry for the Arts has just spent three hundred thousand dollars of public money to massage one of Lloyd Eastlake's investments.'

'Not just Eastlake's, pal. We're all in this. The

Karlcraft Centre project is currently employing a small army of construction workers, most of them union members. It's spending money on everything from cement to door knobs, doing its bit for the local economy. When it's up and running, it'll revitalise much of the central business district, create hundreds of retail jobs and generate millions in government revenues. Putting the arts to work lubricating that process is a job well done, wouldn't you agree?'

Who was I to demur? I told Ken Sproule I owed him a lunch and rang off. 'Wakey, wakey, hands off snakey,' I called through Red's door. 'We aren't going to get much quality time together if you sleep all day.'

He got up and went straight around to Tarquin's place. By the time I'd finished breakfast and read the papers it was getting on for ten o'clock. I found the card with Eastlake's phone numbers on it and looked at it for while, thinking about the story Giles Aubrey had told me.

Like old Giles said, the genie was out of the bottle. Routine police procedures to identify Marcus Taylor would inevitably connect him with Victor Szabo. Shit, it had taken me about five minutes. Aubrey was in a confessional mood. Sooner or later, the whole thing would start to come unravelled. Spending public money on art was risky enough. Spending it on a fake would make us look like idiots, unfit to govern. Angelo would be directly in the firing line. A way would need to be found quietly to scotch the whole thing. I called Eastlake on his mobile and told him I'd appreciate an opportunity to talk to him about the Szabo acquisition at his earliest convenience.

'I understand,' he said. 'Looking out for Angelo's interest PR-wise.' Exactly. Eastlake said he was on his way to the Toorak Road Deli and suggested I join him there.

I went up the back lane and stuck my head in Faye and Leo's kitchen door. Faye had her hands in the sink and Leo had his head in the fridge. 'Where's the cake?' he said. The boys were on the floor glued to the television. There were no cartoons at that hour and they were reduced to watching a rural affairs documentary on mad cow disease.

'That reminds me,' I told Red. 'You'd better ring your mother.'

'It's right in front of you,' said Faye. 'So, Murray, what do you think of Claire? Tarquin, turn that TV off. We're going in ten minutes.' The Curnows, it transpired, were about to leave for Leo's mother's seventieth birthday party and would be out all day.

'Come and ring your mother.' I dragged Red out the back door. 'Then I'll show you where the rich people live.'

The rich people live in Toorak. Skirting the city centre, we crossed the river and headed into its leafy precincts. In hushed cul-de-sacs and meandering avenues, we peered and craned like tourists at the mansions of the filthy rich. Sydney, I informed Red, had plenty of fat cats and flash rats. But for your genuine, copper-bottomed blue-blood, you couldn't go past Toorak.

Cruising past the French Provincial farmhouses and Californian haciendas, the ivied walls and gravelled driveways, we drove the Charade down Toorak Road, a street where all the shops are boutiques and even a carton of milk costs more. The Deli was at the city end, a see-and-be-seen place with Porsches at the kerb and fourteen different kinds of freshly squeezed juice. Eastlake's Mercedes was parked across the road, between a red convertible Volkswagen with an Airedale terrier on the back seat and a Volvo station wagon with P-plates and surfboards on the roof rack.

Spider Webb was standing beside the Merc, looking into the window of a menswear shop called Pour Homme. We parked further down the block, outside one of those places that sells Groucho Marx lamp stands, pink neon telephones and musical birthday cards. A clip-joint for rich kids. Red lit up at the sight of it, so I peeled off ten dollars. Take your time, I told him. And if you shoplift, don't get caught.

The Deli was somebody's gold mine. Cappuccinos to the gentry. *Pain au chocolat* with the accent on the accent. Mobile phones in clear view. Blondes with perfect hair and beesting lips. Jewish husbands with melancholy expressions and big gold Rolexes. Lawyers in leisure-wear.

Lloyd Eastlake was in his element, sitting in a prime booth wearing tennis whites with navy piping. Sitting opposite him was a well-groomed woman in her late forties with big sunglasses and a brittle mouth. The sunglasses were pushed up on top of hair that had the panel-beaten finish rich women spend a fortune acquiring in the taxidermy salons of society hairdressers.

Eastlake saw me enter and waved me over. 'Murray Whelan,' he said. 'My wife, Lorraine.'

So this was the boss's daughter whose hand had given young Lloyd his leg up in business. Lorraine looked like she'd been repenting ever since, consoled only by the diversion of spending as much of his money as possible. She was just leaving.

'I hope I'm not interrupting your game,' I said sociably, an obvious tennis reference.

'Lorraine doesn't play,' said Eastlake. 'Do you, darling?'

'Nice to meet you,' said Lorraine. She'd forgotten my name already. As she headed towards the exit, a ruddy faced man with real estate written all over him moved to fill the vacuum. Eastlake deflected him with an easy gesture, signalled for more coffee and told me to sit down. 'You don't look too happy,' he said genially. 'Angelo not paying you enough?'

'Sorry to be the bearer of bad news,' I said, getting straight down to it before some social fly buzzed over and landed on us. 'I think we've got a problem.'

'Have we?' His expression brightened with amusement at my earnestness.

'You and me both,' I said. 'The Szabo isn't authentic. I'm afraid you've been had.'

His eyes narrowed, assessing me anew. 'You've been hiding your light under a bushel.' His tone was still playful on the surface, but there was a cool undercurrent. 'Didn't know you were such a scholar.'

'I was up Eltham way yesterday and I met someone called Giles Aubrey. He used to be Victor Szabo's dealer.'

At the mention of Aubrey's name, Eastlake leaned forward, beginning to take me seriously. 'Giles Aubrey,' he said. 'There's a blast from the past. So, tell me, what's the old bugger been whispering in your ear?'

'He said *Our Home* was painted by someone else.'

'Oh, did he just?' Beneath the flippancy was a tinge of irritation he couldn't quite hide. 'Did he say who?'

'Szabo's illegitimate son,' I said. 'Marcus Taylor.' Eastlake gave me a blank stare. 'The guy they fished out of the National Gallery moat.' It all sounded a bit far-fetched. 'Anyway, that's what he told me.'

Eastlake drew back and deliberately widened his eyes, like I was pulling his leg. When he saw that I was serious, the amusement drained from his expression. He pursed his lips and rubbed his chin, as though digesting the significance of what I had just told him.

A waiter arrived and put cappuccinos in front of us. Eastlake studied me carefully, as though attempting to discern my reliability. Then he made up his mind. Picking up his spoon, he leaned forward. When he spoke, it was in hushed, confidential tones. 'Can you keep a secret, Murray?'

I didn't reply, but he was welcome to continue.

'I'm not the one being had,' he grinned. 'You are.'

EASTLAKE BUILT a floating island of sugar on the froth of his cappuccino and watched it slowly sink. 'Giles Aubrey is a bitter and twisted old man,' he said. 'And he's been spinning you a line. I don't suppose you happened to mention to him how much we're paying Karlin for the picture, did you?'

'I might have said something about it,' I allowed.

'And that's when he came out with his story?'

'He was very convincing.'

'Aubrey can be, by all accounts. You wouldn't be the first he's taken in. Lots of authentic Szabo embroidery, I imagine. This bit about the suicide in the National Gallery moat, this whatsisname . . .'

'Marcus Taylor.'

'That's a nice topical touch. Aubrey saw the story on the news, no doubt, and grabbed the opportunity to make a little mischief.'

'Why would he want to do that?

'Ancient history,' said Eastlake. 'Old wounds. Aubrey genuinely believed in Victor Szabo, but he never succeeded in making anything of his career. Szabo probably even cost him money. Seeing the sort of figures Szabo's pictures are currently fetching must really piss him off. But the money, I suspect, is the least of it. He's jealous of Fiona Lambert getting all the credit for securing Szabo's posthumous reputation. It was Fiona who found *Our Home* in Karlin's collection, pegged it as a benchmark work and suggested that the CMA acquire it. Casting doubts on the authenticity of *Our Home* would be the perfect way to undermine her reputation.'

This made a certain amount of sense. Perhaps Aubrey had seized on my phone call as an opportunity to exact a little belated revenge on Fiona Lambert. But that still didn't explain everything. 'The drowned guy, Taylor,' I said. 'He left a note. A manifesto, the press were calling it. Angelo thought they might beat something up. So I went to his studio yesterday morning, just before Max Karlin's brunch, and took a look around. He'd painted a perfect copy of *Our Home*.'

Eastlake slowly sipped his cappuccino, studying me over the rim of his cup. 'You're quite the eager beaver, aren't you?' he said. 'But I'm not sure what you're getting at.'

'Neither am I,' I admitted. 'It just seemed like an odd coincidence, given what Aubrey told me later.'

'It's not unusual, you know, for younger artists to make copies of landmark paintings. Just proves what I said. *Our Home* is a masterpiece.'

'But Taylor also had a photograph of himself with Victor Szabo. Doesn't that tend to corroborate Aubrey's story?'

Eastlake indulged me, amused by my persistence. 'I've got a picture of myself with the Prime Minister.

That doesn't make me his love child.'

Put like that, my concerns were all starting to feel a bit far-fetched. 'Looks like I've been wasting your time,' I said, burying my face in my own coffee.

'On the contrary,' said Eastlake. 'You did the right thing coming to me. We *have* got a problem. The art world thrives on gossip. Giles Aubrey's malicious inventions could do a lot of damage.'

'Aubrey can say what he likes,' I said. 'But he can't prove anything. By his own admission, Taylor was the only other person who could confirm his story – and he's dead.'

'You miss my point,' said Eastlake. 'We're talking perceptions here. The value of a work of art is a fragile abstraction. If word gets around that doubts exist about the authorship of *Our Home*, similar speculation could easily arise about the integrity of other works in Max Karlin's collection. Suggest that one picture isn't what it's purported to be, people might wonder about the others. A person in your position, close to the Minister for the Arts, has a certain credibility. What you say gets heard, passed on, amplified.'

'I think I understand the situation, Lloyd,' I said pointedly, resenting the implication that I needed to be warned not to go blabbing Aubrey's story all over town. 'But I'm more concerned about potential embarrassment to Angelo than the market value of Max Karlin's art collection. In either case, the question is to make sure Aubrey stays quiet. He agreed to keep the story to himself yesterday, but who knows how long that will last.'

Eastlake had already figured this out. 'Call his bluff.

Make him put up or shut up. If he took Karlin's money knowing that *Our Home* wasn't authentic, that's criminal fraud. Mention the prospect of prosecution and I bet he'll fall over himself to sign a statement confirming the picture's authenticity.'

A more informed discussion with Giles Aubrey was certainly on the agenda. 'I'll go and see him tomorrow,' I said.

'You do what you think advisable, Murray.'

Business done, I accepted a second cup of coffee and eased back into my surroundings. The Deli's cafeteria decor was obviously not its prime attraction, no more so than the quality of its profiteroles or the freshness of its juices. The customers were there for each other. As we were talking, Eastlake had been fielding social signals from the other booths. Spotting his opportunity, the beetroot-faced realtor table-hopped over, cup in hand. 'Hey, Eastie,' he said, wagging his tail. 'How's that new Merc of yours running?'

Eastlake introduced us, first names only. Malcolm was wearing a Gucci shirt that might have done something for a man twenty years younger. 'Seen Lloyd's new car?' He jerked his head back towards the street. 'High performance auto-mobile like that and he gets a chauffeur to drive it. That's like having the butler fuck your mistress. What do you drive, Murray?'

'Something smaller,' I said. Then, since the subject had come up, 'Good drivers easy to find, Lloyd?'

'Noel?' Eastlake was back at ease, expansive. 'I didn't find him,' he said. 'He found me. You know the Members' carpark at Flemington?'

Malcolm squeezed in beside me, ready to catch any

gems of wit and wisdom Lloyd Eastlake might care to drop. The Members' carpark was where the silvertails held their chicken and champers picnics on Cup Day. Not a place you needed to be a regular race-goer to know about. I nodded. Go on.

'Last spring racing carnival, it was. I was out there with your predecessor, Ken Sproule. Terrible man for the gee-gees, Ken is. We've had a pretty good day and we're both well over the limit. So we get to the car and Ken decides he's not going to let me drive, not in my condition. It's starting to rain and there we are, standing next to the car . . .'

'That was the 450 SLC, right?' chipped in Malcolm. 'The two-door coupe.'

'. . . arguing the toss about whether I'm in a fit state to drive. Anyway, this bloke comes along, he's doing the rounds, working for some car-detailing firm. They go around during the afternoon, checking for dents, rust spots, that sort of thing. They put their card under the wiper – flaking chrome, cracked light, whatever – and a quote for the job.'

I could just see it. Spider Webb prowling the toffs' carpark with a twenty-cent piece in one hand and an eye to the main chance.

'So Ken gets an idea. This bloke can drive us into the city, take the car overnight, cut and polish it, drop it off at my place in the morning. It's either that or walk through the rain to the main gate, get a cab, come back the next day for the car. So I said okay. Next morning, there's the Merc in my driveway, spic and span, never looked better. It hadn't been running at its best, and he had a few ideas about that. Ended up looking after my wife's car as well. When I moved up to the SEL, I needed a driver and put him on full-time.'

Malcolm loved it, the adventures of the cavalier millionaire. 'Hundred and fifty grand's worth of vehicle and you handed the keys to a complete stranger?'

Not a bad story, but it sounded like pub talk to me. And a funny way to hire a bodyguard. Through the Deli's plate-glass front window, Spider was visible across the road. He was sipping from a polystyrene cup and lazily chewing gum at the same time. Blank-eyed, bored, watchful. Drip dry. 'This is the guy with the ears, right?' I pushed mine forward by way of example. The wound was healing nicely. 'Thought I saw him down near the Arts Centre yesterday morning.'

A pair of social lions prowled over, her in an Alice band, him in a track suit, faces from the CMA opening. Eastlake tossed me their names. 'You remember . . .' I remembered I had someone better to spend my time with. Offering my seat, I said hello, made my excuses and went to find Red.

His ten dollars had bought a roll of mints and a small electronic game in the shape of a spaceship. The mints weren't bad. I was trying to wheedle a couple more out of Red when we crested the Punt Road hill and hit the tail end of a string of traffic that ran all the way to the river.

Throwing a hasty left at Domain Road, I cut past the Botanic Gardens and through to St Kilda Road. The traffic was lighter there, although the Arts Centre had attracted quite a crowd. Had Marcus Taylor's famous death, I wondered, prompted a renewed interest in the Old Masters? The gelati vans were back in force and delinquents on skateboards were surfing the steel waves of the sculpture on the lawn next to the Concert Hall. Red was drawn like a magnet to the sight. On impulse, I pulled into a vacant parking space.

A juggler had set up shop beside the sculpture in front of the State Theatre, a hideously ugly brown lump. The sculpture, not the juggler. The juggler was dressed as King Neptune and had three carving knives and a flaming firebrand aloft simul-taneously. I thought I knew how he felt. Just as he finished, an octopus on stilts appeared through the crowd. 'Check this out,' I told Red. 'It's harder than it looks.' Especially since one of the stilts had a bend in it. Red wasn't interested in some promenading fish. His interest lay with the skateboarders. I told him to run ahead, that I'd join him in a few minutes.

Jumping up onto the parapet of the moat, I threaded my way past parked backsides and headed towards the entrance of the National Gallery. The parapet was a little less than a metre across, about the width of a standard table. Not exactly an acrobatic challenge. But then Marcus Taylor didn't have a great track record when it came to tables. It would, I could see, have been quite easy for someone with a few drinks under his belt to slip and knock himself out on the hard grey basalt. But what was Taylor doing walking along the parapet? He was coming from the other direction and the most direct way to the YMCA did not lie along the front of the building.

I went the way I'd have gone if I was Taylor, skirting around the back. At the stage door of the Concert Hall, I found the same guy on duty who'd let me into the

Arts Ministry the previous morning, and got him to unlock the YMCA. The same air of scrofulous melancholy pervaded the place, but not the same silence. As the lift juddered open at the third floor, Lou Reed advanced down the corridor to meet me.

He was coming from one of the formerly locked rooms. A woman in bib-and-brace overalls stuck her head through the open door and watched me advance, her eyes narrowing. 'If you're a journalist,' she said, 'you're a bit late. I already told that lot who were here yesterday everything I know. Which is nothing. The guy was a hermit.' She had a stick of charcoal in her hand. Behind her I could see big sheets of parchment paper taped to the walls. They were covered in black squiggles that might, given a couple of million years, have eventually evolved into horses. Or dogs. Or giraffes.

'If I look like a journalist, I can assure you it's not intentional.' I nodded towards Taylor's end of the corridor. 'I'm a sort of friend.' Well, Taylor was in no position to contradict me.

'Oh,' she said, scowling. 'I didn't . . .' She was going to say she didn't know he had any, but stopped herself in time. 'Didn't have a lot to do with him. Like I said, he kept to himself.'

'There was a painting he was working on last time I was here,' I said. 'I was sort of interested in it.'

'Help yourself,' she said, turning her back in disgust. 'Everyone else has.'

When I opened Taylor's door I discovered what she meant. Taylor's rooms had been plundered of almost anything of value. The camp stove had been nicked, the microwave oven, the desk lamp, even jars of used paintbrushes. Most of the books had gone from the brick-and-board case. A half-dozen back copies of *Veneer* remained, a thin tome entitled *The Necessity of Australian Art* and a dog-eared copy of *A Fierce Vision*. I thumbed through it. A sheet of tracing paper marked the plate of *Our Home*, the principal details precisely transferred to a pencil-drawn grid. Using such a template, a competent draughtsman could easily have enlarged the image to actual size and transferred it onto canvas. It told me nothing I didn't already know, that Marcus Taylor had whipped up a pretty fair version of *Our Home*. Whether it was his first or second attempt, why he'd done it, and where it had gone, were all questions that remained unanswered.

Taylor's dog-eared little collection of photographs was still in the desk drawer. When I compared them with the sketch in Fiona's book, there wasn't much doubt that Victor Szabo's life-drawing model was the woman in the photo. The young hippy that could have been Taylor could still have been Taylor. Szabo was still definitely Szabo. I put the snaps in my pocket.

The cheap plastic-covered stamp album was still there, too, with its paltry contents of low-denomination recent releases. Stamp collecting was a hobby that had never captured my imagination. But waste not, want not. If Red didn't fancy the album, some other child might. That little girl, Grace, for example. Philately might not get me everywhere, but it would give me an excuse to go calling on her mother.

The bankbook was still slotted into the crevasse between the desk and the wall where I'd dropped it in my haste to flee. I hooked it out with a bent coat-hanger and found myself looking at the most interesting thing I'd seen all day.

Critically unappreciated he might have been, but Marcus Taylor was clearly finding a market for something he was doing. Over the previous six months, he'd made a number of deposits. The sums varied from twelve hundred to four thousand dollars, totalling nearly twenty thousand. Not a bad little nest egg for a man whose grant application form said that his sole income was unemployment benefits.

I pondered its meaning. But not for long. Red would be wondering what had become of me. I dropped the bankbook back behind the desk. It felt like evidence. Of what, I didn't know. Sticking the stamp album under my arm, I headed back along the side of the National Gallery. A gang of young hoons was stampeding down the footpath, pushing a shopping trolley full pelt. One of them was crouched inside the cart, gripping the sides for dear life, screaming insanely at the kid doing the steering.

'Help!' he was screaming. 'Murder! Murder!'

THERE WAS only one S. Fleet in the White Pages with a CBD address. Little Lonsdale Street. The western end, down towards the railway yards. Funky. Low rent. About the right place for a loft. Fifteen minutes walk from the Arts Centre. A five-minute drive.

'Wait here,' I told Red, parking around the corner. 'I won't be long.'

'Shoosh,' he said. His head was bent and his thumbs were furiously manipulating the liquid crystal blips of his hand-held electronic game. 'I'm going for the record.' The stamp album, understandably, had failed to impress. It lay discarded on the back seat.

'Ten minutes,' I said. 'Then we'll go have some fun, just you and me.' He didn't look up.

The Aldershot Building was six floors of faded glory, a Beaux Arts chocolate box dating from the boom of the 1880s. Barristers from the nearby law courts might once have had their chambers here, wool merchants, pastoral companies, shipping agents, stockbrokers. Then the boom had gone bust. The mercantile bourgeoisie moved out and the wholesale jewellers and sheet-music publishers moved in. In time, as the pigeon shit mounted on the curlicued plinths of the facade, these became two-man tailor shops and fishy photographers, doll doctors and dental technicians. Eventually, the strict prescriptions of the fire department had driven away even these modest entrepreneurs.

But the Law of Unintended Consequences supersedes even the Prevention of Fire Act and the tenants squeezed out by the prohibitive cost of overhead sprinklers and CO_2 extinguishers had been replaced by bootleg gayboy hairdressers, speakeasy desktop publishers and loft dwellers – all of them on handshake leases with blind-eye clauses. At the Aldershot, no-one was really there and if they were they were just visiting.

Flyers for dance clubs were taped to the wall of the small ground-floor vestibule. Among them, beside the lift, was a much-amended hand-written list of tenants. Salina Fleet was on the sixth floor. I took the lift, a modern job not more than forty years old with cylindrical bakelite buttons that stuck out like the dugs on a black sow. It opened straight onto the corridor. Salina's was the first door along.

She didn't answer at first. I knocked, waited, knocked again. A reggae beat was coming from somewhere, emanating from the very bones of the building, dreams of Jamaica. I knocked again and was about to turn away when the door opened a chink and Sal peered tentatively through the gap.

'Oh, it's you.' Her mouth gave me a jumpy, automatic smile and her eyes tried to find their way around me into the hall. They were cold and glistening like she'd just been polishing them and had to put them back in to answer the door and they weren't warmed up yet. Her once-fruited lips were thin and pasty. Unconsciously raising a little finger to them, she tore off a half-moon of nail.

'Don't worry,' I said, harmlessly. 'I haven't come to take you up on your offer.'

The skin was drawn tight across the bridge of her nose, accentuating the bird-like cast of her face. It was a face about five years older than when I'd first seen it. She didn't open the door any further and she didn't invite me in.

'Sorry to drop by out of the blue,' I said. 'But I've heard that they're pretty well decided that Marcus's death wasn't suicide. Thought I should let you know.'

She accepted the news as though already reconciled to the possibility. Her neck flexed in a tiny bob, pecking an invisible grain of wheat. 'Part of me hoped so, in a way. I can't blame myself for an accident, can I?'

'I was a bit abrupt yesterday,' I said. 'If you'd like to talk about it.' I looked at the floor. 'As a friend.'

She reached out through the gap in the door and put her hand softly on my chest. 'You're a sweet guy, Murray. Really, you are. But I'd rather be alone.' She gave me the most bathos-drenched look ever practised in front of a mirror, sighed heavily and stepped back.

She'd tried that one before. Last time, it had nearly worked. Before the door could shut, I had my foot in it. Through the crack, I could see a bed. On the bed was a suitcase. 'Going somewhere, Sal?'

'How dare you!' she spat through the gap, putting her shoulder to the door. 'You can't just force your way in.'

My thirty-kilo advantage sat inert against the door. 'Talk to me,' I said. 'Please.'

The pressure on the door diminished somewhat. 'This official, or what?'

'Or what,' I said.

She backed away silently, letting the door fall open. Her lack of pretence at hospitality was refreshingly unrehearsed.

What Salina called her loft was a large high-ceilinged room that might have once been a typing college classroom or the workshop of a manufacturing milliner. Chipboard partitions had been installed to create separate kitchen and bathroom areas, the floor had been sanded back and the place stocked with oddments of retro furniture of the Zsa Zsa Gabor On Safari variety. The wardrobe was a metal shop-display rack on castors, half empty. The bed took up the rest of the space, unmade beneath a scattering of clothes and a small, half-packed suitcase. The ashtray contained about five thousand half-smoked green-tinged butts.

'Nice,' I said.

My opinion was a matter of supreme indifference to Salina Fleet. 'What's this all about?' she demanded.

A little of the old Sal had returned. She was wearing Capri pants with a pink gingham shirt knotted at the midriff and hoop earrings. She was still in mourning, though. The Capri pants were black. A bit of bluff might have got me through the door, but it wouldn't get me any further. She'd backed herself against a window sill and folded her arms tight. She wasn't going to take any bullying.

I wasn't going to give her any. By way of emphasising that my intentions were honourable, I turned my back to the bed and perched on the arm of a zebra-patterned sofa. 'Suicide or accident, Marcus Taylor's death is a hot story. You're not the only one the press have been talking to. All sorts of stories are flying around. My job involves keeping one step ahead of the pack.'

That was only part of it, of course. In the final analysis, it wasn't the Protestant work ethic that was gunning my engine. It was my frail ego. I had the distinct impression that my string was being jerked. By whom and to what end was not yet apparent. But I didn't like it. Not one little bit. 'You being on the Visual Arts Advisory Panel, I thought you might be able to advise me.'

'Stories?' Feigning nonchalance, she put a cigarette in her mouth and flicked a disposable lighter. 'What stories?'

'Let's start with yesterday first. You went to the YMCA to get a picture, right? But someone had beaten you to it.' Her lighter wouldn't fire. She kept flicking the wheel with her thumb. I got out mine, walked over to the window and lit both of us up. 'Right?'

'I told you.' She exhaled Kooly. 'I went to get some personal things.'

'Toothbrush? IUD? Little things that slip easily into a folio case.'

'And to make my private goodbyes to Marcus.'

'By coming on to me?'

'I was upset. Vulnerable.'

We wouldn't get far heading down this track. I took myself back to the zebra. 'Tell me about Marcus. How did you get involved with him?'

She shrugged. 'How does anybody? We met last

winter. At an exhibition. He tried to lobby me for a grant. He was hopeless – insecure and arrogant at the same time.' All the things that women can't resist. 'I was on the rebound. We ended up in bed. You know how it is.'

I nearly did. 'And so he got his grant.'

That was below the belt. 'It was a committee decision, based on artistic merit.'

Now we were getting somewhere. 'Good artist, was he? As good as his father, Victor Szabo?'

'Where on earth did you get that idea?' Apparently the suggestion was ludicrous.

'Like I said. Stories are flying around.' I took the photos out of my pocket and showed her the snap of Szabo with the kid that might have been Taylor. 'Like father, like son. And from what I've heard, there wasn't just a taste for the booze in old man Szabo's genes. Marcus inherited a dab hand for the brush. He could knock out a passable version of almost anything, I understand. Not that I'm any judge, but what I've seen of his work certainly confirms that view.'

Her eyes widened. 'You've seen it?'

'It?'

She didn't say anything for a while. She was too busy giving me the slow burn. It could have popped corn at five paces. Lucky I was wearing my asbestos skin.

When that didn't work, she tossed her head back and studied the way her cigarette smoke rose in a lazy coil towards the ceiling. I studied it, too. Ascending effortlessly in a solid unbroken column, it reached higher and higher, an ever lengthening filament of spun wire, stretching up towards the embossed tin panels far above. Then, just as its destination seemed within reach, it wavered, broke into an ephemeral mass of swirling spirals, and dissipated.

'There was never any misrepresentation on my part,' she said abruptly. 'I want that clearly understood.'

'Absolutely.'

She started pacing then, stalking the right approach. 'If this thing gets taken any further, I want protection.'

Protection? From whom? What the hell was she talking about? 'I understand,' I said. 'You don't want to be the one that takes the fall?'

Her point taken, Salina moved into negotiating mode. 'Damn right,' she said. 'Marcus's image production was a perfectly valid form of post-modern discourse, right out there on the cutting edge. His pastiche-parodies of actual artworks effectively deconstructed the commonly held notions of value, authenticity and signature. They were a critical response to the pre-eminence of the so-called famous artist.' She paced, delivering a dissertation. 'His pictures were never mere copies. If his images were subsequently misread as such by others, that's not my problem. It was not my role to impose a monopoly on meaning. Legitimate appropriations, that's what they were. There was never any attempt on my part to pass them off as originals.'

Sometimes, not often, but sometimes, it's as simple as that. *Eek and ye shall find*. Unless my grasp of art-speak was even more tenuous than I feared, Salina Fleet had just told me that Marcus Taylor had been knocking up fakes and that she'd been marketing them for him.

'And these "appropriations"' – I hooked my fingers around the word and rolled it over my palate, savouring its supple resonance – 'included a "pastiche" of Victor Szabo? A "parody" of *Our Home*, perfect right down to the engine number on the motor-mower?' She nodded. I was on the right track. 'Like you say, a perfectly valid form of artistic practice. So where is it now?'

That pulled her up short. 'Christ!' she gasped. 'You mean you don't know. I thought . . .'

'You thought what?'

But the shutters had come down. She'd been trading on the assumption that I knew something I didn't, that I knew who had the duplicate Szabo. Her hands were shaking. She crossed to the door and flung it open. 'Get out,' she hissed. 'You bastard.' It came to me that she was very much afraid. When she wasn't acting she was quite convincing. 'Out. Out.'

'Who do you want protection from? I can help.'

'Just leave,' she commanded icily, her mouth again tearing at a fingernail. 'I refuse to comment further without a lawyer present. If you don't get out, I'll start screaming.'

She didn't give me much alternative but to do as she asked.

'Under the circumstances,' she said, as I stepped past her. 'I think it best if I resign from the Visual Arts Advisory Panel.' Since trafficking in dodgy artworks was hardly an ideal qualification for membership, that sounded like a good idea. I didn't get to tell her so. She'd already shut the door.

Fifteen minutes had elapsed since I'd abandoned Red to his computer game. A couple more wouldn't hurt. I called the lift up, pushed the ground floor button and stepped back out. Otis elevator smacked his big rubber lips together, growled and slunk away. I leaned against the wall and lit a cigarette.

It had burned to the filter when Salina came out her door. She'd put on a pair of gold sling-back sandals and was carrying the small suitcase. She saw me and stopped. She was about to say something unpleasant when the lift arrived. It made a clunking noise and its doors slid open. Standing inside was Spider Webb.

Old blank face himself, shades and all, flexing his jaw like a punch-drunk pinhead. He registered first me, then Salina, ten metres beyond. I registered her, too. She looked like a trapped animal. I stepped in front of the lift, blocking Spider's way. He stood there, legs apart, sizing me up. The doors began to close. I stepped inside and the doors slid shut behind me.

None of the buttons were depressed. He'd been coming to this floor. Where else? I punched the ground floor button with the side of my fist and we began to descend. I turned to face the door, the way you always do in a lift. 'You really get around, don't you?' I said.

His hand shot past me and hit the red emergency stop button. The lift slammed to an immediate halt, throwing me off balance. Before I could get it back, Spider had his forearm against my chest and my back pressed against the wall. 'What the fuck you playing at?' he snarled, breathing Arrowmint all over me.

Under the circumstance, I assumed the question was essentially rhetorical. I kicked him in the shins. He stepped delicately sideways as though avoiding a spilt drink and rammed the ball of his open hand into my solar plexus. I got a little irrigated in the visual department at that point and would have liked a little sit down, if at all possible. 'Ummphh,' I said. 'Whodja ooatfa?'

Spider's face was pushed so far into mine that when he opened his mouth I read the maker's mark on his silver fillings. Any closer and we'd have to get engaged. All I could see of his eyes, though, was my own reflection in those fucking mirror shades. Five times in three days I'd seen him, and still I hadn't seen his eyes. A regular Ray Charles, he was. By the look of the reflections staring back at me, he was doing a pretty good job of putting the wind up me. 'You know what's wrong with you, Whelan?' he said.

By then I knew better than to even attempt an answer. I just stood there, nurturing my inner cry-baby and waiting for the liquidity in my bowels to abate. Spider adopted the softly solicitous tones of a psychotic sergeant major. 'You get in over your head. That's what's wrong with you. You gotta learn to take the hint. Lay off where you're not wanted.'

He slammed one of Otis's buttons and the lift resumed its descent. Spider stepped back then and stood, legs apart, casually waiting for it to reach the ground floor. 'You fucking ape,' I said. 'I'm supposed to be impressed, am I?'

Actually I was, deeply. In my line of work, it's reasonably rare to be strong-armed by a gun-toting thug. That sort of thing usually only happens in federal politics. 'I'll go to Eastlake. I'll have your job.' It sounded pathetic, but it was the best I could do. Fuck the macho shit.

The lift hit rock-bottom and the doors slid open. 'You wouldn't do that,' said Spider, cheerfully. 'Not to an old mate.' He made like a head waiter, ushering me out of the lift ahead of him. 'And you shouldn't leave your kid sitting by himself in the car like that. You'll get done for child neglect.'

We stood there, looking at each other. Him in the lift, me outside. Then he smiled. The kind of smile that could stop a clock. He was still smiling when lift doors slid shut.

I turned then and ran. I ran out the front door of the Aldershot Building, down the hill and around the corner. At the intersection up ahead, Salina Fleet was getting into the back of a cab. She must have come down the fire stairs. I hit the Charade at a sprint.

'You should have been here, Dad,' accused Red bitterly, his eyes downcast, his little hands twitching ceaselessly. 'I got 20,000 points.'

RUSSELL STREET Police Head-quarters was straight out of Gotham City, a brick wall with a thousand blind windows and an RKO radio mast on the roof. Calling all cars.

As a functionary of the incumbent government, albeit an insignificant one, I could not but regard the police as my colleagues. Benign and efficient upholders of the rule of law. Our boys in blue. In other parts of our great nation, the rozzers were thick-necked bribe-takers, rugby-playing racist bully-boys, brothel creepers. But nobody said that about the Victoria Police. Defenders of widows and orphans they were. Protectors of the innocent.

But not necessarily of a ministerial adviser with spiralling suspicions, insufficient grounds for the laying of charges and a child's safety to think about. Quite a lot to think about, as a matter of fact. We drove past Russell Street and kept going. 'How about a movie?' I said. Something we could do together. Somewhere cool and dark where we could hide and I could start drawing some mental maps.

'*Die Hard*?' said Red. '*Young Guns*?'

Whatever happened to Pippi Longstocking? Maybe the movies weren't such a good idea. We kicked around a few other potential game plans. We decided to go exploring again.

We covered a lot of territory that afternoon. We covered school, friends, holidays. We covered Wendy. My former consort had taken up with a prosecutor from the New South Wales Crown Law Department. His name was Richard. You didn't need to be Clifford Possum Japaljarri to connect the dots there. 'What's he like?' I asked.

Wendy was a go-getter. It was her go-getting that had got rid of me. In our marriage of equals, some were more equal than others. We didn't fight. We weren't unfaithful – not that I knew about. Wendy was just moving faster than me, aiming elsewhere. It took me nearly ten years to figure that out, her a little less. If this Richard could make her happy, fine. A happy Wendy would be a sight to behold.

'He's okay, I guess,' said Red, an endorsement so insipid it brought a smile to my lips and nearly broke my heart. This Richard might be around for years. Wendy could shack up with whoever she liked, but if Dicky Boy started calling himself Red's stepfather there'd be hell to pay.

Equipped for high adventure in sandshoes and sunscreen, we followed the same route as the previous afternoon. Out the freeway, past the roadside flower vendors, the orchards and stud farms, the go-cart tracks and vintage car rallies. At the Sugarloaf Reservoir, we bought sandwiches and sodas and ate them in the sausage-scented smoke of the public barbecues. The crowds were out in force, clannish Croats and cacophonous Cambodians and stubby-clutching Ockers. Swimming was prohibited and once we'd walked across the weir, thrown rocks into tomorrow's drinking water and watched the spillway fishermen not catching trout, we struck out for more challenging terrain.

The humidity was 110 per cent, the air as thick as Faye's tapenade, wet as a sauna. The sky oozed over us like a clammy slug, threatening to rain, not delivering. At the Christmas Hills fire station, the sheds sat empty. The brigade was out on a call. A troop of Scouts were filling their water-bottles at the tap. Red disdained them from behind the window of a feebly air conditioned Japanese hatchback.

A kilometre short of Giles Aubrey's private road, we parked in a turn-around and skittled on foot down the wooded incline towards the dull sheen of water. A cascade of rocks and leaves dribbled down the slope ahead of us. The river was slow-moving and not much cooler or wetter than the surrounding air. We stripped to our togs and rushed in, thrashing and splashing and laughing.

Half an hour later, rock-hopping our way upstream, we disturbed a full-grown brown snake. In a single fluid motion, it slithered across our path, long as a broom-handle, flicking its tongue. Watching it go to ground in the fissure between two boulders, Red backed against me. 'Wow,' he whispered, awed and not a little afraid. 'Tark will be pissed he missed this.'

A tad more respectful of our environment, we pushed on. Red was still keen, if a little less gung-ho. Even when he charged ahead to blaze our trail, he kept me in sight, looking back over his shoulder to make sure I was keeping up. It grew darker. The clouds were engorged eggplants, roiling and stewing, close enough to touch. A dry stick of lightning forked across the sky.

We waded out of a narrow ravine onto the dry sand-bar downhill from Giles Aubrey's place. Red, spying the rope where he and Tarquin had played reckless Tarzans, ran ahead.

Halfway there, he pulled up sharp, eyes riveted to the ground. 'Dad,' he called sharply, poised between backward retreat and stark immobility. 'Come quick. Snake attack.'

A man lay face-down on the exposed river-bed beside the eroded wall of the bank. One arm was bent behind his torso, the other twisted behind his neck. It was not a natural position and he wasn't moving.

I took Giles Aubrey by the shoulder and rolled him over. He was as light as balsa and dead as a dodo. His face had been pressed flat against the dry quartz sand of the river-bed and was flecked with grains of mica, diamond dust against the blotched pink parchment of his skin.

How long he had been lying there was impossible to tell. He wasn't warm but neither was he particularly cold. How he had got there was easier to determine. A small avalanche of leaves and pebbles lay scattered around his sandalled feet. He had come tumbling down the near-vertical incline of the riverbank, a drop of perhaps ten metres. The fall had been a nasty one and from the ungainly contortion of the limbs, I guessed that death had come on impact.

Red had found a stick and mounted guard. 'Can you see the snake?'

'He fell.' I pointed up towards the vegetable patch, showing what had happened.

'Yuk,' said Red, disappointed. 'Gross.'

Gross indeed. Leaving Aubrey's body where it lay in sand scuffed and churned from the boys' play the previous day, we climbed the embankment and back-tracked to where his descent would have begun. The old man's duck-headed walking stick lay on the ground at the top of the bank. His prostrate form lay imme-diately below. Picking up the cane, I silently pointed out the skidmarks that traced a path down the slope. Red nodded gravely, as though absorbing some impor-tant moral lesson. This is what happens if you go too close to the edge.

A crack like a gunshot split the air, the temperature dropped ten degrees and the atmosphere condensed itself into raindrops. One by one they began to fall, so slow you could count them. They were as big as golf balls, so fat and heavy they raised craters in the dust. Then all at once it was pouring. Rain churned the earth, turning it to mud.

We dashed for the shelter of the house. Red beat me. We were both already saturated. When I came through the door, he was at the phone, offering me the hand-piece. I assumed it had been ringing when he burst inside, the sound drowned in the downpour. I put it to my ear. 'Hello,' I said.

There was no-one on the line, just a ringing tone, terminating abruptly in the faint hiss of an answering machine tape. 'Thank you for calling,' announced a patrician voice. 'Regretfully, I am unable to respond personally at this time. Please leave a message.' Short, to the point, polite, confident. Phillip Veale.

I hung up slowly, my brow furrowed into a question. 'Last number re-dial,' Red explained to the family idiot. 'They always do it on *Murder She Wrote*.'

'What makes you think it's murder?'

Red shrugged. He didn't. He was just following correct television procedure. 'Now dial 911,' he told me.

'Triple zero in Australia,' I informed him, dialling. 'It was an accident. He was very old and he fell over. And don't touch anything else, okay?'

As I finished giving the emergency operator the details, I became aware of a noise. A repetitive thunking. A low-pitched pulse, barely audible over the drum beat of the rain on the roof. Hanging up, I cocked my ears and tracked the sound. It was coming from the stereo, one of those Bang & Olufsen jobs like an anodised aluminium tea-tray. Aubrey must have had a thousand records, the edges of their covers squared off in perfect order in a set of custom-built timber shelves. I lifted the stylus arm onto its cradle and picked the record up by its edges. Faure's *Requiem*, von Somevun conducting. A little light listening for a sticky Sunday arvo. I slipped the record into its sleeve.

In Aubrey's wardrobe, I found a gaberdine overcoat. By the time I'd scrambled down the bank, it seemed like a pointless gesture. His clothes and hair were drenched and little rivulets of rainwater were forking and branching around his twisted limbs. The correct procedure, probably, was to leave him where he lay.

Let him lie there, open-mouthed amid the puddles until appropriately qualified people arrived and did what appropriately qualified people do.

But I'd taken tea with this man, eaten one of his gingernut snaps. Not to have picked him up out of the dirt would have felt like a calculated act of disrespect. Of myself as much as of him. Besides which, the river was beginning to rise. Rain-pitted water was inching towards the body. The cause of his death was patently obvious, written in the clearly visible trajectory of his fall down the riverbank. I stood for a moment looking down at the second wet body I had seen in as many days. Then I draped the coat over Aubrey and carried him up to the house. I think the coat weighed more.

'What you told me yesterday,' I asked, as we trudged together through the smell of wet earth and the drumming of rain on leaves. 'What was true and what was lies? And what did you talk about with Phillip Veale?' But Giles Aubrey made no answer.

If moving the body was a problem, nobody told me. Nobody told me much at all, really. I'd only just finished laying Aubrey out on his bed when the ambulance arrived. The two-man crew ignored the rain which had eased to a steaming drizzle. I didn't really know the man, I explained. My son had found the body.

'These old people,' said the driver, not unsympathetically. 'They do insist on living alone.'

The label on a bottle of pills on the bedside table bore the name of a local doctor known to the paramedics. She was phoned and agreed to come immediately. She would, I was told, sign as to cause of death. A nearby undertaker was also called. Procedures were in motion. Red and I were superfluous. We'd walked halfway back to the Charade before I realised that they hadn't even asked my name.

Our drive back into town was subdued. My attention was focused on Sunday drivers, poor visibility and slippery roads. 'You handled that well,' I told Red. 'Not many kids your age have seen a dead body. How do you feel?'

He fiddled with the radio, unfussed, immortal. 'Life's a bitch,' he said. 'Then you die.' The catchphrase in my mind remained unspoken. 'Did he jump? Or was he pushed?'

We made it to the movies, after all. Not *Die Hard* but *Moonwalker*. First we ate cheap Chinese, then we sat side by side in the dark and watched Michael Jackson scratch his crotch for ninety minutes. My mind floated free, searching for a thread to cling to in the maze of possibilities, to bind the fragments of fact and conjecture together.

Marcus Taylor makes a minor scene at the Centre for Modern Art. What were his words? 'This edifice is built on a lie.' Six hours later, he's dead. A note found in his pocket raves about corrupt hands on the levers of power. 'You do not know what you are buying.' A picture vanishes from his studio.

Salina Fleet, my lucky break turned sour. She claims to be Taylor's lover and blames herself for his suicide. Then she plays down the relationship and accepts without surprise the proposition that his death was accidental. Volunteering the information that she was selling his 'appropriations' and demanding protection, she realises she's said more than she should and clams up. Then she flees in fear. Not from me. Her bag was half-packed before I arrived. From Spider Webb.

Spider, me old mate. The hot-shot bodyguard warning me off. Off what? The sixty thousand dollar question. Or the six hundred thousand dollar question? The common link between Salina and Spider – Taylor's vanished painting, *Our Home* Mark 2. And Lloyd Eastlake? Where did he come in to the picture? Or didn't he? And Giles Aubrey, with his incredible tale of undetected fakery. Was he, literally, the fall guy?

By the time Michael Jackson transmogrified into a flying saucer and went into orbit, I knew one thing for sure. It was something I'd known before we came into the theatre. As long as Red was in town, as long as there was the slightest chance that Spider Webb's implicit threat was real, the only business I'd be minding was my own.

Back outside on the street, the drizzle had stopped and the cloud ceiling had lifted. 'Look,' said Red, pointing upwards. 'Michael Jackson.'

I looked where he was pointing, to where the moon glowed like a candle behind a paper screen. It hung low in the sky, immediately above the towering steel skeleton of the Karlcraft Centre. 'This edifice is built on a lie,' I heard Marcus Taylor saying.

'Tricked ya,' crowed Red. As we crossed the street to the car, I reached out and took his hand. He wasn't such a big boy that he wouldn't let me hold it.

M Y NEW desk was real wood. My new chair had adjustable lumbar support. The new morning was washed clean from the night's rain. The outlook for Monday was a mild, blue-skyed twenty-eight degrees. My shoes were shined and just enough phone-message slips had accumulated to confirm that I was a man worth knowing.

But turning up at 8.45 a.m. on my first official day at my new job with a pair of ten-year-olds in tow was hardly the ideal way to strike fear into the hearts of the Arts Ministry pen-pushers.

Red was with me because his flight back to Sydney didn't leave until 9.20 that evening and, for a few hours at least, our quality time had to take a back seat to my day job. Tarquin Curnow came along because of a deal I'd cut with Faye and Leo the night before.

The predicament we faced that morning was a common one for the time of year. All over town, parental noses were due back at the grindstone. But the school term had not yet resumed. For another week, mothers and fathers would be forced to improvise child-care arrangements. Fortunately, Leo was employed at the university, a place where the concept of work is still pending definition. We agreed that if he could slip away at lunchtime and mind the boys for the afternoon, I would keep them occupied for the morning. Exactly how, I wasn't sure.

'You two can play computer games on my Macintosh,' said Trish, who'd already set up Checkpoint Charlie at Agnelli's door. 'Just keep the noise down and don't get in my way.' Trish was still adopting a wait-and-see attitude towards me, but she'd had a soft spot for Red ever since he was a baby.

The cool change had made it possible to sleep comfortably for the first time in a week. And I hadn't wasted the opportunity by dreaming of Spider Webb. One of the first lessons you learn in a political party is patience, to defer to *force majeure*, keep your powder dry and bide your time. I'd decided to bide mine until precisely 9.30 that evening, the moment at which Red's plane would be airborne and cruising north at an altitude of 10,000 metres and a speed of 500 knots. As of then, and not before, Spider Webb and the mystery of the missing painting would be at the top of my agenda.

In the meantime, while the boys sat in a corner of the ministerial reception area defending the galaxy from space invaders, I had a different fish to fry.

But first I had to catch it. Since my original idea of putting Angelo Agnelli and Max Karlin together and monitoring developments had proved abortive, the time had come to start asking direct questions about my boss's move into the world of campaign finance. I went to my new desk, picked up my new telephone and rang Duncan Keogh at party headquarters. 'Murray Whelan here,

Duncan,' I said. 'Calling from Angelo Agnelli's office.'

That was as far as I got. 'Jesus,' cut in Keogh, irritably. 'Every man and his dog in on it now, are they? Tell Agnelli not to be so damn impatient. A day or so isn't going to make any difference. If we withdraw the term deposits before maturity there'll be penalties. As to the cash account balance of' – he shuffled some papers around – 'of $207,860, that was invested in Obelisk Trust on Friday afternoon, just as Angelo instructed. Tell him he'll have to be satisfied with that for the time being.'

My new chair was ergonomically correct, but that didn't stop me nearly falling out of it. In itself, the idea of getting a better rate of return on party savings was a good idea. Dickhead Duncan should have done it himself, months ago. And if Obelisk paid the best rate, so much the better. Keep it in the family. But a 6 per cent boost in interest wouldn't fill the coffers to the extent Angelo had been talking about. If he was moving this fast on basic housekeeping matters, what was he doing on the door-knocking front? What favours was he offering where the big donations were to be found?

As I struggled to digest what Keogh had just told me, Agnelli himself appeared at my door. He pulled his cuff back and tapped the face of his wristwatch. 'Veale's briefing,' he mouthed. 'Coming?'

'Angelo's here with me now,' I said down the phone. 'I'm sure he appreciates your efficiency.' Abruptly hanging up, I made a face like a man who'd just disposed of a nuisance. Agnelli, leading off in the direction of the conference room, showed no interest in who I'd been talking to.

The Briefing-of-the-Incoming-Minister ceremony was a text-book exercise. Veale and a brace of deputy directors laid bare the ministry's policies, resources and processes in a professional and lucid manner. Agnelli nodded sagely throughout. I took notes. 'Any questions?' said Veale, after an hour.

The question I most wanted to ask Veale remained unasked. The mystery of Giles Aubrey's phone call would have to wait for a more appropriate occasion. I asked a few little ones instead, just to show I was on the ball. About the Library Services Review Working Party and the International Festival Economic Impact Task Force. About the advisory panels that recommended grants. I picked one at random. 'The Visual Arts Advisory Panel, say. What's the procedure governing selection and appointment of members?'

'Individuals with expertise are nominated by the panel chairperson.' One of Veale's deputies answered for him. 'Subject to the minister's approval, of course.'

Which would be given without a second thought. No minister had the time or inclination to vet the membership of the hundred and one committees needed to keep a healthy bureaucracy ticking over. He or she was guided by the judgment of the relevant chairperson. In this case, Lloyd Eastlake.

That about wrapped up the briefing. Ange took me into his office and spread a copy of the tabloid *Sun* across his desk. 'Seen this?' he demanded.

I'd scanned the newspapers over breakfast and found nothing about the floater in the moat. For one dreadful moment I thought I'd missed something, that Agnelli was about to bore it up me for dereliction of duty. But he had the paper open at a section I never bothered to read, the social page. *New cultural supremo Angelo Agnelli lends his presence to charity bash in aid of the Centre for Modern Art*, said the caption. The photograph showed Ange standing between Max Karlin and Fiona Lambert, *Our Home* in the background.

'How's that for an auspicious start?' glowed the new supremo. 'Lining me up with Max Karlin was one of your better ideas.'

For a moment, I was tempted to inform Agnelli that I'd overheard his conversation with Duncan Keogh, that I knew he'd ordered the investment of a fair whack of the party's fighting fund in Obelisk Trust. State my concerns and do my best to convince him that he was headed into dangerous waters. But my years of handling Agnelli had taught me that direct contradiction was a tactic unlikely to succeed. You can't push on a rope, I reminded myself.

'Nothing about corruption in high places, I see.' Agnelli cast yet another admiring glance at his photograph and closed the paper. 'Looks like that body in the moat business is dead in the water.'

The press was quiet on the subject, I admitted. 'At the moment.'

'Speaking of water,' Agnelli went on. 'I'm off on an inspection and orientation tour of catchment resources and storage facilities. The Water Supply Commission is laying on a helicopter. Won't be back until tomorrow morning.' A joy ride into the hills, in other words. Come lunchtime, he'd be assessing the water quality of Lake Eildon from a pair of water-skis behind the official reservoir-inspection vehicle. 'Think you can see to it that the wheels don't fall off the Arts while I'm gone?'

Bugger the Arts, I thought. With Agnelli out of the office, the coast would be clear to escape and make the most of what little time Red and I still had together. It could be months before I saw my boy again. 'I've got more than enough to keep me busy,' I said.

'Not too busy to write a speech for me, I hope,' said Agnelli. 'I see from the diary I'm booked to open some art exhibition at the Trades Hall tomorrow evening.' By profession, Angelo was a lawyer. Early in his career, he'd specialised in industrial accident compensation cases and he still saw himself as the worker's friend. 'I'd like to say something about ordinary working people enjoying the benefits of high culture,' he instructed. 'And put in lots of jokes.'

I'd just fed Agnelli into the lift with my assurance that his speech would be a masterpiece when Phillip Veale's secretary buttonholed me in the foyer and told me the Director would like a word. Veale looked up from behind his paperwork with the unfussable equanimity of a kung fu master. 'Shut the door, please, Murray.'

When I turned back, he was perching on front of his desk, pinching the crease at his knee so the action of sitting down did not abrade the fabric of his trousers. 'The minister was satisfied with this morning's little show and tell, do you think?'

'A polished performance,' I admitted. 'It will be interesting to see the impact of Angelo's plans for a comprehensive organisational restructure.'

Veale acknowledged my little drollery with a sigh of resignation. Another minister, another restructure. At the briefing, he had been genial but proper. No ironic inflections, no knowing asides. A man with a finely honed sense of the correct demeanour. Now, pressing his fingertips together, he assumed an attitude of hesitation, as if pondering the most tactful approach to a ticklish issue. He let me share his equivocation for a moment. 'A word of advice,' he began, feeling his way. 'If I may be permitted?'

Sure, I indicated. Fire away.

'As a relative newcomer to the administration of the Arts, you, no doubt, will be learning the ropes for some time. And you will, I fully understand, be keen to cultivate diverse sources of information. In doing this, it would be wise to keep in mind just how small and incestuous the arts world can be. Egos are involved, many of them remarkably fragile. Hidden agendas abound. Insinuation and gossip proliferate.'

So far, he wasn't telling me anything I couldn't reasonably be expected to know already. I wondered where this little chat of ours was going.

Veale got to the point. 'Giles Aubrey rang me on Saturday. He told me that you had approached him seeking information of a confidential and sensitive nature. He enquired as to your official status. I told him that you were a member of the Arts Minister's staff.' One of several, the inflection suggested. Not necessarily an important one.

He paused, expecting that I might want to explain myself. Instead, I had a question. 'Did he tell you what I wanted to talk to him about?'

A chastising tone entered Veale's voice. 'As I told you, Giles and I knew each other quite well, at one time. But it's been some time since we've spoken and I, for my part, had no wish to encourage further conversation. Frankly, I found it hard to understand what you hoped to gain by subjecting yourself to the gossip and insinuation of anyone as notoriously self-serving as Giles Aubrey.'

Ah so. I should have realised that Aubrey would check my credentials before talking to me. That explained the phone call. Unfortunately, by the sound of it, he also used the opportunity to re-open an old wound of some kind. Veale now had me on the back foot, and for no good reason.

It was my turn to sound miffed. 'I can assure you,' I said. 'I approached Giles Aubrey on an entirely professional basis, to consult him regarding the valuation of a painting. If he suggested otherwise, he was misleading you. In any case, my contact with him was brief. He died yesterday. A fall, apparently.'

That took the starch out of Veale's shirt. 'Oh,' he said.

A contemplative muse brushed her wings across his features. His thoughts began to turn inwards. Sensing the private nature of his reflections, I made some vague bridge-repairing noises about appreciating his point and quietly withdrew. The sound of crunching eggshells rose from underfoot.

It was past 10.30. The boys were beginning to tire of massacring aliens on Trish's computer. Casting a quick eye over my telephone message slips, I reached for my jacket, ready to go. Just then, reception buzzed to say that I had a visitor, a Mr Micaelis. Assuming him to be an early-bird hoping for an unscheduled appointment, I went out to tell him he was out of luck.

Micaelis was somewhere in his mid-twenties, dark-suited and smelling of Brut 33. He had the slightly put-upon look of the second son of a migrant family. His older brother drove the family truck. His younger brother was studying medicine or architecture. The big plans for him had run as far as accountancy or town planning. Accountancy, judging by the tie. He didn't seem the arty type.

'How ya going?' he said cheerfully. 'Reckon you could spare us a minute?' He handed me his card. It was embossed with a little blue star and a French motto. *Tenez le Droit*. Detective Senior Constable Chris Micaelis, the lettering said. Victoria Police. Well, well. 'Ello, 'ello, 'ello.

We went through the door marked Minister and into my office. Trish shot me a knowing glance as we passed. She hadn't lost any of her street smarts. She still knew a debt collector when she saw one.

Micaelis declined my offer of a refreshing beverage and parked his carcass into the furniture indicated. 'S'pose you know what this is about,' he said.

'S'pose you tell me,' I said.

'This death thing at the weekend.' The cop's studied casualness, we both knew, wasn't fooling anyone. 'Understand you were there when the body was recovered.'

For the briefest moment I wasn't sure if he meant Taylor or Aubrey. Micaelis registered the flicker of hesitation. 'Ms Fleet gave us your name,' he said. Let there be no false delicacy here, he meant. We know that you and the girlfriend were together.

I would share my full concerns with the police in due course, when Red was safe from Spider Webb's threats. In the meantime, I would play it straight, answer any questions put to me and find out what I could. 'That's correct,' I said. 'Salina and I were, uh, strolling in the gardens. We saw the hubbub at the moat and went over. Just as we arrived, they were wheeling the body into the back of an ambulance.'

Sherlock the Greek nodded encouragement. 'Knew Taylor then, did you?'

'Never met him. First time I ever saw him was on Friday evening at an exhibition at the Centre for Modern Art. He was drunk and made a bit of a spectacle of himself, as you're probably aware. I saw him again about 9.30. He was walking alone down Domain Road, even drunker by the look of it. Next time I saw him he was dead.'

Micaelis nodded non-committally. 'And Salina Fleet? Know her well, do you?'

'Not really. I met her for the first time on Friday afternoon here – she's on one of our advisory panels. She was at the exhibition at the Centre for Modern Art – the same one that Taylor was at. I went to the Botanical Hotel afterwards to eat and ran into her again. The pub closed about one and she and I went for a long walk in the gardens. We saw the activity at the moat and went over. She was shocked and upset and that's when you blokes came on the scene.'

Micaelis studied the back of his hand as though consulting his notes. 'So between 1 a.m. and 3 a.m. she was with you. Strolling in the park?'

It was clear what he thought that meant. He was

almost right. 'It was a hot night,' I told him, deadpan.

'Seen her since?' he wondered.

'I saw her early yesterday afternoon,' I told him. 'I dropped in briefly to her place in the city to see how she was feeling.'

'Mmm,' he said, as though I had merely confirmed a known fact. 'And how was she?'

'Naturally she was upset at Taylor's death. She seemed to prefer to be alone.'

Micaelis gave this some consideration, getting up and going over to the window, his hands plunged into his pockets. He rocked on his heels and jiggled a ring of keys deep in the recesses of his pants. 'You don't happen to know where we might find her just at the moment, do you? She didn't come home last night.'

'Perhaps she's staying with a friend,' I suggested.

'Any idea who?' he said pointedly.

'I don't know her that well. Have you tried her work?'

Micaelis didn't need me to tell him how to do his job. '*Veneer* magazine? Not what you'd call a full-time job. They're between issues and haven't seen her for several weeks.'

Nothing in the cop's attitude suggested concerns about Salina's safety. This reaffirmed my decision not to mention Spider's appearance at the Aldershot Building. I went fishing. 'We've been getting mixed signals up here about the cause of death,' I said. 'Do you know yet if it was suicide or an accident?'

'The exact cause hasn't yet been determined,' said the detective senior constable. 'You know the police.' He shrugged absently, as though referring to a slightly eccentric mutual acquaintance. 'Like to have all the facts before making up their minds.'

'But there's something in particular about this situation?' I persisted, pushing it. 'Some reason you want to talk to Salina?'

'Routine procedure, that's all,' he said. 'You'll let us know if Ms Fleet does contact you, won't you?'

The boys were hovering outside my glass door, angling for my attention. No doubt they were bored and keen to make tracks. Micaelis looked at them, then at me. In certain matters, the Mediterranean male mind is an open book. Even as I watched, I saw Micaelis put two and two together and get a resounding five. A married man, I was, having a bit on the side.

'If anything else occurs to you that you think we should know about,' he said.

'I won't hesitate to contact you,' I told him. And I definitely would. In just a little less than twelve hours.

Opening the door, I ushered him to the foyer. The boys ran interference. 'Guess what, Dad?' said Red, tugging at my sleeve. 'Tarquin crashed the computer.'

Trish looked daggers at me over the Macintosh, stabbing at her keyboard, desperately trying to recover her zapped files.

I fed the cop into the lift and we got out of there fast.

I GAVE THE boys three choices. *Gold of the Pharaohs* at the Museum of Victoria, *Treasures of the Forbidden City* at the National Gallery, or an early lunch. The vote went two-nil for a capricciosa with extra cheese and a lemon gelati chaser.

We drove across Princes Bridge and headed through the city towards Lygon Street where the pizzerias and gelaterias were thicker on the ground than borlotti beans in a bowl of minestrone. Just past police head-quarters, where Russell Street becomes Lygon, we hit a red light beside the Eight Hour Day monument. On the diagonal corner, on the tiny patch of lawn outside the Trades Hall, stood a newly erected hoarding. Art Exhibition, it read. Combined Unions Superannuation Scheme Art Collection. Free Admission. Opens Tuesday.

This was the event for which Agnelli had commanded me to write a mirthfully uplifting speech by the next morning. Since I was so close, and since I still had to keep the boys for another hour and a half, I decided to kill two birds with the one casual suggestion. 'See that place, Red.' I pointed to the age-stained Corinthian columns of the Trades Hall's once-grand portico. 'I used to work there before you were born. C'mon, I'll show you.'

A mutinous grumble erupted from the boys. 'We'll only be ten minutes,' I exaggerated. 'Besides which, it's only 11.30 – they haven't lit the pizza ovens yet.'

The Trades Hall had been built in the 1870s, a palace of labour, and a rich example of high Victorian neo-classical architecture. A brick annexe had been added in the 1960s, an erection of expedience, its design informed by the contemporary precept that nobody gave a rat's arse about architecture. We went around the side, drove up a cobblestone lane and parked in an undercroft between the old and the new sections of the building. Little had changed in the thirteen years since my career had begun there as Research Officer for the Municipal Workers' Union. The patina of grime that clung to the walls was perhaps a little thicker. The odours that wafted from the outdoor toilets were perhaps a little ranker. But the same threadbare red flag still dangled ironically from the flagpole. When I told the boys that it was here that the party that ruled the nation was founded, they rolled their eyes and complained about the smell.

'C'mon,' I urged, spotting a small sign that indicated our destination lay on the top floor. 'Want to see the bullet holes from the gun battle where the ballot-stuffers killed the cop?'

'Go ahead,' said Red, unenthusiastically. 'Make my day.'

The story of how, back in 1915, gangsters fought a running battle with police along its first-floor corridor had long been part of Trades Hall mythology. So much so that in the three years I'd worked there I never heard the same version twice. The only point of common agreement was that the bullet-riddled banister had been filched by a souvenir hunter back in the sixties. Which gave me plenty of scope. 'They ran up these stairs,' I improvised freely. 'Firing from the hip.'

We went up a flight of stone-flagged steps eroded in the middle from the innumerable goings up and comings down of the uncountable conveners of the manifold committees of the dedicated champions of labour. On the wall at the first-floor landing was a carved wooden honour board, its faded copperplate listing every General Secretary of the Boilermakers and Gasfitters Union from 1881 to 1963. I touched Red on the shoulder and pointed. R. Cahill, 1903–09. 'Redmond Cahill,' I said. 'Your great grandfather.'

'So where's the bullet hole?' Red said, unimpressed. If I could take the trouble to invent a spurious ancestry, drenched in labour tradition, you'd think the kid could at least pretend to be interested. 'This way,' I lied, leading them along a deserted corridor. The place was so quiet that a regiment of mercenaries could have fired a bazooka down its by-ways without risk of hitting anyone.

The Trades Hall hadn't always been so quiet. In its original form, it was built to accommodate the trade-based guilds whose members had made Melbourne the richest metropolis in the southern hemisphere. In time, it had come to house more than a hundred different unions. The Confectionery Makers' Association, the Brotherhood of Farriers, the Boot Trade Employees' Federation, the Tram and Motor Omnibus Drivers – no trade was so small, no occupation so specialised that its members did not have their own union. Eventually, over a period of a hundred years, every nook and cranny of the place had been colonised. Its once-imposing chambers became a rabbit warren of jerry-rigged offices filled with men in darned cardigans and its hallways bustled with women in beehive hair-dos and sensible shoes.

But those days had long gone. The inexorable march of progress had been through the joint like a dose of salts, amalgamating and rationalising the old organisations into industry-based super-unions with names like advertising agencies and a preference for more up-market accommodation. The AWU-FIME, the AFME-PKIU and the CFMEU had ditched the old dump for more modern digs elsewhere. Apart from the Trades Hall Council, which occupied the new wing, there were few remaining tenants.

The labour movement was not, however, entirely unmindful of its heritage. Bit by bit, as the dollars could be scrounged, the place was being restored to its vanished glory. Plasterers' scaffolding cluttered the stairwells and the smell of fresh paint hung in the air. An art exhibition was about to be staged. Somewhere. If only I could find it. The signs had petered out.

Reaching the top floor, we came face-to-face with a pair of knee-high white socks. They were attached to Bob Allroy, the Trades Hall's pot-bellied long-time caretaker. He was standing on a ladder, hanging a banner above a set of double doors. CUSS Art Exhibition, it read.

'Here's the only man still alive who personally witnessed the murdered policeman's death agony,' I told the boys. By now they'd figured out that my impromptu guided tour was just a pretext and were looking decidedly cheesed-off.

Bob Allroy climbed down from the ladder, wheezing. He was one of life's casualties, never the same since a bag of wheat had fallen on him in a ship's hold in 1953. His entire life since had been more a gesture of working-class solidarity than an affirmation of his usefulness. 'Oh, it's you,' he grunted, recalling my face but unable to summon up a name. He opened one of the doors and I helped him drag his ladder inside. 'Unbelievable, eh?' he panted.

Sure was. The last time I'd seen this room it had been a maze of cheap chipboard and second-hand Axminster, a lost dogs' home for officials of the Society of Bricklayers and Tilers. Now it was a spacious reception room with buffed parquet flooring, hand-blocked wallpaper friezes and freshly antiqued skirting boards. Portable partitions had been erected at right angles to the walls to form a series of shallow alcoves and rows of paintings sat stacked against them, face to the wall, waiting to be hung.

'Art exhibition,' explained Bob, not entirely approvingly. 'The girlie from the cultural office is off sick, so guess who's been roped into doing all the work?'

Bob Allroy wouldn't work in an iron lung and we both knew it. 'Doesn't officially open till tomorrer,' he warned, in case I was thinking of stealing a free look. I wasn't there for an unscheduled squiz, I reassured him, but to rustle up a bit of quick background for a speech I had to write.

Bob moved to one of the windows and licked his

lips, his liver-spotted nose drawn like a lodestone to the revolving brewery sign atop the John Curtin Hotel, clearly visible across the road. The girlie from the arts office, he thought, would be back tomorrow. Better be, if everything was to be ready for the official opening. In the meantime, I'd better see Bernice Kaufman, next door in the admin office. She might know something about it.

This was a definite possibility. There was very little, by her own admission, that Bernice Kaufman didn't know all about. She hadn't been President of the Teachers' Federation for nothing. A couple of minutes with Bernice and, chances were, I'd know more than I'd ever need to about the CUSS Art Collection. More than enough to write Agnelli's speech. Not the jokes, though. I'd have to write the jokes myself.

Bob Allroy ascended his ladder and began screwing light globes into a reproduction etched-glass gas lamp hanging from the ceiling. 'Don't you kids go nowhere near the art,' he warned. 'That stuff's worth a lot of money.'

Seconding that motion, I told Red and Tarquin to amuse themselves for a minute while I did something important. Then I scooted across to the Trades Hall Council, where Bernice Kaufman was holed-up behind a wall of paperwork in an office marked Assistant Secretary. She could spare me a couple of minutes, but only just. 'I don't want to miss my ultrasound appointment,' she said.

You had to hand it to Bernice. In the time it took to say hello, she'd just happened to draw attention to the fact that she was pregnant. You get to be thirty-five,

Bernice had discovered, and your superwoman rating starts to slip if your credentials don't include motherhood, preferably of the single variety. Being the hardest-nosed, most multi-faced Ms in town doesn't cut much ice unless you've also got cracked nipples and a teething ring in your briefcase. So Bernice had scared just enough body fluids out of an organiser from the Miscellaneous Workers' Union to secure herself membership of the pudding club. Not just an ordinary member, of course. Being knocked up would never be the same now that Bernice had a piece of the action.

'Put that cigarette out,' she barked. 'Haven't you heard of passive smoking?'

There was, believe me, nothing passive about Bernice Kaufman. I dropped my fag and ground it mercilessly underfoot. The baby was not due for another five months.

When I explained what I wanted, Bernice didn't believe it. 'I don't believe it,' she said. 'Ministerial adviser for the Arts? Agnelli must be crazy. You're a cultural illiterate.'

'That's why I've come to you, Bernice,' I said. 'I'm after some on-the-job training.'

When I'd convinced her that I really did need background information for Agnelli's speech at the exhibition opening, she reached into a drawer of her filing cabinet and pulled out a thick folder. She was, it transpired, ex-officio company secretary of the Combined Unions Superannuation Scheme. 'CUSS manages several million dollars of union members' money. And while the art collection is only a small percentage of our total assets – its current value is estimated at approximately half a million dollars – it is an important element in maintaining a broadly diversified portfolio. Frankly, the way the financial markets have been performing lately, art is probably our most effectively appreciating investment.'

My amusement must have been too apparent. Bernice changed tack, handing me a page from the file. 'Here's the content guidelines, as laid down by the CUSS board of directors. Keep it. Feel free to quote.'

The emphasis of the collection, read the blurb, was on works that presented a positive view of working life and reflected the outlook and aspirations of ordinary working people. 'Angelo's speech should point out that it includes works by some very prominent artists.'

It did, too. The one-page catalogue Bernice handed me was leavened with the sort of household names guaranteed to reassure the rank and file that its pension funds were not being squandered on the avant-garde. *Potoroo 2* by Clifton Pugh, I read. *Dry Gully* by Russell Drysdale. *Man in Singlet* by William Dobell.

'Did a mob of you go round Sotheby's and Christies with a chequebook or what?'

I didn't take Bernice's withering glance of contempt personally. She thought everyone was an idiot. 'The collection was initiated by the board of directors a little over a year ago, essentially as an investment vehicle. Since purchases of this nature are a specialised skill, we retain an expert consulting firm, Austral Fine Art, to advise us. Austral identifies suitable works for inclusion in the collection, buys and sells on our behalf, takes care of insurance and so on. Up until now, the works have all been held in storage. But a few months ago we decided to put them on show, so our members could better appreciate the investment we made on their behalf. In fact – and this is a point Angelo might also care to make – this is the only time the entire collection has ever been seen by the public.' She put her hands on the edge of the desk and wearily pulled herself upright, levering for two. 'And now I really must go. Can't keep the doctor waiting.'

I walked her to the lift. A waddle was already in evidence. 'So, you'll soon know if it's a boy or a girl – or would you prefer not to find out until the actual birth?'

Bernice might've been up the duff, but she hadn't lost her marbles. 'Information is power, Murray,' she said. 'Don't you know anything?'

Pocketing the pages of bumph she'd given me, I headed back to the exhibition room. Apart from Bob Allroy's ladder and toolbox abandoned in the middle of the floor and the unhung painting lining the walls, it was empty. An icy wave of panic gripped my innards. I should never have let the boys out of my sight. 'Red!' I called. 'Tarquin!' The sound echoed back at me from the deserted corridor.

Suddenly, arms spread wide like music-hall song-and-dance men, the boys sprang from behind the far partition. 'Tricked ya!' they shrieked.

Even as the words left their lips, Tarquin tripped backwards over Bob Allroy's toolbox and slammed full pelt into the step-ladder. The flimsy aluminium tower skidded sideways, rocked on its legs and began to topple over. I rushed forward to arrest its fall and collided with Red. Tarquin, useful as ever, stood open-mouthed. For a moment time seemed to stand still.

The ladder didn't, though. With an almighty metallic clatter, it collided with the upper edge of one of the pictures leaning against the wall, smashing the frame into gilded kindling and squashing the canvas into a buckled heap. The result looked like a piano accordion that had been kicked to death by an electricity pylon.

'Wow,' said Tarquin.

'Shuddup.' I fell to my knees beside the catastrophe. 'Shuddup, shuddup, shuddup.' My heart was so firmly lodged in my mouth that further conversation was impossible.

The picture's frame was utterly demolished, the joints burst asunder, the side panels reduced to four separate pieces of ornately useless timber moulding. The internal framing was a flattened rhomboid from which the canvas dangled in crumpled folds.

Sweaty-handed, I smoothed the tangled mass into the rough approximation of its original rectangular shape. What I saw filled me with a mixture of unspeakable dismay and utter relief.

The mangled picture was a small oil painting. It depicted a solitary stick-figure stockman. He was perched on a gnarled tree-stump beside the mouldering bones of a bullock. His drought-ravaged gaze extended across a blasted landscape towards a featureless horizon. There was no signature. There was no need.

Nobody else did red dirt and rust-rotted corrugated iron like this. Nobody else would dare. It was the trademark, instantly recognisable, of an artist whose rangy bushmen and desiccated verandas had once adorned the walls of every pub and primary school from Hobart to Humpty Doo.

'*Dry Gully*,' I groaned. 'By Sir Russell Fucking Drysdale.'

Red and Tarquin meekly dragged the ladder upright, more abashed by my obviously panic-stricken state than by the damage their game had inflicted. 'Doesn't look too bad,' offered Red lamely.

'Shuddup,' I informed him.

But my boy was a smart lad and there was truth in his statement. The canvas sagged and buckled over its skewiff skeleton, but the actual paintwork appeared to have survived intact. Apart from some very minute cracks, arguably ancient, there was no visible evidence to suggest that the phlegmatic boundary rider had been struck from a great height by a plummeting pile of scrap metal.

And, in light of the fact that the actual art part was still intact, the destruction of the frame suddenly seemed less disastrous. It was just a few pieces of gilded timber, after all. If I acted quickly, it might just be possible to re-assemble the whole thing into some passable semblance of its previous condition before Bob Allroy returned. Particularly since Bob's toolbox was sitting conveniently to hand on the parquet floor.

'Quick,' I ordered the boys. 'Watch the door.' Then, grabbing a pair of pliers and a screwdriver, I bundled up the buggered item, sprinted down the hall to the Gents and locked myself in a vacant stall.

In less time than it took to wedge the ruptured joints of the frame back into place, the futility of my task was obvious. Even in ideal working conditions and with the right tools, the job would have been beyond me. With the timber of the internal stretcher snapped clear through, it was impossible to get any tension in the canvas. The more I fiddled, the more hopeless it became. On top of which, barely a minute had gone by before Red came knocking on the cubicle door. 'Dad! Dad!' he hissed. 'He's back.' There was no option but to face the music.

Holding the picture before me like an icon at a Russian funeral, I advanced down the corridor towards the scene of the crime, its perpetrators in single, guilty file behind me. As we neared the exhibition room, Bob Allroy stepped out the door and pulled it shut. Without so much as a glance our way, he turned on his heels and scurried down the stairs.

'Can't we just leave it here?' said Red, trying the locked door of the exhibition room. 'And run.'

We could. But Bernice knew that I'd been there. And, faced with a demolished painting, Bob Allroy would soon remember that the only other people to visit the unopened exhibition were that guy who used to work downstairs for the MEU and his two kids.

The time was precisely 12.30. Through a window at the top of the stairs I watched Bob cross the street and enter the John Curtin Hotel.

The days when the industrial arm of the labour movement bent its collective elbow in the front bar of the John Curtin Hotel were long gone. But tradition died hard in some men and Bob was one of them. At least an hour would pass before he completed his liquid lunch and returned for his ladder and toolbox.

'Who's Sir Russell Fucking Drysdale?' said Tarquin.

'Shuddup,' I suggested. 'And follow me.'

Scooping up the bits and pieces of *Dry Gully*, I sped

non-chalantly down the stairs. The undercroft was deserted.

'Are we keeping it, then?' said Red, incredulously watching me wrap the picture in an old beach towel.

'Shuddup,' I muttered, throwing a left into Victoria Parade and stomping on the accelerator. What I needed was an art conservator with while-you-wait service.

ARTEMIS PRINTS and Framing was just down the hill from Ethnic Affairs, at the Victoria Parade end of the Smith Street retail strip. Technically, being on the west side of the street, it was located in Fitzroy, a suburb well on the way to total gentrification. But Smith Street, both sides, was universally regarded as Collingwood, an address that could never successfully shed its more raffish working-class associations. As though clutched in the jaws of this ambiguity, Artemis was slotted between a health-food shop called the Tasty Tao and a second-hand electrical goods retailer whose refrigerators were chained together to discourage shoplifters.

It took me exactly seven minutes and fifteen seconds to get there, including parking time.

It was a quiet drive, despite near-misses when I ran the amber lights at two intersections. The boys were concentrating on perfecting their air of contrition and had kept recriminations to a minimum. I bustled them into the Tasty Tao with funds for soymilk ice-creams and instructions to wait at the table on the footpath out the front and stay out of trouble. 'But what about our pizza . . .' Tark started, until he was silenced by a shot across the bow from Red. I took the towel-wrapped bundle of canvas and kindling out of the Charade and pushed open the door of Artemis Prints. A buzzer sounded out the back.

The exposed-brick walls were hung thick with decorator items for the local home-renovator market. Aluminium-framed posters from art museum blockbusters. Georgia O'Keeffe at the Guggenheim. Modern masters. Klimt and Klee. Rustic frames around labels from long-defunct brands of tinned fruit. On the rear wall, beside a curtained archway, hung a selection of sample frames, their inverted right-angles like downturned mouths. Claire, I was pleased to see, carried an extensive range.

She was behind the counter, even more voluptuous than I remembered, serving a teenage girl in skin-tight stone-washed denim jeans and a chemise that showed her navel. Definitely the Collingwood side of the street, probably the Housing Commission high-rise flats. More your Joan Jett fan than your Joan Miro aficionado. 'How much for the non-reflective glass, but?' she was saying.

'It's five dollars more,' said Claire. On the counter between them was a block-mounted poster of a cigar-smoking chimpanzee in a tartan waistcoat riding a unicycle, the glass repaired with tape. Hi-jinx in the high-rise. 'But you get a much better result.'

Claire looked over the girl's shoulder and acknowledged my arrival. Her expression was bland, but her eyes twinkled, inviting me to share the joke. 'I'll be with you in a moment,' she said. 'Sir.'

The teenager gave the non-reflective glass a moment's

lip-chewing consideration and decided to go the full distance.

'I think you'll find it well worthwhile,' said Claire. 'You get a clearer view. It'll be ready to pick up tomorrow.' She was, I sensed, doing it hard. All dressed up for the customers in a lick of make-up, pleated chinos and a sleeveless white blouse. Her chestnut hair, much more ravishing in the daylight, was piled high and held in place with combs.

'So,' she said as the girl left, eyeing my towel-wrapped bundle like it was an unnecessary but not unwelcome pretext. 'Don't say you want me to mount your street vendors too?'

Second thoughts had been assailing me from the moment I walked through the door. A few flirtatious glances over a bowl of tapenade were one thing. Bursting into the woman's shop with a filched artwork under my arm was another. Desperado dipstick and his defective Drysdale. I smiled helplessly and mustered my resolve.

'This may seem a little presumptuous,' I started. 'That is, this might not be the sort of thing you normally do. And even if it is, you might not be comfortable doing it in this particular instance. You really don't know me, I know, but it's sort of an emergency and, well, if you don't feel comfortable, I'll understand perfectly and perhaps you could refer me somewhere else . . .'

At this babble, Claire's lips curled with undisguised amusement. 'An emergency!' She moved aside the cracked chimpanzee to clear the counter. 'As you see, emergencies are our specialty.' If I felt the need to make a bit of a production number, she didn't mind playing along.

'It belongs to friends,' I said, laying my bundle before her. The painting was, strictly speaking, stolen property. If unforeseen difficulties arose, I didn't want Claire implicated as an accessory to a crime. A little white lie seemed best. 'Don't ask what happened.' I cast an accusing backward glance over my shoulder.

Claire followed it out her front window to where the boys sat flicking bits of ice-cream at each other over the pavement table. She gave me a comprehending nod. Detailed explanations weren't necessary. What was parenthood, after all, but a lifelong mopping-up operation?

'And your friends don't know about it yet?' The way she said this suggested that such things were not unknown in her profession. 'You'd like to get it back before they notice it's gone?'

'Exactly.' I began to unfold the towel. She helped me. Her hands were neat and sturdy and when her fingers brushed mine, I felt myself blush. 'The painting itself doesn't seem to be damaged,' I said, keeping my face down. 'Just the frame. All it needs is a few staples, a bit of glue.'

The last flap of towel fell away, revealing what appeared to be the aftermath of a tropical cyclone. Drysdale's lonesome drover, if anything, looked even more despondent. Claire let out an appreciative whistle. 'Is this what I think it is?'

'I'm afraid so. A Russell Drysdale original. But, like I said, the picture itself doesn't seem to be damaged. A few staples, a nail or two . . .'

Under the counter was a black apron. Claire slipped it on, along with a pair of white cotton gloves. Minnie Mouse. 'Interesting,' she said. 'The only other Drysdales I've seen were on masonite board.' She began to separate the pieces of wood, wire and canvas. Ominous diagnostic noises came from the back of her throat.

'Like I said, the picture itself doesn't seem to be damaged.' I smoothed at it uselessly, trying to be helpful. 'A few staples . . .'

She smacked my hand away. 'Let me be the judge of that,' she said. 'There's quite a lot of work needed here.'

'Um,' I said, moving my shoulders from side to side and shuffling from foot to foot. 'The thing is . . .' I looked at my watch.

'How long have I got?' she said, not looking up from probing the debris.

'Half an hour.' I winced sheepishly.

'You have got to be kidding.' But she was already gathering up the ends of the towel.

Through the arch at the back of the shop was a narrow workroom dominated by a long tool-strewn table. Racks of moulded framing occupied one wall. In the other was a window overlooking the side fence. Stairs ran to an upper floor. Clearing away a half-cut cardboard mount, Claire laid the battered picture face-down and snipped away the tangled hanging wire with a pair of pliers.

'You don't know how much I appreciate this,' I said, Mr Sincere.

'Let's just say it's a long time since I've had the chance to work with an artist of this stature.' She removed the stretched canvas from its frame and held it upright. Squeezing the opposing corners gingerly together, she forced the canvas to bulge a little. 'Particularly when he's been hit by a bus.'

Out of its frame, the stretched canvas looked pathetically small, hardly much bigger than a couple of record covers. The edges, long concealed by the boxing of the frame, were a stark white contrast to the murky grey of the rest of the fabric. Claire wrinkled her nose. 'Hmmm,' she said. 'Had this long?'

I looked at my watch. 'About seventeen and a half minutes.'

'Your friends, how long have they had this?'

'Six months or so, I think. Why?'

'Just wondered.' She turned the painting face down and began rummaging through the racks of framing material.

'Hello, Red's dad.' A child's voice came from somewhere behind me. It took me a moment to locate its source. Claire's little girl Grace was peering out shyly from behind the door of a cupboard built under the stairs. Delighted to have surprised me, she opened the cupboard door to reveal a tiny table spread with scrap paper and coloured pencils. 'This is my play school,' she said. 'Mummy made it for me.' Her eyes tracked me across the room as I accepted her invitation to take a closer look.

'Your mummy's very clever,' I said, meaning every word of it. Taking this as a personal compliment, Gracie plumped herself down at the table and began drawing exuberantly with a felt-tipped pen.

'That's the sort of encouragement I like to hear when

I'm working,' said Claire. 'Keep it up.'

She withdrew a length of moulded framing from the rack on the wall and matched it with a section of the broken frame, holding the two together so I could compare them. Apart from a slightly deeper gilding on the old frame, they were nearly identical. 'It'll be quicker to build a new frame than repair the damaged one. This moulding is a fairly common style, so it's highly unlikely your friends will ever notice the difference.' I couldn't see Bob Allroy spotting the switch.

'But first I'll need to take the canvas off the stretcher, replace the broken struts, then re-attach the canvas.' With a definitive smash, she tossed the broken frame into a metal rubbish bin full of off-cut shards of glass.

'Is all that possible in half an hour?' I was getting toey, nervously glancing at my watch, as useful as a scrub nurse at a triple by-pass.

Claire shrugged casually. 'We'll soon find out.' She was enjoying this. Not just the professional challenge, either. She began extracting the tacks that held the canvas on the stretcher.

I paced. A compressor sat on the floor, its hose leading to a pneumatic guillotine on a side bench. Pricy items. Staple guns. Sheets of glass. Tools. Racks of unframed prints. Two metal folio cabinets, not cheap. Cardboard mounts. A whole wall of shaped timber. Add the rent, the rates, utility bills.

Claire, pulling tacks, read my mind. 'Not exactly what I imagined when I left the National Gallery. I saw myself sitting in a trendy little gallery offering the works of interesting young contemporary printmakers to a discerning clientele. The trouble is, ten other places within half a mile had exactly the same idea.'

'Is that why you left the National Gallery, to start this shop?'

'Other way round,' she said.

Gracie tugged at my sleeve and handed me a piece of paper. Two blobby circles in felt-tipped pen, one circle with a hat and currant eyes.

'That's me, isn't it?' The child nodded. Who else? 'Why, thank you. It's lovely.'

Claire looked up, the table between us. 'Sleazebag,' she muttered. In the nicest possible way. It was all I could do to stop myself vaulting the table and giving her a demonstration.

'Other way round?'

'I'd been at the gallery six years, ever since I graduated. That's where I met' – she flicked her eyes towards Gracie, back at her drawing – 'Gracie's father, Graham. He was an administrator. We were together for a couple of years and when Gracie was on the way I applied for maternity leave. No-one had ever done that before. Women who got pregnant were expected to quietly fade away. They said there was no provision, knocked me back.'

'That's discrimination,' I said. Reviewing the National Gallery's employment practices would, I resolved, be my number one priority when I got back to the office. If changes hadn't already been made, they would be damned soon, if I had any influence on the proceedings. We'd see how soon they smartened up if their conduit was squeezed a little.

'I wanted to make an issue of it, but Graham didn't like the idea. He thought it might adversely affect his career. He encouraged me to set up this business, put some money into it. After Grace was born, he got a job offer from overseas. Now he's Director of Human Resources at the Hong Kong Museum of Oriental Antiquities and I'm sticking non-reflecting glass over chimpanzees and framing other people's holiday photos.'

She wasn't bitter, just telling a story. She dropped her voice a register, whether for my benefit or the child's I couldn't tell. 'We don't see him any more.'

'Great,' I said. 'Great progress you're making.' She only had about half the tacks out. Now that she was handling the painting proper, her technique was meticulous, painstakingly slow. The time was 12.58. My feet were inscribing an ever-decreasing circle on the workroom floor.

'For Chrissake,' she said, moving around to my side of the table for no apparent other reason than to accidentally brush her rump against me. 'Stop prowling around like a caged animal. You're making me nervous.'

Jesus, what did she have to be nervous about? I was the one with the crisis on my plate. Maybe, I thought, I should temporarily remove my twitchiness elsewhere. Make more efficient use of my time by taking Red and Tarquin around to Leo while Claire got on with the job, unencumbered by my stalking presence. 'Go,' she said. 'You're no use to me in your current state.'

'The heat's off,' I told the boys, bustling them and their dripping stumps of half-sucked carob-chip ice-confectionery into the car.

The Curnows' place was less than a kilometre away through the backstreets of Fitzroy. Even though I knew it would take me scarcely ten minutes to deliver the boys and return to Artemis, I still had to fight the urge to speed. This painting demolition rigmarole had certainly shot the shit out of my quality time with Red. The one o'clock news came on the radio and I leaned across and hiked up the volume.

Prince Sihanouk had walked out on the Cambodian peace talks. Again. F. W. de Klerk had been elected head of the South African government. Fat lot of difference that would make. Emperor Hirohito had died. Not before time, the old war criminal. Police had refused to rule out suspicious circumstances in relation to the death of the man whose body had been found in the moat of the National Gallery. The weather bureau had amended the forecast top upwards to thirty and the All Ordinaries was steady at 1539.4.

This news – the foul play, not the All Ordinaries – was not entirely unexpected. Salina's disappearance was bound to have raised suspicions, even if none had existed before. The ripples thrown up by Marcus Taylor's drowning were spreading outwards in ever-widening circles. An image of Agnelli on the placid waters of Lake Eildon crossed my mind. I couldn't help but wonder what boats might get rocked before this affair was over.

Leo accepted delivery of the boys with a wave from the Curnows' front door. 'See you after work,' I told Red. 'About six o'clock. We'll have our pizza then, okay?'

'Okay,' said Red, easy-going as ever.

I was back at Artemis Prints at approximately 1.10.06. Enough time for a quick gasper. While I sucked, I perused the offerings in the front window. The least I could do, all things considered, was buy something. The Pre-Raphaelite maidens weren't exactly my cup of hemlock. I settled on a Mondrian print. Remembering my little something for Gracie, I dashed back across the road to the car and retrieved Marcus Taylor's stamp album from where Red had tossed it behind the back seat.

The buzzer rang as I went in the door. When Claire stuck her head around the curtain to see who'd come in, I was standing by the counter like a waiting customer. 'Psst,' I said and beckoned her over. She came cautiously, a questioning look on her face.

'I haven't thanked you properly.' I said it deliberately low so she had to step closer to hear me. Then I took my life in my hands. I put my arm around her waist, drew her to me and kissed her gently on the mouth.

Her lips, soft and dry, yielded tentatively. I inhaled the scent of her hair, apple shampoo, dizzying. She leaned into the kiss, accepting it, returning it. We shifted on our feet, neither of us breathing. Her hands found the small of my back and pressed me closer. The kiss went on. And on.

Suddenly, she broke. We stepped back from each other, both swallowing hard, blinking. 'Your friends,' she said. 'How much did they pay for this painting?'

Her eyes shone with anticipation. 'I dunno,' I shrugged. I'd already done the mental arithmetic, speculated on the cost of restitution. Wondered about insurance. Forty-odd paintings in the CUSS collection, total value half a million dollars. Average price, say $12,000.

Drysdale one of the stars. 'Maybe twenty thousand dollars. Why?'

'Take a look at this.' Claire tugged at my hand, drawing me into the workroom. At the parting of the curtain, her touch fell away just as Gracie looked up from her colouring-in. The stamp album was still in my hand. I held it out to the child. 'Do you like stamps?'

'Stickers?' She grabbed the book avidly, her diffidence forgotten.

Claire stood at the work table, hands on hips, inviting inspection of her handiwork. The replacement frame was finished, indistinguishable from the original. It sat empty. Next to it was the repaired stretcher, a cross-braced timber rectangle, naked of fabric. Beside them was the unstretched canvas of *Dry Gully*. Ochre red and russet brown, it looked like the freshly-flayed skin of some desert reptile. Then there was another piece of canvas, the same size as *Dry Gully*. This one was a rather amateurish seascape that seemed to have been roughly cut down from a larger picture. Finally, propped open with a thick ruler was a reference book, *The Dictionary of Australian Artists*.

'I thought there was something odd about this picture.' With all the exaggerated staginess of a conjurer about to execute a marvel of prestidigitation, she proceeded to show me what. First, she turned *Dry Gully* over and invited me to examine the condition of the canvas. Before, when it hung on the stretcher, it was a dusty parchment colour. Now, it was a fresh-looking chalky white. Attached to the fabric, right in the centre, was a small piece of paper on which was printed an image, some words and a number. As I bent forward for a closer look, Claire whisked the canvas away. 'One thing at a time.'

She pointed to the other canvas. 'When I took the Drysdale off the stretcher, I found this underneath.' To demonstrate what she meant, she turned *Dry Gully* face down on the table and placed the fragment of seascape over it, also face down. The two canvasses fitted together perfectly. *Dry Gully*'s obverse side now appeared the same dirty cream colour as when it was still stretched. 'Two canvases,' said Claire. 'One on top of the other – creating the impression that the painting in front is much older than it really is.'

'Why would someone do that?' I asked.

She now removed the false back and allowed me to examine the little square of paper. It had serrated edges and bore an image of the Sydney Opera House surmounted by the head of William Shakespeare. Australia Post, said the inscription, 43 cents. UK–Australia Bicentenary Joint Issue.

'Big Bill in Tinsel Town,' I said. 'What does it mean?'

'It means that if Russell Drysdale painted this picture,' Claire said. 'He did so posthumously.' Her index finger settled on the biographical entry in the reference book. 'By 1988, he'd been dead for seven years.'

'**Y**OU MEAN it's a forgery?'

Jesus H. Christ. What was it about me? I'd only been in this culture caper three days and the fakes were jumping out of the woodwork at me. First *Our Home*, now *Dry Gully*. Was no representation of the Australian landscape, no work of art safe now that I was in the field?

Claire's professional curiosity was piqued, but she wasn't jumping to any conclusions. 'Not necessarily. It's certainly not an original, but as to being a forgery – well, that depends.'

'Depends on what? Surely it's either genuine or it isn't.'

Claire sucked in her cheeks and held the counterfeit Drysdale up to the light, as if trying to penetrate its secret. 'I'm no expert, but this seems to be a very competent attempt to replicate Drysdale's work. But the fact that it's been done with a considerable degree of skill does not, in itself, make it a forgery. Owners of valuable artworks sometimes have high-quality copies made – to reduce their insurance premiums, from fear of theft, in case of accidental damage. They lock the original away, hang the copy and let people think it's the original. Perhaps your friends did that.'

'What, like a duchess who keeps her diamond tiara in the safe and wears a paste imitation?' Except there were scant few duchesses around the Trades Hall.

'Exactly. Or maybe your friends are just engaging in a little harmless pretension. Bought themselves a replica and told people it was an original.'

What sort of friends did she think I had? 'Not these people,' I told her. 'Not their style.'

'I don't suppose you happen to know if it came with a certificate of authenticity, do you?'

'What's that?'

'A letter provided by the seller giving details of the picture's origins and attesting that it is what it's purported to be.'

I told her I couldn't imagine my friends buying anything without all the paperwork being in order.

'You don't happen to know where they bought it?'

'It was arranged privately, I believe. Through a firm called Austral Fine Art.'

She swung a phone book down from a shelf. 'Never heard of them. But there's no shortage of art dealers in this town.' There was a page of them, including the Aubrey Gallery. But no Austral Fine Art.

'Forgery isn't my area, I'm afraid,' Claire said. 'My only experience has been with inaccurate attribution and genuine mistakes. The National Gallery has a Rembrandt self-portrait that turned out not to be a Rembrandt at all. We changed the caption to "School of Rembrandt" and left it where it was. But deliberate misrepresentation, that's another matter altogether.'

I was deliberately letting her walk me the long way around this, covering all the bases. I already had a grim feeling that I knew what it meant. But I wanted to be absolutely sure I wasn't jumping to any conclusion just because it was the obvious one. 'What do you think the stamp means?'

'Yes,' she said. 'Interesting isn't it? It's obviously some sort of personal mark. A secret signature, if you like.'

'If it's secret, why is it in such a prominent place? Surely that would increase the chances of the deception being discovered?'

'True,' she agreed. 'Perhaps whoever did this intended that it be discovered.'

'But why would a forger want to be discovered? Wouldn't that defeat the purpose?'

'It would if the motive was financial gain. But in some cases I've heard about, the forger was less concerned with money than with fooling the experts. After the critics and curators have waxed lyrical about the unmistakable hand of the master being visible in every brushstroke, the forger pops up and reveals that the picture in question was painted not by Van Gogh in Arles in 1889, but by Joe Bloggs in Aunt Gertrude's garden shed last December.'

How did the declaration found in Marcus Taylor's pocket go? *You so-called experts . . . You speculators and collectors who do not even know what you are buying . . . You are all allowing yourselves to be deceived and defrauded.* There was another line, too. Something about taking action to draw public attention. Since the note was found on his body, the assumption had automatically been that the action he meant was his suicide. But if he hadn't, in fact, killed himself, what could he have been referring to?

'Gracie, sweetheart,' I said. 'Can I borrow back that sticker book for a minute?'

Gracie, having found the stickers already stuck down, was feeling gypped enough. She warily surrendered the album. 'I suppose so,' she said. 'Just for a minute, but.'

The stamps dated from the previous year. Beneath each, inscribed in minuscule block capitals was a name. Some I recognised as belonging to artists. William Dobell was below a stamp commemorating the Seoul Olympics. Runners breasting a tape, 65 cents. Margaret Preston got paired with a possum. The British–Australian joint issue with the high culture theme bore the inscription 'Drysdale'.

The CUSS catalogue that Bernice Kaufman gave me was still in my pocket. I unfolded it and checked the names against those under the stamps. There was a stamp corresponding to every artist in the collection. Thirty-eight names, thirty-eight stamps. The album was Taylor's register of production, his output ledger.

Claire, naturally, was regarding my behaviour with a degree of incomprehension. 'What's all this?' she said.

'Just a minute.' Using *The Dictionary of Australian Artists*, I checked two of the names. Noel Counihan and Jon Molvig. I wouldn't have known their work if it was up me with an armful of impasto, but their names rang a bell. According to the reference book, they were both dead. I tried a name I didn't recognise. It wasn't listed. Nor were three others that were unfamiliar. By the look of it, the CUSS art collection contained only works by dead or undiscovered artists.

If this meant what it looked like it meant, the whole lot were what Salina Fleet would probably call referential images at the cutting edge of post-modern discourse. Fakes.

'For Chrissake, tell me what's going on!' Claire was getting impatient, irritated by my lack of communication. 'This is a joke, right? You're playing an elaborate trick on me, aren't you?'

'I wish I was,' I said. 'Mind if I use your phone?'

'Only if you tell me what's going on.'

Gracie was all ears, galvanised by her mother's response to my evasiveness. When I thrust the stamp album towards her, she went all shy and refused to take it back. I put it on her little desk instead.

'I will,' I told Claire. I put my hands lightly on her upper arms, a conciliatory gesture. She shrugged them away. 'I promise. Just as soon as I find out myself. In the meantime, do you think you can put that picture back together the way it was?'

'Aren't you going to tell your friends?'

'Tell them what? "You know your Drysdale? Well guess what? It's not really a Drysdale at all. And here are the bits and pieces to prove it." I've taken it without their knowledge or permission, don't forget. Right now, the only option is to stick to the original plan and get it back where it belongs before they notice it's gone. That way, I'll have enough breathing room to figure out how to break it to them, or have them discover the truth themselves.'

She was, I could see, far from persuaded. But she was also curious enough to put her better judgment temporarily on hold. 'Phone's on the counter,' she said.

I went out into the shop and dialled the Police Minister's office and asked for Ken Sproule. 'Is that criminal intelligence?' I said. 'What's this I hear on the news about Taylor's death being down to suspicious circumstances?'

The methodical whoomph of a pneumatic stapler came from the workroom.

'I'm as much in the dark as you are,' claimed Sproule. 'Now that it's become a police operational matter, it's strictly arm's length from us here in the minister's office.'

'Come off it. You must have some idea. What's this about the girlfriend shooting through?'

Sproule's ears pricked up audibly. 'How'd you hear about that?'

'So you do know something, then?'

Ken got fatherly. 'A word to the wise, Murray. Don't go dipping your bib in here. The cops are notoriously sensitive to any suggestion of political interference in the operational side of things. Do yourself a favour and keep well clear.'

'Since when does asking a question constitute political interference? Don't be a prick. Tell me what's going on.'

'What's going on is a routine police inquiry into a sudden death,' said Sproule in tones that brooked no contradiction. 'Tell you what,' he softened slightly. 'If I hear anything relevant I'll let you know. Can't say fairer than that, okay?' Okay as in end of issue. Okay as in never.

'Well I certainly wouldn't want to do anything that might jeopardise an ongoing investigation, Ken.'

Sproule, for some reason, thought I was being facetious. 'Don't get your wig in an uproar, Murray . . .'

But I was already hanging up. The stapler had finished its whoomphing and Claire had appeared in the archway, attentive. 'I never did ask about your job,' she said. 'What exactly is it you do?'

It was time I came clean, told her the truth. 'It's hard to explain,' I said. 'I assist the minister.'

The parodic Drysdale was in its new frame, indistinguishable from its pre-accident condition. 'Brilliant,' I said, wrapping it in the beach towel. It was 1.35. Every minute's delay increased the chance of the picture's absence being discovered. And now there was potentially a great deal more at stake than a bit of embarrassment over some accidental damage. 'How much do I owe you?'

This went down like an Elvis impersonator at La Scala. 'You owe me an explanation, for a start.'

'You'll get one, I promise.' I started for the door. 'Soon as I can.'

Soft soap didn't cut any ice around here. Claire blocked my way, hands on hips. 'How soon will that be?'

'I want to see you again. Soon and a lot. But I can't do it today. I've got to get back to work, then I have to take Red to the airport. I won't see him again for a couple of months and I want to spend a little time with him, just him and me, this evening. Let me take you to lunch tomorrow. I promise I'll tell you everything then.'

The curtain was closed, Gracie not in sight. I put my hand on the back of Claire's head. She didn't resist but she wasn't so enthusiastic any more. I gave her a big wet one and bolted out the door, feeling like a fool.

With a good run of green lights, I was back at the Trades Hall in six minutes and at the open door of the exhibition room in another two. My towel-wrapped package was under my arm. Bob Allroy was up his ladder, back turned, his hand in the etched-glass mantle of a reproduction light-fitting. Bob was one of the few men still in regular employment capable of making a day's work out of changing a light globe. I crept across the room and slipped the picture back in place.

'No touching,' Bob growled from above. 'It's moran my job's worth if anything happens to them pictures.'

Returning *Dry Gully* to the collection was one thing, finding out how it got there in the first place was another. That was a question for Bernice Kaufman.

The receptionist was still out to lunch, so I went straight through to Bernice's office. It, too, was empty, as was that of the neighbouring Industrial Officer. But the big fat suspension file labelled Combined Unions Superannuation Scheme was still sitting there, right where Bernice had left it. Lowering myself into the inflatable ring cushion on her chair, I began thumbing.

For all her ferocious efficiency, Bernice was unlikely to win any Institute of Management awards for the neatness of her record-keeping. The CUSS file contained everything but the kitchen sink – minutes of sub-committees, auditors' reports, back copies of the members' newsletter – all of an unedifyingly general nature.

Naturally enough, there was a lot of accounting stuff, including a collection of monthly statements from Obelisk Trust. As of the thirtieth of the previous, CUSS had a balance of slightly more than $6 million in its Obelisk account, half equity linked, half property trust, the first yielding 19.2 per cent, the second 22.8 per cent. Even to a man unschooled in the finer points of finance, these seemed like passably tolerable rates of return. But it wasn't where CUSS kept its cash reserves that interested me so much as where it got its art.

I hit that particular jackpot when I opened a well-stuffed manilla folder and found a sheet of paper bearing the elegantly understated letterhead of Austral Fine Art, Pty Ltd. It was the cover page of a document, dated five months earlier, confirming a number of purchases made by Austral on behalf of the Combined Unions Superannuation Scheme and listing the price of each work. Austral's address was a postoffice box in South Yarra and Drysdale's *Dry Gully*, at $60,000, was its single most expensive acquisition on CUSS's behalf.

Bulldog-clipped to the letter was a swatch of pages, also on Austral letterhead, each headed *Provenance and Certificate of Authenticity*, and consisting of a simple one-paragraph statement, signed at the bottom. The one I wanted read:

Sir Russell Drysdale: Dry Gully (1946)
This painting is the work of the late Sir Russell Drysdale and is from his estate. Austral Fine Art unconditionally guarantees the authenticity of the above named work.

The signature on both the letter and the certificates

was an ornate arabesque, executed in fountain pen and utterly illegible. But the name and title typed below it were decipherable at a glance.

Fiona Lambert, it read, Managing Director.

'**I**NTERESTING?' BERNICE Kaufman loomed in the doorway, her voice dripping sarcasm.

'Ah!' I jumped to my feet, beaming. 'You're back.' I gestured towards the unattended reception area. 'Hope you don't mind me waiting for you in here.'

Bernice's proprietary eyes raked every file, folder and item of correspondence for evidence of unauthorised tampering. 'Forget something?'

I hastened around the desk, relinquishing the Assistant Secretary's throne to its rightful owner. 'I've got an angle for Angelo's speech I'd like to run past you. Get your input.' I tumbled my hands around each other, meshing my fingers like gears. 'How about he emphasises collaboration between the arts industry and union movement?'

'If you were qualified in any way at all for your job,' she advised me primly, 'you would know that the union movement enjoys extensive links with the cultural sector. The Operative Painters and Decorators have, for a number of years, been at the forefront of raising artists' awareness of health and safety issues. Many unions have engaged artists to create works in collaboration with their members. The Building Workers' Union had a poet-in-residence last year.'

A concrete poet, presumably. 'Good points,' I said eagerly. 'Exactly the sort of thing Angelo's speech should mention. What about those consultants you mentioned, Australasian Fine Art, do they have union affiliations?'

Another silly question. 'It's Austral, Murray, Austral. And a CUSS board member with extensive links to the visual arts recommended them, if that's what you mean by union connections.'

'Which reminds me,' I said. 'I'd better get the names of the board members. Make sure Angelo does the acknowledgments right.'

Bernice flicked through the CUSS file and handed me a list. The Secretary of the Trades Hall Council chaired the board. Most of the other names belonged to prominent union officials. Some of them didn't.

'Lloyd Eastlake,' I read out loud. A knot formed itself in the pit of my stomach.

Bernice nodded confirmation. 'You know him?'

'He heads up my policy committee.'

'In that case,' said Bernice, 'I don't have to tell you what an asset he is. It was Lloyd's idea for CUSS to get into art in the first place. Frankly, the rest of the board was lukewarm. But they soon changed their minds. Not only did Austral acquire works by blue-chip artists at very good prices, they found buyers who were prepared to pay considerably more than the works had cost us. The board was so impressed with the investment potential that it immediately upped its level of commitment. It also decided to take a long-term view, to build up the collection rather than just buy and sell on spec.'

'So you must have quite a lot of contact with this Austral crowd? Mind if I take notes? Can I borrow a pen?'

Bernice handed me writing materials. 'Typical,' she clucked. I poised the pen. 'As company secretary,' she went on, 'I am, of course, responsible for the overall administrative framework. But Lloyd insists – and I agree with him on this point – that he handle all direct liaison with Austral himself. That way, individual board members can't try to push their personal tastes. You can imagine what sort of a dog's breakfast we'd end up with if that was allowed to happen.' Not, she felt, that there was any need for Angelo's speech to concern itself with such detail. 'Downplay the investment aspect. Emphasising the cultural benefits to our members would be more appropriate.'

'I agree,' I said. The investment aspects didn't bear thinking about, given what I knew or suspected about the actual value of the works in the room upstairs. Novelty was about the most value they could claim. 'By the way,' I asked. 'How was the ultra-sound?'

Bernice's hand went into her bag like a shot. 'See for yourself.' She handed me what appeared to be a polaroid photograph of meteorological conditions over Baffin Bay taken through the screen door of a low-flying satellite during a lunar eclipse.

'A boy,' I guessed, pointing to what looked like an isthmus extending into the north-west quadrant.

Bernice radiated ambivalent pride. 'Sometimes you surprise me, Murray.'

There were plenty more surprises in store for Bernice Kaufman before her bonny bouncing little numbers man was dragged screaming into the delivery room. But she wouldn't be hearing them from me. Not right away. Not until I'd had a chance to ponder the meaning of the amazing information the past hour had brought to light. 'Thanks, Bernice,' I said. 'You've been incredibly helpful.'

For a brief moment, Bernice's insurgent maternal hormones escaped into her voice box. 'Anytime, Murray,' she sighed wearily. 'Now piss off. I've got work to do.'

Pocketing Bernice's cheap ballpoint pen, I backed out the door and headed downstairs, deep in thought.

Arts was supposed to be a cushy posting. Everybody knew that, for all of Ken Sproule's talk about the culture vultures ripping your flesh. Freebies to the opera and holding the minister's hand at gala soirées were supposed to be the name of the game. Not Spider Webb, dead bodies, police investigations, missing pictures and forgery rackets.

Was it really possible that Lloyd Eastlake knew the paintings in the CUSS collection were fakes? Surely not. A measly half a million dollars worth of pictures was small beer compared with the sort of dough he handled every day at Obelisk Trust. He had too much at stake to engage in such risky business, even if he was that way inclined.

But the moral, legal and financial dimensions were not the only ones to be considered. There was a much more important aspect to all this. The political one. The resignation of the Deputy Premier and the Cabinet reshuffle had been designed to counter a growing perception that the government was financially incompetent, no longer a fit custodian for the public cookie jar. What would happen to voter confidence when it was revealed that the government's appointee as head of the Arts Ministry panel that handed out grants to artists couldn't tell a fake from a fish fork? And that one of its members was brokering forged artworks?

Admittedly, this was not the sort of issue upon which a government stands or falls. But nor was it something you'd want to read about in your morning paper. Not if your boss was the minister responsible. Not if it was your job to see that precisely this sort of thing didn't happen.

Things were starting to get seriously complicated.

Going to the police on this CUSS forgery business was out of the question. Nothing would be gained and much might be lost. A quiet word in the right ear at the right time and the unions could bury their own dead. And, in any case, I was holding firm to my decision not to talk to the cops until Red was safely up, up and away.

But that didn't mean I couldn't make some discreet enquiries of my own in the meantime. The problem was where to start. This needed some nutting out. I drove back to my new office, nutting all the way.

Trish thrust a wad of telephone message slips into my paw as I came in the door. Mendicant terpsichoreans and lobbyist librarians. String quartet convenors and craft marketers. Festival creators and design innovators. People whose calls I was paid to return. 'Thought you'd taken the day off,' she said.

I went into my calm new office, sat at my new desk, looked out my big window and I asked myself the same question I'd been asking myself all the way from the Trades Hall. The inescapable one.

Was Lloyd Eastlake knowingly involved in the faking of the CUSS art collection? And if so, did that mean he was implicated in the death of Marcus Taylor?

Realities were at work here that experience had ill-equipped me to deal with, but that I would very swiftly have to learn to manage if I wanted to keep my head above water.

Back in Ethnic Affairs, I'd encountered my fair share of wealthy men. Some of the richest men in the state were migrants. Not that you'd often find them snoozing in the library at the Melbourne Club. Their own communities knew them as employers and entrepreneurs, as the patrons of social clubs and the doers of good works, and perhaps as other things I made it a point never to inquire about. I'd known them as pleaders for community projects, as genial hosts at national day celebrations, as abstract factors in predictable electoral equations.

But in a very real – meaning political – sense, their transactions and their reputations, their associations and ambitions, were fundamentally a matter of indifference to me. Apart from the one or two who had scaled the Olympian heights of industry, they were generally at a remove from the real centre of power. For all their money and their sectional influence, they were ultimately on the outside looking in. No transgression, error or lapse on their part could really hurt the government.

But not so Eastlake. Eastlake was on the team, one of the boys, a man publicly identifiable with the standards by which we ran the state. A man with a finger in every pie. The party pie, the money pie, the union pie, the culture pie. And some of these pies, unfortunately, now also contained Angelo Agnelli's finger.

I found Lloyd Eastlake's card and laid it flat in front of me on my desk. I built a hedge of yellow phone message slips around it. I tapped its cardboard edge against the blond timber. I buzzed Phillip Veale, two glass partitions away. 'Hypothetically speaking,' I said. 'What's the score on the director of a public art gallery also operating as a consultant to private clients?'

'Hypothetically speaking,' said Veale. 'Probably legal. Possibly unethical. Definitely unwise.' He didn't ask who and I didn't tell him. I couldn't help but feel that our relationship was on the mend.

Then I called a contact at the Corporate Affairs Commission and asked him to look up the company registration information on Austral Fine Art, Pty Ltd. He promised to get back to me within an hour.

Finally, I called Eastlake. Not the mobile number. If he was in his car or on the hoof, Spider might overhear the call. I rang the number that looked like it might be his direct office line. It was. He picked it up after the first ring. 'Where the fuck are you?' he said. 'I've been frantic.'

'It's Murray Whelan.'

'Oh, hello.' He dropped his voice an octave and changed down to cruising speed. 'I thought it was someone else.'

'Are you speaking hands-free?' I like to know exactly who is listening to my conversations. 'Is there anyone else in the office with you?'

'No. I'm alone. Why?'

'Regarding that matter we discussed yesterday at the Deli. I need to talk to you again.'

Eastlake didn't mind indulging my penchant for the melodramatic at the weekend. But, come the working week, he was a busy man. 'Not more of Giles Aubrey's tall tales, I hope.'

'Aubrey's dead,' I said.

'Dead? How?'

'That's what I want to talk to you about. Among other things. Face-to-face and as soon as possible.'

A couple of long seconds went by. 'The soonest I can see you is six.'

Not the most convenient of times, Red-wise, but I was the one doing the asking. 'Fine,' I said. Eastlake gave me Obelisk's address, a downtown office block, and rang off.

Three other people could help me shed light on what was happening. One of them was lying low. One would keep. The other, I decided, might best be caught on the hop.

'Don't worry,' I told Trish's disapproving look as I headed out the door. 'I'm not going far.'

Just across the road and into the trees.

FIONA LAMBERT was wearing a fire-engine-red, thigh-length tunic that emphasised the paleness of her skin and the indelible-ink blackness of her hair. She was standing at the front door of the Centre for Modern Art watching two men in company work-wear drag a flat wooden crate out of a van parked in the driveway.

I sat across the road in my car, watching her watch them.

A young woman in harem pants and a beehive flitted about, getting in the way. I remembered her from Friday night. Janelle Something. Fiona's assistant. The delivery guys negotiated the crate through the door and Fiona and Janelle followed them inside.

Our Home had a new home.

And Ms Lambert, at a guess, would be far too preoccupied for the next little while to participate in the kind of consultative process I had in mind. *Our Home* would have to be uncrated, examined, gloated over, stored away. Slipping the Charade back into gear, I pulled out from the kerb. I had an idea. Not the best idea I'd ever had. But, at the time, it had a compelling sort of logic.

I drove through pools of shade cast by elms and

pines, turned into Domain Road and found a parking spot in a quiet residential side street. Hope Street, said the sign. I left my jacket in the car and walked around the corner.

Domain Road, with its two-storey terrace houses and small apartment buildings, was quiet. A solitary jogger panted along the footpath. I leaned against a parked car and cased Fiona Lambert's pink stucco block of flats. After a couple of minutes, the dowager with the miniature mutt came out the front entrance and carried her schnauzer across the road. She clipped a lead to the benighted animal's collar and led it into the park. Doo-doo time for Dagobert.

When the pair of them had moved out of sight, I went into the flats and walked briskly up the stairs to the landing outside Fiona Lambert's door. I rapped confidently with the little brass knocker, listening for any sound in the flat opposite. There was none. I rapped again, Justin Case. Justin wasn't home, so I angled up the Ming Dynasty pot-plant holder, slid the key from underneath, opened the door and put the key back in place. It wasn't breaking and entering. That would never have occurred to me. I was just dropping around when there was nobody home.

Not that I let myself into people's places on a regular basis. Usually it was the other way around. I'd given a spare key to my place to Faye in case Red ever needed to get in while I was at work and occasionally I'd come home to find she'd left something exotic in the fridge. But this was something new. Just thought I should make the point.

The flat was exactly as I had last seen it. Same

Bauhaus chairs, same boxy sofa, same honey-coloured dining table, same pornographic portrait. Out the uncurtained window, the roof of the CMA was just visible between the trees. If Fiona decided to pop home across the greensward, I'd see her coming through the trees.

The object of my search was vague. Anything to corroborate Lambert's association with the bogus CUSS collection. Anything to connect her with Marcus Taylor, to help clarify the mutually contradictory information I had about their relationship. Had Taylor hated her as the woman who stole his birthright? Or was he providing fake artworks for her Austral Fine Art operation? Was it possible that she had the missing version of *Our Home*? Given what I now knew, Eastlake's line about it being a student copy of a masterwork had taken on a decidedly hollow ring.

The small study opening off the lounge room was the logical place to start. A strictly utilitarian space. Walls bare except for a row of tiny canvases, each no more than four inches square, each a different shade of blue. A ladder-frame bookcase filled with art magazines. A chrome-inlaid Aero desk, tres chic, with matching stainless-steel waste paper basket, empty. A cardboard box containing several dozen brand-new copies of *A Fierce Vision*. A two-drawer filing cabinet. Bottom drawer, stationery supplies. Top drawer, domestic appliance warranties.

On the desk, an Apple computer with a plastic cover. Must learn to use. Postcards. Someone called Vicki saying Budapest was fab. Invitations to exhibition openings. Bills. Gas, electricity, phone. Very ordinary. Visa,

Mastercard, Amex. Denting the plastic to the tune of about twenty-two hundred a month. Clothes and restaurants mainly. Mortgage statement. Nine hundred a month, $86,000 left to pay.

On a salary of, what, sixty grand? Fiona Lambert was living beyond her means. Extravagant but, so far, nothing illegal. Nothing relating to Austral Fine Art. Not so much as a sheet of letterhead. Must keep all that over at the CMA.

Scanning the view out the window on my way, I went up the hall to the bedroom.

Heavy drapes, open a chink. Window overlooking a small courtyard. Enough light to see by. Big contrast to the *Vogue* casualness of the living room. Queen-size bed, black sheets smoothed tight. Cotton. Satin would be tacky. Many big plush pillows, red. Pale carpet, low nap, soft like felt. On the wall above the bed was one huge painting. Not Szabo. Thickly laid-on acrylic paint, high texture, chopped like the waves of a starlit sea. Abstract, tactile, sensual. I could smell clean linen and Oil of Ulan. Red lacquer chest of drawers, antique Japanese. Rice-paper lamps. The whole room reflected back on itself from a mirrored wardrobe occupying entire side wall.

An intensely private atmosphere, redolent of the mysterious feminine. Then again, maybe it was just that I hadn't been in a woman's bedroom for quite some time.

I slid open the mirror-fronted wardrobe and saw a great quantity of clothes, all of them either red, white or black. Enough shoes to make Imelda Marcos's mouth water. About a dozen men's business shirts. Top brands.

Ironed. No half million dollars. No Certificate of Incorporation for Austral Fine Art.

Nothing for me on the rack. I looked in the Japanese chest. For a moment longer than absolutely necessary, I stood staring down at a girl called Fiona's collection of investment-quality lingerie. Nothing tarty. No reds or blacks here. Shell-pink, ivory, cream. Resisting the temptation to touch, I knelt on the floor and looked under the bed. Nothing, not even dust.

Straight across the hall was the bathroom. The chunky vanity basin was littered with toning lotions and night creams. Princess Marcella Borghese Face Mud. A cupboard held thick towels, folded and stacked. A cane laundry basket contained damp towels and a white t-shirt with two interlocked Cs in gold on the front.

The kitchen was expensively spartan: Alessi kettle, Moulinex, crystal wineglasses, stainless steel Poggenpohl appliances. Japanese crackers on an empty bench-top.

By now I was hyperventilating. 'Right,' I said, out loud. Time to go. If Fiona Lambert was up to no good, the evidence of it wasn't here.

One last getaway glance out the window. Fiona Lambert was crossing a sunlit patch of lawn between two pines, headed for home. She was, perhaps, two minutes away. At the far side of the courtyard were rubbish bins, a rear exit to the flats. I opened the door a notch to reconnoitre my getaway and heard footfalls coming briskly up the stairs towards me, a heavy male tread.

Whoever he was, he'd be on the landing in a matter

of seconds. His destination must be the flat opposite. Fiona was still ninety seconds away. It would be close, but an undetected departure was still possible. Closing the door and pressing my back to it, I listened for the man to go into the other flat.

The footsteps came closer. My hearing, all my senses, felt preternaturally heightened. A radio somewhere was broadcasting talkback. Out on Domain Road, a tram clattered by. Somebody's muffler was due for replacement. The footsteps reached the landing. I waited for the jingle of keys or a rapping on the knocker opposite. All I heard was breathing, the wheezing of an unfit man who had just climbed a flight of stairs on a summer day and was pausing to catch his breath. I strained to hear movement, my heart drumming in my ears.

Distantly, the rhythmic click of a woman's heels rapidly ascended the concrete stairs.

The tattoo beat of my pulse became a surf-roar of panic.

The door was about to fly open. My idiotic spur-of-the-moment impulse was about to backfire horribly, to result in my discovery and disgrace. What possible pretext could I find for being in a woman's flat in this way? What would it look like? I'd be taken for a panty sniffer or a petty thief. A pervert, a psycho. How had I got myself into this position? To what idiot impulse had I surrendered my common sense? What outlandish excuse could I invent? I had to think of something and think of it fast.

I did. I hid.

I hid in the first place I found, a louvre-fronted closet beside the entrance to the living room. I took it for a coat closet but found it held brooms and mops and a vacuum cleaner. Shouldering my way between the broom handles, I swung the slatted door shut behind me just as a key snicked into the front-door lock.

A feather duster tickled the back of my neck. The handle of a broom toppled to rest against my cheek. The metal nozzle of the vacuum cleaner was jammed up my posterior crotch. Standing to rigid attention in claustrophobic darkness, I held my breath and awaited the humiliation of discovery.

'Did you bring it?' Fiona Lambert opened her front door and stepped through.

Two silhouettes passed before the downward sloping slats of the louvred panel. Just as they did so, I realised that the closet door had not swung completely shut behind me. A chink perhaps a centimetre wide remained open. From where I was standing, it looked as vast as the Grand Canyon.

'You have the delivery docket?' said a male voice, a deep rumble.

My senses were so acute that I could feel the hair standing up on the nape of my neck, taste the dust molecules in the air, smell the residues of floor wax clinging to the broom bristles. A spider in the dark behind me exuded the glutinous thread of its web. Heat radiated from my body. Sweat gushed from every pore, cascading down my skin and dripping into my eyes. My heart belted against my ribs like the bass riff from a Maxine Nightingale disco hit. The saliva had dried in my mouth and, when I tried to swallow it, crackled like a sheet of cellophane being rolled into a ball. I felt as if I was about to burst into flames.

Two shapes went past, into the living room. Through the gap, I could see the shoulder of a white business shirt. The man wearing it had something tucked up under his armpit, blocked by his torso. He half-turned and I could see the back of his near-bald skull. He was examining a sheet of light green paper. Satisfied with what he read, the man folded the page and put it in his pants pocket.

'Show it to me,' said Fiona impatiently, just beyond my vision.

A sliver of dining table was within my narrow line of sight. The man took the thing from under his arm and put it on the table. It was a shoebox in the distinctive hot pink and silver colours of the Karlcraft chain. He took the lid off and removed banded wads of banknotes. He built them into two piles, each about fifteen centimetres high. The money was pale, the colour of hundred dollar bills. Even from inside a broom cupboard on the other side of the room, it looked like a great deal of money.

'One hundred thousand dollars,' said the jowly voice of Max Karlin. 'Cash.'

'O NE HUNDRED thousand?' Lambert was outraged. 'That wasn't the deal. Where's the rest of my money?'

Holding my breath, I leaned forward until my eye was almost pressed to the crack in the door. My field of vision widened to include a good part of the living room. Fiona Lambert stood staring down at the money on the table, her expression caught between elation and petulance.

Karlin ignored her outburst. 'Aren't you going to offer me a drink?'

'You think you can short-change me, is that it?' snarled Lambert. 'Our deal was for twice this amount.'

Karlin put his hands in his pocket and moved out of view. 'It's all I can afford.' His attitude was take-it-or-leave-it. 'If I really wanted to cheat you, Fiona dear, I wouldn't be here at all. Be reasonable. It's still a great deal of money.'

'Our agreement was for one third of the purchase price of *Our Home*,' complained Lambert bitterly, her eyes never leaving the money. 'By my arithmetic, that's two hundred thousand dollars.' Karlin had gone in the direction of the couch. Lambert turned to face him.

'You think it was easy convincing Eastlake to pay more than double the market value?'

Karlin chuckled indulgently. 'Oh, I don't doubt you were very persuasive, my dear.'

His crossed ankles came into view. I could picture him on the couch, leaning back, his legs extended in front of him. 'It's just that circumstances have changed since we made our little agreement. A year ago, cash was easier to lay my hands on. I was slinging fifty thousand a month in backhanders to the building contractors alone. But things have changed. The money has dried up. My bankers are counting every penny. The other investors are watching me like a hawk.'

Fiona Lambert swung around to face him, bare arms akimbo. 'Sell another one of your pictures.' She was spitting chips. 'Sell two, sell anything. Pay me what you owe me.'

'Even if I thought I owed you anything, I've nothing left to sell.' Karlin indulged her, but he was unsympathetic. '*Our Home* was the last really valuable picture I still owned outright. The rest were sold long ago. I've been leasing them back, keeping up appearances.' Compared to him, he was saying, she had nothing to complain about.

'Liar!' She actually stamped her foot.

Karlin snorted with amusement. 'Take the money, Fiona.' His tone was fatherly, unprovokable. He'd seen all this before. 'Be happy you got anything at all. I'm walking away with nothing. Time was, I was a shoe salesman who liked to collect pictures. Then I decided to be a big-shot property developer. I sold my shops, hocked my pictures, bet everything on one big project.

Now, after fifty years of hard work, all I've got are banks and investors and unions and construction contractors gnawing at my flesh. Jesus, I've even got an art gallery director blackmailing me.' He emitted a dry humourless guffaw, as if this was the ultimate indignity.

'You're breaking my heart.' Little Miss Lambert didn't sound so well brought up now.

'Be grateful you're getting anything, Fiona. I'm only here because of my sentimental attachment to *Our Home*. Because I'd rather see it go to a public art museum than be sold off in a fire sale. And because I'm a man who keeps his word. I used to be, at least.'

'I don't care where you get it,' insisted Fiona sullenly. 'I want my money.'

'Or what? You'll sue me? I can picture the scene in court. I can hear your lawyer explaining how you extorted money out of me.' Karlin came back up onto his feet and gave a sarcastic demonstration. He drew himself up to his full diminutive height and waggled his chubby finger, imitating a lawyer pleading a case. '"They had a watertight deal, Your Honour. She, expert on the works of Victor Szabo, proposed that she would refrain from deliberately raising suggestions that the painting known as *Our Home* was of dubious authorship. He, in return, agreed to sell the work to her gallery and to pay her a secret commission on the deal. Further, Your Honour, she proposed that if he did not comply with her demands she would cast public doubt on the integrity, and therefore the market value, of other art works in his collection. A perfectly normal commercial transaction, Your Honour."' His address to court complete, Karlin wheeled on his feet and headed towards the kitchen door. 'Yes, Fiona, I can just imagine that.'

Lambert was silent, scowling, one foot tapping. Her gaze followed Karlin and flashed across my hiding place like a spotlight playing on a prison wall. I cowered back into the darkness and slowly emptied the exhausted oxygen from my lungs.

Plumbing whined in the wall behind me and water hit a metal sink. Karlin was in the kitchen, running a tap, getting his own drink. Under cover of the noise, I gulped down air and eased the tension in my muscles. My skin was tacky with sweat and my pulse still raced, but the terror of discovery was abating, replaced by a sense of exultation. My instinct in coming here had been vindicated.

This Fiona Lambert was some piece of work. Selling an entirely forged collection of art. Forcing Karlin to sell *Our Home* and blackmailing him into paying her a secret commission on the deal. Inveigling Eastlake into raising the money.

I ran the desiccated rhinoceros of my tongue around the Kalahari of my mouth, cocked my ear for the next amazing revelation and put my eye once more to the crack. So what if I was discovered? Compared with Fiona Lambert's outrageous felonies, cupboard-skulking was a mere social misdemeanour.

Lambert was sitting at the table, staring at the money. Avarice and triumph lit her face. Karlin's voice came from the kitchen. 'Stop squawking and be grateful you got anything. Frankly, my other creditors won't be anywhere near as lucky. The financial empire of Max

Karlin is about to collapse into a pile of rubble and I'm not sticking around to see it happen. I'm on my way to the airport. I'm leaving the country. At five this afternoon, bankruptcy papers will be filed for my private holding company. At nine o'clock tomorrow morning, I'll be in Europe. A liquidator will be sitting at my desk. And the dogs will be fighting over Karlcraft's carcass.'

Fiona Lambert couldn't give a damn about Karlin's misfortunes. Breaking the band on one of the wads of cash, she licked her thumb and started counting. Her lips moved silently like a devotee telling her rosary beads. Karlin came out of the kitchen and when he spoke the sound was so close it startled me. 'Don't bank it all at once. Large cash deposits get reported. And don't start spending it either, not unless you want Lloyd suspecting something.'

'You think I'm stupid?' said Fiona rancorously. 'You think I don't know that?' He'd made her lose count and she had to start again. 'And leave Lloyd to me. I know how to handle Lloyd Eastlake.'

Karlin was standing immediately in front of my hiding place, blocking my view. 'Tch tch. Greedy girl, tch tch.' His shape moved towards the front door. 'Goodbye, Fiona.'

Lambert got up from the table. I leaned backwards and held my breath. The front door opened. 'Bon voyage, Max.' Fiona was caustic to the last. 'And thanks for nothing.' Karlin's footsteps rapidly receded down the stairs. The door was pulled shut and Fiona spoke under her breath. 'You miserable little Shylock.'

Charming.

My big moment, I decided, had arrived. Throw open the cupboard door, jump out and spring Ms Director of the Centre for Modern Art with her hands sunk elbow-deep in ill-gotten loot. Bang her up, dead to rights, with the evidence of her sins piled on the Baltic pine dining table of her over-geared pied-à-terre.

Lambert's silhouette passed the louvred door. I pressed my eye to the crack, waiting for exactly the right moment to make my move.

Her mood had improved remarkably. She kicked off her shoes, sashayed her hips, pumped her arms at her side and sidled across the living room. 'Let me look at you,' she cooed throatily. 'You beautiful, beautiful money.'

She picked up one of the packets of bills and fanned it with her thumb. She kissed it. She slowly ran it over her bare arms, luxuriating in its feel. She squirmed sinuous. 'Money, money, money,' she sang. The tune from *Cabaret*.

Tearing the band off with her teeth, she smeared a fistful of bills across her neck and torso. The loose notes cascaded past her swaying hips and settled on the floor around her feet. She reached for another wad and danced a slow silent rhumba with it, pressing the cash to her belly with one hand and describing a slow circle in the air above her head with the other. She was in a trance.

I couldn't believe my eyes. Turned on by a wad of cash. It was a mesmerising sight. And sexy as all hell. She slid the wad of bills slowly down her body, moaning a low guttural tune in the back of her throat. She moved out of sight. Glassware clinked. She segued back into sight, drink in one hand, money in the other. I'd seen enough. Time to spring.

Bang. Bang. A sharp metallic rapping came from the flat door. I nearly jumped out of my skin. I cringed backwards and my line of sight narrowed.

Startled out of her reverie, Fiona dropped her bundle. She went down on her knees, scrabbling for the bills strewn about the floor. Rap, rap, came the knock at the door. 'Just a moment,' she called, scooping up an armful of loose money, dumping it on the table and going down for more. 'Who is it?'

'Me.' A male. Not Karlin.

'Coming.' She disappeared from my sight briefly, then darted back with a piece of cloth, some sort of throw-sheet off the couch. It billowed above the table and fell loosely over the money. She composed herself, smoothing down her clothes and hair. She came towards me, scooping up her shoes on the way. When she reached my hiding place, she paused to slip on her shoes. She leaned against the louvred door. It clicked shut.

My heart shot backwards in my chest, hit my spine and bounced off. My legs requested a transfer to other duties. I braced myself for exposure. Fiona, oblivious to the pulsating tom-tom of my heartbeat, stepped to the front door and opened it. All I could see was a section of carpet, visible through the downward-raked slats of the closet's louvred door.

'Hi.' Fiona was purring, butter not melting in her mouth. 'What brings you here?' Like this was the nicest surprise she'd had all day.

'Just a chance visit.' The voice sounded familiar.

When I heard it again, I had no trouble putting a face to it. 'I called in across the road to see if the picture had arrived safe and sound. Janelle said you'd come home for lunch, so I thought I'd join you.' It was Lloyd Eastlake.

Things were getting more interesting by the moment. I hung on Lambert's response. She said nothing.

'Aren't you going to ask me in?'

A moment's silence. 'Um. I'm just on my way back to work, actually.' And not really in a position to do any entertaining, what with the flat all cluttered up with hundred-dollar bills.

Eastlake was undeterred. 'Let's have a little drink first. Celebrate your success. The Centre for Modern Art's first major acquisition. *Our Home*, ours at last.' His tone was more than just chairmanly. 'You look a bit flushed. You haven't been having one all by yourself, have you? You naughty little girl.'

She played along. 'Okay, I admit it. You caught me at it. But I really must be getting back. The picture has to be stored away properly. You know what Janelle's like.'

'What's the hurry? Janelle will be fine.' The tone was playfully wheedling, but there was a possessive edge to it. 'You haven't got someone in there with you, have you?'

'Like who?' She laughed the idea away, resenting the inference.

'An attractive woman like you,' he said, turning it into a compliment. 'Could be any one of a million men.'

This all had an air of easy intimacy to it. I began to suspect I knew what Fiona had meant when she said she knew how to handle Lloyd Eastlake. 'I just love it when you get jealous.' Playful sarcasm. 'Married man and all.'

'C'mon. How about that drink.' Eastlake didn't want to stand in the door. He was coming inside. Like it or not.

I was breathing through my skin, willing myself invisible. Eastlake's shoes appeared in the louvre-framed square of carpet in front of the closet. Suddenly, the outline of Fiona's red dress pressed back against the door. The louvres bulged inwards and the whole door creaked on its hinges. Fabric rustled against fabric. Fiona had grabbed Eastlake and pulled him against her. Another sound came – part moist sucking, part sibilant inhalation, part low moan. They were going the smooch, the full mutual tonsillectomy by the sound of it.

The vixen! 'Hmm,' she murmured appreciatively. 'I do find it exciting, I must admit. Getting *Our Home* at last.'

Lloyd Eastlake wasn't a man to pass up an opportunity. 'Hmm,' he agreed. Now that she'd started him up, there was no stopping him. The cupboard door bowed inwards. All I could see was the bare backs of Fiona's calves, her ankles, her fire-engine red shoes. Eastlake's shoe slid between hers, the light grey check of his trousered leg rubbing against her bare flesh.

Movement traced the silhouette outline of Fiona's body. Something slid behind her, cradling the small of her back. Through the slats of the louvre, I could clearly see the individual hairs on the back of Eastlake's hand. My mouth turned to a desert. It seemed inconceivable that they couldn't hear my heart beating. I could hear every breath they took, distinguish their individual rhythms. I might as well have been in bed with them.

They might as well have been in bed with each other. The pace of their breathing quickened, the volume of their slurping noises. Eastlake's hand was tugging up the hem of Lambert's dress. Her knickers were pale lilac. His hand slid into them, down into the valley of her buttocks. Her feet eased wider. 'Hmm,' he murmured. 'I'll have to buy you an expensive painting more often.'

She moaned encouragement. Eastlake's hand was out of her knickers. He was down on his knees, tugging at them. Her legs closed. A flash of lilac slid past her white knees. Through the inverted V of her thighs, I saw him shake free of his suit jacket. He reached down and opened his trousers.

All the blood in my body had converged in my groin. I could have got a job as a coat hook. The pulse in my ears was beating a rhythm like the time-keeper on a slave galley. Faster. Faster. Ramming speed. I screwed my eyes shut and tried to think of something else. Anything else. Humpity, humpity, went the door, threatening to burst in. Bang, bang, bang.

I peeked, knowing already what I would see. Fiona's feet had vanished, raised off the floor. Little ridges of red dress were being forced into the gaps between the louvre slats. So too was the bare flesh of Fiona Lambert's arse. One red shoe lay on its side. The other had vanished. Eastlake was still wearing his. I could see their stitching. Four-hundred-dollar shoes. Only the tips showed. His trousers were round his ankles. His calves were braced. His knees were buckled. His thighs were thrusting.

Bang, bang. I closed my eyes and searched my mind for some distracting thought. I peeked again, then squeezed my eyes tight.

Eastlake's trousers were Prince of Wales check. This was the pattern favoured by the sharpies, part of the uniform. Wide Prince of Wales check trousers and skin-tight maroon knit tops. That's what Geordie Fletcher wore.

Geordie Fletcher and the horrible twins, Danny and Wayne. I was back at the Oulton Reserve. Round and round I was spinning, biffed and bashed at every turn. My life was in the hands of a gang of brain-dead sharpies. Spider, my supposed protector, was in league with the enemy. My hand was curled tight around the neck of a bottle. A potential weapon, but tangled in the folds of my coat.

Suddenly, it came free. I brandished it like a club. Dizzy with vertigo, I staggered sideways and fell. The bottle hit the concrete path. Broken glass scattered in a pool of spilt alcohol. I was on my knees breathing in the acrid smell.

'Fucking idiot. You wasted it.' Geordie Fletcher had me by the collar, hauling me to my feet. This was it. The cat-and-mouse game was over. I was about to be beaten shitless. The twins had stopped their jeering and fallen silent. Big brother was going to show them how it was done.

More fool him. The neck of the bottle was still in my hand, a hard knife-edged cylinder. Slashing side-ways, I caught Geordie unawares. My blow sliced across his thigh, opening a gash in his pants. Blood sprayed into the air.

Geordie jumped back. Amazement lit his face. My fear became exhilaration. I thrust the bottle neck in front of me, daring them to try anything. The Fletchers circled, Geordie's surprise turning to rage. Spider Webb elbowed his way between the twins. 'Put it down, Whelan,' he said. 'Don't be a dickhead.' Somewhere in the dusk beyond the tea-tree, car doors slammed and footsteps raced towards us. Every sharpie in town was about to descend on me. There was blood everywhere. 'Come on, you little cunt,' Geordie yelled. 'Have a go.'

I did. I rushed him. Spider grabbed my arm, twisting it. 'Drop it. Drop it.' Pain shot through my elbow. The bottle neck fell from my hand. Broken glass crunched underfoot. Geordie kicked me in the balls. The pain was searing. Spider's face was in mine. 'Fucking idiot.' Bent double, eyes welling, I retched.

The galloping feet arrived. Hands grabbed my hair, jerking my head back. I swung wildly, no longer caring what happened. An adult had me. A police uniform. A sergeant's stripes. I recognised the face. I'd seen it in the hotel, drinking with my father after closing time. Open handed, he whacked the side of my head so hard that I saw stars and my teeth nearly fell out. 'You're coming with me, son.'

'Come! Come!' urged Fiona. 'Yes. Yes.' She said some other things, too. Things I won't repeat here.

The pace of Eastlake's thrusting increased. The closet door quaked in its frame. An anchovy smell tinged the air. Rumpity, rumpity. Casanova let out a plaintive groan. Hissing like a braking steam train, he slowed to a halt. Suddenly, all was still.

Eastlake disengaged with a suction-cup slurp. Fiona

Lambert's bare backside separated from the louvres and her feet found the floor. Her dress fell back into place. She let out a long breath. I wished I could do the same. 'You tiger,' she said. 'That was wonderful.'

With a dull thud, Tiger Eastlake slumped back against the wall opposite. He swallowed, caught his breath. 'You came?'

'Uh-huh.' She might have fooled him, but she wasn't fooling me.

'You sure?' His voice was post-coitally dreamy.

'Would I lie to you?' Her real love, I knew, was lying on the dining table. The knee-trembler had kept him out of the living room for a while. But what was she going to do now? Push him out the door? Her back was still pressed against the closet. 'Now I really do need a drink. Be a darling. There's an open bottle in the fridge.'

Eastlake's hands came down and his pants went up. A zipper zipped. He took a step closer. Nuzzling sounds. He was compliant. His shoes swivelled in the direction of the kitchen. As he moved away, Fiona's back came off the door. I sensed, rather than heard, her flit across the living room.

From the kitchen came the rattle of a refrigerator shelf. Bottles clinked. A cork was withdrawn. A cupboard opened. Glass nudged glass. I could have done with a drink myself. And a cigarette. I like one after-wards.

'I don't suppose Max Karlin personally delivered the painting, by any chance?' called Eastlake. There was a well-practised familiarity at work here. The easy way the switches went on and off. This sex business between him and Fiona had been going on for some time. But the casualness of Eastlake's question was a little too studied. He had something on his mind.

'Max?' Miss Innocence was relaxed. The dough must have been safely out of sight. 'Haven't seen him since Saturday. Why?'

She came over, picked up her knickers, went back into the living room. 'Where's that drink?'

'I've been trying to contact him all day.' Eastlake came out of the kitchen. 'He's not returning my calls.'

I remembered his anxious grab at the phone when I'd rung. Poor Lloyd. His timing was lousy. Thirty seconds earlier and he'd have run into Karlin on the stairs.

'I really should be getting back to work,' Fiona said. Not, of course, with any of her previous door-blocking urgency. They were like a married couple. He wanted her to listen while he complained about his hard day at the office.

'Sorry to burden you with my worries,' he said. 'I know you hate shoptalk. But if you hear from Max, tell him to call me immediately. There's a rumour going around that he's getting cold feet. The Karlcraft Centre is at the don't-look-down stage. The whole thing is in danger of falling over if Max loses his nerve right now. Obelisk has sunk a lot of money into Max Karlin. More than I was authorised to lend him. I've staked Obelisk's whole future, and my own, on Max's success. If he goes belly-up, he'll take me with him. The least he could do is return my calls.'

'You worry too much.' Fiona played the wifey part, smoothing his fevered brow. 'He's probably just in a meeting or something. It'll be okay, you'll see. If he rings to check that *Our Home* has arrived okay, I'll tell him to call you straight away.'

Eastlake was pacing about while Fiona made reassuring noises. I couldn't quite make out what was being said. My whole body ached from the effort of standing to attention. Carefully, I moved my wrist into a position where I could read my watch. Thirty minutes I'd been standing there. It felt like years. I needed to urinate. Suddenly, something jolted my heart back into my mouth. I heard the sound of my own name.

'That reminds me,' Eastlake was saying. 'You don't have to worry about Giles Aubrey any more. That Whelan guy rang me, said he was dead. I knew I shouldn't have told you what Whelan said Aubrey told him. You've probably been worrying about it.'

'Dead?' she said, only mildly curious. 'How?'

'Whelan didn't say. All very enigmatic, he was. I'm meeting him later, so I'll find out then, I suppose. Anyway, there's one less problem.'

'Oh, I was never really worried about Giles Aubrey.'

Yet again, I couldn't believe my ears. But the logic was overwhelming. The story Aubrey told me – whether true or not – had the potential to derail the CMA's purchase of *Our Home*. Lambert had put a great deal of effort into making sure the sale went ahead. She had a lot riding on its successful conclusion. She could hardly just stand by and let Giles Aubrey ruin her plans. A woman as young, fit and ruthless as Fiona Lambert would have no trouble pushing a frail old man down a steep riverbank.

'I'll just try Max again.' Eastlake came closer and I

heard a distinct grunt as he bent to pick up his hastily shed suit jacket. Blip, blop, blip. Mobile phone dialling noises. Silence. Glasses tinkled. The kitchen tap ran again. Fiona, clearing up. Eastlake got through, asked for Karlin. 'Still not back? Okay. Same message.'

My bladder was full. If I didn't get out of that fucking closet soon, I'd have to start paying rent.

They were at the door. 'Remember, if Max calls . . .'

'Don't worry. I'll tell him . . .'

'I don't know what I'd do without you.' Eastlake spoke in tones of unalloyed affection. Jesus. The schmuck was in love.

The door closed. Lambert waited a beat, then let out a long sigh of relief. She moved down the hall. Seconds later, the pipes in the wall behind me started up. From the direction of the bathroom came the sound of running water, then of teeth being brushed. Brush, brush, brush. Then the shower started. Above the cascade of the water, I heard the screech of a curtain being tugged along a metallic rail.

Leaning lightly on the cupboard door, I popped it open. Reassuring myself that no-one was coming up the stairs, I drew the flat door shut behind me. My shirt was drenched in sweat and draped with cobwebs. My hands were shaking. I gulped air. My breath came in short pants, dressed for the weather.

I hurried downstairs, gripping the banister.

DROPLETS OF moisture flashed in the sunlight. Sprinklers played across the lawns of the Domain. Children ran between the trees squirting each other with water pistols. Senior citizens at picnic tables poured streams of steaming tea from thermos flasks. After what felt like an eternity trapped in that broom closet, my bladder was about to explode.

Tilted forward at the waist like a particularly obsequious Japanese, I scuttled across Domain Road and cast about for a public convenience of some description. The only facility in sight was a shoulder-high bed of red and yellow canna lilies. Advancing into its leafy interior, I proceeded to irrigate its tuberous root structure.

Below the waist, I sighed with relief. Above the neck, I struggled to make sense of all that I had just observed. Some things were crystal clear. Others were murky and obscure. I had a growing sense of dismay and responsibility.

That Fiona Lambert was some piece of work. And she definitely had Lloyd Eastlake's measure. Our Man in the Arts, puffed up with smug vanity, was a soft target. Particularly by the time Fiona Lambert had finished working her charms.

Scam one was the CUSS set-up. Eastlake, doing his girlfriend a favour, had put the art investment business of the Combined Unions Superannuation Scheme her way. This entailed a conflict of interest on his part, both as a director of the CUSS and as chairman of the Centre for Modern Art, but he had probably done no more than what a thousand other company directors did every day of the week. His hot-shot lover, however, had taken full advantage of the opportunity to slip the unsuspecting CUSS an entirely fabricated art collection. The sheer scale of her audacity was staggering.

Scam two was the Szabo deal. Eastlake, persuaded that *Our Home* was an absolute must for the CMA collection, had exerted his influence with both the government and Obelisk to fund its purchase. Fiona, meanwhile, had forced Max Karlin to sell the picture and cut herself in for a piece of the action.

My presence within the stand of lilies, I was suddenly aware, had not passed unnoticed. An amorous couple reclining on the lawn nearby were beginning to cast hostile glances towards where my head extended above the leaf line. I turned my back to them, lest they get the wrong idea.

Was it really possible that Lambert could have got away with her CUSS fraud if not for the accidental depredations of a pair of skylarking ten-year-olds? Would Taylor's forgeries have remained undetected in the face of public scrutiny? And why had Taylor been colluding with Lambert? According to Giles Aubrey, he hated her guts. Had the whole Szabo–Taylor story been a product of Aubrey's notorious tendency to misrepresentation? Or had Marcus Taylor eventually become reconciled to his father's ambitious young bit of cheesecake? Or had his broker, Salina Fleet, handled customer relations? Was it possible that he had no idea that Lambert was the buyer of his 'appropriations'?

Did canna lilies, I wondered, benefit from the occasional dose of concentrated uric acid? This slash was taking on the proportions of an Olympic event. Marcus Taylor. Perhaps he, too, tried to piss in somebody's garden. Maybe he thought he'd found the perfect way to avenge himself on Fiona Lambert. Maybe she had unwittingly given him the opportunity to engineer her downfall. Maybe he had wanted his forgeries to be discovered, as evidenced by the stamp on the back of *Dry Gully*. But not for the reasons Claire had postulated – not out of a forger's vanity – but to discredit and destroy Fiona Lambert.

For months he had toiled in obscurity, producing an entire collection of fake art works in his ratty studio at the old YMCA. For months he had bided his time, waiting for just the right moment. For the moment when he could reveal that his perfectly innocent postmodern tributes had knowingly been passed off as the real thing by Fiona Lambert.

But something even better had come along. The CMA's acquisition of *Our Home*. An irresistible opportunity – not just to avenge himself on Lambert – but to strike a blow against his dead father as well. Frustrated by his inability to obtain anything but the most meagre recognition of his own achievements as an artist – a paltry grant can be even more insulting than none at all – Taylor had manufactured a carbon-copy of *Our Home* with the object of compromising the integrity of Victor Szabo's entire artistic output. Oedipus meets Hamlet on the banks of the Yarra.

At long last, the call of nature rang less stridently in my ears. Drained, I parted the broad green leaves of the cannae, stepped back out onto the lawn and gave the scandalised lovers a cheerful wave. Through the trees, I could see the white facade of the Centre for Modern Art. A scenario, part memory, part specula-tion, began to take shape.

Poor little Marcus Taylor. He really was a fuck-up. He painted his duplicate *Our Home*, but then got pissed and cocky and tipped his hand at the CMA opening. That little performance of his must really have set the cat among the pigeons. No wonder Salina Fleet had looked so nervous when he got up on that table and started waving his arms about. She knew what he was going to say. He'd given her a sneak preview of the notes to his speech a few moments before, out in the back garden.

Fiona Lambert was a cool customer, though. She didn't betray herself, even though she was the one with most at stake. Later that night, while supposedly home in bed, she caught up with Taylor and sunk him and his troublesome plans in the National Gallery moat.

The sky was blue. Birds were singing. The grass was green and cool underfoot. I walked back towards Hope Street, where the Charade was parked, through a beauti-ful summer afternoon. I wondered how she had done it. How she'd managed to get Marcus Taylor's uncon-scious body up over the parapet and roll it into the water. Knocking him out would have been the easy part. He was practically legless the last time I'd seen him, staggering down the Domain Road footpath.

His big moment had come to nothing. But he still hadn't played his trump card. *Our Home* Mark 2 was still on its easel back at the YMCA. His day would come. Just you wait, he said. Just you wait.

Through an intermittent stream of traffic, I could see the very spot where I'd heard him mumble those words. Pausing beside an enormous Moreton Bay fig, I leaned against the trunk and recalled the scene.

Taylor coming one way. Me going the other. Up ahead of me, the Botanical Hotel. Ahead of Taylor, Lambert's flat and, a fifteen-minute walk away, his own room in the YMCA. The disappearing tail-lights of Lloyd Eastlake's Mercedes.

Rewind further. Up in the flat. Fiona on the phone. Out the window, standing less than fifty metres from where I was currently standing, also on the phone, Spider Webb.

The Missing Link. I'd been battling to put Spider into the picture. He and Fiona Lambert were, after all, far from a natural pair. But now that I began to put the pieces together, an alliance between the two of them made a certain sort of sense. Each was working Eastlake from a different direction – Spider looking for the main chance, Fiona needing help to work her gold mine.

Spider. Warning me off. Tidying up the loose ends. Loose ends like the fact that Taylor had gone to the bottom of the moat with his keys in his pocket. So somebody had to go back the next morning and retrieve the duplicate Szabo and dispose of the evidence of the

Austral forgery factory. Loose ends like the fact that I'd got there first and had to be locked in the basement with Willy the Whale. Loose ends like Salina Fleet.

I thought again of Salina's reaction at the moat. Those frozen expressions on her face, caught by the flashing ambulance light. Shock, panic, fear. Did she guess what had happened? Was her insistence that Taylor had killed himself a hastily improvised way of protecting herself, of demonstrating that she could be trusted to keep silent? And her appearance at the YMCA? Was she acting on her own initiative, hastening to clear out all evidence of Taylor's work? Or was everyone just after Taylor's version of *Our Home*?

Then I had come along, sticking my bib in. Not content to remain locked in the basement of the YMCA, I'd kicked up a racket. When Salina inadvertently released me, I put her on the spot. She was a fast thinker, but not entirely convincing in the clinches. And, by then, I'd seen the picture on the easel in Taylor's studio. By then, I was starting to make a real nuisance of myself. I sought out Giles Aubrey, a man who could be relied on to grab the first opportunity that came his way to stir the pot, and gone running to Eastlake with what he told me. But Eastlake, in turn, told Lambert. So Aubrey had ended up at the bottom of the nearest river-bank with a compound fracture of the *corpus delicti*. At least Sal had the sense to make herself scarce.

As I stood there, concealed by the grey folds of Moreton Bay fig, contemplating my responsibility for Giles Aubrey's death, Fiona Lambert came out of the block of flats. Hands empty, teeth shining, looking exceptionally pleased with herself, she crossed Domain

Road and walked towards the Centre for Modern Art.

It was, I decided, time to blow the whistle on Ms Lambert. Get the cops on the case while she still had the hundred grand stashed in her flat. Detective Senior Constable Chris Micaelis would be hearing from me, I resolved, very soon. Just as soon as I'd made a couple of phone calls.

Once Fiona Lambert disappeared into the CMA, I hurried to the Charade and headed back towards the office. It was getting on for 4.30 and the ebb tide of early rush-hour traffic had begun to flow out of the city. Anybody with half a brain had already clocked-off and was headed for the beach.

Something I'd overheard in Fiona Lambert's flat was exercising my mind. The world of high finance was *terra incognita*. It was time I got hold of a tourist guide. Even as I turned into St Kilda Road, I was pulling up in front of the Travelodge and fishing in my pockets for coins.

I could find only notes. This meant that before I could use the pay-phone, I was compelled to go into the bar and buy myself a drink. A shot of Jamiesons with a beer chaser. I needed to be both alert and relaxed. I fed the change in a phone in the lobby and called the *Business Daily*. 'You're a finance journalist,' I told Faye Curnow.

'If that's a news tip,' she said. 'You're a bit late.'

'Matter of fact, I do have a tip,' I said. 'A scoop. But first tell me about Obelisk Trust. It's like a bank or a building society, right? Government guaranteed.'

'Don't you believe it. High returns, high risk.'

'And what if I told you that Lloyd Eastlake has been

sinking large amounts of Obelisk money into the Karlcraft project without his board's approval?'

'I'd say that he might well soon regret it. The rumours are flying thick and fast that the banks are about to refuse to roll over Karlin's loans. If that happens, he'll have no alternative but to file for bankruptcy.'

'How would he go about that?'

It wasn't complicated. 'You lodge some forms with the Federal Court. A court-appointed trustee moves immediately, shuts the doors and starts liquidating your assets. Your creditors howl like stuck pigs. Then they sit around for the next ten years not getting their money back.'

'So what would you say if I told you that, even as we speak, Max Karlin's lawyers are approaching the court, bankruptcy forms in hand? And that, further, I've got my life savings in Obelisk Trust.'

'I'd tell you that if you don't get your money out of Obelisk by close of business tonight, you can probably kiss most of it goodbye. And I'd ask you how reliable is your information about Karlin.'

'Straight from the horse's mouth.'

'Then you'd better get off the phone. I've got a story to break, and you've got a hasty withdrawal to make. Thanks for the tip.'

I didn't get much thanks for my next call. In fact, I got a flea in my ear. 'Murray Whelan here,' I said. 'Calling from Angelo Agnelli's office.'

'What now?' barked Duncan Keogh.

This wasn't going to be easy. The last time I'd rung the finance committee chairman, I'd hung up on him. 'It's about that deposit with Obelisk Trust.'

'Thought I told you I'd done it.'

'You did,' I said. 'Only there's been a bit of a rethink in the strategy department. Angelo wants the funds withdrawn immediately and put back where they were.' Eastlake wasn't the only one who could play at this exceed-your-authority game. 'Like you said this morning, Duncan. No need to get our shirt-tails in a flap.'

Standing at a pay-phone in the lobby of a budget hotel with a finger in one ear to drown out the muzak bouncing off a tour party of Taiwanese dentists' wives was not the ideal location for a conversation of this nature.

'You tell Agnelli from me,' said Keogh. 'That I'm still the finance committee chairman, not some bank clerk, and if he wants something done he should have the courtesy to call me himself, not get his office boy to do it.'

This was great. Keogh had finally decided to grow a backbone. 'Listen, Duncan . . .' But Duncan wasn't listening. It was his turn to hang up.

This was not good. I went back into the bar and bought myself another beer. With the option of bluffing Keogh now closed, the only way left to get the party funds out of Obelisk before the balloon went up was to call Agnelli and have him speak to Keogh. That would entail a great deal of explanation. Frankly, given the choice, I'd rather have gone straight back up to F. Lambert's kitchen, stuck my bare hand into her high-speed Moulinex blender and thrown the switch.

I racked my brain for a plausible lie. It was a fool's errand. The truth, or a passable facsimile of it, was my only option. But first I would have to get through to the ministerial hovercraft plying the distant waters of Lake Eildon. I gorged the pay-phone with coins and dialled Agnelli's mobile. 'The mobile telephone you have called has not responded,' said a female robot. 'Please call again shortly.'

Shortly? Just how much time did she think I had? It was exactly five o'clock. If Obelisk kept standard business hours, it had just shut its doors for the day. I hung up. The phone ate my change.

I dialled the Arts Ministry and asked Trish for a precise fix on my employer's whereabouts and contactability.

'Somewhere in transit,' she said vaguely. 'Not due back in town until later tonight. Why, is there a problem?' Trish's discretion was a one-way valve. Nothing came out, but she was always open to input.

'No problem,' I said. 'Any messages?'

My contact at Corporate Affairs had called. Austral Fine Art, Pty Ltd, was an off-the-shelf number with a paid up capital of two dollars, incorporated the previous year. Its sole shareholder was a Lloyd Henry Eastlake of Mathoura Road, Toorak.

This took a moment's consideration. If Austral was Fiona Lambert's company, how come Eastlake owned it? What a sucker. He even had his name on the corporate shell his girlfriend used to doublecross him.

Right at that instant, the structure of Austral Fine Art was the least of my worries. Unless I did something pronto, our campaign funds would disappear into financial never-never land. Which in turn meant that Angelo Agnelli, rather than being carried shoulder-high through the next election-night victory party, would be lucky if he was allowed to slink away and commit harikari with a blunt raffle ticket.

My meeting with Eastlake was at six o'clock. But if I could get through to him, before then, perhaps he could see his way clear to reverse Keogh's deposit. In a deregulated world of round-the-clock electronic banking, surely Eastlake could authorise an after-hours transaction. Maybe there was still scope for some fancy financial footwork. I didn't need to tell him the truth. I could say I'd been tipped off by a *Business Daily* journo.

Eastlake's direct line was engaged. So was his mobile. I looked up Obelisk in the book and rang the number. Yes, said his secretary, Mr Eastlake was in. But no, he couldn't take my call. He was currently in conference and absolutely could not be disturbed.

The 'in conference' bit was a nice touch, spoken with the strained plausibility of a nuclear power plant press officer during a meltdown. Eastlake was either still desperately trying to track down the elusive Max Karlin, or the penny had finally dropped and he was on the phone trying to parley his way out of financial ruin.

My name had nudged the secretary's memory. 'Mr Eastlake just asked me to contact you, Mr Whelan. Regarding your meeting at six. He said can you please meet him at the Little Collins Street entrance to the Karlcraft Centre. He said he wants to show you some of the public art there.'

A building site was an odd place for a business meeting, but I wasn't arguing. Eastlake was perhaps hoping to find Max Karlin there, too. He'd have to settle for me. It had just gone five-fifteen. Enough time to drive back to the Arts Ministry, park the car and walk the three blocks into the city. Calling the cops could wait.

Famous last words.

THIRTY STOREYS of concrete and steel skeleton towered upwards. A construction hoarding ran along Little Collins Street, thick with show posters and aerosoled graffiti. Iggy Pop. Leather is Murder. On the footpath opposite, an endless stream of home-bound shoppers and office workers flowed out of the Royal Arcade, sparing only a passing glance at the big Mercedes parked tight against the hoarding. Construction Vehicles Only, read the sign, 6 a.m to 6 p.m.

The hours were a fiction, a pretext for the council to issue parking tickets. Building industry hours are 7.00 a.m. to 4.30 p.m. and the only remaining evidence of construction vehicles was a powdery sludge in the gutter, the hose-down water from long-departed concrete trucks. A pink slip nestled beneath the Merc's windscreen wiper.

Spider Webb was nowhere in sight. I wondered exactly where he was. If he was lurking about, I doubted he would try anything smart with Eastlake present.

Not that Eastlake's presence was apparent. The building site was deserted. Through a chain-mesh gate in the hoarding, all I could see was a maze of scaffolding, piles of sand, stacks of breeze bricks, the silvery worm-casings of air-conditioning ducting. I rattled the padlock and peered inside, finding only shadows and silence.

Down a side alley was a smaller gate. An open padlock dangled from its bolt. It led directly into an access walkway, a two-metre-wide tunnel of whitewashed plywood extending into the interior of the site, its walls streaked and pitted from the casual buffeting of loaded wheelbarrows and the elbows of apprentice plumbers. Safety Helmet Area, said a sign. No Ticket, No Start.

I didn't have a ticket, at least not one from the Building Workers Industrial Union, but I started anyway. I headed along the unlit passageway, breathing plaster dust and the smell of polymer adhesives, hearing nothing but my own footsteps, hoping I was headed in the right direction. Forty metres in, the tunnel doglegged sharply, ramped upwards and opened onto a broad balcony of raw concrete.

An immense atrium extended before me, as vast as the interior of a cathedral. Muted sunlight filtered through a glass ceiling high overhead. A series of galleries lined the sides, ascending three storeys above me. From the floor, two storeys below, a forest of scaffolding sprouted upwards, clinging to the edges of the jutting balconies and wrapping itself around the row of columns that marched down the centre of the great space. The whole place was the colour of ashes.

Lloyd Eastlake was sitting on a pallet-load of ceramic tiles at the edge of the balcony, staring out into the void. One hand was resting on the metal piping of a temporary guard rail. The other was supporting his chin in the manner of Rodin's *Thinker*. Whether this disconsolate pose was deliberate or not, I couldn't tell. But it spoke volumes. Here was a man who had heard the news.

He turned at my approach and slowly rose to meet me. His arm swept wide in a grand, operatic gesture. 'Welcome to the Karlcraft Galleria,' he declared, his voice larded with irony, his words instantly swallowed up in the empty vastness of the place. 'Come. Admire.'

We stood together at the guard rail and gazed at the vista spread before us as if it was some marvel of nature, some wondrous subterranean grotto. 'Over forty thousand square metres of retail space. Nearly a hundred fashion boutiques and specialty stores. Five bars, three restaurants, a cinema.' Eastlake spoke as though offering me dominion over the cities of the world. 'Above us, twenty-eight floors of prime commercial office space. Below us, parking for a thousand cars.'

I remained silent, not knowing how to respond. Eastlake was inviting me to share the loss of his dream. I could hardly tell him that parking for a thousand had never been one of my visions.

'Even as a hole in the ground it was impressive,' he went on, wistful now. 'Sometimes I'd come here and just look for hours on end. Watching it take shape. Imagining what it would be like finished.'

That, at a guess, was about three months away. The finishing-off was well under way. All the essential structure was there. The escalators sat ready to roll, sheathed in protective cardboard. Stacks of plaster sheeting, pallet-loads of tile and marble, plate glass, rolls of electrical conduit lay everywhere, giving the place an air of having been abandoned in haste.

It was not entirely abandoned, though. Across the concrete canyon, on the level below, something flickered at the periphery of my vision. I leaned forward and squinted, trying to penetrate the shadows. All I could see was the doorway of an embryonic boutique, the pitched angle of a sheet of plate glass. Nothing moved. A play of the light, perhaps.

Eastlake was wearing the same Mickey Mouse tie as when I had first met him. He'd pulled it down a little and undone the top button of his shirt. Close up, his eyes were distracted, a little wild. His skin was the colour of putty. His forehead glowed with the slightest patina of perspiration. It was the closest to dishevelled I could imagine him.

'I heard about Karlin,' I said. By that time, it could hardly have been a secret.

'The bastard,' said Eastlake, flat and expressionless, almost without rancour. '"No hard feelings." That's what he told me. "No hard feelings. It's just business." Can you believe that?'

Karlin was right, I thought. Concentrate on the basics. I wasn't there to console Eastlake. I had problems of my own. 'What does this mean for Obelisk?' I said. 'For the funds Agnelli invested last Friday?'

Eastlake seemed not to have heard me. He was leaning out over the edge of the guard rail, looking straight down. 'See that?' he said.

Immediately below us, a drop of two storeys, was a section of mosaic flooring. The newly laid tiles were

bright in the half-darkness. The pattern was a cornucopia spilling forth the fruits of abundance. 'Public art,'
he said. 'As a major investor, I was able to insist on
the inclusion of murals, sculptures . . .'

His voice trailed off. He turned and picked up a
terracotta tile from the pallet behind him. Casually, he
tossed it over the balcony. Twenty-five metres below, it
hit the horn of plenty and exploded like a grenade. 'So
Angelo wants his money back, does he? Well, you tell
him that he's not alone. I want my money, too. And
I've lost a damn sight more than he has.'

Eastlake threw another tile, then another, flinging
them out into the void. Four, five, six he hurled, rapid
fire, grunting with the venomous exertion of it. They
bounced off scaffolding, struck columns, ricocheted
downwards. The harsh clashing of hollow metal and
the shattering sound of breaking glass filled the air.
Across the reverberating emptiness, well out of range,
one part of the shadows seemed lighter. A shape like a
man stood immobile, watching.

As abruptly as it began, Eastlake's cathartic rage
halted. Taking a handkerchief from his jacket pocket,
he placidly wiped his hands. 'Obelisk is finished. As
Karlcraft's principal unsecured creditor, it will be lucky
to get ten cents in the dollar.' Despite his pretence at
composure, he was wound tighter than a spring.
'Obelisk customers, I'm afraid, have done their dough.
All thanks to Max Karlin's cave-in to the banks.' He
shook his head in disbelief. 'And to think that only
yesterday I was concerned about maintaining the value
of his art collection.'

We had moved to the reason for our meeting. 'Giles

· Aubrey died of a fall,' I said. 'Or that's what we're supposed to think. Personally, I have my doubts.'

Eastlake smiled thinly, continuing to wipe his hands. 'And this is why you insisted we meet? Face-to-face, as you put it. So you could share your doubts?' He put his handkerchief away, did up the top button of his shirt, straightened his neck and slid the knot of his tie into place. The obscure inferences of a nut-case were the last thing Lloyd Eastlake needed at a time like this. This meeting, a pit stop in the journey of life, was now at an end. He turned to go.

I could see his point. Time to start getting down to detail. 'I intend to share my suspicions with the police. And, unfortunately, you are involved.'

That stopped him in his tracks. 'Me? How?'

'Because of your ownership of a company called Austral Fine Art,' I said. 'And because of the political implications arising from its dealings.'

'What's Austral got to do with Giles Aubrey? What political implications?'

It was a long story and I had to begin somewhere. 'This afternoon,' I said, 'purely by chance, I discovered that one of the paintings in the Combined Unions Superannuation Scheme art collection is a forgery. A painting supplied by Austral Fine Art. It is quite likely that other works sold by Austral are fakes. Further, I suspect that the person who organised the fraud was responsible for the deaths of both Marcus Taylor and Giles Aubrey. We both know who I'm talking about.' I leaned back against the guard rail and let the implications of my words sink in. 'Don't we?'

Eastlake stared at me with frank amazement. He

tilted his head and searched my eyes, as though attempting to discern my motives. He appeared to conclude that I was stark raving mad.

It was a perfectly understandable reaction. Not only had he just suffered a reversal of his financial fortunes. Now he was being told that the woman he loved had been taking advantage of him, and that she was suspected of murder.

'These are remarkable allegations,' he said at last. 'Can you prove them?'

I did my best to look sane. 'The evidence is largely circumstantial at the moment, I admit. But once a proper investigation begins, the outcome will be inevitable. If I felt I could hold off taking my suspicions to the police, I would. But you understand that I can't be party to concealing activities of this nature.'

'Why are you telling me all this?' Eastlake was genuinely perplexed.

'Don't be dense.' Did he want me to spell it out for him? 'Think about the political implications of your little peccadillo. You've set yourself up as Labor's man in the arts. You'll have to immediately resign from the Visual Arts Advisory Panel, the CMA chairmanship and the various other government appointments you hold.'

Eastlake was utterly incredulous. 'Have I got this right?' he said. 'You're telling me that you've held off informing anyone of your suspicions until you had the chance to ask me to resign my official positions?'

Not strictly true, but I nodded anyway. 'I know it's a case of shutting the gate after the horse has bolted,' I said. 'But I think you'll agree that your position will be untenable once this gets out. The sooner you act the better.'

Eastlake seemed to give this suggestion some thought. He bent his head and ran a hand slowly through his hair. We were standing about three paces apart and I could see the bald patch on the crown of his head.

Suddenly, it came towards me. Eastlake's shoulder rammed full-strength into my upper body. His leg went behind my heels and swept my feet out from beneath me. I tilted backwards, off balance, and felt myself pivoting over the guard rail. One arm flew out wildly, scrabbling for equilibrium. The other shot desperately towards my attacker, my fingers raking the air.

'Oumphh,' I said, caught in a wave of vertigo. Then I toppled backwards over the rail and pitched weightless into empty space.

M Y RIGHT hand closed around something soft and smooth. My shoulder joint wrenched violently in its socket, jerking me upright. I was no longer falling. I was dangling in mid-air.

'Urrgh,' said a voice above me. The thing in my hand was Lloyd Eastlake's Mickey Mouse tie. Somehow I'd managed to grab it as I went over the rail. I hung from it, one-armed, swinging like a pendulum. My feet scissored the empty air. My free arm flailed upwards. 'Urggh,' said the voice again.

Lloyd Eastlake's face stared down at me. His lips were purple. His eyes bulged. His windpipe was pinned against the horizontal bar of the rail. My weight was dragging him down, strangling him. The fingers of my left hand found the tie and gripped it. I held fast, two-fisted, and felt the silky noose tighten further around Eastlake's neck.

His arms flew over the rail. He grabbed his rodent-infested neckwear and started hauling it upwards, desperately fighting to relieve the pressure. The thin fabric began to slide from my grasp. My elbows sawed against the raw concrete lip of the balcony. My feet windmilled helplessly, two storeys above the hard floor.

As Eastlake pulled upward, the clenched knuckles of my right hand struck the bottom pipe of the guard rail. I let go the tie and lunged for it. My fingers wrapped themselves around smooth metal. It took my weight. With my left hand I immediately refastened my grip on the tie. But the pipe was too thick for my fingers to encircle. It was already slipping from my grasp.

All this was happening very quickly. I tried not to look down. I looked up, past the Mickey Mice. Eastlake reared above me, his throat now clear of the top rail. One hand was tugging at the middle of his tie, the other was clawing at the knot. Spit was dribbling from his lips. His eyes were utterly whacko. He had tried to kill me and now both of us would die.

Not if I could help it. I released the tie with my left hand and grabbed the bottom rail. Eastlake flew backwards, out of sight. Now I had the rail by both hands, I began to haul myself upwards. Over-arm chin-up. Never my best event. My bicep muscles quivered. They felt like jelly. My cheek grazed the concrete rim. Then my chest. Then my sternum. It was like trying to climb out of a swimming pool without the resistance of water to push back against. I twisted and jived in mid-air, struggling to swing a leg up over the edge of the balcony.

Now I could see Eastlake. He had collapsed on his backside. His hands tore at the garrotte around his neck. He sucked at the air and wiped his spit-flecked lips with the back of his hand. His palms went flat to the floor and he began to lever himself upright. His mouth was a smear of murderous intent. One swift kick and I'd be cactus.

'Wait,' I wheezed. If I could buy a few seconds, I might get my arm over the rail. 'Fiona Lambert's not worth killing me to protect. She's just using you. She got a cut of the Szabo deal. Karlin was in her flat this afternoon, just before you. Making the pay off. She knew he was leaving the country and didn't tell you.'

Eastlake was back on his feet, dusting off his pants. He took two steps towards me and raised his foot.

'You wanted proof,' I grunted, my knee finally finding the edge of the balcony. 'Look in her flat. You'll find a Karlcraft shoebox full of cash.'

'Bullshit.' Eastlake's voice was a rasp. His heel came down hard on the knuckle of my right hand.

'Arrgghh,' I screamed and felt my fingers begin to loosen. Scrabbling to shift my balance onto my knee, I heard the sound of running feet. It was coming from below and behind. 'The cops,' I winced through gritted teeth, pain throbbing up my arm. 'I told them I was coming here.'

It was no use trying to bluff him. Eastlake was beyond reason. His face was a blank mask. His eyes were empty. The sound of running footsteps became a high-pitched twittering. Bats, I thought. The squeaking wheel of a supermarket trolley. A choir of heavenly angels come to carry me aloft. The bells of hell.

I had, I realised, got it all horribly wrong. Eastlake wasn't doing this to protect Fiona Lambert. He had his own reasons for wanting me dead. Austral was just as much his scam as Lambert's. Maybe more so. It was he who had killed Taylor and Aubrey. And I was next on his list. That's why he wanted me to meet him here. You stupid idiot, I thought. You've brought this on yourself. You deserve to get yourself killed.

Eastlake's heel came down again. One. Two. Both hands. I was going to die. All I had left was a vindictive lie. 'Your darling Fiona's fucking Karlin, you know.'

'Liar!' He pressed the sole of his shoe flat against my chest. His hands curled around the guard rail. With a great heaving grunt, he pitched me backwards. The pipe slid from my faltering grip.

Once again, I plummeted into the abyss.

My whole life began to flash before my eyes. It's true. It happens. A great soft tit filled my mouth. My mother stabbed me with a nappy pin. My first day at school. Sister Mary Innocent raised the yard-long blackboard ruler and brought it down with a mighty whack on the back of my bare legs. My knees buckled and gave out beneath me. I crumpled into a heap.

I was on a small platform of loose planks. It was the top of a mobile scaffold, the kind painters use to reach really high ceilings. Someone had pushed it beneath me while I was clinging to the railing above. That squealing noise was the rolling of castors. I had plummeted a grand total of perhaps four metres. From above came the sound of running feet. The scaffolding tower began to tremble and sway. Either we were having an earthquake or someone was climbing rapidly up the ladder braced to its side.

Adrenalin surged through my veins. My fight or flee reflex went into overdrive. There was nowhere to flee to. Rolling up into a crouch, I grabbed hold of the nearest cross-piece of scaffolding. Wincing at the jolt of pain in my fingers, I braced myself for action.

A hand closed around the top rung of the ladder.

Then another. I saw a chunky gold pinky ring. Spider Webb was coming to finish me off.

Webb's head appeared, sunglasses pushed up on top of his sleek hair. Bobbed down like a Cossack dancer, I kicked out at his head.

I missed. Spider put his forearm up and easily deflected the blow. 'Fuckwit,' he snarled. 'Thought I told you to stay out of this.' He cocked his head, motioning me to silence. Rapidly retreating footfalls reverberated off plywood walls. Eastlake was hightailing along the access walkway. Spider's head disappeared. He was clambering back down the ladder. It was all very hectic and not at all self-evident.

'Wait,' I blurted. Would somebody please tell me what the hell was going on? Creeping forward on hands and knees, I peered over the edge of the tower. Spider slithered to the floor. Weaving his way between drums of pre-mixed grouting, he sprinted towards a stairway leading to the upper concourse.

Whatever the hell was happening, I had no desire to be left alone. Not with Eastlake still rampaging around the joint. Not this far from *terra firma*. I swung myself down onto the rungs of the ladder and gingerly climbed to the ground.

The ground was good. I liked it a lot. I let its reassuring presence seep upwards through the soles of my shoes. I was shaking like a leaf. The memory of Sister Mary Innocent had always affected me that way. At the bottom of the stairs was a skip overflowing with carpenters' off-cuts. As I went past, I grabbed myself a club-sized length of timber. It was only lightweight pine but it had some tremendously reassuring nails sticking out the end. Nobody was going to mess with me.

Nobody tried. The upper balcony was deserted, the whole site silent as a grave. I loped through the access walkway, headed for the exit. I took the dogleg corner wide, ready for anything. Nothing like being on the receiving end of an attempted homicide to get the old glands pumping.

Spider was in Little Collins Street. Pedestrians were coursing around him. He'd run hard and was doubled up, catching his breath. The back end of Eastlake's Mercedes was barrelling through a green light at the far end of the block, past the flashing No Turns sign. 'Shit,' said Spider, standing erect and sliding his visor back down over his eyes.

I had no idea exactly where this big-eared lug fitted into the scheme of things. I no longer flattered myself that I had any grip at all on the scheme of things. The only thing I knew for sure was that Spider Webb had just saved my life. And that gets you a lot of points in my book. I nearly kissed him.

'Fucking psycho,' I said. 'Your boss is a fucking psycho.' Two approaching women, spotting the cudgel in my hand, veered to the other side of the street. A weapon was now probably superfluous. I tossed it back down the alley.

'He is now,' said Spider, like Eastlake's behaviour was entirely my fault. 'And Christ alone knows where he's headed.'

Christ and yours truly. 'Fiona Lambert's place,' I said. 'Bet you anything.'

'Why there?' Spider didn't find the idea by any means obvious. 'What did you tell him?'

'I told him that his girlfriend's been cheating.' I was beginning to get a very bad feeling about having told Eastlake that. And the other bit. The bit about her and Karlin. I'd been thinking on my feet, so to speak. The lie hadn't bought me any more time. But judging by the expression on Eastlake's face when he stomped my knuckles, it had certainly hit home.

'Shit,' said Spider again. 'No wonder he flipped out.' His neck went up and his head radared about.

'What's going on, for Chrissake,' I demanded. 'Tell me.' I was starting to sound like Claire.

'Later.' Spider took off up the street, head swivelling as he went, like he'd mislaid something. 'Wait,' I yelled, and headed after him.

The rush-hour traffic was beginning to ease, but Swanston Street was still busy. It was the main thoroughfare through the central business district and the route for all cross-town trams. A row of them was banked up at the traffic lights. I was three paces behind Spider and one step ahead of him. Given the rate the motor traffic was inching ahead, there was a better than even chance that a tram would beat a Mercedes to Domain Road. 'Please, Noel,' I pleaded. 'Tell me what's going on.'

Spider didn't answer. He was too busy joining the crowd of pedestrians surging across Swanston Street, weaving through the gridlocked cars towards the green and yellow trams. The foremost was a Number 8. *Toorak via Domain Rd*, read the destination board.

Halfway across the street, Spider stopped abruptly and bent to the driver's window of a black Saab. As I caught him up, he reached inside and snatched a car phone from the ear of the driver and began punching in numbers. The chinless wonder behind the wheel couldn't believe it. Spluttering, he tried to open his door, demanding his toy back. Spider held the car door shut with his foot and clamped the phone to one of his auricular protuberances. 'C'mon, c'mon,' he urged. Then, quickly, 'He's headed for Lambert's place. Get there fast. He's finally flipped.'

He tossed the mobile back into the Saab driver's lap and sprinted for the trams. The lights went green, airbrakes hissed and the front tram lurched forward. Spider swung himself aboard just as the door began to glide shut.

I wasn't so fast. I raced alongside and swung myself up onto the running board. The tram was crowded. Standing room only. It crossed the intersection, gaining momentum, headed for Princes Bridge. Faces peered out at me, some amused, some alarmed. The door slid open and a rough hand hauled me aboard.

'You in a hurry?' the conductor scowled. She had a nose ring and was wearing acid-proof work boots with her green uniform skirt and blouse. 'Ta!' I said and began shouldering my way into the press of hot bodies, pursuing Spider towards the front of the carriage.

My fellow passengers parted before me like the Red Sea. And with good reason. My grime-streaked shirt-tails were hanging out. I was clutching my throbbing right shoulder with a swollen red hand. My half-healed ear had started bleeding again. I was panting heavily. And an aromatic wet patch extended down my trouser leg from crotch to knee. Apart from everything else that had happened in the preceding twenty minutes, I had evidently contrived to piss myself.

Spider had got as far as the front window. He was squeezed between a couple of strap-hanging white-collar types, doing his best to pretend he didn't know me. 'Piss off,' he hissed, squaring his glasses on the bridge of his nose, smoothing his hair and twiddling his jewellery. I pushed myself right up against him. The salary-men cringed back and averted their eyes. 'Persistent bastard, aren't you?' Spider muttered, craning over the heads of the seated passengers, monitoring the passing cars on the road outside.

'You'd better believe it,' I warned. 'And until I get some answers, I'm sticking to you like shit to a blanket.'

Spider shrank back, but he started talking. 'Eastlake's been tickling the till,' he said. 'He syphoned Obelisk Trust funds into his own account and used them to play the stock market. It worked okay for a while. But when the crash happened in October '87 he lost the lot. Ever since then, he's been running a round-robin, paying Obelisk depositors their dividends out of their own capital. Karlcraft Developments was his only hope for a big win, a way to cover his losses. He lent the project every penny he could raise. As long as Karlin stayed afloat, he had a chance of survival. Now that Karlin's folded, the whole Obelisk house of cards will fall over. Eastlake's looking not only at personal financial ruin but prison time for fraud.'

'He's also been selling forged art,' I said, not to be entirely outdone. 'He's been using a front called Austral Fine Art.' The guy had just tried to kill me, so I was keen to sink the boot in.

Spider pushed my head aside, tracking a stream of passing cars. 'We know all about Austral,' he said. 'That's why we suspect he killed Taylor.'

Spider's metamorphosis was happening a bit fast for me. 'What do you mean "we"? Who's "we"?'

The tram was hurtling down St Kilda Road at a steady clip, approaching the war memorial. The greenery of the parkland raced along beside us. It wasn't the only thing. As we slowed to disgorge passengers one stop short of the turn into Domain Road, a blue Mercedes sped by, a grim-faced Lloyd Eastlake at the wheel. Spider began elbowing his way to the door, me right behind him. The conductor blocked our way. 'Fez please.'

I fumbled in my pocket. Spider pulled out a wallet and flipped it in her face. She was looking at it sceptically when I reached past and dumped a fistful of change in her palm. 'Two all-day travel cards, please,' I said. The tram rounded the corner and accelerated up the slight incline of Domain Road. As the connie punched our tickets, I reached up and jerked the communication cord. The tram's clicketty-clack crescendo reached its peak and it began to decelerate. The door slid open.

Eastlake's Mercedes was pulled up on the park side of the road. It was empty, its boot open. Spider hit the bitumen running. Me too.

I ran around the back of the tram and narrowly beat a stream of oncoming traffic to the footpath in front of Lambert's block of flats. When I looked back, Spider was still on the far side of the road. He'd thrown open the Merc's driver-side door and was reaching across to the glove compartment.

Fiona Lambert was not a nice person. But if Eastlake did anything violent to her, it would be because of what I'd told him. I turned and started into the flats, almost colliding with the old chook with the schnauzer. 'Well I never!' she exclaimed, clutching the hapless pooch to her bosom.

'Me neither,' I said, and started running up the stairs.

THE DOOR of Fiona Lambert's flat sat carelessly half-open. Behind it, bananas were being gone in no uncertain terms. The sound was coming from the direction of the bedroom. 'Bitch!' Eastlake's voice was shrill with indignation. 'To think that I killed for you.'

The spare key was in the lock. Fiona Lambert's security consciousness was appalling. 'You're crazy,' she was saying, over and over, sounding very convincing.

I was all ears, panting, imagining the scenario, figuring the options. Shivers were running up and down my spine. Eastlake had a lead of, what, five minutes. Time enough to burst in, launch into a truth and consequences confrontation, maybe get rough. A glass container shattered. Definitely get rough.

He was having a busy few days with the rough stuff, Chairman Lloyd. Getting quite a taste for it. The targets were easy. Marcus Taylor, drunk and emotional. Giles Aubrey, frail and disposable. And me. I'd gone to him like a lamb to the slaughter. He'd been showing me some public art and I'd gone too close to the edge. Dangerous places, building sites.

But the motive here was different. With Taylor and

Aubrey and me, it had been about money and staying out of prison. This was personal. He'd called me a liar back there at the construction site, but he'd been quick to believe. The seeds of doubt must already have been there, waiting to flower. Deep-seated doubts about his true worth, perhaps. A self-esteem problem. Something to do with the business that transpires between rich men and expensive women.

Money, reputation, ego, sex. If he couldn't have it any more, nobody would. No pre-meditation here, no calculating the odds. Now it was all just cataclysmic rage. 'Take it, take it,' Fiona was crying. 'It's yours. Take it.'

She'd folded, shown him the money. Bad move, sister. It wouldn't satisfy him, only prove the point that the whole world was against him. The deck stacked. The game over.

A shoe box of petty cash wouldn't fix anything. The raw sound of a slap came through the door.

Spider's running footsteps echoed up the stairs towards me. Time for the Coalition Against Domestic Violence to start getting pro-active. I pushed the door open and entered the flat. An ornamental candlestick sat on the hall table, a drooping blob of burnished silver. I snatched it up and began down the hall. 'Don't. Please don't,' Fiona Lambert was begging.

I stepped into the bedroom doorway. What I saw is fixed forever in my mind.

Eastlake had his back to me. He was bending slightly at the waist, one arm thrust out rigidly in front of him. Fiona Lambert was beside the bed, one knee on the floor as if genuflecting. She'd been showering. Again.

A very hygienic girl. Her hair was half-dried and she had a pale yellow towel wrapped around her body. One hand was clutching it closed. The other was raised to her cheek, touching a blazing red welt. Her eyes were as big as dinner plates and she was doing her effortless best to look tremendously contrite. A shattered jar oozed moisturising cream onto the carpet.

On the bed was the bright pink Karlcraft shoe box. Its lid was off. The money was back in its banded bundles, neatly stacked. Spread out beside the box was a painted canvas, the edge frayed from where it had been cut from its stretcher. A red-brick suburban dream home. Blue sky.

Eastlake jabbed his extended hand towards it. 'Look at it!' he ordered. 'It's perfect. You'd be a laughing stock if I hadn't done what I did.'

But her eyes were turning towards the door. Eastlake spun around, his arm still extended. In his hand was a gun. The gun from the glove compartment of the Mercedes. He stuck it in my chest.

The gun had crossed my mind as I ran up the stairs. I thought Spider was reaching across to the glove compartment to get it. For some reason, Eastlake and the gun were an association I had simply not made. Guns were for bodyguards, bank robbers, cops. Committee-chairing, well-suited Melbourne businessmen didn't go packing firepower. Not even homicidal ones. Wrong again, Murray.

'You!' accused Eastlake. Me, the guy who kept turning up like a bad penny. Me, the interfering busybody he'd last seen disappearing over a second-storey balcony. He looked at me like I was an apparition. 'You.'

As if to confirm that I was flesh and blood, he prodded me in the chest with the barrel of his Smith & Wesson. His Black & Decker. His Gulf & Western. Whatever the fuck it was, my Daliesque candelabra had met its match. I let it slip to the floor.

Back at the Karlcraft Centre, Eastlake had been hyped-up and homicidal. But his actions had a certain logic. Criminal, but rational. He was disposing of a potential threat. Now, he'd come completely uncorked. The windows to his soul were wide open and the view was not a pleasant one. Like a tantrum-wracked child who could neither believe how far he'd gone nor conceive of how to get back, he was simultaneously thrilled and appalled by his own behaviour. A disconcerting combination of emotions in a man with a gun against your chest at point-blank range.

Even as Eastlake's berserk eyes locked onto me, Fiona Lambert saw her opportunity. She began to come up off her bent knee, backing away. As she rose, she reached out to steady herself against the edge of the bed. Her towel slipped to the floor, exposing her nakedness. Instinctively, she snatched up the canvas from the bed and covered herself. It was an odd moment for modesty and there was an almost coquettish aspect to the gesture, as if she hoped that her vulnerability might offer her some defence.

It didn't. Eastlake, reacting to her movement, swung the gun around. Fiona cowered back, raising the picture in front her body protectively, as if to shield herself from his sight. At exactly that moment, Eastlake fired.

An explosive crack reverberated through the confined space. The bullet punched a neat round hole straight through the front door of *Our Home*. Fiona Lambert staggered and fell backwards onto the bed, the painting draped over her face, covering her head. Her naked body twitched and went limp. It was stark white against the black sheets. Colour co-ordinated to the last.

Eastlake's hand jerked at the recoil and I lunged forward. I caught him in mid-turn and the barrel of the gun twisted upwards. It went off again and blew the top off his head. Blood and brains went everywhere.

The two reports echoed in my ears. The smell of cordite filled my nostrils. Eastlake was still on his feet, the gun still in his hand. He sort of teetered. I was moving backwards, partly reeling from the scene before me, partly being dragged from behind. The gun hit the floor and Eastlake crumpled like a wet rag.

Then I was stumbling backwards down the passageway. Spider Webb was dragging me by the collar. 'Far canal,' he said. He didn't hear any argument from me. Perhaps twenty seconds had elapsed since I'd entered the flat.

From the direction of the street came the wail of an approaching siren. Spider released me and ran into the living room. He looked out the window, cursed, then dashed out the front door. I drooped against the passage wall, shitless.

A low moan came wafting out of the bedroom. With my back pressed against the wall, I sidled up to the doorway and peeked around the corner. The gun came into sight, half covered by Eastlake's inert torso. The moan happened again. It was coming from behind the painting. I stepped over Eastlake, flicked the gun away with the toe of my shoe and raised the punctured canvas.

A gory furrow started at the bridge of Fiona Lambert's nose and ran the length of her forehead, parting her hairline. Her eyelids, caked with blood, fluttered. Her mouth goldfished. She moaned again. The bullet had only grazed her. She'd need a lot of aspirin and a very good cosmetic surgeon, but she'd live. She also had great tits. Pity she wasn't my type.

Sliding an arm under her shoulder, I propped her limp white body upright. The shoe box lay beneath her. A hundred thousand dollars. It didn't look like much any more. I propped Fiona up with a pillow, scooped up the box, dashed into the bathroom and dropped it into the laundry basket. 'Noel,' I called. 'Come quick. She's still alive.'

Footfalls thundered up the stairs. A small dog yapped germanically in the distance. I settled Fiona Lambert's head in my pee-drenched lap and pressed the towel to her brow. Suddenly, the room was full of men, some of them in uniform. The one named Detective Constable Micaelis was calling Spider 'sir'.

I SAT IN the living room on Fiona Lambert's white sofa in my pissy pants and bloodied shirt and waited my turn, watching sundry coppers traipse through the front door and listening to their cryptic confabs. Apart from the odd glance, most of them paid me so little attention I might as well have been part of the furniture. A couple of classic plain-clothes types wandered in at one point and had a cursory sniff at the fittings and fixtures. 'Now that's what I call art,' one of them said. He was looking at the Szabo above the mantel, young Fiona in the buff.

The real thing was in the bedroom being worked on by an ambulance crew. We'd propped her up and the bleeding had pretty well stopped by the time the paramedics arrived. She was in deep shock, they said. I wasn't feeling too well myself.

I scrounged a coffin nail from one of the dicks and was just lighting up when Fiona was helped out the front door, held up by the armpits. They'd put a bandage around her head and got her into a bathrobe. She was almost walking, but she wasn't talking and she didn't look at all glamorous. Spider and Micaelis went downstairs with her, then came back inside a couple of minutes later. Micaelis did the talking.

'How ya doing?' he said. 'I reckon we'll need a statement, eh? How about you accompany Detective Senior Sergeant Webb to the station, while I make sure Ms Lambert gets to the hospital, okay?'

'Sure.' It wasn't like I had much choice. 'But I need to call my son first.' Red's flight was at nine-twenty and it was already seven o'clock. Micaelis looked to Spider for confirmation. 'I wouldn't want to be done up for child neglect,' I said. 'Sergeant Webb.'

Spider pointed his chin towards the phone. 'Make it quick.'

'And I'd like to do something about this.' I stood up and framed my crotch with open palms. 'My thighs are starting to chafe.' Micaelis didn't think it necessary to refer that one up the chain of command. I smelled worse than the back of the grandstand at the Collingwood football ground. 'Use the bathroom,' he said. 'Make it quick.'

Tarquin answered the phone at the Curnows'. 'Something's come up,' I told Red when he eventually came on the line. 'See if Leo can find the spare key to our place, pack your bag and wait for me. Sorry about this.'

'No worries,' Red said, the voice of experience. I'd been late before. We'd still managed to get to the airport on time. It was only forty-five minutes away. Thirty-five with a tail wind and a good run at the lights.

Leo came on the line and I repeated what I'd just told Red. 'Can do,' he said. Faye was still at work and he was feeding the kids. 'You don't happen to know where Faye keeps the lettuce, do you?'

I went down the hall and looked in the bedroom door. Eastlake was still on the floor. He wouldn't have to worry about his bald patch any more. A woman cop was standing on the bed with a camera, getting an overhead shot. What with five detectives plus their reflections in the mirrored wardrobe door, it looked very crowded in there.

The bathroom was immediately opposite. Stripping off my pants and underpants, I turned on the tap and started sponging myself with one of Fiona's fluffy towels. I could see the cops behind me in the mirror. Spider looked across and saw me standing there bare-arsed in my shirt-tails. 'What is this?' he said, reaching over to pull the door shut. 'A fucking nudist colony?'

I grabbed the pink shoe box out of the laundry basket and stepped into the toilet cubicle. The box contained ten bundles of hundred-dollar bills, each about two and a half centimetres thick – an inch in the old dispensation. One thousand pictures of a man in a grey ski mask.

My jocks were in a pretty deplorable state. Pulling them back on was not a pleasant experience. I distributed the cash evenly around the waistband. It bulged a little, but at least it was dry. I sucked in my breath, buttoned up my pants and left my shirt hanging out. When I checked the result in the bathroom mirror, I looked like a candidate for Weight Watchers. This would never work.

'Here,' said Spider, half-opening the door. A clean shirt sailed through the air and landed at my feet. 'Found a dozen of these in the wardrobe. The owner won't be needing them any more.' Spider Webb was turning out to be a real gent.

Eastlake was two sizes bigger than me. His crisp white Yves St Laurent fell like a tent over the bulge at my midriff, perfectly concealing it. That's why the rich look so good. It's all in the tailoring. 'Ready,' I told the cops, wiping my face. With my cash assets concealed and my shirt hanging out, I could have been the President of the Philippines.

A small crowd had gathered at the front of the flats, so we went out the back way. A prowl car was waiting in the access lane with a uniformed constable behind the wheel. He was eleven, maybe twelve years old.

The money felt a little uncomfortable at first, but I got used to it. It's extraordinary how much cash you can carry on your person, I thought. Almost as extraordinary as the number of times you put your hand in your pocket and find nothing at all. I got in the back seat and Detective Senior Sergeant Webb got in beside me.

The ride into town was almost nostalgic. The only other time I'd been driven to the station in the back of a police car was the trip from the Oulton Reserve to the Preston cop shop. As the major offender in the affray, I had the prestige vehicle. The Fletcher twins rode in the back of a brawler van. Geordie Fletcher was driven off to hospital blubbering about an unprovoked attack and calling the cops cunts. Spider, who'd managed to weasel his way out of the whole thing, had been sent home.

On the way to the station, they told me I'd be charged with attempted murder, aggravated assault, going armed with an offensive weapon, possession of intoxicating liquor in a public place while a minor, assaulting police, hindering police, disorderly behaviour, offensive behaviour and resisting arrest. At fifteen, it sounded like a lot. I'm not 100 per cent on this point, but I think I may have burst into tears.

But nothing the cops said was as demoralising as the look on my father's face. After an hour's solitary in the lockup, I was ready for anger. What I got was silent, unanswerable disappointment. It wasn't the brawling. That was bad but not unprecedented for a boy my age. It was the liquor. The bourbon could only have come from one place. And that meant guile and deceit.

'I ought to give you a hiding,' Dad said when we got home. I wished he had. There was no getting out of the Brothers, though. I was back at St Joey's before you could say muscular discipline. It was either that or boarding school, so I considered myself lucky. From then on, my rebellious instincts were channelled into joining Young Labor and handing out how-to-vote cards at council elections. The police, needless to say, were never heard from again. This was less out of mercy for me, I concluded, than consideration for the tribulations of a recently bereaved publican. Either that or Geordie Fletcher – guided by some sharpie code of *omerta* – had refused to make a formal complaint. I never saw him or his brothers again.

Spider Webb's mind must have been turning over similar ground. He sat there for a while, chewing his cud and practising his thousand-yard stare. Then, as we passed the Arts Centre, he spoke. 'So,' he said, as if making a commonplace observation for no other purpose than to break the silence. 'Still a fuckwit after all these years.'

The money was sticking into my bottom rib. I straightened up a little and hoped that it didn't look like a summoning of my dignity.

'Remember that night in the park when you tore that Fletcher kid's pants with a piece of broken glass?' said Spider, smiling to himself at the memory. 'Him and his brothers were just fooling around, having a bit of fun, stirring you. All of a sudden, you went ballistic. Tried to take them all on. I'll never forget the look on Geordie Fletcher's face when you ripped his precious strides. If they hadn't been so baggy, you'd probably have cut him.'

You'd think a detective sergeant would have more highly developed powers of recall. 'I did cut him,' I said. 'There was blood everywhere.'

'Yeah,' said Spider. 'Yours. You gave yourself a blood nose when you fell on the ground. You always were a loose cannon.'

'Yeah?' I jerked my thumb back over my shoulder, back the way we'd come. I didn't remember any blood nose. 'I suppose all that was my fault? I suppose it was my fault that Eastlake tried to push me off a balcony?' Actually, it was. I'd practically begged him to do it. But Noel Webb wasn't to know that.

'If you hadn't stopped me talking to the Fleet woman yesterday,' he said, 'there's a fair chance that we'd have questioned Eastlake by today. Possibly even charged him. I doubt if he'd have tried anything under those circumstances. Even if you'd given him the chance.'

Now I was being taken to task for my gallantry. 'How was I supposed to know you were a cop? The way you were coming the heavy, flashing that gun of yours. I thought you were up to no good.'

'If I remember correctly,' said Spider, remembering correctly, 'you were the one throwing your weight about. I merely suggested that you refrain from involving yourself in matters outside your authority. When you refused to take the hint, I emphasised my point by showing you Eastlake's gun.'

'I thought it was your gun.'

'What would a chauffeur be doing with a pistol?'

'Why would I assume it was Eastlake's gun? I thought you were his bodyguard.'

'It's not all that uncommon for rich men to own a weapon,' said Spider, like he was stating a self-evident truth. 'Eastlake had three. All licensed, of course. But he always kept them at home. When I found that one in the Mercedes on Saturday morning, it was unusual enough to make me think he might be getting unstable.'

We were crossing Princes Bridge. A pair of sculls came gliding out from beneath the pilings and raced each other upstream in the direction of the Botanic Gardens, the water flashing at every dip of the oars. I turned my head and followed the rowers' progress until a truck in the next lane blocked my view. 'I thought you were working some sort of scam on Eastlake,' I said.

'Yeah?' Spider shifted his gum from one side of his mouth to the other. 'What gave you that idea?'

'That,' I admitted, 'is a very good question.'

We rode the rest of the way in silence. It was preferable to having Noel Webb tell me how many ways wrong I'd been. As the car pulled up in front of police headquarters, Salina Fleet was coming down the steps.

She was back in her serious costume. Beside her was a balding middle-aged man in a dark suit carrying a briefcase. They didn't look like they'd just won Tattslotto.

I got out of the police car, fluffed up my kaftan and wondered what Salina and I might say to each other this time around. We didn't say anything. Salina's mouth was just starting to open when Noel Webb stepped onto the footpath behind me. Salina's jaw snapped shut like a trap. She and her companion executed an almost perfect left turn and the two of them wheeled off down the footpath together.

'You were always wasting your time there,' said Webb. 'I could have told you that all along.'

If I hadn't been standing in front of police headquarters, I might have made some appropriate reply. As we entered the building, Spider stuck his sunglasses in his shirt pocket, screwed off his pinky ring and spat his gum into a fire bucket. His ears seemed less prominent.

'**W**AIT HERE for the present,' I was told. The present was a long time coming. I waited ten minutes. I waited fifteen minutes. Seven-thirty came and went and it still hadn't arrived. I began to entertain serious doubts that I'd get Red to the airport in time, even with a force-nine gale behind me.

'Here' was an interview room on the fifth floor. It had a little window in the door, a narrow laminex table fixed to the wall, a tape recorder and two plastic chairs. For some reason, I half-expected the door to be locked. Maybe all that padding around my waist was weighing on my conscience.

Next to the interview room was a sort of open-plan office. The sign on the door said Fraud Squad. It was deserted. Except for the tireless DSS Webb and his Hellenic sidekick, the bunco team was clearly a nine-to-five sort of outfit. I picked up a phone. Nobody jumped out of a waste paper basket and demanded to know what I thought I was doing.

Faye answered, home from work. Fresh from chasing her big story on Max Karlin. 'I'm at the cop shop,' I announced. As quickly as I could, I told her that Lloyd

Eastlake had committed suicide and that I'd been with him when it happened.

'How awful,' said Faye. 'Can I use this information?'

'Possibly,' I told her. 'But I can't discuss it right now.'

She took that to mean I couldn't speak freely, so she changed the subject. 'The boys tell me you paid a visit to Artemis Prints this afternoon,' she said. 'You sly dog.'

This was not an ideal time for a gossip session. 'Did the boys tell you why I was there?'

'No. But I can guess.'

'I bet you can't,' I said.

'Speaking of Claire,' she said. 'Wendy rang. She tried to call you at Ethnic Affairs and they referred her to Arts. Arts said they didn't know where you were. And you weren't at home. So she called here. Anyway, she said to remind you to make sure to get Red to the airport on time.'

That was thoughtful of Wendy.

At least the subject was back where I wanted it. 'Listen, Faye,' I said. 'Can you do me a favour? If I'm not there by 8.30, do you mind driving Red to the airport?' That way, at least he'd get back to school on schedule, even if it meant that next time I wanted to see him I'd probably have to appeal to the full bench of the Family Court.

'Sure,' said Faye. 'You poor dear.'

I'd just hung up when Ken Sproule arrived. I'd been wondering when he'd turn up. His transition from Arts had been a smooth one. Ken's short-sleeved business shirt and polyester tie were clearly in their element in the hugger-mugger world of the gendarmerie. He was bouncing about on the balls of his feet like a champion full forward angling for a mark.

'Been in the wars, I hear, Murray,' he said. 'Thought I told you to watch out for them cognoscenti.'

He gave me a good looking over, as though appraising my bloodlines for stud purposes. 'You're okay, though, aren't you? No missing limbs? No internal bleeding?' He didn't look in my mouth, but he was only half joking. Clearly, he'd been thoroughly briefed.

'Shaken but not stirred,' I assured him. 'But your mates the rozzers are keeping me on tenterhooks. Eastlake didn't succeed in killing me, but the suspense of hanging around here just might.'

Ken took me back into the interview room and shut the door. 'You got the big picture, right?' He was bouncing around so much the room felt like a squash court. 'Paper-shuffling at Obelisk Trust. Eastlake suspected of knocking off the bloke in the moat.'

I had that much of it, I agreed. 'Plus the Combined Unions Super Scheme art fraud.' I didn't want him thinking I was a complete slouch.

'How'd you hear about that?' He was impressed.

'Buy me lunch one day,' I said. 'I'll tell you all about it.'

He didn't press the point. 'As you can well imagine,' he said. 'The manure has really hit the ventilator. Major construction project goes bust. Mutual fund chief executive dead on the floor. The business community is going to have kittens.' He beamed at the sheer horror of it.

He straddled a chair, folded his arms over the back-rest and dropped his voice a notch. 'And to cap it off, the city's finest now find themselves in the embarrassing situation of having left a homicidal maniac on the loose for three days longer than absolutely necessary. They had grounds for questioning Eastlake on Saturday. If they had, most of this shit could have been avoided. They didn't because the fraud squad guys decided their undercover investigation into the Obelisk fiddle took precedence over the Taylor homicide investigation.'

The implications of what he was saying were clear. People were dead because of a police fuck-up. 'If this gets out,' he said. 'The boys in blue will have very red faces.' The fixer's fixer had at last found something worthy of his mettle. If Ken Sproule could square this one away, the Chief Commissioner would be eating out of Gil Methven's lap for years to come.

Sproule jumped up and gave another display of shadow boxing. 'It's going to take some fancy foot-work to get our ducks in a row on this little baby,' he said. 'You with me?'

'I don't see why I should be.' Spider Webb might have saved my life but, if what Ken said was true, only after he'd put it at risk in the first place. I had no reason to want to let the cops off the hook. And Ken hadn't exactly been 100 per cent frank with me last time I'd spoken to him, so I was in no big rush to do him any favours.

Sproule didn't smoke but he had some cigarettes. Was this standard interview-room procedure, I wondered? The informant smoked a hearty cigarette and agreed to co-operate with the authorities. I drew the smoke into my lungs and waited for the phone book around the head.

He straddled the chair again like he was doing the bad cop/good cop routine as a one-man show. 'What's the first rule of government, Murray? The one that precedes and supersedes all others. The *sine qua non* of political power.'

I didn't know Ken could speak Latin. And he was a philosopher as well. It was a surprise-packed day.

'Keep the cops happy,' he said. 'That's the paramount rule of political survival. Cause if the cops are unhappy, life just ain't worth living. Doesn't matter if you're Joseph Stalin or Mahatma Gandhi. It's a universal truth.'

'What do you want me to do?' I said. Ken's logic had an unarguability to it that I just couldn't argue with. And I might, at least, find out what he had in mind.

'Good boy.' He got up and started pacing again. If this kept up much longer, I'd get dizzy and pass out. And then Ken would start to go through my pockets and find what I had in my Reg Grundys. 'Everybody wants the lid put on this thing as fast as possible. The Chief Commissioner has okayed it for you and me to sit down with the cops involved and see if we can't come up with a result that everyone can live with.'

'Two conditions,' I said.

Ken was ready for that. He would have thought less of me if I hadn't asked. 'Gil Methven is prepared to say that Eastlake resigned from all his official Arts positions as of the end of last year,' he said, correctly anticipating my first demand. 'That way, none of this will reflect on Angelo Agnelli as current minister. What's your other condition?'

'That depends on how long this little pow-wow takes,' I said. 'And it's more of a favour than a condition. I might not even need it. But it's well within your power, if I'm any judge. I'll tell you what it is at the end of the meeting.'

As a matter of principle, Ken Sproule didn't like dealing in the dark. But he didn't have much time to manoeuvre. The press would already be making a beeline for the Domain Road flat. 'Okay,' he scowled. 'Let's go. And try not to give too much cheek. The cops have long memories, you know. Mind your manners.'

It wasn't my manners I was worried about. It was the spondulicks in my dank underdaks. They were beginning to itch. If I didn't get them out of there soon, I'd have a very nasty rash.

We went upstairs to a conference room with venetian blinds on the windows and rings from coffee cups on the tabletop. Webb was already there and two other cops I'd never seen before, both in their fifties, one in a suit, the other in uniform. You could tell the one in the suit was a senior officer by the cast of his face and way Noel Webb approached him on all fours. The one in uniform was an Assistant Commissioner. I knew that because his epaulette insignia consisted of crossed silver batons in a laurel wreath surround. Also because he was wearing a name tag that said *Eric Worrall, Assistant Commissioner – Crime*. Eric was a gaunt, expressionless man who could have got a job walking behind the hearse in a Charles Dickens novel.

The guy in the suit was introduced as Chief Inspector Brian Buchanan. He was all neck and looked like he'd gladly bust Santa Claus for driving an unregistered sleigh.

None of the cops were delirious with joy about me and Sproule being there and they didn't go to a lot of trouble to conceal the fact. Having to share trade secrets with a couple of political flacks was bad enough, never mind that one of them had his shirt hanging out and smelt like he should have been in the care of the Salvation Army. I tried to take up as little space as possible and resist the urge to scratch.

Micaelis arrived just as we'd finished the introductions. Assistant Commissioner Worrall waved us into our seats. 'This is strictly informal,' he said. 'And strictly confidential. The objective is to pool our information and determine a course of action. Agreed?' Ken Sproule and I nodded. Worrall handed the running of the meeting to Buchanan.

'Let's get on with it,' said Buchanan. He had a pencil in his hand and pointed at Micaelis with it. 'What did the Lambert woman have to say?'

'She's on pain-killers, sir, but reasonably lucid.' Micaelis' hitherto pally demeanour was no longer in evidence. 'She says she has no idea why Eastlake attacked her. Claims they'd been lovers for about a year but never quarrelled. She says she'd seen him earlier today and he was agitated about business matters, but otherwise normal towards her.'

Which meant, as I had hoped, that she had enough cunning not to mention the money. She probably wondered why Micaelis didn't ask her about it.

'What about the other one?' said Buchanan. 'Fleet.'

Micaelis had a sheaf of paper in front of him. 'She

contacted us this afternoon and came in with her solicitor while I was in attendance at the Lambert residence. She had a statement already prepared.' He shuffled the papers around until he found what he wanted, referring to it as he spoke. 'She and Eastlake were both on the committee that recommends arts grants. Last August, about the time that applications were being considered, she was having a relationship with Marcus Taylor. She recommended him for a grant and spoke highly of his technical skills and his' – Micaelis' finger found the exact phrase – 'his post-modernist sensibility in relation to the validity of quotation and appropriation.'

'What the hell's that supposed to mean?' Buchanan pointed his pencil at me. He seemed to think I was an art expert.

'It means he could do good fakes,' I said.

'You can get a grant for that?' For a man who thought he was an orchestra conductor, Buchanan was harbouring some deep cultural insecurities.

'Only a small one, sir,' said Micaelis. 'And Fleet thinks that was only to keep her happy. But, a few weeks later, Eastlake approached her wanting to know more about Taylor. In particular, he wanted to know if she thought Taylor could paint him some pictures in the manner of certain well-known artists. He even produced a list.'

Sproule spoke, addressing himself to the Assistant Commissioner. 'The background here relates to the Combined Unions Superannuation Scheme. Eastlake had persuaded the CUSS to invest hundreds of thousands of dollars in an art collection, using a front called

Austral Fine Art. The collection was a fiction. It existed only on paper. He used the money to keep his Obelisk round-robin going. He probably had in mind that when the Karlcraft project eventually paid off, Austral could recommend liquidating the collection. He got away with it for nearly a year, pretending to buy and sell artworks. But then the CUSS board decided it wanted to have an exhibition. Got all excited about the idea. Eastlake had no option but to play along. Suddenly he needed real paintings.'

Micaelis resumed. 'Fleet approached Taylor on Eastlake's behalf. She claims she was never party to any deception he may have subsequently engaged in, but she clearly knew what was going on. Taylor began producing paintings of the kind Eastlake required. The pictures were painted in his studio at the old YMCA building. Fleet informed Eastlake when they were ready. They were then picked up by Senior Sergeant Webb.'

'The sergeant was already working undercover as Eastlake's driver,' Buchanan explained to Worrall. 'Part of a long-term fraud squad investigation of Eastlake's activities in relation to the Obelisk Trust.'

Ken Sproule tipped me a quiet wink. A vision came to me of the Members' carpark at Flemington, of Sproule convincing a well-tanked Eastlake to hand his car keys to Noel, the helpful man from the detailing company.

'Eastlake assumed I had no interest in his business affairs,' said Webb. 'I had access to his home, his office, documents, telephone conversations and so on. We were well on the way to establishing a strong case against him in relation to Obelisk when this business with the paintings began. My instructions were to collect them from Taylor's studio – as many as two or three a week for nearly three months – and store them in the garage of Eastlake's house in Toorak.'

'We suspected these paintings related to some illegal activity,' said Buchanan. 'But our main focus was on the Obelisk investigation and it was only after the events of last Friday night that we began to realise the significance of the art works.'

By then, I'd worked out that Buchanan was the fraud-squad head honcho. He and Webb were very concerned that Assistant Commissioner Worrall adopt a favourable view of their activities. 'And exactly what happened last Friday?' said the big chief.

Yeah, I thought. Exactly what did happen? I leaned forward in my seat and adjusted my underpants under the rim of the table. There was a slight rustling sound.

Noel Webb cleared his throat and worked his jaw as if he wished he hadn't chucked his chewy away. 'About 9.30 on Friday night, I was driving Eastlake along Domain Road when we passed Taylor staggering drunkenly down the footpath. We picked him up and Eastlake had me drive the two of them around while he talked to Taylor about some particular painting. Something special, by the sound of it, in the style of a painter called Szabo. First he tried to convince Taylor just to let him see the picture. Taylor said he had it hidden away somewhere and nobody was going to see it until the time was right. Eastlake had a bottle of scotch and plied Taylor with it, but he wasn't getting much joy. Taylor wouldn't say where he had the painting. Eastlake offered him money for it, sight unseen. Twenty grand. Taylor reckoned that Eastlake was just trying to find out where the picture was hidden. Taylor was maudlin drunk. He kept going on about Fiona Lambert, how he was going to settle the score with her. He had no idea that she was Eastlake's bit on the side. Meanwhile, I was driving around in circles through the Domain.'

Police headquarters weren't centrally air conditioned. The cooler in the window frame kicked in with a whirr like an asthmatic fridge compressor. Noel Webb had our undivided attention.

'After a couple of hours of this, Eastlake told me to park the car and dismissed me for the night. This was across the road from the National Gallery. I hung around for a bit, watching, but all they were doing was sitting in the back seat talking and drinking. I left them to it and went home.'

He paused at this anti-climax, as if offering us the oppor-tunity to ask questions. Assistant Commissioner Worrall had one. 'Can somebody enlighten me on the significance of this conversation?'

Micaelis could. 'According to Salina Fleet, sir, Taylor had a grudge against Lambert. She'd knocked him back for an exhibition of his real pictures, told him they weren't up to scratch. Plus there was some sort of bad blood relating to a dead painter by the name of Victor Szabo. On Lambert's recommendation, the Centre for Modern Art recently purchased a painting by this Victor Szabo. So Taylor got the idea of painting a copy of the Szabo and using it to discredit Lambert in some way. He was getting quite het up about it, apparently. Fleet realised this might cause problems for Eastlake and alerted him to the fact. She also tried to dissuade Taylor. But he got drunk and went off half-cocked at an exhibition at the Centre for Modern Art last Friday night, threatening to blow the whistle.'

I thought it was about time I said something, just so I didn't get taken for granted. 'I was there,' I volunteered. 'Taylor had been drinking, psyching himself up, and he fell over mid-speech. Made me cut my finger on a broken champagne glass.' I held up the damaged digit. Worrall looked at me like I'd just given him further grounds to doubt the wisdom of the Chief Commissioner's information-sharing policy. 'Because Taylor was drunk, nobody paid any attention to what he was saying,' I said. 'But it must have given Eastlake a scare. If Taylor made himself the centre of an art-world brouhaha, the whole CUSS fraud would be at risk.'

Webb took up the narrative from there. 'The next morning, I'd just heard about Taylor being found dead when Eastlake told me to go clear out his studio. He particularly wanted any paintings of a house with a lawn-mower.'

Buchanan held up his hand and stopped him there. 'Sergeant Webb sought instruction at that point,' he told Worrall. 'At that time, on the basis of information to hand, the cause of Taylor's death was still unknown. Eastlake may have been involved, or he may just have been taking advantage of the situation to cover his tracks. So rather than jeopardise a successful ongoing undercover investigation, I instructed Sergeant Webb to carry on as normal.'

'In the meantime,' said Micaelis, 'Salina Fleet had

seen Taylor's body being recovered. Her immediate assumption was that Eastlake was responsible.'

The penny dropped. 'Bastard!' I said. Everyone looked at me. '"Bastard!" That's what Salina Fleet said when she saw Taylor's body. She must have meant Eastlake. I thought she meant me.' They all looked at me then like maybe I should explain why she might think such a thing. 'Sorry,' I said to Micaelis. 'Please go on.'

'Fleet panicked. She thought that if Eastlake was prepared to kill Taylor, then maybe she'd be next. She immediately started talking up the suicide scenario, hoping to send a signal to Eastlake that she was no threat to him.'

Noel Webb cleared his throat. 'As instructed by Eastlake, I went to the YMCA and searched Taylor's studio. I found a painting that fitted the description Eastlake had given me and put it, and a number of other sketches and paintings, in the boot of Eastlake's Mercedes.' As he said this, he fixed me in a steady gaze, inviting me not to contradict him or elaborate on his story. Discussions about people being locked in basements for their own well-being, I clearly understood, had no part in these proceedings.

Assistant Commissioner Worrall wasn't interested in fake paintings. He had homicide on his mind. 'How does any of this relate to the Taylor death?' He looked at his watch like maybe somebody should get to the point. I checked mine, too. 8.07 p.m. It was beginning to look like I definitely wouldn't be seeing Red again for some time.

Chief Superintendent Buchanan was all for getting

back to the point, too. He wanted it made clear that his decision to keep Spider undercover hadn't resulted in a killer being allowed to run loose. 'At that time, the only evidence to connect Eastlake with Taylor's death was purely circumstantial.' He tapped his pencil on the table, punctuating his points. 'The medical evidence suggested an accident. When we sought to question Fleet about inconsistencies in her original statement, the one suggesting suicide, she couldn't be found.' He gave me a meaningful look. I kept my trap shut. The coppers were too clever by half for the likes of me.

He tapped again. 'It wasn't until this afternoon that more substantial information came to hand. The scotch bottle found with Taylor's body had two sets of prints on it. The second set didn't match any we had on record. Sergeant Webb lifted a set of Eastlake's dabs off his vehicle for comparison, but the match didn't come back until late this afternoon. As you know, sir, they're pretty under-resourced down there.'

Here Worrall looked at Ken Sproule to make sure he took the point.

'Then Fleet turned up,' Buchanan went on. 'She'd spent the night at the Travelodge, she said, thinking things over. Apparently, she was under the misapprehension that Sergeant Webb, acting on Eastlake's instructions, was planning to kill her. She brought her lawyer with her and gave us a fairly detailed statement. Also, as a result of enquiries among taxi drivers working that night, a driver . . .'

'Stanislaw Korzelinski.' Micaelis must have been hoping for an A-Plus in note taking.

'. . . reported seeing two men fitting the general descriptions of Eastlake and Taylor on the moat parapet about the time of death. He says that one was lying down and the other appeared to be shaking him by the shoulders. Either that or banging his head on the stonework.'

Buchanan dropped his pencil and it rolled into the centre of the table. We all looked at it. We all saw the same thing. Eastlake, remonstrating with the drunken Taylor, knocking him unconscious and rolling him into the water.

Assistant Commissioner Worrall waited until the pencil came entirely to rest, studying it down his thin bony nose. 'Very well,' he said, at last. 'Point taken. Now how does all this bear on the current situation, the shootings in Domain Road.'

Chief Superintendent Buchanan pressed his point home. 'Whether Eastlake killed Taylor intentionally or not will probably never be known. What we do know is that the imminent financial collapse of Obelisk Trust was going to both ruin Eastlake personally and bring his fraud to light. So killing Taylor solved nothing. The pressure of this knowledge, and various other factors, drove him over the brink. As evidenced by his unprovoked attack on both Mr Whelan here and on Fiona Lambert, he was no longer in control of his mental faculties.'

'These other factors,' I said. 'Would they include the murder of Giles Aubrey?'

Sproule kicked me under the table.

'Who?' said the Assistant Commissioner – Crime.

'A retired art dealer,' said Buchanan, quickly. He

made a drooping movement with his wrist that might, arguably, have been a gesture of casual dismissal. 'Marginal to the case. He died of a fall yesterday after- noon. We have no reason whatsoever to suspect foul play.' The police, too, bury their mistakes.

'As to the business in the Domain Road flat,' said the Assistant Commissioner. 'I have been given to under- stand that Eastlake, having shot Miss Lambert, turned the gun on himself.'

He looked at Sproule. The other three coppers looked at me. Nobody said anything. Me least of all.

'That's it then,' said Worrall. 'An open-and-shut case. Suicide brought on by pressure of business. Now it only remains to tie up the loose ends.'

Micaelis was still young. He hadn't quite got the whole message. 'We'd have to prove Fleet knowingly conspired to defraud, sir,' he said. 'Very difficult with her co-conspirators dead.'

'And without a complainant,' said Sproule good- naturedly, doing his best not to take the mickey. 'I've already spoken to our friends at the Trades Hall. The board of the Combined Unions Superannuation Scheme has no interest in further investigation of this matter. Its art collection no longer exists. It never did.'

The westering sun had turned the venetians to burnt sienna. There wasn't anything left to say. Assistant Commissioner Worrall pulled his navy blue sleeve back and looked at his watch. I could have told him if he'd asked. 8.12 p.m.

Worrall stood up, nodded and briskly left the room. It must have been his turn to ride the goat at the Masonic Lodge. Buchanan reached across the table and picked up his pencil. Noel Webb pushed his chair back, blew out a long stream of air and took a packet of gum out of his pocket. Senior Constable Micaelis gathered his papers together and squared off the edges. Ken Sproule cracked his knuckles and looked exceedingly pleased with himself.

'Ken,' I said. 'About that favour.'

THE WHITE Commodore V-8 with the chequer-board stripe down the side flashed its twin blue lights, whooped its siren and swung across the path of the metallic green Laser reversing away from the kerb. I jumped out and jerked open the Laser's rear door. 'Out of the car and spread 'em,' I barked.

Tarquin cowered back. Red, faster off the mark, gave an ecstatic grin.

'Tricked ya!' I said.

Faye reached back from the driver's seat and biffed me around the ear. 'Scared the shit out of me,' she said.

Ken Sproule, true to his grudging word, had managed to get a traffic division squad car placed at my disposal. 'It's only to save him the trouble of running his own red lights,' he explained to the despatch officer. Even on a quiet Monday evening, running red lights was strictly the prerogative of the constabulary.

As we raced through the intersection outside the Trades Hall, the caretaker was removing the CUSS art exhibition sign. An unprecedented burst of efficiency from Bob Allroy. One less speech for me to write.

On my lap in the front seat was a black plastic bin-liner. 'What's in the bag?' Ken said as I emerged from the toilet in the police garage, tucking my shirt into my pants. The hundred-dollar bills that had been pressed against my skin were as soft as suede and I had inky smudges like tread marks on my spare tyre. 'Dirty laundry,' I said.

Faye nosed her Laser back into the kerb. The boys got out and extended their attention to the figure in blue behind the wheel of the police car. His sunglasses were the same kind as Spider's. I was beginning to think that the Police Co-operative Credit Union owned shares in Ray-Ban. 'This officer is going to drive us to the airport,' I told Red. 'Hop in.'

Tarquin, green with envy, demanded to be allowed to come along for the ride. 'Next time,' I said. 'But you can sit in the back seat for a minute while I talk to your mum.'

Prompted by my remark on the phone, Faye had success-fully grilled the boys on the true reason for our flying visit to Artemis Prints. She'd followed up with a call to Claire. 'She didn't sound very impressed, Murray,' she said. 'She thinks you took advantage of her better nature. She was quite keen on you, you know. For a while. But I'm afraid you've blown it. So what's all this about friends of yours with a forged Drysdale? And what's that smell?'

A proper answer to those questions would take three days, a whiteboard, a flow chart and a breach of confidence. I gave Faye the thirty-second version. 'Wow,' she said, mentally reaching for her keyboard.

'This is absolutely not for publication,' I warned.

'Within the life of this government.' The money in the bag in my hot little hand, of course, I did not mention.

'Look!' called Tarquin. He'd pulled something out of a box on the back seat of the prowl car and was waving it out the window. It was a deep red stick of waxed paper about as long as my arm. 'Extra-length dynamite!'

It wasn't, but it might as well have been. It was an emergency flare. Two kilograms of compacted magnesium with a ring-pull activator cap. I reached over and deftly relieved Tarquin of its possession. 'My wrist,' he squealed. 'You've broken my wrist.'

In what seemed like no time at all, we were barrelling down the Tullamarine freeway with the roof lights flashing, the siren wailing and Constable Speedy Gonzales of the Accident Appreciation Squad making the rest of the traffic look like it was standing still. 'I'm sorry your visit was so boring,' I told Red. 'Next time, we'll do something more interesting. Go fishing, maybe. And we'll definitely have that pizza, I promise.'

Speedy dropped us at the terminal with ten minutes to flight time. 'Told ya,' I informed Red, although we were too late to get him a window seat. We embraced at the departure gate. 'See you later, Dad,' he said. 'Sorry about busting the picture.'

'Do something for me,' I asked. 'Tell your mother I've got a new girlfriend.'

'You haven't really?' The kid squinted at me dubiously. 'Have you?'

'No,' I said. 'But you never know your luck. And don't mention the dead body. Or the snake. Or the painting. Or the police car. Or the dynamite.' I started to reach into the plastic garbage bag, thought better of it and fished a twenty out of my wallet. 'In case you need a beer on the plane,' I said. 'And your teeth still look fine to me.'

We embraced again. Then he was gone.

If anyone needed a beer it was me. I hadn't eaten since breakfast. I found an airport eatery with a tray-race and a neon sign that read Altitude Zero. I got myself a tray and ate something they claimed was lasagne. Ate it all. Right down to the plate. That's how hungry I was.

It was eleven before I'd got a cab back to the Arts Centre, picked up the Charade, put the black plastic bag under the seat and drove home. Home sweet lone-some home. I stepped inside the front door and reached for the light switch. Intuition stopped my hand stopped in mid-movement. I bent my head to the darkness of the hall and listened. The muted rustle of paper. An infinitely faint flush of light beneath the door into the living room. An electrical charge in the atmosphere. Someone was in the house. My hand went sweaty around the black bag.

Streetlight flowed through a gap in my bedroom curtains. Nothing out of order there. I flicked the money under the bed. The only thing in the room vaguely resembling a weapon was the bedside lamp. It was either that or a lumpy pillow. With the lamp cord wrapped around my wrist, I advanced noiselessly down the hall, put my shoulder to the door and pushed it open.

Claire was lying on the couch, her red hair lit by the feeble fluorescence emanating from the kitchen nook. She looked up over the top of an open book. 'Pretty dense,' she said. *The Rise and Fall of the Great Powers*.

'You'll ruin your eyesight.' I knelt on the floor and plugged in the lamp. 'How did you get in?' Not that I was complaining.

'Your security is abysmal,' she said. 'But your friends are terrific. Faye gave me the key. She also told me what's been going on. I thought I'd save you the price of a lunch.'

The face of Sister Mary Innocent flashed before me and dissolved. 'Don't go away,' I said. 'I've just got to take a quick shower.'

'Not a cold one, I hope,' said Claire.

When I came out of the bathroom, Metternich was on the floor and Claire was in my bed. Luckily, I'd changed the sheets. I do that every time I get a new job. 'I don't know about this, Murray,' she said.

'Me neither.' I dropped my towel to the floor and she could see that I was lying. I lay down beside her and put my head between her breasts, my ear over her heart. It didn't hurt at all.

F EW THINGS remain secret for long in the modern office. Even through two plate-glass walls I could read Angelo Agnelli's face like the fine print on a rent-a-car contract. If Ange had got any sun while he was inspecting those mountain lakes, it wasn't showing in his complexion.

My boss's ashen face wasn't the first reading I'd done that morning. Over a two-egg breakfast with Claire, I'd taken in the headlines. The *Age*, doing its best at broadsheet restraint, led with KARLCRAFT DEFAULT PROMPTS OBELISK SUICIDE. The *Sun* concentrated on the human interest angle with LOVE NEST DEATH PACT. Faye's piece on the front page of the *Business Daily* took a more soberly fiscal line. FUNDS SINK IN WAKE OF LIQUIDITY DRAIN.

Agnelli had read them, too. They were spread across his desk in front of him. He'd been sitting there, staring down at them, for what felt like a very long time. I knew that because I'd been watching him ever since he'd arrived. He told Trish he was not to be disturbed, shut his door and sank into his seat like a condemned man assessing the comfort of the electric chair.

A minister is rarely alone and almost never lost in silent contemplation. It was a sight to behold. From time to time, Angelo's leonine head would rise and he would peer over at me. I was pretending to read *Craft Annual*. His hand would extend towards the phone, hover, then withdraw. His fingertips would drum on the desktop. His gaze would again lower.

Eventually, the suspense got too much for me. Undeterred by Trish's gorgon bark, I invited myself into the ministerial presence. 'How was the water?' I said. 'Dam and be damned, as they say in Tasmania, eh?'

Angelo broke off from his self-guided tour of purgatory and regarded me bleakly. 'Damned's the word,' he said. 'Sit down.'

Angelo Agnelli was not a bad man. He was no better or no worse than he ought to be. He was vain and his ambition exceeded his abilities. So what? In a politician these are not failings but the minimum requirements for the job. Why else do it? Angelo was a minister because enough people thought he should be one. Those people, for better or worse, were my people. Perhaps they didn't know Angelo quite as well as I did. But they had not entirely misjudged him. He was occasionally a fool, but he was not an idiot. He could be petty, but he was rarely malicious. Others, perhaps, could do his job as well, or even better. But it was Angelo, not others, who signed my pay cheque at the end of the week.

If there was to be a pay cheque. Just as well I'd taken out insurance.

I did as I was bid and sat down. The glorious morning sunlight pouring through the floor-to-ceiling windows might as well have been acid rain. Angelo stared at it in blank-faced silence for a long moment.

Then he rapped abruptly on his desk as though calling his internal caucus to order. 'About your future here,' he said. 'Things have not necessarily transpired as entirely advantageously as initially anticipated.' He sounded like the freshly-mouldering Hirohito announcing the capitulation of Japan.

'You're not satisfied with my performance?' I asked.

Now that Ange had set his course, he had no intention of allowing himself to be distracted. 'I was going to tell you about something today,' he said. 'Get your input and so forth. But events appear to have overtaken me.'

He slapped the papers on his desk with the back of his hand. He stood up. It was getting momentous. He began to address me as though I was a plenary session of state conference. 'I am responsible . . .' he began.

His mouth, unaccustomed to this phrase, did not know what to do next. He began again. 'A situation has arisen . . .' That was better. 'A situation has arisen whereby it may be possible for me to be seen to be responsible for the diminution of a significant component of the party's campaign funds.' There, he'd said it.

'Really,' I said. 'How could a situation like that have come about?'

'Against my better judgment,' he said. 'I allowed myself to be persuaded to become involved in the affairs of the finance committee.' He didn't say who had done the persuading. My preferred candidate was the invisible little Angelo sitting on his shoulder, the one in the red suit with the horns and tail.

'A bad call was made. The long and short of it is that as a consequence of subsequent events, events beyond my control . . .' He glared down at the newspapers with an expression he'd borrowed from Charlton Heston for the occasion. 'I am no longer able to confirm your ongoing employment. As soon as the implications of this situation become more widely appreciated, my position will no longer be tenable. In fact, I will have no option but to tender my own . . .' He searched for the word. He didn't have far to look. It was on the tip of his tongue. 'Resignation.'

For the sake of Angelo's finer feelings, I feigned surprise. 'Really!' I said. 'Is it that bad?'

As ideas went, it was worse than bad. Resignation would be an admission of culpability. A free ride for the opposition. A step closer to power for the true grafters. The smug, despicable, self-serving, incompetent, sanctimonious blue-bloods of the old-school-tie brigade. The enemies of the human race. The Liberals. The ice was thin enough beneath the government without the heat given off by Angelo Agnelli sweating over his failures.

'I'm a little confused here.' As I spoke, I reached across Agnelli's desk and drew the phone towards me. 'It was my understanding that finance committee affairs were Duncan Keogh's responsibility.' Agnelli's phone was as state-of-the-art as the desk it sat on. 'Shouldn't we hear what Duncan has to say about all this?'

Before Agnelli could stop me, I pecked out Keogh's number and pushed the hands-free button. The speaker went brr-brr and Keogh's irritable hello came down the line, loud and clear. 'Murray Whelan here, Duncan,' I said. 'Calling from Angelo Agnelli's office.' My call sign.

Agnelli, exhausted from the unaccustomed rigours of self-examination, slumped back into his chair and buried his head in his hands.

Duncan wasn't having a very good morning either. 'Tell Angelo I can't get anybody at Obelisk to talk to me. All deposits have been frozen and they reckon they can't deal with us preferentially just because of our association with their former CEO. Especially because of that. They say everybody wants their money and we'll just have to wait our turn. They don't have any idea how long that might take.' He was talking twenty to the dozen and his sweat was oozing through the phone speaker. 'Rumour is that it wasn't just the Karlcraft collapse that tipped the balance. That chickenshit prick Eastlake stuffed things up right and proper. We might be lucky to get back anything at all.'

He went on and on like this for quite some time, sinking the silent Agnelli ever deeper into the slough of despond. Then, barely pausing to draw breath, he changed tack. 'Okay,' he said. 'I admit it. I should have withdrawn the money yesterday afternoon. But Agnelli should have called me himself.'

At the mention of his name, Angelo shuddered visibly.

So far, I hadn't said anything. Personally, I found Keogh's remarks perplexing. 'I don't know what any of this is about, Duncan,' I said. 'But Angelo couldn't possibly have called you yesterday afternoon as, for some reason, you seem to think he should have. He was out of town on ministerial business. And you're the signatory to the finance committee accounts, aren't you?'

Keogh, sensing slippage in the rug under his feet, switched to the offensive. 'You tell Agnelli I'm not wearing this alone,' he snarled. 'He said at our meeting on Friday that he'd be backing me all the way to Cabinet.'

'What meeting was that?' I said.

Angelo took his head out of his hands.

'You know very well what meeting. The one in Agnelli's office at Ethnic Affairs.'

This didn't sound at all right to me. 'Are you sure about this, Duncan?' I said. 'Angelo hasn't mentioned any meeting to me. You kept minutes, did you?'

'Of course I didn't keep minutes.' Dunc was getting quite snappy by this stage.

'Was there anyone else at this meeting, Duncan?' I wondered. Some good was coming of Eastlake's death already. 'Anyone who can back you up on this?'

A tinge of luminescence had begun to creep over Agnelli's eastern horizon.

'You still there, Duncan?' I said. For a while the only sound coming out of the speaker was the steady bubble of boiling blood and the rustle of the rug beneath Keogh's feet reaching escape velocity. Then Duncan made a manly lunge for the soft option.

'You tell Agnelli that he can tell the Premier that if I can't get our funds out of Obelisk by close of business tonight,' he said, courageously taking it upon himself to do the noble thing, 'he'll have my resignation on his desk first thing in the morning. You can also tell Agnelli to go take a flying fu . . .'

Fortunately, I'd been keeping count. It was my turn to hang up. The green had by now drained entirely from Agnelli's gills. He looked like he might soon be sitting up in bed, sipping beef tea and receiving visitors. But I could see that he was still somewhat troubled.

'Keogh's a suck-arse little prick,' I told him, hoping to allay any sense of responsibility he might have for the demise of the soon-to-be-ex finance committee chairperson.

But it wasn't his conscience that was bothering Agnelli. That stunted faculty was already slouching back to its cryogenic cave. 'Keogh might take the fall,' he said. 'But the party's still down the tubes to the tune of $200,000.'

'That's quite some tune,' I admitted. 'Would it help if I hummed the first few bars?'

I picked the package off the floor beside my chair where I'd put it when I came in and spilled the contents onto Agnelli's desk. Less reasonable expenses. A packet of fags, two tram tickets, last night's lasagne and the dry-cleaning of a pair of strides.

Agnelli stared down at the small mountain of cash. 'Fuck Jesus fuck.' From Ange, that was high praise indeed. 'You rob a bank or something?' He must have been confusing me with Lloyd Eastlake.

'An anonymous donation from an intimate acquaintance of a former party member,' I explained. 'A strong believer in discretion. You and I are going to be buying a lot of raffle tickets in the next few months.'

Angelo was deeply appreciative. The moolah vanished into his bottom drawer, the newspapers went into the waste basket and my appointment as his cultural counsellor was immediately confirmed.

'I don't think I've got the stamina,' I said. 'Not if yesterday was any indication of the pace.' He really needed someone with the proper background for the job. 'An Italian, perhaps,' I suggested. Machiavelli. Houdini. Alfa Romeo.

But I did agree to stay in place on a temporary basis. 'Only until I've had a chance to put some proposals in front of you regarding retrospective amendments to the National Gallery's policy on the granting of maternity leave,' I said. 'After that, I'd like a chance to spread my wings in Water. If that's okay with you.'

It was, and that's where I've been ever since. The view from the office isn't as good as the one at Arts. And the only openings I get invited to are new sluice gates. But it's not as stressful here. And it's getting to the point where I can stand up on the skis for nearly fifty metres at a stretch.

Now that the eighties have officially drawn to a close, there's a lot of media rhubarb about what it all meant. Much breast-beating and decrying of all the glitz, the greed, the gullibility. Much calling on us to put the past behind us, tighten our belts and look grim reality square in the eye.

Myself, I don't know that there's all that much wisdom to be found in hindsight. Sure, we learn from our mistakes. But only from the ones we've already made, so the lessons have limited applicability. And whenever I hear that stuff about belt-tightening, I can't help but think how much bigger some people's belts are to begin with. And this is coming from a guy who knows a thing or two about cashed-up waistlines, remember. And about the mad glint in the eye of reality.

Max Karlin's in the belt-tightening business these days. He's living in Gdansk, advising the Polish government on the application of free-market principles to the footwear industry. Perhaps he can find a place in his operations for Duncan Keogh. At last report, Duncan had let his party membership lapse and was calling himself a freelance management consultant. Not getting a lot of what you might call work, from all accounts.

The Karlcraft Centre was completed only three months behind schedule, although not under that name. It's now called Absolute Melbourne. Current ownership resides with a fluid consortium of Singaporean shipping magnates that Faye tells me are looking to unload it onto a Dutch insurance company as soon as the Foreign Investment Review Board rubber stamp gets back from having its worn-down lettering refurbished. For the opening ceremony, an ice-rink was installed in the Galleria and the Australian Opera performed *Gotterdammerung* in costumes designed by Ken Done.

The shops don't seem to be doing much business, though. And there's so much un-let office space upstairs that you could run a fifty-head dairy farm on some of the floors. Claire and I had a drink in there a couple of weeks ago, in the tapas bar on the second level, overlooking the mosaic floor. 'How's business?' I asked the tapas barman.

'Dropping off,' he said.

The children's wear boutique opening onto the horn of plenty was having a clearance sale. I bought Grace a pair of Osh-kosh overalls marked down from a hundred dollars to thirty-nine ninety-five. Still a bit rich, I know, but nothing's too good for my Gracie.

Claire is back at the National Gallery. One of the recommendations of the Human Resources Policy Review Committee was that former employees whose termination was the result of discriminatory industrial relations practices be given hiring priority if positions became available due to natural wastage. When one of the conservatorial staff was pensioned off with prostate cancer induced by chronic cadmium yellow exposure from handling too many French Impressionists, Claire got his old job.

Not that she goes near the Monets. She's in the Australian section. From what I can tell, she spends most of her time with a pair of tweezers and a magnifying glass, sticking ochre blobs back on Aboriginal dot paintings with Aquadhere general-purpose wood glue. But she feels her professional skills are much better employed than they were at Artemis Prints and Framing. Plus she doesn't have to work Saturday mornings. She sold Artemis for the cost of the stock and cleared twenty grand on the outstanding mortgage, so the property boom was not without its upside, while it lasted. The place is now called Fred's Head Shop and sells extra-width cigarette papers, blown-glass water-pipes and framed posters of Bob Marley. So some connection with the arts remains.

Speaking of art, the real authorship of *Our Home* remains a mystery. To me, at least. Very few other people know or care about its existence. The version with the bullet hole and the blood stains is in the vault at the new Police Museum, along with the bullet-riddled banister from the Trades Hall. The version which belonged to Max Karlin was eventually de-accessioned by the Centre for Modern Art. It now hangs in the collection of the Victa Motor Mower Company, although this is probably more because of its subject matter than its authorship. It was recently the subject of a doctoral dissertation published by the PIT Department of Cultural Studies entitled *(Sub)liminal Penetration in the (Sub)urban Landscape.*

Public interest in the works of Victor Szabo never scaled the heights Fiona Lambert hoped and the planned retrospective exhibition was cancelled due to lack of funding. The content of future exhibitions at the Centre for Modern Art will be determined by its interim curator, Janelle. It was Janelle who phoned Fiona Lambert that night at the flat. She rang to say that Fiona had left her keys behind, yet again. Fiona popped over and picked them up as soon as she'd brushed me and Lloyd off. Then she had an early night.

Fiona is now Assistant Curator of Naive Pottery at the Warracknabeal Regional Gallery. It's a bit of a come-down, I suppose, and a fair way from the bright lights. But that's probably the way she prefers it, given that she looks like she's had a zipper installed in her fore-head. She probably still thinks the cops pinched her dough.

Salina Fleet, on the other hand, has gone from strength to strength. The commission she was charging on Marcus Taylor's knock-offs was more than enough to cover the cost of her relocation to New York, where she is now performance art commentator for *Flashy'n'Trashy*, a theoretical journal financed by the Sony Corporation. The name Fleet, it transpired, was a legacy from an early and soon discarded husband.

Her maiden name was Fletcher. Makes you wonder, doesn't it.

Obelisk's depositors were eventually paid out at forty-five cents in the dollar. So Agnelli's brief foray into high finance just about broke even – if you count Fiona's contribution. Even better than break-even if you add in the two trips to Bali, the three microwave ovens and the fourteen dinners-for-two we won in raffles and kicked back into the cause.

Red was a bit pissed off that I didn't keep the trip to Bali and take him along. He's been there twice now with Wendy and Richard. He reckons it's cool although he did get embarrassed when his braces set off the metal detectors at the airport. My alarm bells certainly rang when I saw the bill. But I insisted on paying the whole lot, not just half. It's my genes they're designed to compensate for, after all.

Wendy and Richard got married. In a church. Wendy wore white. 'More oyster, really,' said Red. 'Puke-a-rama.'

He's coming down next month and I've got the use of the Water Supply houseboat on Lake Eildon. Tarquin is coming too, just for the first few days. Unfortunately there's very little chance he'll drown. The water level is too low.

The drought has been going on for nearly a year now. Quite a challenge, policy-response wise. Sometimes we pray. Sometimes we dance.

The election will be late next year. We're hoping to dance it in. We definitely don't have a prayer. Not even with *Nea Hellas* behind us, to the hilt.